I0586475

Gone Before Spring

Sheila Solomon Shotwell

For colindanny 1981-2017

Gone Before Spring
Sheila Solomon Shotwell

© 2017 Sheila Solomon Shotwell All Rights Reserved. Updated content. Visit the authors website at www.sheilasolomonshotwell.com or find her on Facebook.
ISBN 978-0-9994225-1-9

There came a time when the risk to remain tight in the bud
was more painful than the risk it took to blossom.
– attributed to Anais Nin

Chapter One

Cathy Cicerelli stood at the end of my driveway looking like she'd just sucked on a lemon.

"C'mon, we're gonna be late for Mass."

"I never told you to wait for me," I said.

Cathy Cicerelli was a year younger than me. My mom and I moved into the neighborhood in the middle of fifth grade, (in a blizzard on my birthday, in fact), and Cathy and I started playing Barbies two days later. Cathy drove me crazy all summer. She hid under her bed every time there was a tornado alert, just like she did when she was nine, not to mention a bunch of other babyish stuff. I always knew Cathy swiped my Barbie's blue net birdcage hat. Nobody else in this whole city ever had one because my Aunt Maxine sent it to me from Hartford, Connecticut. How did she expect me not to wonder why her Barbie had one clear out of the blue and mine had disappeared? I stopped playing Barbies in sixth grade. Right before I got my first period, I threw the whole case of stuff into the back of my closet.

Most of last summer was spent playing the radio and staring at the crack in the ceiling above my bed. I'd rather have been doing that than trudging toward school. Even though this was my fourth year at St. Bonaventure, or as the boys called it, St. Boner's, I still dreaded the first day. I'd always dreaded the first day of school and I also dreaded getting Miss Fitzgerald, better know as Fizzytits, for my homeroom teacher. She was at least eighty years old.

There were only two good things about school starting. Number one was that my sister went back to college. It's a miracle we survived after spending three months together. Everything I said or did made Renee furious. She always said there was no doubt in her mind that when I grow up there will be poopy diapers all over my house and mold growing in my refrigerator.

The second good thing was finally being in eighth grade. Everybody looked up to the eighth graders. Even if you weren't the slightest bit popular, you were still cool for being in the oldest grade. For the past three years we studied everything about them. Their clothes, their hair, and of course who hangs out with who. I could hardly believe it. I would officially be an eighth grader as soon as I walked into St. Boner's.

"You wanna go to the park after school?" Cathy asked me cautiously as she pushed her thick glasses against her face.

"Nah, I'll probably be going with Peg and Irene, or maybe we'll hang around in Alger Heights. After all, tomorrow's a full day. Then we'll only have weekends for fun stuff."

It wasn't so bad walking to school with Cathy, but I somehow had to convince her that we wouldn't be spending time together. It would be a little easier this year since eighth graders were in their own separate wing at school.

My plan was to hang around more with Peg and Irene. They liked to shop at Mitchell's Young At Heart in Alger Heights and keep track of the Top 40 songs on WLAV just like me. Cathy was never a fan of The Beatles, let alone The Rolling Stones. Back in the old days, when my Barbie made out with Paul McCartney, she just looked confused.

As it turned out, the morning went by pretty fast. I did get Miss Fizzytits for homeroom, but it ended up being worth it because around eleven o'clock, she forgot that she'd already unbuttoned the little jacket over her blouse an hour before. It was very warm in the classroom and she had taken it off and hung it on the back of her chair. So while she was explaining the class rules about using the giant dictionary in the back of the room, she unbuttoned her blouse and removed that. There she sat in a yellow slip with her wrinkly grayish chest and shoulders completely exposed.

Gone Before Spring

Gerard Waterman fell sideways out of his chair and rolled around on the floor in my aisle. I couldn't believe my eyes. Of course he was ordered to the principal, Sister Mary Edith's office, which wasn't unusual for him.

After school, we all stood around outside in little groups.

"Ruth Ann, you should come with us to the football game on Friday night," Irene said. I wasn't sure if my mother would let me go, but maybe she would if she had a date with Larry.

For most of the years since my parents' divorce, my mom didn't have a boyfriend. But for the last few months Larry came over a lot. Back when we lived in the apartment, I got out of bed to go to the bathroom and passed the TV room and saw them kissing. They were in side by side chairs and their faces were all smashed together. It made me feel sick. They nearly jumped out of their seats when they heard me. Larry ran his fingers through his thinning red hair and my mom straightened her blouse.

"What are you doing up?" she'd asked me, as if I was the one doing something wrong.

Larry was okay sometimes. He took me to see *A Hard Day's Night* a few days after the kissing episode and didn't say a word when tears rolled down my face over the sight of the Beatles. He even told my mom that he'd enjoyed the movie.

One night he showed me how to make a Chef BoyArdee Pizza and while we were waiting for it to come out of the oven, he sketched a pretty cool picture of my penny loafers with an ink pen. Then he stopped coming over for about a year and my mom went back to reading Harlequin Romances on the couch in the evenings, and eating chocolate cream drops. Toward the end of seventh grade, Larry started coming over again.

"I'm not sure about Friday," I informed the girls. "But I'll meet you by the slides at one o'clock."

As I rounded the corner of my street, I noticed Cathy a couple of blocks ahead, walking with her little brother, Frankie. He was smacking his plaid book bag against her as they walked. I unlocked the side door that led to the kitchen and went straight to the refrigerator. My mom was at her secretary job at Lowry Piano. I took out the stuff for a honey loaf sandwich and while I was spreading mustard on the bread, my Siamese cat, Reddy jumped up on the counter. I kissed the top of his head, even though he wasn't supposed to be up there. "Where's Ruff?" I asked him.

My dad had given Ruff and Reddy to me the summer after third grade. While they were still tiny kittens, we took them on a short vacation and snuck them into the hotel. They meowed all night, climbed the drapes, and in the morning we were told to go to another hotel.

That seemed like a million years ago, and looking back, I realized my dad gave me the kittens so I'd feel better about him getting an apartment with Wilma. I didn't have to go visit them again until spring break which was fine with me. It felt weird to be around Wilma even though she did look a lot like my old platinum bouffant-haired Barbie. Except Barbie didn't constantly have a cigarette in one hand and a martini in the other.

* * *

On Friday, I couldn't decide what to wear to the football game. My mom finally said I could go when I called her at work that day around four o'clock.

"Well, I guess if Peg's mother is driving and picking you up, and you come right home after, it's okay," she'd said.

"Oh thanks, Mom. I'll clean the house with you all day Saturday," I offered.

Now I was sorry I'd made the offer because a bunch of the girls were planning to rent tandem bikes and ride around the Alger Heights neighborhood. I'd have to work on that one tomorrow.

In the meantime, I needed to find something to wear. I didn't have much to choose from. We were required to wear ugly green uniforms at St. Bonaventure's, and only one day a month was declared "color day" so we could get our uniforms washed. Color day was a pain in the neck for me before I started babysitting and buying some of my own clothes. I still shudder when I remember the day in sixth grade that I wore a print shift my sister sewed for me. I'd grown several inches since the last time I wore it, and Sister Peter Verona humiliated me in front of the class by requiring me to tie my mohair sweater around my knees to cover up.

I decided the herringbone culottes and tights would be a good choice and they still fit. My mom told me I might be done growing now that I'm almost five feet tall and everyone in our family is short. I pressed my hands as hard as I could on the sides of my hair. For some reason, during summer vacation, my hair went from being slightly wavy to very wavy. I planned to buy Curl Free as soon as I got another babysitting job. All the models in the magazines had straight hair, usually blonde. I couldn't think of a worse curse than having curly brown hair.

Just when I had decided to change out of the culottes and into jeans, Peg's mom pulled into the driveway. Irene was in the car as well as Peg, and each of their younger sisters, who are in sixth grade and best friends just like Peg and Irene. I used to envy their regular family life because it was so different than mine, but seeing their fathers come home grouchy or their little sisters borrow their stuff without asking, I realized the benefits of our small family.

"Well, don't you look cute tonight?" Peg's mom remarked as I squeezed into the backseat with the other girls. That truly felt like a compliment because Peg's mom was from New York and my mom always says that she had "Jackie Kennedy style."

When we got to the football field, people were rushing past us and climbing the bleachers as fast as they could.

"We always sit around here when my dad brings us," Irene said, leading the way.

I didn't want the girls to know I'd never even been to a football game, let alone one with my dad. My family's idea of entertainment was going to plays. My sister majored in theater in college so I was always dragged to plays like *Oh Dad, Poor Dad, Someone's Hung You In The Closet, And*

9

I'm Feeling So Sad. We never paid attention to sports. I didn't have any idea what was happening on the football field, but I tried to clap and cheer along with everybody else.

At halftime, a few boys from our class came over and stood in the aisle by us. They were throwing their heads back and tossing peanuts into their mouths. Gerard Waterman got one caught in his throat and the other boys all smacked as hard as they could on his back until it came flying out of his mouth and landed in Peg's hair.

"Get it out, get it out!" she yelled and made him remove it.

The rest of us huddled together screaming, "Ewww!"

There was one boy in the group I'd never met. He was in the other seventh grade class last year and was not in my homeroom this year. I'd noticed him in the hall because he was taller than the other boys. My stomach got a funny grabby feeling when I caught him looking at me with his dark blue eyes. I turned my head away really fast.

"Tom LaBelle was looking at you," Irene's younger sister whispered a little too loudly in my ear. I poked my elbow into her side and stared straight ahead, pretending to be interested in the football game which was starting up again.

The second half of the game was way more interesting. I was just as excited as the others when the score was tied in the fourth quarter. We were all standing on the bleacher and screaming when our team scored a touchdown and won the game. All of a sudden, my loafer slipped off the edge. I tried to catch myself so I wouldn't fall onto the person in front of me. My left shin smacked into the bleacher just as the lady stood. I was relieved the woman had gotten out of the way, but I felt a warm oozy feeling through my navy blue tights.

"Good grief, are you okay?" Peg asked as she put her arm around me.

"I don't know," I said as I sat to look down at my leg. My tights were ripped and soaked with blood and it was throbbing.

"Here's some ice." Tom LaBelle offered his large Dixie Cup to Peg to hand to me.

"I'm such a klutz!" I tried to laugh so I wouldn't look like a big baby in front of everyone. The girls helped me to my feet after I rubbed some of the ice on my shin bone.

"Thanks," I said smiling as best I could at Tom LaBelle. I wasn't sure what to do with his cup of ice so I just carried it with me.

* * *

When I got home I didn't mention falling at the game. My mom and Larry were on the couch watching TV and sharing a bowl of popcorn. I hurried past them and went upstairs to take care of my leg. After I peeled my tights off and washed it, it really didn't look that bad. There was a scrape and I knew I'd probably have a bruise the next day.

After I turned out the light I heard Cathy calling me through the window. Her brother's room was right across from mine and we had talked back and forth a lot in the summer. I pretended I couldn't hear her as I looked over to my dresser where the moon was shining on Tom LaBelle's Dixie Cup. I fell asleep listening to my transistor radio.

* * *

My leg felt stiff the next morning when I shuffled into the kitchen. My mom was sitting at the table which was covered with the monthly bills and her checkbook.

"Why are you walking like that?" she asked me.

"I slipped on the bleacher last night. It's no big deal."

"That needs peroxide or something."

"Of course peroxide," I said, throwing up my hands. We never had Bactine like normal families or stuff like Scotch Tape and Band-Aids. Adults, especially my mom's relatives, often made comments about how difficult it was for my mom, not having a husband and raising two daughters. I always felt bad about that and tried not to complain too much. Thankfully, two other kids in my grade also had divorced parents. At my last school I was the only one in the class from a "broken home," and kids asked questions all the time about what it was like. I would tell them that sometimes me and my mom would go out for a candy bar or a popsicle at ten o'clock at night. Their eyes would grow big and I could tell they didn't believe me.

"I was hoping you could vacuum the living room and dining room," my mom said as she dabbed a peroxide soaked tissue on my leg.

"I can," I answered quickly, still hoping to rent tandem bikes with my friends in the afternoon. My mom said it all depended on how I felt after vacuuming because riding a bike would require a lot of bending. She also wanted me to straighten my room and dust mop under the bed.

As it turned out, she let me rent the bicycles with the girls. She even gave me the seventy- five cents for the rental fee. There were six of us altogether and my partner was Mary Lou Bender, who lives down the street from Peg and Irene. She sits next to me in science class and wears scarves around her pony tail every day.

We pedaled through the Alger Heights neighborhood where the houses looked much newer than the ones in Madison Heights where I lived. The two neighborhoods were separated by Garfield Park where everyone swam in the summer.

After an hour of riding, we decided to stop at Miller's ice cream shop. Right when we walked in, the lady behind the counter was handing an ice cream cone to Gerard Waterman. As soon as he took it from her, the large scoop of Fudge Ripple fell off his cone and landed on Marty Whitman's foot. We all burst out laughing when he picked up the ice cream with his hands and handed it back to the lady.

"Here," he said.

She gave him a dirty look and plopped it into the sink. "I suppose you want a new one?"

He turned to us and shrugged. Then we all started shoving one another around because the juke box was playing a song that we'd been singing loudly while we were riding our bikes. It was turning out to be an especially fun day. I had never really hung around more than one or two friends at a time, and it felt surprisingly good to be in a group. Just as I was about to lick my Blue Moon ice cream, I felt a tap on my shoulder.

"How's your leg?" It was Tom LaBelle, and when I looked up at him I felt the grabby feeling again.

"Oh, it's okay I guess, thanks. And thanks for the ice last night."

"Well, it looked like a bad cut. Good thing you didn't have to get stitches. I did last year when I ran my toboggan into a tree."

"Yeah, that was pretty cool. There was blood all over the snow," Teddy Zukowski chimed in. "C'mon, LaBelle, let's go." He yanked on the back of Tom's shirt. Tom waved at me as he took a few steps backward.

"Hmm...I think somebody likes Ruth Ann," Irene said. "Between last night and just now, there is no doubt."

"Just because he gave me some ice when I was bleeding, and then asked about it today?"

But I knew inside what Irene was talking about. I felt it too, because when Tom talked to me, he looked right into my eyes. Almost like he was searching for something. And I wanted to know what it was.

Chapter Two

In history class on Monday morning, Marty Whitman leaned forward from his seat behind me and said, "Hey, I live next door to Tom LaBelle and he asked me to ask you if you like him." I turned my head slightly sideways, but didn't dare answer him because our history teacher, Miss McHeartland never missed anything and would let you know it. Sure enough, I saw her Scottish plaid skirt come flying toward us just before her teacher's edition of *This Land Is Our Land* came down squarely on Marty's head. I knew if I had turned my head one more inch in his direction, I would have been clobbered too.

After dinner, I was in my room doing homework and my mom hollered up the steps.

"Ruth Ann, there's some boys here to see you."

I jumped up and looked in the mirror, tried to flatten my waves and then curiously made my way downstairs.

"They're in the driveway. Who are they?" she asked.

"Well, I don't know. I haven't seen them yet."

I went through the kitchen to the side door, and saw Marty Whitman and Tom LaBelle on their bikes.

"Hope this is okay. Peg told me where you live," Tom said.

"Oh it's fine," I said through the screen. I wasn't sure if I should stay in or go out.

"Are you girls going to the carnival at Miracle Mart on Saturday?" he asked me.

"I didn't know there was one, but maybe."

There was that grabby feeling again. It was kind of like the feeling I had when I watched *A Hard Day's Night*, but more grown up.

"Well, we're going in the afternoon. You girls should try and make it over there. Hey, I heard you almost got the teacher's manual on your head along with Marty today."

He and Marty snickered as Marty popped a wheelie in the driveway. I noticed that they both had monster stickers plastered on their bikes.

"Those are hideous," I said.

"No they're not. They're cool. We collect 'em." Tom smiled at me mischievously and then I think my heart actually fluttered. I'd heard the expression, but I didn't know it could really happen.

* * *

On the way to school the next morning, Cathy handed me something wrapped in wax paper. "Here, it's my mom's homemade bread, that you love. You haven't come over on Monday nights the way you used to."

The best part about living next door to the Cicerellis, was the cooking, no question about it. Cathy's parents were from Italy and her mom cooked the most delicious food I'd ever tasted. Every Monday she baked Italian bread and loved it when I came over to have some. She especially loved the way I would go on and on about how she was the best cook I ever met and how I always begged her for her secret salad dressing recipe. She made salad dressing from a tin gallon of olive oil that had pictures of ladies in nightgowns, picking olives.

"You'll get the recipe when you grow up and get married," she always told me.

"Was that Tom LaBelle who came over to your house last night?" Cathy asked me. "He is the only thing the girls in my class talk about!"

"Yeah, he stopped by with Marty Whitman. I guess they're next door neighbors." I was trying my best to sound casual. Cathy's eyes were even more magnified behind her glasses and her hair was frizzier than usual.

"Wow, wait 'til I tell Theresa Sullivan and those other girls. They won't believe it! They are completely in love with Tom LaBelle!" Cathy blurted out.

"It's not that big of a deal, Cathy," I said.

I was a little worried about what she'd say to the girls in her class, but I did kind of want them all to know.

* * *

On Saturday, my mom drove me, Peg, Irene, and Mary Lou to Miracle Mart so we could go to the carnival that had been set up in the parking lot. She didn't mind driving us because she wanted to do some shopping in the large discount store. Mary Lou's dad would be picking us up at five o'clock.

We wandered around eating cotton candy and looking at the various booths and rides. We heard an uproarious laugh that we knew had to be Teddy Zukowski. He had the loudest and most contagious laugh in the whole school. We spotted him standing at a shooting booth with several boys including Tom LaBelle. Before we could decide whether or not to walk over to them, Marty spotted us and we saw him poke Tom in the ribs. The two of them walked away from the group and came over to us.

"Hi Ruth Ann," Tom said softly. It was the first time he'd called me by my name. "How about a ride on the Ferris wheel?"

Before I knew it, we were in line and he was handing two tickets to a guy as if the whole thing was planned out. When I climbed into the seat I bumped my leg on the bar and winced.

"Are you okay?" he asked me.

"Oh I'm fine, it's just that bruise from the football game."

"No kidding? Wasn't that two weeks ago?"

"Um, no I think it was just last week. It's really okay, I guess I'm a slow healer."

The ride started kind of jerky and our seat rocked back and forth as we ascended to the top. Tom laced his fingers through mine and we held our hands together on top of his thigh for the rest of the ride. We didn't talk the whole time and when we got off, Gerard Waterman hollered out to us, "Hey LaBelle, what'd you do to her? She's bleeding all over!"

I looked down and sure enough, my leg was bleeding through my

16

beige tights right where I'd hurt it at the football game.

"You must have had a scab," Tom said as we both stopped in our tracks and looked down.

"Yeah, I guess I bumped it harder than I thought, when I was getting on. It doesn't hurt, though. It's fine." I was sorry I'd worn my culottes with the beige tights and wished I'd worn my blue jeans like Peg and Irene.

I felt like such a toddler, getting hurt all the time. Mary Lou whispered in my ear that she didn't have a Band-Aid in her purse, but she had a Kotex. I punched her in the arm and laughed. It made me realize that a cut on my leg wasn't as embarrassing as some other things.

Peg was coming toward us with a large red stuffed rabbit and her face was almost as red as the toy. It turned out that Marty had won it throwing darts at balloons and had given it to her, which made me wonder what was cooking there.

We spent the rest of the time joking around, eating caramel corn and watching Teddy Zukowski and Gerard Waterman flirt with every girl around. A guy in a gorilla costume came up behind them when they were following a pretty girl and crashed cymbals above their heads. That was the best laugh of the day to see them jump a foot off the ground.

* * *

On Sunday afternoon, Tom called me on the telephone and asked me to meet him at the park by the swings. My mom was out with Larry, so I just left a note on the dining room table. I was supposed to be doing homework, but I figured I deserved a break and the park was only a block from my house. I applied my Bonnie Bell lip gloss extra thick and then on second thought, wiped some off. My mom would never let me wear make-up. It was time to bring that subject up again.

Tom was sitting on his bike near the swings when I got there. His eyes were the exact color of the Midnight Blue crayon in my old Crayola box, the giant one with sixty four colors. The breeze lifted his dark hair

17

from his forehead and he looked so handsome, I felt woozy.

"Wanna swing?" he asked as he grabbed hold of the chains and sat on a swing. I sat on the one next to him and twirled around so the chains crossed each other.

"I think Marty likes your friend, Peg," he said.

"Hmm, that kind of explains why he gave her his prize yesterday."

"Maybe we could all go to the movie next Saturday at the Four Star. *Fantastic Voyage* is gonna be there and I hear it's really good. You want a push?"

He got off of his swing and pulled me back far before letting go. I was sailing through the air.

I hollered, "I'll ask Peg when I call her tonight. We can probably do that. But she always goes everywhere with Irene. Will it just be you two?"

Tom said he'd call a few other guys because he said it didn't really matter to him who all went. But I thought he looked a little disappointed when he stopped pushing me and went back to his swing. I wondered if he was wanting a double date. I didn't even know if Peg liked Marty.

Just as my feet started dragging on the ground, I looked up and there was Cathy and her little brother. Her hair was in curlers with a baby blue thing tied around it, which reminded me of my Barbie's missing birdcage hat. She was carrying a picnic basket, so I figured she was coming from her Aunt Mary's house on the other side of the park. Frankie had a foil covered plate in his hands. She was staring at us and her mouth was open.

"Hi Cathy, been to your Aunt Mary's?" I asked her.

She nodded and didn't even close her mouth. If the curlers weren't bad enough, Cathy was wearing an outfit that I swear she'd had since fourth grade. I wondered what Tom thought.

"Yeah, this is stuff for our mom's birthday party," Frankie answered.

I suddenly remembered that we were invited to that and it was at five o'clock. I waited until they were almost to our street and then I said, "I really should be going. Those kids are my next door neighbors and my mom is making me go to their mom's party and I haven't even finished my English paper."

I got off the swing and took a couple of steps backward. Tom came over toward me and put his finger under my chin.

"You're so pretty," he said.

I just rolled my eyes and shook my head.

"I really have to go." I waved my hand at him and turned to run.

"Don't forget to call Peg," he shouted at me.

I turned around as I ran, nodded and waved again. All I could think about was, *Tom LaBelle said I was pretty, Tom LaBelle said I was pretty…*

* * *

The party at Cathy's house was crowded and there was a whole long table of Italian food from all of her aunts. I filled my plate twice. Mr. Cicerelli kept bringing platters of chicken and steak from the grill in their driveway. No matter what they served, it was always covered in Mrs. Cicerelli's homemade tomato sauce.

I was waiting for a chance to get Cathy alone. I finally saw her go upstairs, so I followed her to her bedroom. I noticed a pair of scissors on her desk and a book of ballerina paper dolls, but I glanced away quickly so she wouldn't see that I noticed them.

"Hey Cathy, do me a favor, okay, and don't say anything to your mom about seeing me at the park today."

"Yeah, with Tom LaBelle!" she replied.

My mom and Larry were still gone when I got home, so I'd thrown away the note that I'd left. I decided it wasn't worth mentioning because I had a feeling my mom wouldn't have approved of my being alone with a boy at the park.

"Did Frankie tell your mom?" I asked.

"No, he probably forgot."

Just then Cathy's cousin Tony came running into the room.

19

"Help! Frankie's stuck in the clothes chute, help me get him out!"

Sure enough, Frankie's bottom half was in the clothes chute and his head and shoulders were sticking out. We both pulled as hard as we could on his arms and when we finally got him out, Frankie wasn't wearing any pants. When we all realized his pants had come off and gone down the clothes chute, we fell on the floor laughing, including cousin Tony. Frankie's face was all red and then he started crying while holding his hands in front of his privates.

"I used to fit in there. Don't tell Mommy, Cathy. She'll kill me," Frankie said.

"Okay Frankie, it's a deal, but only if you forget you saw Ruth Ann at the park today and go get some pants on." We burst out laughing again and all fell over in a heap.

Frankie nodded and rubbed his eyes with the back of his hand. After he and his cousin were back in his room, Cathy turned to me and said,

"I have an idea! How 'bout I tell Teresa Sullivan and those girls that I went to the park with you guys and Tom LaBelle pushed us both on the swings?"

"But Cathy that's not true," I said.

"So? It doesn't matter. C'mon. What can it hurt?"

I could tell Cathy felt like I owed her now. She wanted so much to be popular and had no idea how to go about it. I looked over at the paper dolls again and decided maybe this would help her grow up a little.

"Well, I guess it's okay, just so they don't talk to me about it," I said.

I wasn't even sure who Teresa Sullivan was. Thankfully, they were in a different wing at school. We only saw the seventh graders at Mass and we had to sit with our own grade. There wasn't much chance I'd have to talk to them about it and I was pretty sure they would never talk to Tom. She motioned for me to follow her down the stairs.

"C'mon, you gotta try the cake I made. It's a Betty Crocker Cherry Chip.

20

Chapter Three

Angela Droski, one of the girls who rented bikes with us, invited me to her birthday slumber party. I couldn't wait to go to her beautiful old house with the huge room over the garage where the party would be. It was so big that she invited twenty girls. Her bedroom looked like it was from another century with a lavender eyelet canopy bed and a collection of antique purses on the wall. Next to her bed was a large, pink flowered pitcher sitting in a bowl that people used for washing in the olden days.

We all rolled our sleeping bags out in the giant room and tried doing levitation. I swear we got Mary Lou Bender about four feet off the ground. After that we stood on the corner tables and pretended to be go-go dancers while we played records. Then we shoved each other off the tables onto the pile of sleeping bags. It was a blast. Some girls fell asleep right after midnight, but a few of us talked into the wee hours. Around four in the morning somebody got the idea of trying to make Amy Jo Burke pee in her sleeping bag because she was the first person to fall asleep. I was having a hard time staying awake and had just snuggled down in my own sleeping bag, when they stuck Amy Jo's hand in a bowl of warm water. She sat up and looked around, then got up and rolled her sleeping bag into a bundle. Mary Lou pointed at her pajama bottoms which were all wet.

"You're all mean, you're a bunch of brats! I'm going home." She grabbed her stuff and charged out of the room. Nobody followed her and Angela was asleep, so we stayed put.

"I didn't think it would work," Irene said with her eyes bulging.

"Don't worry, she just lives across the street and down a ways."

After that, everybody fell asleep. In the morning, Mr. and Mrs. Droski made pancakes for all of us and Mr. Droski tried to be funny by singing the Beatles song, *Love Me Do* at the top of his lungs. I thought about my dad. He's really funny too and I wondered how he'd act if I had a slumber party and he was there in the morning. It could never happen though since he lived two hours away and I only had one friend in his town.

Mrs. Droski came into Angela's room while we were getting dressed to see if anyone needed a ride or anything.

Just as she turned to leave, she stopped right by me as I was stepping into my jeans, and said, "Oh my, Ruth Ann, what happened to your leg?"

" I fell against a bleacher at the football game and then I bumped it again on the Ferris wheel."

"Well, keep an eye on that so it doesn't get infected. It looks pretty bad."

I smiled at her for being so motherly. I couldn't imagine my mom noticing a friend's injury. She was too busy to even notice mine. I don't undress around my mom if I can help it. Back in fourth grade I got one boob for some reason. My mom and sister made a really big deal out of it and made me feel like a freak. Then about a year later, when my sister was working downtown at Wurzburg's Department Store, she came home one day with a training bra. I was so mad at my mom for letting Renee buy the bra, instead of the two of us going downtown together. She said they wanted my sister's employee discount.

By the time my boobs were almost the same size they teased me about "developing." Then all of a sudden I had pubic hair and my sister walked into the bathroom as I was getting out of the tub. The teasing went through the roof after that, like it didn't happen to every girl. So, from then on I always locked the door when I was changing or bathing. Especially if my sister was home. She and my mom were more like friends than mother and daughter, and it always felt like they were ganging up on me. It made me feel better when I noticed that most of the girls were beginning to fill out. I was tired of having the biggest boobs in our class.

* * *

Because of the slumber party, none of us could go to the movie on

Gone Before Spring

Saturday. We all agreed to spend the day doing chores and homework so we could possibly go on Sunday. I was so tired that I fell asleep by eight thirty that night. The last thing I remembered was lying in bed and recalling the slumber party in sixth grade where we girls all practiced making out so we'd be ready when we really did make out with a boy. I couldn't believe that was only two years ago. It was pretty embarrassing when I thought about it. I fell asleep listening to the song, *Itchycoo Park* on my transistor radio.

* * *

All six of the "Tandem Riders", as we liked to call ourselves since the day we'd rented Tandem bikes, went to the Four Star Theatre on Sunday. A few other girls from the slumber party also went, but Amy Jo wouldn't go, because she was still upset about the peeing incident. When we filed in, Tom and Marty, and a couple of other boys waved us over to the rows they'd saved. Peg was practically deposited next to Marty, and Tom made sure I was next to him. It all happened very fast.

The movie was pretty interesting. People were traveling through somebody's blood stream. Before long, Tom's arm was around my shoulders. My heart was beating very fast because I was pretty sure this would be the day I'd get my first kiss, from a boy at least.

The movie was almost over and somebody in our row dropped a bottle on the floor. When I turned to look, Tom brushed his lips across mine. His lips tasted like the Good and Plenty he'd eaten earlier. We both looked straight ahead at the screen after that with our hands interlaced like on the Ferris wheel, but this time they were resting on my thigh. I couldn't even concentrate on the movie. Maybe the kiss had been an accident. I'd probably turned my head too quickly and ran into Tom's lips by accident. Maybe he didn't even mean to do it. But then he wouldn't be holding my hand. Or would he? My heart was beating in my ears. My first kiss. Or almost-kiss. Or accidental kiss. I wondered if he felt the same way. Maybe not because maybe this wasn't his first kiss. Then I felt a little ping in my heart.

* * *

The next weekend Tom went with his family to Canada for his grandma's birthday. I thought it was very cool that his family was French Canadian. There was something romantic about it. I had babysitting jobs on both Friday and Saturday nights, so on Saturday I went to Mitchell's Young at Heart in Alger Heights to put a corduroy suit on lay-away. I was the last girl in the Tandem Riders to get one. They were print A-line skirts with matching jackets and the style was to wear a ribbed Poorboy top under the jacket. I picked one that was cadet blue with an olive print. I was excited because I already had an olive Poorboy that would match it.

I had decided to wait on the Curl Free because I had a new magazine with Twiggy on the cover with directions inside on how to make your hair straight by rolling it up with empty frozen orange juice containers.

* * *

Tom called me on Sunday night when he got back in town.

"I really missed you," he said.

I was surprised he said that and replied, thanks, which sounded so dumb when I thought about it afterwards. I wished I had told him that I missed him too.

Cathy pumped me about him every chance she got when we walked to school. Thankfully, she knew better than to say anything around Frankie. He was a little loudmouth. Already, Mrs. Cicerelli had hollered over the backyard fence to me while she was hanging up her laundry.

"I hear you gotta boyfriend."

Instead of answering her, I hollered back, "Your hair looks really nice, Mrs. Cicerelli. You must have gone to the beauty shop."

"Thank you very much, and why don't you come by anymore on Mondays for bread? I've got some cannoli in the house right now I made for the Altar Society. Come on over and I'll give you one."

I wondered who had blown it, Cathy or Frankie. Or maybe, Mrs.

Gone Before Spring

Cicerelli had seen me step outside to talk to Tom and Marty when they stopped by on their bicycles.

My mom finally asked me who they were and what they wanted. She was watching her favorite show, *The Man from U.N.C.L.E.* Her hair was in curlers and she was smoking a Salem cigarette. Ruff and Reddy were curled up next to her on the couch.

"Does this kid think you're his girlfriend?" she asked during the commercial.

"Yeah, I guess so. He's really nice. He's French Canadian."

I don't know why I said that. I guess I hoped she'd think about that instead of the girlfriend/boyfriend part. I went upstairs to take a bath and as usual I brought my radio into the bathroom to listen to in the tub. Music made me forget all the stuff I wanted to forget and remember the stuff I wanted to remember. It all started after I bought my first record in fourth grade, *Can't Buy Me Love*, by the Beatles. At the time, it helped me forget how much I missed my dad and it distracted me from thinking about having only one boob.

I usually used my mom's bubble bath when I bathed, but she seemed to be out of it. I leaned back for a while and sang along to a song I didn't really like. Without the bubbles, it was easier to see my body. Then I lifted my left leg to try and turn the hot water faucet with my toes. That's when I noticed my leg. The spot where I'd hurt it weeks before was much bigger. It was red with white crusty edges. It looked at least three inches longer than it had been. When I got out of the tub, I leaned over and patted it dry very carefully. The white, crusty part had split open a little bit and was bleeding. After I put on my nightgown, I decided I better show my leg to my mom.

She was standing in her closet with the light on, probably trying to figure out what to wear to work the next day.

"Hey mom, remember when I banged my leg at that football game? Well, it kind of looks worse." It didn't seem like my mom was listening.

She was holding a checkered skirt up that I hadn't seen her wear in a long time. She had turned it around and was looking at the back of it.

"Hmm, what did you say?" I repeated to her that my leg looked worse and then she laid the skirt on her bed. I put my leg up next to it. She studied it for a few seconds and then she told me to move over by her nightstand where she switched the lamp on.

"That looks like psoriasis."

"Like you had when I was little?" I asked. She nodded and looked at it more closely.

"I really think that's what it is. It looks just like it," she said.

I felt panicky, remembering my mom's skin when I was in kindergarten. She had round red spots on her arms and chest and there were little tubes of medicine all over the house that never seemed to help. Then I thought of the commercial on TV that talked about "The Heartbreak of Psoriasis." The people on the commercial really looked heartbroken and now I might be one of them.

"There's not much they can do for it. You'll just have to ride it out. We'll keep an eye on it, but mine went away, so yours probably will too."

I was glad it was fall and I wouldn't have bare legs for a long time. It would be gone by spring when I wore shorts. I made a mental note to get tights to match my new suit. If I wore nylons, people might ask me questions.

* * *

Maureen Abraham, one of the other Tandem Riders, called me the next night and invited me to her birthday party. It was going to be a "mixed party," for boys and girls because she was turning fourteen. She had started school a year later than us and was a little older. Later on that night Tom called and we realized we would both be turning fourteen in January. I was four days older than him.

On Saturday, the day of the party, I rolled my hair up on the frozen orange juice containers and taped my bangs down with Dippity-do and

26

pink hair tape. I was determined to have straight hair for the party. Peg and Irene had come over to my house the day before when my mom was still at work and we tried ironing my hair. We had read about doing that in fashion magazines. It didn't work. It just made my hair feel like hay. Maureen also had wavy hair and she told me Curl Free didn't work for her and I shouldn't waste my money. The Alger Heights girls seemed to understand my allowance was small and that I had to pay for many of my own things.

I decided I should hunt in my closet to find something interesting to wear to the party. I dug around and found an old wool skirt that still fit my waist. Now it was a mini skirt because it was from a couple years before. Its light aqua color matched a mod print blouse my Aunt Dorothy had sent me last year that I'd hardly ever worn. I couldn't believe what a great outfit it made. I decided to push the sleeves way up to look more casual. Then I turned sideways in front of the mirror to see if the blouse looked good untucked. That's when I noticed my left elbow. It had two small scaly patches on it that were red and raised. I held my elbow up to the mirror and inspected it more closely. Just what I thought...more psoriasis. There was no question about it because it looked like the small spots my mom had when I was little.

When one of my favorite songs came on the radio, I turned it up louder and rolled my sleeves down below my elbows. I danced a little in front of the mirror because I figured the boys wouldn't dance at the party, but the girls might. When I twirled around, I looked over and there were Cathy and Frankie waving like fools from Frankie's window. Those little spies! I huffed over to the window and drew my curtains closer together. I stuck my tongue out at them and then felt a little sorry in spite of my embarrassment.

* * *

The party was in Maureen's basement. Her mom had hung yellow crepe paper and balloons from the ceiling to make it look festive.

"I'm so glad you're here. Come meet my friends from the cottage," Maureen said.

She introduced me to six kids. A couple of them looked a little older than us. A girl, in a striped mini dress named Deanna, was sitting on a boy's lap so I knew Maureen's parents were somewhere else in the house. I set my gift on a table. I was quite pleased with it. It was twelve lip glosses all stuck together to make one long one that you pulled apart. They were all different flavors like peppermint and root beer.

I looked over and a few of the cottage kids were dancing to a song by the Kinks, even some of the boys. Maureen took me by the hand and brought me into the group to join them. I wasn't very confident about dancing in front of people, but I knew it would be more noticeable if I said no. It was more fun than I figured, especially since I was the only person from St. Bonaventure's besides Maureen.

A bunch of our own kids came down the stairs and it got really crowded. More people started dancing and we were all putting Bugles on our fingers and feeding them to each other. I felt somebody's eyes on me and when I turned around, Tom was standing by the snack table drinking from a Dixie Cup. He was looking right at me and his eyes were smiling. It reminded me of the night I first met him when he gave me the ice. Then I swore in my head because I remembered falling and that seemed to start this whole damn psoriasis thing. I suddenly felt scared in the middle of all that fun. I squeezed through the crowd and headed toward Maureen's little basement bathroom. I was glad it was in the opposite direction of Tom.

As soon as I shut the door, tears came to my eyes. I looked in the mirror and blinked hard, then dabbed with toilet paper, so tears wouldn't roll through the blush my mom had finally let me wear. I took a deep breath and looked at my cute outfit in the mirror. I was so proud that I had put it together myself. It was actually cuter than most of the clothes out there and with the dark green tights and rolled down sleeves, nobody knew my skin was different than anybody else's. I just wouldn't think about it tonight.

When I came out of the bathroom, the party was even more crowded. Maureen's parents were placing birthday cake and ice cream on the side table and replenishing the punch.

"Want some punch?" Tom handed me a Dixie Cup and then tapped his against mine as if we were toasting. I guess that made a little sense because it was my first boy/girl party and probably everybody else's from St. Bonaventure's.

"You look so nice tonight," he said into my ear. And when he did I felt his lips touch my ear ever so softly. Shivers went right up my spine. I just smiled at him because I didn't know what to say. My very favorite song came on, *How Can I Be Sure*, by the Young Rascals. I always sang it at the top of my lungs in my bedroom and used my hairbrush as a microphone. Tom took my cup and placed it on the table by his, and then he put his arms around my waist to begin dancing. I put my arms around his neck like the kids did on American Bandstand when they slow danced. Everyone around us backed up and watched for several seconds and then a few other couples joined us. I couldn't believe it, I was probably the first girl in my class to slow dance with a boy and he was the cutest boy in the whole world. My heart was beating very fast and I was sure his was too.

After the song, we joined some kids in the other part of the basement who were playing Twister. Tom and I stood by the sidelines holding hands, but laughed with everyone else when Teddy Zukowski's pants ripped straight up the back seam as he stretched his leg over Marty's head.

"Here, put this on," Mary Lou said as she handed Mr. Smith's raincoat to Teddy from a hook on the wall.

For the rest of the night, he ran around pretending to put fires out with an imaginary hose.

As people meandered back to the room where the record player was, Tom led me by the hand into the laundry room. He closed the door and took me into his arms and kissed me in a very grown up way. We kissed like that a few times and each one was longer. I felt almost woozy and would have liked it to go on and on, but I got nervous about Maureen's parents finding out and telling my mom. If my mom and sister ever got wind of this, there's no telling what they'd say or do. I'm pretty sure they expected me to play Barbie dolls with Cathy until I was in high school.

Chapter Four

A couple of days after the party, my other elbow had spots and so did my right knee. They were beginning to itch very badly and the one on my leg was starting to feel like a burn. I showed my mom and she reassured me that it would "run its cycle" and I shouldn't worry about it. In fact, she said, worrying would make it worse.

My dad called on Wednesday night to say he'd be coming to town on Sunday. It would be the first time I'd seen him since I spent a week at my grandma and Aunt Dorothy's house in August. He only lived a mile from them, so I saw him a lot. He also took off work a couple of times and we explored junk stores and hung out on his houseboat. He wanted me to stay with him and Wilma now that I was older, but I told him maybe next time, when I come in the spring.

He got to our house around noon on Sunday. My mom and I had just gotten home from church.

"Hey Sport, whatcha wanna do?" he asked me after I slid into the front seat of the Cadillac. My dad was a used car dealer, so I never knew what kind of car he'd show up in.

"I don't care," I shrugged.

"The usual?"

"Okay by me." Our "usual" was the Public Museum. We loved to walk around and look at the exhibits, especially the diaorama scenes of Indian villages and buffalo. We always ate lunch at Holly's restaurant across the street before going to the museum, and then we'd go back for a hot fudge sundae after we finished.

"So, your mom tells me she thinks you came down with psoriasis."

I was surprised to hear that because I didn't even know they'd talked and I really didn't think my mom would tell him since she seemed so unconcerned. My dad pushed his hat back and started the car.

"You know, I had that during the war, myself."

"Are you kidding me? You had it too?" I asked. He made a funny face and nodded.

"Yes, I did. And you probably don't want to know where I had it."

"You mean?" He nodded again. I could not believe it. I didn't just have one parent with this disgusting condition, I had two! And one of them had it on their privates!

"Did mom catch it from you?"

"Oh no, it's strictly a non-contagious disease. I asked Wally." Oh great, I thought. He asked Wally. Wally was his pharmacist friend who my dad treated like his personal doctor. Last summer, my hay fever got really bad while I was visiting him and he took me to Wally. Another time I got my period while I was visiting and my dad went to Wally's for "supplies." I waited in the car.

My dad handed me a small paper bag and inside was a tube with the "Heartbreak of Psoriasis" stuff. Of course he got it from Wally.

"Try this Sport. It might work, it might not."

When we were eating our lunch at Holly's, my dad brought the boyfriend thing up. Apparently, my mom had filled him in on that too.

"So, what's this I hear about a guy named Tom hanging around?"

"Tom? Oh yeah, he's been hanging around, I guess."

I was relieved that he wasn't very nosy about it. He seemed more interested in knowing if my mom had a boyfriend. I told him Larry was pretty nice, but I really hadn't seen him around as much lately. I didn't ask my mom questions because I didn't want her to ask me many either.

My dad came inside our house to fix the toaster and tighten a doorknob. He was great at fixing things. Larry tried, but wasn't too hot at it. My mom says it's because he's "the artistic type."

"Well, Sport, I got a two-hour ride and it gets dark earlier these days. I should hit the road," my dad said as he scratched Ruff and Reddy's ears and necks.

My mom had oven fried chicken cooking and I hoped she'd ask him to stay. Not that she ever had before, but they seemed friendlier today for some reason.

"Put that stuff on your skin like the directions say on the tube. You'll be fine in no time." He lifted me off the ground when he hugged me goodbye. I breathed in his scent of suede, cigars, and Old Spice. I stood on the porch and waved while he backed the car out of the driveway. He honked the horn several times and I watched his car turn the corner by the park. As usual when he left, my stomach felt like I'd swallowed a ball of clay.

When I came back into the house, the phone was ringing. It was Cathy.

"I just saw your dad leave. Did you have a good time with him?"

Cathy caught me sobbing on my back steps once when my dad left. It was the first spring that we lived here. She's the only person who knew how hard it was for me to say goodbye to him. My other friends liked to hear me talk about how funny he was. I would tell them about his crazy antics, like the time he pulled over and did the twist right on the highway when Chubby Checker came on the radio.

"We went apple picking today and my mom made pie. Wanna come over and watch *The Ed Sullivan Show*?"

I remembered The Supremes were going to be on *Ed Sullivan* and for some reason, hearing Cathy's voice made me feel better.

"Or you can come earlier and watch *Wonderful World of Color.*"

Back in fifth and sixth grades Cathy and I would often watch *Walt Disney's Wonderful World of Color* together with her brother. I thought maybe for old time's sake, it wouldn't hurt.

"Let me see how long my homework takes. I'll come over after," I told her.

I went upstairs to the bathroom and opened the tube of the heartbreak stuff. It had a terrible smell that made me feel about five years old because I remembered my mom using it. I put a little bit on my first spot, which seemed to be growing bigger every day.

After I finished my homework, I went next door. We sat on the floor in front of her console TV, eating apple pie.

"What's that smell?' Cathy sniffed in my direction.

"Oh shoot, can you smell it?" I asked her. She nodded.

"It's some medicine my dad brought me for my skin. I have this condition that he used to have and so did my mom. But they don't have it anymore and mine will probably be gone soon too."

"Where is the skin condition?" Cathy searched my face. I told her how it started on the injury and that there were a few other places.

"Can I see it?" she asked. First I pushed up the sleeve of my sweater and showed her my smallest spot. That's when I saw that another spot had popped out right by it.

"Well, I guess there's two now," I said. She asked to see my leg. I pushed my jeans up.

"Does it hurt?" she asked.

I nodded. "This one does. The others itch really bad."

Mrs. Cicerelli called from the kitchen, "Who needs another piece of pie?"

It was so delicious that I couldn't resist. She seemed so thrilled I was at their house, that she couldn't even hide it. She came out to the living room and lifted a piece out of the pan and onto my plate. Then she pointed the pie server at Cathy and said through gritted teeth,

"Caterina, you didn't wash that casserole dish like I told you!"

Cathy put her arms over her head in defense. Mrs. Cicerelli would often get so angry at Cathy and Frankie and then in the next breath be gushingly sweet toward me. I found it pretty amusing.

After my bath, I used the heartbreak stuff sparingly, because of the smell. My mom said the main ingredient was tar and that's why it smelled so bad. I tried Vaseline before bed to help with the burning, and decided to check more often to see if I had new spots. Maybe this would be it and I could concentrate on getting rid of the ones I still had.

* * *

The following Saturday, Peg and I went to the Four Star Theatre and met Tom and Marty there. Irene was out of town so Peg's mom didn't think too much of her going alone with me. We were worried she'd have to drag her little sister along, but she didn't want to go since Irene's little sister was gone too.

The boys told us to meet them in the balcony which I had never been in before. I had rarely gone to the movies at this neighborhood theatre. My mom and sister and I usually went downtown for movies. I noticed that Marty's arm was around Peg as soon as the lights went down and Tom encircled me in his arms when the movie started. I lost count of how many times we kissed. He even kissed my neck and ears very softly. There weren't many people in the balcony. I noticed it was mostly kissing couples.

Every now and then it crossed my mind that I had around eight small, ugly, red sores and one large one under my clothes. If Tom knew about them, I wondered if he would he be kissing me right now. Thankfully, they weren't on my face or hands, I thought to myself. But then I panicked. *Could* people get psoriasis on their face and hands? It had crossed my mind the other night, but I hadn't allowed myself to think about it again until now.

I broke out of Tom's embrace and excused myself to go to the ladies room. As I headed toward the stairs, I noticed three girls standing in a cluster, giggling. When I looked at them, they stopped. I thought they looked familiar. I was glad the bathroom was empty so I could study my face closely in the mirror. So far, there didn't seem to be any sign of psoriasis there or on my hands.

After the movie, the four of us walked around Burton Heights. We strolled the aisles at Woolworth's. Marty picked up a pet turtle so his legs were wiggling in the air. Peg and I yelled at him to stop because the turtle looked so helpless. Both of the boys tied chiffon scarves on their heads and dangled purses from their arms. We doubled over laughing. In the jewelry aisle, Tom slipped a ring on my finger and leaned over to my ear and said, "With this ring, I thee wed."

He brushed my lips with his and I felt so lightheaded, I had to grab hold of the counter. I heard a voice in my head asking me, *Am I falling in love?*

As we passed down the aisle of lotions, powders, and first aid items, Marty grabbed something from the shelf, then turned to us and said,

"Hey look, you guys, it's the "Heartbreak of Psoriasis." I was mortified, not only had he chosen that product, he said it in the exact voice they used on the commercial. My heart felt like it sank to my feet as Peg and Tom laughed.

* * *

The next day was Renee's birthday, so my mom and I drove to Mt. Pleasant, the town where she attended college. I hated the ride there except for the last stretch, where there were so many houses made from field stones that my sister and I never got the same count. I loved field stone houses and fantasized about living in one someday.

Renee lived in a tiny apartment with a friend and it was as neat as it could be because my sister was a cleaning fanatic. In fact, when we got there, she was racing around dusting and plumping pillows on the couch. After we convinced her the place looked fine, the three of us went to a nearby restaurant for an early dinner. While we were waiting for our food, Renee talked about the plays she planned on auditioning for. Just as the waitress was setting our food in front of us, Renee piped up and said,

"Hey, Ruth Ann, I almost forgot. Mom told me you have psoriasis all of a sudden. Let me see."

I shot her the most wicked glance I could and then smiled up at our timid looking waitress as she placed my fried perch in front of me. I felt a little like Mrs. Cicerelli showing my totally different emotions for two different people. I hit the bottom of the ketchup extra hard as I aimed it at my French Fries. A splatter of it landed on Renee's pink cashmere sweater.

"You little brat, you did that on purpose!"

"I did not!" I shot back.

"Both of you, cut this out right now. We are in public," my mother said, as she dipped her napkin in her water glass and handed it to my sister. Renee took the napkin from my mother and marched off to the restroom. I squeezed my lemon wedge onto my perch and peppered my coleslaw.

"Do you have more new spots you haven't told me about?" my mother asked.

I shook my head as I sucked on my straw. My sister returned and heaved a loud sigh as she sat down again. It appeared that she had been successful in removing the ketchup stain. Knowing Renee, I figured she invented a magic stain potion that she carried in her purse. She took such amazing care of her personal items that it was almost frightening.

"Did you hear from your father?" my mother asked Renee.

"Oh yes, the usual. His perfunctory phone call and a card with money."

My sister did not share the same affection for our dad as me. She always said that if I remembered the bad stuff like she does, I'd feel the same. I actually did remember some of the bad stuff, but it made a different impression on me, I guess. I knew he wasn't perfect, but I felt like my dad really liked me in a way I wasn't so sure about my mom and Renee. It always felt like I was in their way and that they'd have a lot more fun without me.

After dinner, we drove around the campus and stopped at the Dart Discount Store, which was actually open on Sunday. I looked at records and make-up while my mom bought Renee a new rug and lamp for her apartment.

* * *

"Renee, hurry up and blow your candles out. They're half melted!
"She's thinking of the best wish," my mom said.

I hoped it was to be finally done with college since she was twenty-two. My mom gave Renee a matching set of skirt, sweater and slacks in a dusty blue color, and the new Barbra Streisand album. I gave her a silver circle pin to wear on her collar that had an R in the middle. I also gave her Mallow Cups, her favorite candy that she often ate in front of me without sharing, even though there were always two in a pack. That's kind of why I got those for her, a little dig, I guess.

"Thanks, Ruth Ann," Renee said as she leaned over and kissed my cheek.

We left Mt. Pleasant around five o'clock and I slept most of the way home. I was glad that my mom was content listening to the radio because I wasn't in the mood to talk about any "new spots" or boyfriends.

Tom called when we got home and we talked for a half hour because his parents were gone. Normally, they didn't allow him to talk on the phone for very long because they didn't like the line to be tied up. I thought about telling him about my psoriasis, but then I decided against it because it would hopefully be gone by spring when I was wearing shorts and short sleeves. So we mostly chatted about friends, teachers and music. Tom said his favorite band was The Doors and he wanted them to be my favorite band. I had so many favorites, it was hard to choose "the one." We did decide that *Light My Fire* was "our song."

"I gotta go. I just heard my parents drive in. Promise me that every time you hear *Light My Fire,* you'll think of me, and I'll do it too. I mean forever, 'til the end of time."

"I promise," I told him.

Then he whispered into the phone, "I can't wait to kiss you again, bye." I got all fluttery over that.

* * *

My mom had left instructions to rake the front yard when I got home from school. Even though it was the end of October, it was warm enough to go without a jacket. Cathy came out of her house with two pieces of hot, buttered Italian bread fresh from the oven. She held one out to me on a light green napkin.

"Thanks, Cath. I need a break." I motioned for her to follow me to my front steps.

"I can help you if you want," she offered.

"Oh, that's okay, I only have to do the front today. We're still waiting for the leaves to fall from the backyard tree."

Cathy got quiet for a minute and then started scratching on the front walk with a stone. I got the feeling she had something on her mind. Then she looked up.

"If somebody was saying something about you that might or might not be true, would you want to know?" she asked me.

"It kind of depends on who's saying it, but yeah, I guess so."

"Well, Teresa Sullivan and her little group called me over to them on the playground today and told me they saw you making out with Tom LaBelle at the movies on Saturday."

So that's who those giggling girls in the balcony were at the movie.

"What if I was?" I asked.

Cathy's eyes were like dinner plates behind her glasses, and I thought her frizzy hair was going to spring off her head.

"I thought sure they were lying, 'cause they're jealous," she said.

"Well, maybe they are jealous, but they aren't lying," I said as I brushed the crumbs off my lap. Then I stood up and started raking as Cathy sat there with her mouth open. I thought of how she never even liked our Barbies to make out with Ken.

39

Chapter Five

The Tandem Riders and a few other kids were going to the football game on Friday night. I was glad to have a babysitting job for lots of reasons. For one thing, after the fall I took at the other game which started off this "Heartbreak" stuff, I wasn't the biggest football fan. The second thing was that I would probably earn enough at the babysitting job to get my print corduroy suit off lay-away.

On Friday afternoon, when I was washing my hands in the girl's bathroom, Maureen Abraham came up to the sink next to mine. "Are you going to the game tonight?" she asked me.

"No, I have a babysitting job."

"I'm not going either." She pulled two brown paper towels out of the container on the wall.

"Hey, do you wanna come and babysit with me?"

"Okay, that sounds fun."

I had been wanting to get to know her a little better, partly because she seemed very nice and I felt closer to her in age since she was the only girl in our little group who was older than me. Most of the other girls had turned thirteen in the last few months and I was going to be fourteen in less than three.

My babysitting job was right across the street from my house. I'd been babysitting for them for two years. Steven and David were seven and nine years old and pretty easy to handle. The only problem was that Steven occasionally walked in his sleep and had to be guided back to bed. It didn't bother me, but their mom said it frightened other babysitters. Mrs. Harris was a widow, and she went on dates sometimes or out with her girlfriends. She had no problem with Maureen coming over. When I came downstairs from putting the boys to bed, Maureen was just hanging up the phone.

Who was that?" I asked her.

"Teddy Zukowski. He and Gerard Waterman are coming over, but just for a minute. I loaned Zukowski two dollars and I need it, so he's bringing it over. He lives so close that it was easier for him to come here than to my house."

I wasn't comfortable with the boys coming over. I didn't think Mrs. Harris would be happy about it, and this was my best job.

"That's not a great idea, Maureen. My house is right across the street. My mom might see them."

"I know that, Ruth Ann. Don't forget, I came to your slumber party in sixth grade."

I groaned inside. That was the "girl make out party," when my sister came down the stairs and screamed at us that we were keeping her awake.

"I told them to come to the back door through the alley," Maureen said as peeked out the kitchen window.

They showed up fifteen minutes later.

"C'mon girls, we brought a deck of cards, let's play a game or two." Teddy pulled the cards out of his pocket and shuffled them in his palms. I looked at the clock. It was a quarter to nine and Mrs. Harris wasn't due home until after eleven. I looked at Maureen and she had her head cocked sideways in a pleading sort of way. There was something about the twinkle in her eye that made me give in.

"Okay, but you guys have to be out of here in an hour." We all pulled out the chairs and sat around the dining room table.

"Girls, the game is strip poker," Gerard announced.

"You're kidding, right?" I couldn't believe that Maureen was laughing as she looked at her cards. I got the feeling this was not her first time at this and that maybe she'd played with her cottage friends.

I had never played any kind of poker even though I'd watched my dad play at the car lot more than once. It wasn't long before we all lost our

41

shoes and socks.

"Off with your pants, Waterman," Teddy chuckled.

Gerard removed his belt. I was glad Maureen and I were both wearing triangle scarves over our hair, because that's what we removed next. I was watching the clock carefully, because there was no way I was going to take off anything beyond the sweater I was wearing over my blouse. For one thing, how would I explain the sores all over my arms and legs? All of a sudden, we heard a car in the driveway, and we all froze.

"Quick, go out the front door, hurry," I ordered.

Maureen and I threw their socks and shoes at the boys, shoved them outside, and pushed the dining room chairs in as fast as we could. We grabbed our own shoes and socks and plopped down on the couch just as Mrs. Harris and her date entered the kitchen through the back door. We were out of breath and I hoped they didn't notice, as we both sat facing the TV set.

"Hi Ruth Ann," Mrs. Harris said. "Don't worry, we're not in for the night.

We decided to go bowling, so I just stopped home for my bowling ball."

I introduced her to Maureen and it really looked like she didn't suspect a thing. I was relieved when they left and also relieved that strip poker had been cut short. I felt like an idiot for going along with it, but I had been too scared to argue. I was afraid of it being obvious that I had something horrible to hide.

"What luck we both had these scarves on," Maureen laughed as we tied them back on.

As I adjusted the scarf, my finger went over a bump on my head. It felt scaly and raised and it made me think of how the spots on my skin had been looking lately, which was very white and scaly.

"What's the matter?" Maureen asked me. I thought about telling her, since she seemed so trustworthy and kind. Then I quickly decided to keep quiet. I needed to keep reminding myself of how much time there was until spring.

"Oh nothing, I just need to switch shampoo brands. What kind do you use?"

Just then, Steven came bumping into the living room and even though his eyes were open, I could tell he was walking in his sleep. Maureen and I both giggled. I turned him around and headed him back to his room. I tucked him in and closed the door. When I came downstairs, Maureen was on the phone again. I was worried because I was afraid she'd called the boys back over.

"Hey, do you ever go on the beep-line?" she asked me. I shook my head.

"It's so cool, if you dial your own number, you get a busy signal and you can hear kids shouting their phone numbers. After you get a phone number, you hang up, call them back, and talk to them. Watch how I do it."

Maureen hollered into the phone, "What's -your -num-ber?" Then she wrote a phone number down and yelled, "Hang -up-I'll- call -you- back!"

"This is soooo fun. I did it last week with my cottage friends," Maureen said as she dialed the phone. We spent the next half hour talking to two boys who lived in a nearby suburb. We told them we were sixteen and that we both had long, straight hair and that I actually looked a lot like George Harrison's girlfriend, Patti Boyd. Maureen said she was so tall that she had a hard time fitting in her sports car. When we got off the phone, we laughed our heads off.

"That was so cool," Maureen said. "I can't wait to try it again."

"Yeah, it's kind of fun to be tall and have straight hair." And clear skin, I thought to myself.

* * *

The next morning, Peg called and said she was trying to get all the Tandem Riders to take the bus downtown to go shopping. I had planned to get my suit off lay-a-way at Mitchell's Young at Heart, but I decided I could do that another day. As I was getting dressed, I saw that there were a couple of more spots on my leg near the original one. A feeling of dread came over me as I realized that I was getting more and more new spots.

It was fun taking the bus with Peg, Irene, Mary Lou, Angela, and Maureen. The girls all decided that the first thing we had to do was look for the new kind of patterned nylons that were the latest style. I got quiet when I heard them all talking about it. There was no way I was going to be able to wear the nylons without telling them about my skin.

"Hey, let's go to Parklane Hosiery on Ottawa before we go to the big stores," Angela suggested. I had never been in the store. It was very tiny with only one employee and all they sold were nylons and garter belts. The nylons all came in flat boxes, which the lady pulled out from drawers in cabinets. There were several patterns to choose from. I chose a pair in the color of cinnamon with a tiny diamond pattern. They seemed like the ones that would cover my legs the best.

"Let's eat lunch at Wurzburg's coffee shop," Irene suggested as we walked down Monroe Avenue. I was in full agreement because I always loved to stop at the book department you passed through on the way. When I was younger I'd stop and flip through the Nancy Drew books and occasionally my mom would buy one for me.

We stopped in the Junior Miss department as soon as we entered the store. We were dying to see the latest Villager and Ladybug brand clothes that all the coolest girls in high school wore. I found a mint green cable cardigan that I loved so much I clutched it to my cheek. After I looked at the price tag, I talked myself out of love.

"I have a great idea!" Mary Lou said. "Let's go in the dressing room and put on our new nylons."

Unfortunately, all the girls agreed with her and ran toward the dressing rooms. I lagged behind, pretending to be matching the sweater to a skirt.

"You coming?" Maureen turned to me as she followed the other girls.

"I'll be right there." I wasn't sure what to do, but I darted into one of the cubicles so I could think. I took the nylons out and draped one over my arm. In spite of the color and pattern, they were still see-through. I unhooked the navy blue stocking that was on my bad leg and cursed myself for wearing them. If I didn't have my garter belt on, I'd have a great excuse to leave the nylons in the box. I decided to try anyway.

"These look even better than I thought they would," Peg hollered to us.

I studied my leg in the mirror and could only see angry looking red sores with white scales. The nylon fabric irritated my skin and it hurt, and the color and pattern didn't disguise much at all. I felt sad that I'd spent my babysitting money on something I couldn't really wear. Now it would take another job to get my suit off lay-away. I put the nylons back in the box and zipped up my bench-warmer coat. When I came out of the dressing room, the girls were in a cluster looking at the cute stick pins you got if you purchased an item from the Ladybug line.

"Why didn't you put on your new nylons?" Mary Lou asked me as she glanced down at my legs.

"I decided to save them," I said as I held a Ladybug earring up to my ear in the mirror.

"Well, let's get to the coffee shop," Angela said. "I'm dying for onion rings."

We walked through the book department and I glanced longingly at the Nancy Drew books. It seemed like a long time ago that I'd read them, and, I thought to myself, a time when I didn't have hideous skin.

Chapter Six

Between classes at St. Boner's, we had to walk in a circle along the wall and not speak. When we came to the door of our classroom, we were expected to enter and quietly take our seats. Tom and I were not in any of the same classes, but we always looked at each other and smiled as we circled. I noticed that he didn't look my way on Monday as I headed toward science class. He just looked straight ahead. I wondered what was going on.

I took my seat next to Mary Lou who was wearing an orange striped scarf around her ponytail. Sister Bartholomew (better known as Sister Barfalottoyou) was glaring at me. Then I remembered her "final warning" to me on Friday. She said if I hadn't cut my bangs by Monday, "I'd be sorry."

She thought my bangs were too close to my eyes. Thanks to Dippity-do hair gel, and the pink hair tape, I had been pulling off a very mod hairdo that I thought looked quite British. As soon as everyone took their seats, she called me up to the lab table which had a large mirror attached to it so the class could watch her occasional experiments.

"Just look at yourself," she screamed. She grabbed hold of my bangs and jerked my head back and forth. The DNA model teetered on the corner of the table as I looked at my class in the mirror. Most of them had their hands over their mouths to keep from laughing.

"What did I tell you on Friday, missy?"

"Lots of things, Sister. Mostly I remember that you said cilia are the little hairs that wave in our cells."

"Yes, I did say that, you sassy girl, and I also told you to get rid of this not so little hair that's hanging in your eyes, did I not?"

"Yes, Sister, you did."

"And how MANY times did I tell you that last week?" She jerked my head back even harder.

"I'm not sure, Sister."

By this time Sister Barfalottoyou was so red I thought her face might explode. She pulled me backward by the bangs all the way over to her desk. The entire class burst out laughing and so did I, even though I was sure she was going for her scissors. Instead, she removed the six inch metal clip from her clipboard, yanked my bangs completely back, and inserted the clip to keep the hair off of my forehead. She turned me toward the class and then pushed me toward my chair.

"Take your seat and don't take that out of your hair until you go home this afternoon. Either you cut that hair tonight or I'll do it for you tomorrow."

I took my seat and instead of feeling embarrassed, I felt strangely comical. I could almost see my dad shaking his head and rolling his cigar around in the corner of his mouth. When I looked around at my classmates, it looked like they'd all been crying, they'd laughed so hard. I'm pretty sure nobody learned anything about DNA for the rest of the hour.

When we walked around the circle in the hall, I was quite a spectacle. I saw Tom sneak a peek at me and his eyes grew wide, even though he'd ignored me earlier. At the end of the day, he caught up to me on the sidewalk.

"I bet your head feels different without that clip!"

"Much lighter, that's for sure. Barfalottoyou is pretty ridiculous, huh?"

He threw back his head and laughed really hard.

"I was kind of mad at you before that happened, but there was no way I could stay mad when I saw you in the hall with that thing on your head!"

I pretended that I hadn't noticed Tom ignoring me earlier. "Why were you mad?"

"Were you gonna tell me about playing strip poker at your babysitting job?"

"You're kidding, right? We took off our shoes and socks. Oh yeah, and our scarves!"

"Yeah, but what if the lady hadn't come home?"

"Trust me, that would have been the end of it, no matter what."

I looked into Tom's eyes and thought about telling him about my disgusting skin disease, but I stopped myself. There was something about the way he smelled that was so irresistible, I was afraid of losing more chances to bury my face in his neck.

"Well, see that it doesn't happen again," he said with his finger under my chin. Then he looked around and quickly gave me a peck on the lips before anyone could see us.

When I got home, I rummaged in the bathroom drawer for some scissors. As usual, I couldn't find any, just like when I needed Band-Aids or other necessities. I had my hand on the telephone receiver to call my mom at work when it began ringing. It was Maureen.

"Hey, wanna come over and do homework?" I was tempted because she had the new record, *To Sir, with Love* by Lulu. I loved singing with the song when it came on the radio.

"Well, maybe. Hey, do you guys have any hair scissors? I need to cut my bangs."

"We do have some and I could cut your bangs."

That sounded like a good idea to me, so I grabbed my homework and cut through the park to her house. Maureen's Pomeranian, Teeny, beat her to the door and jumped all over me when I walked into their family room.

"Come with me, mademoiselle, the beauty shop is right this way," Maureen said. As I followed her up the stairs, I noticed the framed silhouettes of each person in her family that were hanging on the wall. It seemed like every family had these, except for mine.

Maureen's room was pink. I sat on a pink bench in front of a pink dressing table and she draped a pink towel around my neck. She put *To Sir, with Love* on the record player and turned it up loud.

"Close your eyes," Maureen said as she picked up the scissors.

"Don't take too much off," I warned her. "Just enough to get Barfalottoyou off my back." Maureen nodded in agreement and began carefully snipping away.

"I don't know how you stood having that thing on your head all day. I think I would have thrown it at her after an hour. Hey, your scalp is really white." I felt Maureen lift my bangs, so I opened my eyes.

"Turn toward the window more. Gee, it's really red in places too. Does it hurt? What could this be?"

I felt an instant lump in my throat. This was it. I hadn't looked at my scalp very closely, even after finding the spot at my babysitting job. I got up and looked in the round mirror over her dressing table. Sure enough, my scalp in the front was covered with psoriasis. I took a deep breath and sat down hard on the bench. Maureen was standing very still with the scissors in the air. The record had stopped playing.

"Oh it's just this skin condition that I inherited from my mom. I have it lots of places, but you can't catch it from me, I promise."

"Oh, I didn't even think of that. How long have you had it?" I tried to hold back, but I couldn't. Tears rolled down my cheeks. I took the ends of the pink towel and wiped my face. As bad as I felt, I was glad Maureen was the first of my girlfriends to find out besides Cathy.

"Please don't tell anyone else, at least not yet. I'm pretty sure it won't last long 'cause my mom had it and hers went away after a few months. You know those commercials about the 'heartbreak of psoriasis'? That's what I have."

"What does the doctor say?" Maureen asked.

"Well, I haven't gone yet."

"Why not?" I felt funny that Maureen looked so surprised.

"My mom is so busy working. She doesn't get home 'til five thirty or even later sometimes, and doctor offices are closed then, and I really haven't shown her all my spots."

"Ruth Ann, she might get really mad if you keep it from her. You know how moms are. Maybe my mom could take you to the doctor. She's not that busy."

"No thanks. That's really nice of you, but I'm okay for now. Let's put the record back on and get my bangs cut." I could tell Maureen wanted to talk about it more, but I just wanted to change the subject. She shrugged, gave me a little hug and then started cutting my bangs. She did a better job than I would have and at least I'd be off the hook in science class. As I inspected my hair in the mirror, I was shocked to see Maureen striking a match and then lighting a cigarette she had between her lips.

"Want one?" she asked me, holding out a pack of Winstons. I hesitated and then decided it wouldn't hurt to try. I coughed and choked after the first couple puffs and then Maureen switched the record to *Stop in the Name of Love* by the Supremes.

We sang together in front of her mirror holding out our hands in a stop motion every time the word *stop* was sung. Then we put blue eye shadow on and pinkish white lipstick and Maureen blew four perfect smoke rings. I felt happier than I had in a long time. It felt good that Maureen knew about my psoriasis and that she didn't think I was gross.

* * *

My mom was just pulling into the driveway as I walked up.

"Where've you been?" she asked as she came out of the garage.

"I went to Maureen's house so she could cut my bangs. Sister Bartholomew said she wouldn't let me back in class unless I did. In fact, she humiliated me in front of everybody."

"Well, I doubt it was that bad, Ruth Ann. Hey, your friend did a pretty good job," she said as she inspected my bangs.

"Are you kidding? She made me wear a giant clip from a clipboard on my head, ALL DAY! And that's not all, now I have psoriasis on my head.

Maureen saw it when she was cutting my hair."

My mom sighed loudly as she unlocked the side door.

"I had a really rough day at work, Ruth Ann. And now I have to figure out what to have for dinner. I better not get a call from that nun tonight. I'm not in the mood."

I slammed my bedroom door and threw my school books on the bed. With my face as close as possible to the mirror, I lifted my bangs up to see how I looked all day with the clip on my head. While I was walking home from the park, I began worrying that the kids had seen the psoriasis on my scalp while I was wearing the clip. As I inspected closely, I decided that you couldn't see it unless you were very close like Maureen was when she was cutting my bangs.

"I guess I better keep Barfalottoyou and her clip as far away as possible," I said out loud to myself in the mirror.

Chapter Seven

Maureen invited a bunch of us to her house on Saturday because her parents were going to the cottage to close it up for the winter. They were planning to have dinner with friends and wouldn't be back until late. Maureen was especially excited because her new boyfriend, John O'Rourke was coming over too. He was new in our school this year and she'd had a crush on him since the first day. When I got to her house, Peg and Irene were already there. They were trying to help her pick out an outfit.

"Wear this," Irene said, holding up a pink fuzzy sweater.

"No, I'm really sick of pink. Yellow is my new good luck color," Maureen said as she applied Ice Blue Secret deodorant to her underarms.

"Are you sure your parents are staying out late?" Peg asked.

"They might even stay overnight. If they start playing cards after dinner, they'll go 'til midnight. And it's an hour and a half away from here. Don't worry, we'll have the whole house to ourselves and I'll have a whole Johnny to *myself*." Then she puckered up in the mirror and applied Kiss Me Pink lipstick.

When the boys arrived, Maureen put *Sunshine of Your Love* on her parent's stereo. We all stood around laughing at her mother's collection of Hummel statues. She had over fifty of them on a shelf above the television. Gerard picked one up and I thought Maureen was going to have a heart attack.

"Put that down this instant, Waterman!"

"Okay, I won't hurt the little guy," he said as he handed it back to her. Then Maureen played *A Whiter Shade of Pale* and Tom held out his arms to me to slow dance and so did Marty to Peg. Gerard shrugged and held his palms up to Angela. She rolled her eyes, shrugged back, and let him dance with her. Irene and Teddy were fighting over a can of Redi-Whip that they were squirting into their mouths. John was paging through a Life magazine on the coffee table and Maureen was looking at me with a *what should I do?* look on her face.

"Ask him!" I mouthed the words to her over Tom's shoulder. She had talked about dancing to this song all week. She tapped him on the shoulder and gave him that bewitching smile of hers. He looked up from the magazine while still holding a corner of the page. I could tell he was trying to act surprised that people were dancing and that Maureen was pulling him off the couch. As soon as they began to dance, Teeny started nipping at the cuffs of John's jeans.

When the song started playing a second time, Marty reached over and switched off the lamp. Tom immediately kissed me and it lasted for at least a whole minute. Then he took my hand and led me into the living room and onto the couch next to the baby grand piano. We kissed several times with our feet on the floor but our top halves lying down. Then I felt Tom's hand slide under my shirt and onto my bra. I wasn't sure if I wanted him to stop or not. When he started fumbling with the hook in the back, I sat up.

"What's the matter?" he asked.

"I don't know," I answered truthfully. I felt kind of confused.

"C'mon, you're my girl. I thought about you all week." Then he kissed me again and lowered me back down. I got a tingly feeling. It reminded me of how I used to feel when Barbie would answer the door to Ken with her shell pink negligee undone. The record had ended in the other room and wasn't switching off. I figured everyone was making out because all I could hear was the clicking sound of the needle on the record.

"Hey, LaBelle, we gotta go," Marty was standing in the doorway of the living room. By this time, my blouse was unbuttoned, and we were pretty tangled up.

"Okay, give me a sec," Tom said over his shoulder.

"I love you," he whispered into my ear. My heart was beating very fast. Nobody had ever said those words to me.

"I love you too."

"I'll call you tomorrow," he said as he stood up.

All the boys were moving toward the door when we got back in the family room. Maureen had a huge smile on her face, so I knew things had gone well with John. The girls left shortly after, except for me because I was sleeping over.

When we got to Maureen's room, she lit a Winston and took a big puff. She put her other hand on her hip and smiled at me in a knowing way after she blew the smoke at the ceiling.

"He got to second, didn't he?"

"What do you mean?" I tried to play dumb. I knew she was talking about second base.

"C'mon, Ruth Ann. You guys have been together for over two months, and I can tell by the look on your face." I leaped onto the pink chenille bedspread and Teeny started yapping his head off. I hid my face in the pillow, but it was no use. I was laughing hysterically. I loved how Maureen just said things straight out.

"Okay, you win! YES! There, are you happy?"

"On or under?"

"What?"

"On or under your bra?" I threw the pillow at her and it knocked a curler out of her hand.

"Good thing my cig is in the ashtray! If you don't tell me, on or under, I won't tell you a thing about Johnny."

"Okay then. Just a little bit under. Now c'mon, tell me all about you and Johnny.

"Well, I think he's kind of shy. We mostly talked the whole time, about his old school and stuff like that. But he did kiss me twice before it

54

was time to go. I'll tell you what, I haven't felt like this about any boy from St. Boner's before.

We didn't turn out the lights until after midnight. Maureen's parents had called and said they were spending the night at the cottage. We were snuggled in the twin beds in the dark and I felt so grown up with her parents gone.

"Hey, Ruth Ann?"

"Yeah?"

"Does Tom know about your skin problem? What's it called again?"

"Psoriasis. No, he doesn't know about it."

"Do you have it on your chest or anywhere like that?"

"No, thank God." At least, not yet, I thought to myself.

"Well, that's good anyway. Tonight was fun, wasn't it?"

"*Really* fun. Thanks for having me over, Maureen."

"Are you kidding? I'm so glad we're friends."

"Me too."

* * *

My sister came home the night before Thanksgiving. My mom was making a Jell-O salad when Renee came bursting through the door.

"Why hasn't anybody raked the front yard?"

I was sitting on the window seat in the dining room, talking on the phone to Tom. I put my hand over the bottom of the receiver.

"Just a minute, Tom. Renee, I've raked three times. Those are the backyard leaves that blew into the front." My mom came out of the kitchen, drying her hands on her apron. She walked over to Renee and kissed her cheek.

"Hi honey. You know how long it takes for those leaves in the back to fall. We plan to finish up on Friday. I have the day off." Renee picked up Ruff and he licked her cheek. Reddy brushed up against her legs.

"Well, at least the cats aren't dead. I'm glad somebody's paying attention to *them*." She glared at me.

The next day, we carried the Jell-O salad and a green bean casserole over to the Cicerelli's. They had invited us to Thanksgiving dinner. Their house was full of cousins running all over and babies crying. They had to set up three tables for everyone to fit. I was surprised that Mrs. Cicerelli's turkey didn't have tomato sauce and I was glad that she'd made her yummy bread. I hadn't had any in several weeks.

After dinner, Cathy and I went up to her room. She wanted to show me two outfits her mom had bought her for the school holiday program. She had to pick out which one she wanted to keep.

"Gee, Cath, when is your mom gonna start taking you with her to buy clothes? Have you ever even asked her?"

Cathy shrugged and pushed her glasses up on her nose.

"Maybe you should start by saying you don't like either one and then go pick out your own choice." I felt bad saying that, but I figured it was for her own good. The orange corduroy jumper was bad and the plaid dress even worse.

"I'm not good at picking out clothes like you are. Hey, would you go with us?"

Going shopping with Cathy and her mother was the last thing I felt like doing. It crossed my mind that I'd smoked two cigarettes and let a boy unhook my bra. Cathy would probably go right under the bed like there was a tornado if she knew.

"Pretty please. You're so smart about cool clothes. My mom would probably take us to lunch at my uncle's restaurant too." I told her I'd have to see.

* * *

The next morning Renee woke me from a sound sleep.

"Get up right now, Lazy. It's time you started helping Mother around here. This place is a sty! Just look at this." She held her finger up after sliding it across my dresser.

"It is not a sty, Renee. And for your information, I help her all the

56

time. Leave me alone!" She slammed my door and started vacuuming the hallway. There was no way I could sleep in now.

When I got downstairs she was vacuuming around me as I sat at the dining room table eating cinnamon toast and reading the comics. I knew she was doing it to irritate me, so I pretended not to notice. Then she moved into the TV room and switched the vacuum off.

"What on earth is this?" Renee hollered. My mom came into the dining room with a laundry basket. We both went in to see what she was talking about. Renee was pointing at the carpet in front of the couch.

"Oh honey, that's from Ruth Ann scratching. The skin on her legs is flaking off. I just vacuumed it the day before yesterday."

"Oh my God, that is so disgusting, I can't even believe it. And why are *you* doing the vacuuming? She should be doing it!"

"Renee, she can't help it. The itching is terrible."

"Well, maybe the itching *is* terrible, but she's old enough to clean up after herself!" I looked down at the floor and saw the white flakes. I felt like a gross monster.

"I hate you Renee! Go back to Mt. Pleasant!" I ran out of the room and up the stairs. When I got to my room I began sobbing into my pillow. My sister had been mean to me many times before, but this time she'd outdone herself. I wished with all my heart that *she* would get a horrible case of psoriasis.

While I was washing my face with cold water and Noxzema, my mom came into the bathroom and sat on the edge of the bathtub.

"Don't feel bad, Ruth Ann. You know how Renee is about cleaning. She didn't mean to hurt your feelings. And she's about to get her period any minute."

"Ruth Ann, telephone," Renee shouted from downstairs.

"It's probably Cathy. She wants me to go shopping with her and her mom and I don't want to."

"Why don't you go with them, honey? They're such good neighbors and you and Cathy used to be so close. I know you've kind of outgrown her, but think about how she must miss you." I groaned.

"I'll tell you what. You go with them and I'll give you the last few dollars to get your suit off lay-a-way."

That sounded like a pretty good compromise to me, even though I knew my mom was trying to make up for Renee being mean.

* * *

Cathy was in the dressing room at Mitchell's Young at Heart. She was trying on a brown Poorboy sweater that I thought she'd look good in because of her brown eyes. Mrs. Cicerelli was chatting with Mrs. Roshevsky, the owner. My suit was draped on my arm in a plastic bag and it was all paid for. While I was trying to find a print skirt to match Cathy's top, Mary Lou and Angela walked up to me.

"Hey Ruth Ann, what are you up to?" Mary Lou asked.

"Oh, hi. I'm just helping my neighbor pick out an outfit."

"Your neighbor?" Angela asked. Just then, Cathy stuck her head out of the dressing room curtains. As usual, both her glasses and her hair looked enormous.

"I think this is too tight, Ruth Ann," Cathy said before she spotted the girls. Her face turned red when she noticed them and she poked her head back in. I shook my head and rolled my eyes at the girls.

"She's your neighbor? Doesn't she go to St. Boner's? I think I've seen her before. Why are you hanging around with *her*?"

"Who do we have here?" Mrs. Cicerelli asked. I introduced her to Angela and Mary Lou and they walked away quickly. I hoped Mrs. Cicerelli hadn't noticed me making fun of Cathy. I hadn't meant to, but I was embarrassed to be shopping with the Cicerellis. I was also embarrassed that the girls hadn't been more friendly. I looked over at Mary Lou's paisley scarf on her ponytail. I got a sudden urge to yank it off, open the door and let it blow away.

* * *

Gone Before Spring

While we were eating pizza at Uncle Alfredo's restaurant, I forgot all about not having any leftover pumpkin pie or stuffing at home. His pizza was the best I'd ever had. Mrs. Cicerelli disappeared into the kitchen to talk to her brother and Cathy and I laughed about the time we had been there for Frankie's birthday and he'd fallen off his chair.

"We got the new *TV Guide* and guess what movie's on Shock Theatre next Friday?" Cathy asked. My mouth was full of pizza, so I just shrugged.

"*Bucket of Blood*! Can you believe it? Remember when I stayed over at your house and we watched it?"

"How could I forget? You spent the whole time hiding behind our couch."

"I did?"

"You sure did. And your mom said you didn't sleep for three nights after."

"Yeah, but don't forget. I was only in the fifth grade."

"You really think it'd be any different now?"

Cathy nodded as she chewed. I was about to remind her that I'd found her under the bed during a tornado alert just six months ago, but her mother returned to the table.

"You girls should have some salad with that. Let me get some salad from the kitchen."

"No, Mom. We don't need any. We're full." Cathy wiped her mouth on a napkin.

"All right, all right. So, are you happy with your new clothes? Ruth Ann did a nice job, picking out, didn't she?" Mrs. Cicerelli pinched my cheek. I was glad she wasn't insulted about taking the other things back.

"I like the new clothes, Mom. Thank you." Cathy seemed a little glum all of a sudden. Good thing I hadn't mentioned the tornado.

59

Chapter Eight

My mom said I could have two friends overnight for *Bucket of Blood*. I had told everyone at Angela's slumber party about the movie because it was one of my favorites. It was all about a bunch of beatniks who hung out at a coffee house, and one of them started killing people and covering them with clay so everyone would think he was an artist and that the dead people were statues he made.

I was having such a hard time deciding who to have over besides Maureen. When I got home from school on Tuesday, my mom called me from work.

"Larry wants to take us out to eat tonight and he told me you should pick the place. Where should we go?" I hadn't seen Larry in a while, but I'd noticed that he'd been calling my mom again lately. Then a scheme popped into my head.

"Kewpies or Fables, either one."

"Let's go to Fables," my mom said. Larry loves their olive burgers."

That night after our waitress had taken our order, Larry looked right at me and asked, "So, Ruth Ann, what have you been up to?"

"Well, my favorite scary movie is on TV this Friday and Mom said I can have two friends overnight. The problem is that I can't decide who to invite because there are six of us in the Tandem Riders and..."

"The Tandem Riders?" The thing I liked about Larry was that he didn't tease and he really seemed interested in stuff.

"Yeah, we started calling ourselves that after we rented tandem bikes the first week of school. And we do a lot together, so this will be hard."

"And I remember the last slumber party when you girls stayed up all night," my mom said.

"Mom, that was on my twelfth birthday! I'm almost fourteen.

Anyway, Renee was a witch that night. She ruined the whole thing." I wished I could forget that practice make-out party.

"She's right, Marla. Eighth graders are way more mature than sixth graders. They're practically in high school," Larry said, as he placed his napkin in his lap.

My scheme was working. I knew Larry would be on my side and that my mom would not want to seem grouchy. She shook her finger at him, but was trying not to laugh.

* * *

The next morning, when I shuffled into the kitchen to make toast, there was a note from my mom propped against the toaster. It said I could invite all the Tandem Riders to the overnight. *Good old Larry*, I thought to myself.

After school on Friday, I moved the coffee table out of the living room and pushed the couch back, so we'd have room to spread our sleeping bags in front of the television. Ruff and Reddy were following me because they always love it when we changed things around. One good thing about Renee was her decorating hobby. She made new curtains with matching pillow covers last summer, and it really made our downstairs look better.

Maureen came early and helped me put the snacks out on our dining room table. My mom promised to make caramel corn later and the girls were excited about that when I'd mentioned it at school. By 7:30, everyone had arrived and we decided to go up to my room and put our pajamas on. All the girls rifled through their bags, pulling sweaters over their heads, talking and laughing loudly. Then I realized that I had forgotten to stash my pajamas in the bathroom cupboard. I had planned on changing in there, so nobody would see my psoriasis. I opened my top drawer and pretended to be looking for something.

"My mom must have left our clean laundry in the basement. I'll be right back."

61

Only Mary Lou seemed to hear me as I left the room and went downstairs.

I knew there were no pajamas in the basement, so I wasn't sure what to do. My mom was sitting on the window seat in the dining room, talking on the phone. She gave me a funny look when I passed her. I stood in the laundry room looking around and could hear the girls' laughter through the vent. I closed my eyes and willed myself not to cry. I had to quit being such a big baby about this. When I went back to my room, the girls were looking at my records and magazines.

"Is there a record player downstairs?" Angela asked. Then Mary Lou chimed in.

"Hey, where's your pajamas?"

"I guess they're not dry yet."

I hated to lie, but couldn't think of another excuse. I felt envious when I saw how carefree the girls were about changing in front of each other. At least it was so cold that we'd had snow flurries earlier in the day. That meant I could wear my flannels and they would give better coverage.

"Let's take the records down and get some pop," I said quickly to change the subject.

The girls followed me into the kitchen where I handed out 7-up, Coke, and Orange Crush. Maureen asked me to play *Let's Spend the Night Together,* and we all stood around the hi-fi singing, and using our pop bottles as microphones. When the song ended, I saw Irene staring toward the kitchen doorway. I turned around and there were my mom and Cathy standing side by side. Cathy was still wearing her school uniform and she was holding a plate in front of her. Apparently my mom had let her in through the side door and we were so loud I hadn't heard her.

"I didn't know you had company," Cathy said. "My mom baked those anise cookies you love, so she wanted me to bring some over."

I wasn't sure what to say because I was really surprised.

"Oh, thanks Cath." I turned toward the girls.

Gone Before Spring

"This is Cathy, my next door neighbor. Her mom is the best cook I've ever known."

The girls all said hi, but Cathy barely replied. I took the plate from her and said, "Flip the record over and play *Ruby Tuesday,* you guys." I led Cathy to the kitchen with the plate in my hands.

"You want a bottle of pop, Cath? There's Orange Crush." She shook her head and said, "That's okay. I'll just go. I wanted to know if you could sleep over and watch *Bucket of Blood*, but you already have plans for it, I guess."

I'd recently heard my mom say that she "felt like a heel" when she forgot her sister's birthday. Now I understood what a heel felt like.

"I'm sorry I didn't invite you, Cath. I just thought you'd feel weird 'cause you really don't know my friends. But hey, go get your pajamas and stay over." Cathy looked down at my jeans and sweater.

"Where are *your* pajamas? The other girls all have their pajamas on. Why don't you?"

I thought about busting out with the truth because Cathy did know after all, but I changed my mind.

"C'mon, Cath, stay over. My mom's gonna make caramel corn later." That's when Cathy's eyes welled up with tears. She turned around and walked down the steps to the side door. I followed her, not knowing what to say. I thought of all the times we used to spend the night together and my mom would make caramel corn. One time we'd even slept in a tent in her back yard. I decided to pretend I hadn't noticed her tears.

"Well, tell your mom thanks for the cookies and I'll see you soon."

I closed the door after watching Cathy walk down the driveway. I felt like the meanest person alive. When I turned around, Maureen was standing there with something rolled up in a bundle.

"Here's your PJs. I got them out of your drawer. Go put them on in the basement, like they just came out of the dryer."

I loved Maureen. She was turning out to be a really good friend. And a smart one.

* * *

We were all sitting on our sleeping bags messing around with our hair and painting each other's toenails. Maureen had just painted my pinkie toenail with shocking pink polish, when Mary Lou bent her over to the side and pointed at the part of my leg right above my ankle.

"Eww, what's that on your leg?"

I felt my heart flip-flop. Peg turned her head to the side and studied my leg. Then the rest of the girls leaned in to see. I felt like dying. Maureen looked up at me like she was trying to figure out what she should do. Since I was hesitating, she glanced at all of them and shrugged.

"It's just a little skin thing, like an allergy," she said and then bent over and began painting the toenails on my other foot.

"How long have you had it?" Mary Lou asked, with a disgusted expression. I realized that it wasn't worth holding back anymore.

"I've had it a couple months. It's called psoriasis. My mom had it and it went away after a few months."

"You caught it from your mom?" Angela asked.

"No, it's not contagious, I promise. It's like something you inherit, I guess. Don't worry, nobody can catch it from me."

"Is that the only place you have it? Does it itch? Does it hurt? Is that why you haven't worn your new nylons?"

I felt overwhelmed and was trying to answer one question at a time, when I heard a light tap on the window. I looked up and saw Tom. He was on the front porch looking in. Irene screamed and everyone turned toward the window.

"You guys, it's just Tom. Shush up or my mom will come down." My mom had promised she'd read in her room until it was time for the caramel corn. I opened the front door and Tom stood there with a silly grin. Then I realized I was wearing my pajamas with the Siamese cats all over them. Marty was behind him with Gerard, Teddy and John. The girls

64

were giggling and hiding behind the door.

"Can you come out?" Tom was almost whispering.

"Well, maybe for a minute. My mom's upstairs, so she might not notice. Just a sec."

I closed the door softly and held a finger to my lips. Then I took the *Beatles VI* album out of the jacket, put it on the turntable, and turned it up as loud as I thought I could without my mom noticing. I pointed to the coat tree and we all got into our jackets and shoes and tiptoed out the front door. We left the door open a crack so we could get back in without knocking. When I got on the porch, Tom grabbed my hand and led me behind our garage. It was really cold and had started to snow again. Tom had a wool scarf around his neck and his face was very red. He leaned down and kissed me so tenderly that I started crying.

"What's the matter? Did you miss me?" I swallowed hard and nodded. I figured that he may as well think that because I wasn't sure why I was crying.

"Seriously? Aww." He pulled me toward him and held me close. I buried my face in his scarf and started sobbing. I felt angry that Mary Lou had acted so disgusted by my skin, but grateful that Tom had come when he did and saved me from the questions. Now I felt like I didn't deserve such a nice, cute boyfriend since I had hideous skin he didn't even know about. He patted my eyes with his sleeve.

"Aren't you having fun with your friends?" he asked. I nodded, then shook my head and then shrugged. He started laughing. "Gee, you're pretty mixed up tonight, aren't you? Hey, do you have your period or something? That's exactly how my sister acts when she has hers."

I couldn't believe Tom mentioned anything about my period. I had never talked to a boy about periods. I was kind of shocked, but at the same time I felt like we really were a couple now. I shook my head and stood on my tiptoes and kissed him in the most romantic way I could. I got the "Barbie negligee" feeling all over under my pajamas, which surprised me because they certainly weren't see-through. After we kissed several more times, Tom placed my hand on the front of his jeans.

"See what that kiss did?" I wasn't completely sure what he meant, but I had a pretty good idea. I recalled our old Sears Catalog that I had cut up for paper dolls. I would stare at the bulges on the men's underwear page and wonder how it would feel to have all that extra stuff in your underpants. One thing I did know, was that side one of the album was close to being over and we needed to get back in before my mom discovered we were outside.

"I have to get back in. My mom will kill me if she's knows we're outside with boys."

"Okay, I'll call you tomorrow. Maybe I can come over or something." I nodded and we walked back toward the front door. Maureen and John were kissing by the elm tree.

"Hey you two, we gotta go back in." Neither of them said anything. They just looked at me and smiled.

We snuck back in and the record had already ended. My mom walked in just as we were hanging up our coats.

"What's going on, Ruth Ann?"

"Nothing. It's snowing again, so we wanted to run around in the back yard."

My mom looked very suspicious and I could tell she knew something was up.

"Well, I don't know what time your movie comes on, but I'm making the caramel corn now. I've had a long day and need to go to sleep. Don't you dare open that door again. Do you hear me, young lady?" I nodded and hoped like mad that the questions were over.

Bucket of Blood wasn't as scary as I remembered. It was actually pretty funny. It had cool background music, though, and the girls liked it. We decided it was the Tandem Riders movie and that *Let's Spend the Night Together* was our song. I felt a little sad about it, though, because it had kind of been my movie with Cathy and she had walked in when we were all singing the song. I couldn't stop thinking about the look on her face when she was standing there with those cookies.

My mom made french toast for everyone in the morning and after the girls left she told me that Larry was right. Eighth graders were more mature than sixth graders because sixth graders didn't run outside to kiss boys in the back yard. Then she told me to vacuum the living room and change the kitty litter.

Chapter Nine

It stayed very cold for the whole next week. We all got excited because the park at the end of my street made an ice rink every year, and we heard it might be ready by Saturday night. Roller skating was one thing, and ice skating, another. I was terrible at roller skating. Back in sixth grade I had knocked over the entire Hokey Pokey line when I couldn't stop on those stupid rubber tips. I had to yell, "Look out!" Then I ran straight into the wall. After that I just sat at the snack bar and ate French Fries. But for some reason, I could manage pretty well on ice skates and Renee's old pair still fit me.

On Saturday morning, while I was helping my mom defrost the refrigerator, my dad called.

"Hey Sport, how 'bout coming for a visit after Christmas? Or do you have big plans?" I hesitated, because even though I missed my dad, I was looking forward to hanging out with the Tandem Riders and of course, Tom. I didn't want to hurt my dad's feelings, though, so all I said was, "Not really."

"That's okay, you think about it. Hey, how's that tar stuff working on your skin? Did it help?"

Again, I didn't know what to say. It hadn't helped my old spots, but since I hadn't got any new ones in over a week, I was slightly hopeful.

"Yeah, I think it's a little better."

"Well, you gotta keep at it. Put it on every night before bed, ya hear? And I'll call you back in a few days after you talk to your mother, okay? And if that stuffs not workin', just tell me so I can talk to Wally. He can probably fix you up with something else. Bye, Sport. Be good."

"What did your father want?" my mom asked as she placed another bowl of hot water in the freezer.

"Not much. He asked about my skin, mostly."

"How *is* your skin. You haven't mentioned it lately." My mom lit a cigarette and leaned against the kitchen counter.

Well, you haven't asked lately, I thought to myself.

"It's fine," I said as I lifted a big chunk of ice out with a spatula and then threw it into the sink. " Can I go ice skating tonight? They finished the rink."

"Down the street, at the park? Who with? You sure have an active social life these days. I suppose that Tom's going."

I just kept chipping away the freezer.

* * *

All the Tandem Riders, except Irene, went ice skating that night. We met in the warm-up house where we put on our skates and they sold hot chocolate.

"Do you know what you're getting Tom for Christmas?" Maureen asked me.

"No, I haven't even thought about it. Are you getting John something?"

"I'm buying him Brut Cologne and I've been hinting that he should get Ambush for me because Brut and Ambush go together." I recalled the day we bought our patterned nylons and had stopped to sniff Ambush in the perfume department.

Just then, Tom and Marty walked in with their skates over their shoulders.

"Wow, the ice looks great! It's never been this smooth before," Tom said as he sat next to me on the bench. I took off my regular socks and replaced them with my red wool skating socks. Mary Lou and Angela were sitting across from me.

"Do you still have that skin disease on your legs," Mary Lou asked. "What's it called, Sore-itis?"

I looked up at her and tried to act like she'd asked me about the weather or something else I didn't care about, even though I wanted to strangle her with her ponytail scarf. Tom had been about to place his foot in his skate, but he stopped and looked up.

"Yes, I still have it."

I was about to tell her it was psoriasis, but Maureen blurted out. "Ruth Ann, you want hot chocolate? I'm getting one before I go out."

Peg turned to Mary Lou and said, "Can I borrow fifty cents?"

I got the feeling the other girls were trying to cover for me because of Mary Lou's big mouth.

"No thanks, I'll wait 'til I come in for a break," I told Maureen while trying to say thank you with my eyes. Tom held his hand out and led me to the door as I wobbled on my skates. He was acting like he thought I was going to fall over. When we got out on the ice I filled my lungs with the frosty air. The stars were twinkling and it could have been a perfect night if Mary Lou hadn't shown up. I was trying to remember if she'd ever been so mean to anyone else. Tom took my hand.

"Ready?" I nodded as we began skating.

After we got about half way around the rink, he looked at me and said, "What the heck was Mary Lou talking about?"

"Oh, you mean about my skin?" Again, I was trying to act like it wasn't a big deal. "It's something I must have inherited from my parents. I just got it a couple months ago."

"Why didn't you tell me before?"

"Does it matter? I didn't think it was worth mentioning, I guess. My mom's went away really fast, and mine probably will too."

He stopped skating and pulled me back. "Of course it doesn't matter. I love you, that's what matters, right?" I swallowed hard and nodded. John and Maureen came skating by, and John grabbed Tom's stocking cap off his head. Tom went flying after him and Maureen circled back to me.

"Are you all right?" she asked. "I wanted to slap Mary Lou for asking

70

you about your psoriasis right in front of Tom. She did that on purpose."
As we started to skate, Peg caught up with us.

"Just so you know, I told Mary Lou she needed to leave you alone
about your skin problem. I think she's jealous of you or something."

"Jealous? Of me? That doesn't make sense," I said.

I thought of Mary Lou's long straight hair and big blue eyes. Not to
mention her darling house that actually had a white picket fence.

"Thanks Peg, but don't turn around. Here she comes."

Mary Lou and Angela skated up to us. "Why aren't you guys
skating?" Angela asked. "You're gonna freeze if you don't keep moving."

I noticed instantly when the song on the loudspeaker switched to
Light My Fire. Less than thirty seconds passed before Tom skated up to
us, took me by the hand, and said, "C'mon, Ruth Ann, this is our song."
As we skated away, I saw Mary Lou staring at us with a very weird look
on her face. Could that be it? Did *she* like Tom, I wondered. When John
and Maureen went by, I noticed he was wearing Tom's hat on top of his
own.

"I thought you went after him to get your hat back," I said.

"I started to, but then Mary Lou Bender stopped me to say she was
sorry that I found out about your skin. She said she just figured I knew."

"What did you say?"

"I told her I didn't care one way or another and I didn't know why she
did."

I reached up and kissed Tom's cheek. Then he kissed my lips lightly.
I was glad we weren't under the big spotlights. Even so, I saw Teresa
Sullivan and her friends from Cathy's class staring at us from the other
side of the rink.

"We better watch it," I told Tom.

"What do you mean? This is our song. Do you know how much I
want you with me, whenever I hear it? For once, you *are* with me."

He kissed me again. This time a little longer. I felt pretty worried.

71

This was a very public place and I was afraid it would get back to my mom. She and Renee were always talking about girls with bad reputations and I was sure this is how those stories got started. When the song ended, I looked around for Maureen. I waited until she came by, then I grabbed her.

"I'm ready for that cocoa, if you are."

* * *

In science class on Monday, I tried to act as normal as possible toward Mary Lou. In fact, I even told her that I liked her polka-dot scarf. It seemed to me she was a little standoffish. It also seemed like Sister Barfalottoyou was giving me a few too many glances. Lately, I'd been trying to sweep my bangs to the side so I could grow them out. I called Maureen after school and asked her to help me with my hair. I didn't want Barfalottoyou coming at me with her scissors like she'd threatened. Maureen came over and brought all her hair stuff in a little red suitcase.

"You have to plaster your bangs over with the tape and wear it all night while you sleep. That will keep them from falling into your eyes and hopefully keep Barfalot off your back."

Ruff was brushing up against her ankles while she worked on my hair. Reddy jumped up on the dressing table.

"I love coming over here," she said to me in the mirror.

"You do, really?" I asked her. " How come?"

"Well, I don't know anyone with Siamese cats, and I've actually never had a friend whose parents are divorced. I have to admit, it's pretty cool that your mom's gone so much. Don't you think it's cool?"

"I guess so." I decided not to tell her about the times my mom had gone out after work and not told me. It didn't bother me now, but it sure had when I was in fourth grade.

"Seriously, though. Your sister's in plays and everything. You guys almost seem French or something."

"Hmm, that's one way to look at it, I guess. I've always felt like a freak, especially in this neighborhood. And of course with the nuns at school."

Maureen put her arms around my neck and spoke to me in the mirror.

"I can't believe we've known each other for two years, but we've only become good friends in the past two *months*. Look at all that time we wasted."

"Yeah, but at least we're making up for it now," I said.

"You are right about that. Hey, wanna go on the Beep-Line?"

* * *

I babysat for Steven and David two nights that week and also for a new family around the corner. With Christmas coming up, I needed the money. Maureen had talked me into the Brut idea for Tom and she said John was going to mention Ambush to him. The two of them had gotten pretty friendly lately and Maureen and I were glad about that.

I still hadn't told my mom that my dad wanted me to come for a visit during winter break. I wondered if he'd called Renee, too. She had a whole month off from college. I usually visited him in the spring and summer, but I figured that maybe he was anxious for me to stay with him and Wilma. The one time I went to Saginaw during winter break, Renee and I stayed with Grandma Gertie and Aunt Dorothy, and it seemed kind of weird, because they didn't have a Christmas tree. Just like my dad, they're Jewish. I wondered if my dad would have one now that he was married to Wilma, since she wasn't Jewish. But even though I was a little curious, I really wanted to wait until spring to visit them.

On Saturday afternoon, all of the Tandem Riders were going to The Four Star Theatre to see *To Sir, with Love*. None of us saw the movie when it was shown downtown in the summer, and we were all excited about going. We had seen previews and pictures in magazines and it was so thrilling to have a movie about teen-agers who lived in London. We all wanted to dress like LuLu, the girl who sang the title song and was in the movie.

I decided to wear the cranberry, corduroy bell bottoms that I'd gotten for my birthday last year. Cranberry had been the popular color last year, but at least they still fit. The mod print blouse that I'd dug out to wear to Maureen's party matched pretty good. As I buttoned up in front of the mirror, I noticed three new spots on my stomach, and one on my chest. My heart sank because it'd been a couple of weeks since I'd gotten any new ones. I stomped my foot and said, "Damn it!" I didn't care, this called for swearing.

"Ruth Ann, you better hurry up and get these dishes done before you go," my mom yelled up the stairs.

"Just a minute!" I burst out. I really hadn't meant to sound that mad, but I was putting the heartbreak stuff on the new spots and I still needed to fix my hair before Peg's mom came to pick me up.

To Sir, with Love was so good that I didn't think about those *damn* new spots even once during the movie. When we got out on the sidewalk in front of the Four Star, we all began talking at once.

"Aren't you glad Sir decided to keep on being a teacher?" I said to the girls.

"Yeah, I thought sure he was going to leave that awful school," Peg said.

"You know when he got really mad, about that thing burning in the little stove? What do you think it was?" Angela asked us.

"C'mon, don't you know? It was a Kotex!" Mary Lou was practically shouting.

"A Kotex?" Irene looked shocked.

"Well, whatever they call them in England. They call diapers nappies, you know."

"I was so happy that the kids ended up liking Sir and that they seemed better in the end," Maureen said.

"If you ask me, I think you look a lot like LuLu," I said to Maureen.

The other girls all turned toward Maureen and studied her for a few seconds.

"Hey, you know something, she does," Irene said. "Maybe you should start wearing one big dangly earring like LuLu did at the school dance."

"They'd really love that at St. Boner's, wouldn't they?" We all burst out laughing at the thought of that.

Chapter Ten

Renee came home on Monday night. She walked right in the door and turned a cushion around on the couch.

"Didn't either of you notice the zipper was showing on that cushion?"

My mom gave her a quick hug and then lit a Salem. I got up to answer the phone. It was my dad.

"Hey, Sport, what's new?" he asked me.

"Not too much. Thursday's my last day of school and I've gone ice skating a couple of times."

"Oh yeah? Do you have skates?"

"I've been wearing Renee's old ones. She just got home. Want to talk to her?"

"Well, sure, in a minute. It turns out Sport, that next week's not a good time for you to come here. Wilma's sister's coming from Vegas and they've made all kinds of plans. But listen, I'm gonna send you some money. You buy somethin' you've been really wanting. Maybe I can make it over there for our birthday. Okay, Sport? Now put your sister, on and we'll talk real soon."

I held the receiver up to Renee. She was holding Ruff and scratching under his chin.

"It's Dad. He wants to talk to you."

"Is he coming to get you next week?" my mom asked as she crushed her cigarette into the ashtray.

"No, he's busy. He said he might come next month for our birthday."

My mom shook her head. "I'll believe that when I see it."

My dad and I have the same birthday. He always said I was the best present he ever got. I loved hearing that when I was a little kid, but now I wasn't so sure he ever meant it. At least he didn't ask about my psoriasis. I didn't want to tell him that I had new spots, and if I'd gone there for a visit, he would have made me show him my skin. He'd probably have taken me to the pharmacy to see Wally about it. Boy, it was a good thing Wilma's sister was coming from Vegas, so I got out of the visit. I did wonder if they had a Christmas tree, though.

* * *

Maureen found out that Miracle Mart had the best price for Brut, so we went there with her mom on Friday afternoon since it was our first day of Christmas vacation. I got honeysuckle dusting powder and lotion for my mom along with a fuzzy white scarf. For Renee, I bought a ceramic statue of a Siamese cat that had plastic eyelashes, a book of Life Savers, and a new eyelash curler. I thought the eyelash curler kind of went with the cat. I had hoped to buy my mom something she could wear to work. She was always worrying about what to wear, but I just hadn't saved enough. I decided that I'd put an outfit on lay-a-way for her birthday. I didn't have to worry about my dad because Renee and I always sent him a box of cigars.

We went back to Maureen's house to wrap our gifts. They had about ten rolls of wrapping paper, ribbons in any color you wanted and three packages of scotch tape. Her mom had left to do more shopping so we cranked up the hi-fi and sang, *What the World Needs Now,* three times. Afterwards, we made a bowl of chocolate frosting from a mix and sat on stools in her kitchen eating it with two spoons.

"So, when are you and Tom exchanging gifts?" she asked me.

"I don't know. What about you and John?"

"Probably not 'til next week, since Christmas is the day after tomorrow. His grandma and grandpa are here and they're really busy. Hey let's go to my room and smoke a Winston before my mom gets back."

* * *

When I got home, Renee was pulling white angel hair apart and placing it in swirls over each light on the Christmas tree. She was playing her new Barbra Streisand Christmas Album.

"Thanks a lot, why didn't you wait for me to help decorate?" I asked as I set my bag of gifts on the floor.

"You can help with the ornaments. The lights and angel hair require way more patience than you have, Ruth Ann. Larry's taking us to the Fiesta Cafe for tacos, so go do something with your hair."

"Do something with my hair? What do you want me to do with it, Renee? Put a wig on it?" I stomped up the steps. Renee always dominated the Christmas tree. Even when my mom and I hung ornaments, she would move them around where she wanted, so there wasn't any use in helping. I looked in the mirror at my hair. I thought it looked better than usual. Renee probably hadn't even looked at it. She just always had to pick on me about something.

When I heard shouting outside, I looked out the window. Cathy and Frankie were throwing snowballs at each other in their back yard. I saw Cathy run behind the garage. I opened up my window and scooped some snow up to make a snowball. I threw it as far as I could, but it missed Frankie who I'd aimed for. Cathy poked her head around the other side of the garage and looked up at me.

"Get him Ruth Ann. He deserves it! He just put snow down my neck."

There were snow shovels in their driveway and I figured they were supposed to be shoveling, so I decided to go over and help them for a few minutes. Cathy and I had barely talked since the slumber party night when she'd brought the cookies over. I grabbed our shovel and went next door to the Cicerelli's pushing the shovel all the way to the back, making a path. It had only snowed a couple of inches, so it was kind of fun.

"Hey, what are you doing here?" Frankie asked me.

"I'm checking up on your work sir, which you haven't even started."

"Oh yeah? Well here's some work for you."

Frankie threw a snowball at me which missed my face by only an inch. I ran behind the garage where Cathy was still hiding. Her glasses were fogged up and she was wearing a red stocking cap with a huge pink ball on top.

"Hey, your brother's getting a pretty good arm, you know it? What have you been up to?"

Cathy seemed happy to see me. I figured enough time had passed since my slumber party.

"Nothing, really. My cousins from New York are coming for Christmas."

Cathy had talked about her cousins from New York ever since I'd met her. I couldn't believe they were actually coming and I was just hearing about it now.

"Wow, Cathy that's so cool. You must be really excited."

"Yeah, my mom's been cooking for days. She's making bread right now. Want some?"

A snowball went whizzing by the side of the garage.

"I came over to help you shovel. C'mon, let's put Frankie to work."

Frankie was chasing a neighbor boy around the side of their house, so Cathy and I shoveled alone.

"I noticed Renee's home."

"Oh yeah, she's over there right now blaring Barbra Streisand and playing with the angel hair."

"Oooh, I love how Renee does the angel hair."

Cathy was right about that, our tree always looked magical with the lights shining through the poofy swirls of cottony stuff. I guess it's another one of those things that made us "seem French," since everyone else used tinsel on their trees.

"Of course, she started decorating the tree while I was shopping with Maureen."

"What presents did you buy?"

" Well, I got Brut cologne for Tom."

"You bought *him* a present? Oh my gosh. Wow. You did?"

"Cathy, he's my boyfriend. That's what you do."

"Oh. Okay. Is he buying one for you too?"

"Sure, I guess so. It's not that big of a deal, really."

I heard my mom pull into our driveway. She got out of the car and waved at us as she walked to the fence. She had a big smile on her face, probably, because I was hanging out with Cathy. My mom didn't smile after work very often.

"Ruth Ann, Larry's on his way over to take us out to the Fiesta Cafe."

I whispered to Cathy, "That's because Fiesta Cafe is Renee's favorite place and my mom wants Renee to like Larry."

"Hi there, Cathy, would you like to go out for tacos with us?"

"Tacos? I've never had tacos before. I think I have to help my mom. Our cousins from New York are coming tomorrow."

"That's right, how could I forget? Your mom's talked of nothing else for weeks. I can't wait to meet them."

Weeks? It felt weird not to know important things about Cathy's family.

"Well, I'll see you, Cath. Have fun with your cousins." I started to walk down her driveway.

"Okay, thanks. Hey, Ruth Ann, I was just wondering. Did your skin get better yet?" I shook my head.

* * *

Tom called me the next morning and asked if he could stop by with his gift. I figured it was better not to tell my mom and Renee. It turned out lucky because they were out grocery shopping when he came to the side door. I decided to ask him in since it was cold and he was holding a gift. How could my mom argue with that? He had only been in our basement recreation room until now, but I led him through the kitchen to the living room.

"Wow, what's that white stuff on your tree?" he asked.

"Angel hair. We have it every year. It's my sister's specialty, I guess."

Tom handed me a small box wrapped in silver foil with a red and silver bow.

"My sister wrapped it for me."

"She did? So she knows about us?"

He nodded. I had seen his sister, Jeanette, at Mass. She was a junior in high school.

It was Ambush, of course. When I handed him his gift, he smiled. I couldn't decide if he felt as silly as I did or not. His gift was wrapped in the only paper from Maureen's house that seemed all right for a boy. It had pine cones all over it.

After he opened the Brut, he set it on the coffee table and kissed me. We leaned back on the couch and began making out. Reddy jumped up and started scooting the ribbons around.

"I shouldn't have started this. I have to get going," Tom said. "But you're so irresistible, I can't believe it."

I felt kind of weird making out on our couch, in front of my cats, and in the complete daylight. It was way different than Maureen's couch in the dark, but Tom's eyes just drew me in. I knew exactly what he meant by irresistible. I thought of the whole Cicerelli family right next door. Even the cousins from New York were there.

I sat up quickly and smoothed down my hair.

"Yeah, my mom and sister will be back anytime, so you probably should go."

"Well, I'm really glad you're not going to your dad's next week. Maybe we can go to the movie."

He leaned forward and kissed me, and I looked to see if his eyes were open. At first they were closed, but then he opened them and we were looking right into each other's eyes while we kissed. I got the Barbie negligee feeling more than I ever had before. I stood up quickly.

"I'm *so* sorry, but you really better go."

81

He gave me a very mischievous look like he was picturing *me* in a pink negligee that was flying open. Then I thought of my body covered with red sores and remembered how I looked underneath my jeans and sweater. If he saw me in a negligee, he'd probably run out the front door, screaming. I walked him to the side door where we had one last kiss.

I left my Ambush on the coffee table on purpose. Renee noticed it two seconds after coming into the house.

"Where did this come from? And what's this mess?"

She was crunching the silver paper up before I could I even answer. I snatched the striped bow because I wanted to save it.

"It's a present from Tom, my boyfriend."

Renee laughed as my mom walked into the room.

"Look, she got a present from her *boyfriend*."

"Ruth Ann, was that boy in here while we were gone?"

"Just for a minute. I couldn't help that you were gone."

"Well, that's just great. You can bet your life that all the neighbors saw us leave, and him show up. You should *not* have let him in here, Ruth Ann."

"Oh, for cryin' out loud!" I said as I grabbed the Ambush.

"Well listen to that. She sounds just like Dad." Renee said as she opened a box of miniature candy canes.

"I'm sorry I'm not in the fifth grade anymore. You two want me to be ten years old forever. I can't stop myself from growing up and neither can you!"

"Lower your voice, right now, young lady. Don't you forget, this is Christmas Eve."

My mom lit a cigarette, and Renee started hanging the candy canes on the tree.

"Get out there and put the groceries away," my mom said, after she blew out her match.

* * *

Gone Before Spring

Later that night, I saw Tom and his family at Midnight Mass. They were in the second pew from the front. Since I was wearing my mod corduroy hat and Renee's old Chesterfield coat, I felt like I was pulling off the British look pretty well. When I walked back from communion, Tom's sister, Jeanette, smiled at me. I tried to imagine Renee smiling at Tom or any of my girlfriends even, and it wasn't possible. I turned around and looked back at Tom. He had turned around too, and was grinning at me. It made me completely forget about the host in my mouth that I was supposed to be concentrating on.

* * *

When I came downstairs the next morning, Ave Maria was playing on the hi-fi. The first gift I saw under the tree was a guitar. My mom and Renee were beaming.

"How do you like *that*?" My mom gestured with her head toward the guitar. I wasn't sure what to say. I had never asked for a guitar. What I'd really hoped for was a navy pea-coat, like all the other girls were wearing. My maroon bench-warmer was on its third winter and way too short.

"*And*, it comes with lessons at Farrell's Music Studio," my mom added while continuing to beam.

"Wow, I can't believe it," I said.

"I made this for you to wear while you play your guitar," Renee said. "Go put it on, so we can take a picture."

Renee was holding up a granny gown. I'd seen them in *Seventeen Magazine*. It was brown with little daisies all over it.

"It's really cute, Renee, thanks. But, I'll put it on later, okay?"

"C'mon, Ruth Ann. Your sister has worked really hard on this. Go put it on for her. She's anxious to see how it fits."

I knew there was no use arguing. I went upstairs and took off my Siamese cat pajamas. Renee was good at a lot of things, but making clothes was not one of them. Every time she made me something, it was crooked or tight or off in some way or another. Sure enough, the sleeves were too tight on my upper arms. But, when I looked in the mirror, all I could see was the psoriasis on my elbows, which had gotten very bad, and the newer spots on my lower arms. "Oh great," I said to myself. "What should I do now?"

I grabbed a cardigan sweater out of my closet and put it on over the granny gown and then went downstairs. My mom and Renee were bringing out mugs of cocoa and a plate of my mom's date pinwheel cookies that I thought about all year. The Doris Day Christmas album was playing and Renee was singing along. She stopped as soon as she saw me pick up a cookie.

"Ruth Ann, take off this sweater. I want to see how it fits." She was peeling the cardigan right off me.

"Don't Renee. It's cold in here, and it fits great. You don't need to see it."

My mom came in with a coffee cake and the camera.

"Ruth Ann, sit in front of the tree and pretend you're playing the guitar, so we can take your picture."

"But she won't take off that sweater. Do you know how long it took me to make that granny gown?"

Renee's voice had that tone that meant we were in for trouble. My mom was very excited about the guitar. I really wanted her to stay in a good mood, so I took the sweater off and picked up the guitar.

"That's it. Now, sit right against the tree and look down like you're playing a song. Gee Renee, it fits her good. Maybe a little tight in the sleeves."

"Wow, look at your arms, Ruth Ann. That psoriasis is getting worse."

"Good thing you pointed that out, Renee. I wouldn't have noticed." I felt like spilling my cocoa on her favorite fuzzy slippers.

My mom snapped two pictures. Then she set the camera down and handed me my Christmas stocking.

"Look what's *right* on top," she said as much to Renee as to me.

Gone Before Spring

I pulled out a tube of the "Heartbreak" stuff.

"I noticed you were almost out of it, so I thought you could use another one. I figured one more tube and you should be over this whole thing."

"Thanks, Mom. I do need another one."

Our Christmas stockings were always full of stuff that we needed. This time mine also held a toothbrush, hand lotion, two pairs of knee socks, and a pack of tissues for my purse.

My other gifts were a stocking cap with a long tail, for ice skating, a flannel nightgown, a package of "days of the week" underpants, and the album, *Sgt. Pepper's Lonely Hearts Club Band* which, beside the pea-coat, was something I'd really hoped for.

Chapter Eleven

A couple of days after Christmas, Maureen and I took the bus downtown. I decided to use the money I'd received from my dad, Grandma Gertie, and Aunt Dorothy, to get a pea-coat. My mom said it was better to wait anyway, since now they'd be on sale.

"Hey, we should go to the photo booth at Kresge's and get our pictures taken," Maureen suggested as we stepped off the bus.

"That's a great idea. This *is* our first time downtown, with just the two of us. Do you mind, though, if we look for my coat first?"

I found a pea-coat on sale in my size at Herpolsheimer's department store. Afterwards, we rode the kiddie train that was on the ceiling in the basement of the store. It was surprising how much fun it still was to glide over people's heads, and tables of sweaters, socks and underwear. We felt silly, but in a good way. Wurzburg's department store still had all their mechanical decorations in the windows. When we stopped to watch them for a few minutes, I felt kind of sad about not being a little kid anymore.

"Do you have any idea why this makes me feel like crying?" I asked Maureen.

She put her hands on my shoulders when she answered me. "You know what? I love you, 'cause we're exactly the same person in so many ways. I was just trying to figure out why *I* feel like that."

At Kresge's we each bought a roll of pink hair tape, and then we sat at the lunch counter on stools, sharing french fries and a grilled cheese sandwich. We laughed so hard in the photo booth that Maureen fell off the bench and almost pulled me down with her when she grabbed the corner of my coat. We used six quarters and both of us took home three strips of pictures. I studied them on the way home, wondering if it was the last time I'd take pictures without a face full of psoriasis.

Gone Before Spring

* * *

When I got up the next morning, my sister was standing on a foot stool in the kitchen. The counters were covered with dishes.

"I hope you know, you're sticking around here today to help me," she said. She was unrolling shelf paper. I turned from her and opened up the refrigerator.

"Ruth Ann, hand me the scissors! Can't you see what I'm doing?"

"I'm not even awake yet, Renee," I said. The telephone was ringing.

"Don't you dare make any plans with whoever that is! Do you hear me?"

It was Tom. We decided to meet that night at the skating rink. I figured my mom would let me, if I worked around the house for a few hours.

In the late afternoon, I decided to take a break, since I'd been helping Renee all day. It seemed like a waste of time. The old shelf paper looked fine to me. I flicked on the television to watch a rerun of *Leave it To Beaver*. Renee came charging into the living room.

"Oh no you don't! It's time for *Dark Shadows*." She turned the station without a second thought. She had dominated the TV all summer watching her spooky soap opera. She'd even gotten me hooked on it the last few weeks before she went back to college. I hadn't watched it since then. I sat on the edge of the couch, out of curiosity.

"Ruth Ann, stop scratching! I can't concentrate when you do that."

I hadn't even realized I was doing it. My legs were so itchy lately that I scratched them until they bled.

"Okay, never mind. I was gonna stick around and watch this with you, but I forgot that I'm *way* too disgusting to be in the presence of your royal highness." I got up and walked out.

"All right, I'm sorry. I guess you can't help it. C'mon back and sit down, but wash your hands during the commercial."

* * *

Ignoring Renee, I went upstairs and put my new album on, cranked up the song, *I'm Fixing a Hole,* and sang as loud as I could. Singing made me feel better and drowned out *Dark Shadows* from downstairs. I patted my bloody legs with a wet washcloth, then toweled them off gently and applied Vaseline. I put on my new stocking hat, and turned sideways in the mirror to admire the snowflake pattern and the tail which reached the middle of my back. Maybe if I was wearing it when my mom got home from work, she'd be happy to see me in it, and would let me go skating.

Another thought popped into my head. If I had dinner ready when my mom got home, that would surely put me on her good side. I went down to the kitchen, and looked in the refrigerator. Our holiday leftovers were gone and there wasn't much to work with. I found a box of Noodles Romanoff in the cupboard, and there was enough lettuce and a tomato to make a salad. As soon as I started, Renee yelled at me from the living room.

"Are you making a mess in there?"

"*No*, I'm making dinner."

My mom walked in with a bag of groceries just as I was setting the table. She had picked up some stuff for dinner and for the next couple days, but gave me a big smile anyway. I wasn't sure what she was smiling about the most, not having to cook, or me wearing the new hat while *I* cooked. I figured I'd be skating and kissing Tom in no time.

As I shook the salad dressing bottle at the dinner table, I asked my mom if I could go skating after dinner.

"As a matter of fact, I was just speaking with Francesca outside, and she said Cathy got skates for Christmas."

Uh-oh, I thought to myself.

"I told her you'd take Cathy skating the next time you went, so this is perfect. I know she's anxious to try them out."

"But, Mom, I'm meeting Tom there. He called earlier."

"That's no reason you can't take Cathy. I don't want you meeting that boy all by yourself, anyway."

"It wouldn't be all by myself. I have other friends, you know. And why are you calling him, *that boy*? His name is Tom."

"Listen here, young lady, I don't care whether you go or not. You can stay home the rest of vacation as far as I'm concerned. You either call Cathy to go or you don't go at all!"

I looked over at Renee as she reached for the pepper and could tell she was trying very hard not to smile.

"I hate you both! And I know you both wish I didn't even live here!"
I shoved my chair back and stood up to leave.

"Maybe I should go live with Daddy. At least *he* loves me!" I took off the stocking cap and threw it at the table, where it landed on the salad.

"Oh, sure, he loves you. He doesn't have to live with you," Renee hollered.

I ran up the stairs, slammed my bedroom door and threw myself face down on the bed.

"Damn that Cathy," I said into my pillow. "I wish the Cicerellis would move!"

Or maybe I should move to Saginaw with Dad, I thought as I turned over and looked at the ceiling. My mom opened my bedroom door.

"Ruth Ann, you have two choices. You either get on the phone and invite Cathy to go skating, or you stay in this house the rest of winter break." She tossed my hat at me and closed the door loudly. I threw my pillow at the door.

It just didn't seem fair. Last year, I hardly had any girlfriends, let alone a boyfriend. Now I was in a whole new group of friends and the cutest boy at St. Boner's liked me. But I was covered with a hideous skin disease and my mom was trying to either keep me in the house or make me hang around the most boring girl imaginable. I picked up my hat and thought of the one Cathy would probably wear if she came with me, the one she had on in her backyard.

A thought came to me. I had helped Cathy pick out better clothes at Mitchell's Young at Heart, maybe I could fix her up a little before we went. I called her on the upstairs phone and invited her to go skating, but I told her to come over to my house first. Just as I figured, she was wearing the red hat when she knocked on my bedroom door.

"Hey, Cath, come on in for a minute. I was just thinking, you would look so cute in this. Can I try it on you?" I showed her my black knit headband that I usually wore.

"You mean, instead of my hat? My Aunt Mary made this for me."

"Let me just see, Cath."

She took her hat off and I pulled her hair back into a ponytail. The headband made her look older. I handed her my lip gloss and she put some on. Then I brushed a tiny bit of blush on her cheeks. She looked so much better, I couldn't believe it.

"Wow Cath. Take a look."

She seemed surprised at her reflection in the mirror.

"You're right. I look different."

"Well, let's get to the park. Its six thirty already." I sprayed some Ambush behind my ears and then I lifted Cathy's ponytail and sprayed some on her.

Tom was already putting on his skates when we got to the warm up house.

"Hi, I thought you'd beat me here. This is Laurent. He's my friend from Canada and he just got here a couple of hours ago." A boy with dark eyes and a beautiful smile, stood and shook my hand.

"Nice to meet you. This is my next door neighbor, Cathy. You've met Cathy before, right, Tom?" Tom nodded and said hi to Cathy and Laurent shook her hand. We sat across from them and took off our boots.

"Laurent's dad and my dad have been best friends since they were kids, and they're here for a visit. I thought they were coming tomorrow, so that's why I didn't tell you on the phone."

"Well, I didn't know Cathy got skates for Christmas. But she did, so she came with me and hopes she can stand up once she gets them on." I looked over at Cathy and she was nodding.

"Maureen and John are out on the rink and a bunch of the other kids."

Right after Tom said that, Mary Lou and Angela came in.

"Hey, Ruth Ann, nice hat," Angela said as she pulled off her mitten "Did you get that for Christmas?"

"Oh look, it's her little neighbor friend again. Didn't we see you trying on clothes at Mitchell's? *What grade* are you in?" I didn't like the tone in Mary Lou's voice. Cathy looked up from untying the knots in her laces and just looked blankly at Mary Lou.

"Hi Tom. Who's *your* friend?" Mary Lou asked him. Tom introduced Laurent to the girls, but I noticed he didn't stand and shake their hands. Mary Lou went over and sat next to him.

"I've been to Canada twice. Where do you live? Are you staying all week?"

She was trying her best to engage Laurent, but he didn't seem to be listening.

"Can I help you, Cathy?" Laurent got on the floor and pulled Cathy's laces out of the holes and began lacing them up like he did it for a living. Angela was holding a cup of hot chocolate out to Mary Lou, but she wasn't even aware of it. She was staring at Cathy and Laurent with her mouth open.

Laurent finished lacing Cathy's skates, helped her up and led her to the door by the elbow. I admired her pony tail as she went out, and wished that I'd tied a scarf around it. I figured that would have really burned Mary Lou up, to see her style copied, but she was already smoldering anyway.

"See you out there," Laurent said to us over his shoulder.

"Well, she couldn't be in better hands," Tom said. "Laurent's the star of his hockey team."

Out on the ice, I saw Laurent helping Cathy by the edge of the rink.

He let go of her to demonstrate how to stop, but she began wobbling and almost fell. He steadied her and took her hand. Maureen and John skated up to us.

"It's so good to see you," Maureen said as she hugged my arm. "I wasn't sure you were gonna make it. Look at you in your new pea-coat and hat."

I did feel pretty stylish, but my scalp was beginning to itch terribly under the new hat. I'd noticed the past couple days that the psoriasis there was getting much worse.

"Yeah, my mom wouldn't let me come unless I brought Cathy," I gestured toward her and Laurent.

"That's Cathy? Who is she with?" Maureen clapped her mittens together when I told her how I'd fixed Cathy's hair and how Mary Lou's flirting had been squashed.

It started to snow and the wind was kicking up, so several of us decided to go inside for a cocoa break. I pulled off my hat as soon as we got in and sat by the girls on a bench. Tom and Laurent brought hot chocolate to me and Cathy.

"Why isn't the snow melted from your coat, Ruth Ann?" Mary Lou asked. "Look at your shoulders."

I felt everyone's eyes on me and then wanted to die on the spot. Maureen brushed off my left shoulder. Cathy was sitting on my other side and brushed off my right shoulder when she saw Maureen do it.

"Oh my God, is that dandruff?" Mary Lou asked.

"Ruth Ann has *psoriasis*, Mary Lou," Maureen said. "In case you've forgotten."

I looked over at Tom. I was pretty sure he had heard all of this, but he was blowing on his cocoa and talking to the boys, pretending not to hear. Mary Lou seemed to raise her voice even louder.

"Well, I didn't know you could get that on your head. Ruth Ann, didn't you say your parents both had it? How did that happen? Haven't they been divorced practically your whole life?"

Maureen stood up and faced Mary Lou.

"Know what, Mary Lou? You and I need to talk. Privately."

Mary Lou crinkled her forehead, looked at Angela, and then up at Tom, who had turned toward all of us at the sound of Maureen's voice.

"Are you coming?" Maureen asked her.

"Am I coming where?"

Maureen pulled Mary Lou up from the bench and led her to a corner of the warm-up house. Tom turned toward me, smiled, and shrugged. Then Teddy Zukowski and Gerard Waterman walked up and started slugging him and goofing around. I was glad they had caused a distraction. I was so embarrassed about the whole thing, but even more so with Cathy there.

"How long is Tom's friend staying?" Angela asked me.

I was grateful that she was changing the subject. "A few more days, I guess."

"We'll see you out there," Tom said to me as he, Laurent, and the other boys walked toward the door.

I nodded and smiled. I wasn't sure I felt like skating anymore, but I knew the worst thing I could do was go home.

"I'm really sorry, Ruth Ann. I didn't mean to embarrass you," Mary Lou said.

Maureen was standing next to her with one hand on her hip.

"Okay, sure."

"C'mon, Angela, let's skate," Mary Lou said. "That's what we came here for." Angela followed her to the door, but turned and looked back at us with that, "I'm sorry" look on her face.

"Like hell she didn't mean to embarrass you," Maureen said.

I glanced sideways at Cathy to see if she'd heard Maureen swear. She wasn't even paying attention, though, 'cause Teresa Sullivan and her friends had just walked in. They looked at Cathy and then at us, and

Teresa put her hand over her mouth and said something to the other girls. Maureen noticed the whole thing and sat next to Cathy on the bench.

"You look great with your hair pulled back, Cathy," Maureen said to her, as she draped an arm across Cathy's back. "Well, girls, shall we hit the ice?"

I was dying to ask Maureen what she'd said to Mary Lou, but I didn't want Cathy to hear, so I decided I'd wait and call her when I got home.

We skated for another half hour, just long enough to admire Laurent's impressive skating, and to be sure Teresa Sullivan and her friends saw him and Tom stop to chat with us. My mom would have said, "They were pea-green with envy."

* * *

Tom was busy with Laurent for the next few days. Renee came up with one project after another when she wasn't learning lines for her next play. We cleaned closets and drawers, painted the woodwork in the dining room, and washed the windows on the inside. Ruff and Reddy followed us from room to room as we worked, looking for patches of sunshine to lay in, and Renee constantly nagged at me to stop scratching.

I babysat for the new people again on Saturday. They lived a couple of blocks away from our house, so my mom said I had to get rides from them both ways when it was dark. They just had a four year old boy named Ralph. We played Tiddlywinks and colored in his cowboy coloring book. He went to bed as easily as he had the last time I'd watched him. They warned me not to go in the basement because there were puppies down there and they said they were fine on their own. I heard puppy sounds through the floor but tried to block it out. The last thing I wanted was to cause trouble and not get asked back.

Ralph's parents were different than anyone I knew. His dad had slicked back hair that he ran his comb through before he left the house. I'd always heard guys with hair like that were called "greasers." Ralph's mom had black hair that was teased very high into a beehive hairdo and she

94

wore lots of black eyeliner. Their TV was broken, but I didn't mind because I was reading *Gone with the Wind*, and since they didn't come home until 1a.m., I was able to read several chapters.

They asked if I could come back the next night which was New Year's Eve. I said yes, even though I usually had to get permission first. I had been waiting for a New Year's Eve job offer because it was the only night you could be guaranteed to make five dollars. My friends and I all counted on it. I knew my mom wouldn't mind because she had a date with Larry and my sister was going to a party. My mom had been especially nice to me the past few days, because she'd heard from Cathy's mom that Cathy had the "best time of her life," at the skating rink.

* * *

The next night, Ralph's parents told me he could stay up a little later since it was New Year's Eve.

"Hey, sorry the TV's broken. Tough break, bein' New Year's Eve. It should be fixed by the next time you babysit," Ralph's father said.

"Oh, that's all right. I have this really long book." I held up my copy of *Gone with the Wind*, and said I hoped to make more headway. There was a record player in their dining room, but I wasn't interested in their records which were mostly Elvis. He was truly a "greaser."

I made Jiffy Pop and it burned a little, but Ralph didn't mind. He was such a sweet little boy. It was the first snack food they'd left for me. At most babysitting jobs, the people would leave chips and pop at least. Sometimes there would be dip or ice cream bars, especially on New Year's Eve.

Tom and I talked on the phone for two hours after I put Ralph to bed. Ralph's parents hadn't called the other times I'd sat there, so I wasn't worried about the telephone line being busy. We talked about everything from our families to our favorite food. He told me he missed the scent of Ambush.

"Well, I really miss your Brut too," I said.

"Hey, what's with that Mary Lou, anyway? Was she giving you more grief about your skin?"

My heart sank. I was hoping he hadn't noticed the episode at the warm-up house.

"Yeah, sort of. I guess she can't understand why everyone isn't perfect, like her."

"Perfect? I would never call her perfect. Hey, Ruth Ann, can I ask you something? Does your skin thing, what is it called, psoriasis? Does it hurt or anything like that?"

"It hurts sometimes, and other times it itches like crazy."

"Oh, that's kind of awful. You're so pretty, though, that it doesn't matter otherwise. You know that, right?"

"That's nice of you to say. I sure don't feel pretty, with or without psoriasis."

"You don't? Huh. I don't really get stuff like that about girls. My sister's always goin' on about how hard it is and everything. Oh, shoot, I gotta go. I hear my parents comin' in. Bye, I love you."

I hung up the phone and thought about what Tom had said. I looked in the mirror over the broken TV and couldn't see what he meant by pretty. I saw my "sallow coloring" as my mom called it. She always said it was from my Jewish side. I saw the dark circles under my eyes that my mom admitted were like hers, and my hair, which no matter how hard I tried, refused to lie down flat. I wondered if boys said things like that just to get you to kiss them, or even more.

Chapter Twelve

Once we got back to school, all the teachers seemed to talk about was the science fair. I knew it was a big deal in eighth grade, but I'd avoided thinking about it. Most kids got tons of help from their fathers, and the teachers acted like they didn't know.

Last year we had to do a project for the social studies fair. My mom had brought home lots of molding scraps from the furniture factory, next to where she worked. Some of them had designs that looked Greek to me, so I had fashioned a Greek temple out of them, by looking at a picture in my geography book. It was lopsided and had to be re-glued over and over. I got a B- on the project, but I was sure that was due to Sister Verena feeling sorry for me. She probably knew my dad didn't live with us. I thought I deserved a C or C+ at best.

On the way home from school, Cathy told me that Teresa Sullivan and her friends had cornered her in the girls bathroom to find out about her skating night with me, the week before.

"Yeah, they want to know if you and I are close friends like we used to be, and if Tom comes over to your house every day, and all kinds of stuff like that."

"All kinds of stuff like what, Cathy?"

Frankie ran up and bashed into Cathy with his Jetsons lunchbox, then he pulled off her red hat, and ran away with it. I decided that maybe Frankie wasn't so clueless. That hat needed to go away for good, as far as I was concerned. It seemed that my fashion lesson hadn't stuck.

"Oh, I don't know exactly, but I did tell them we were all doing homework together one night this week. I mean you, me and Tom. Not Laurent, of course, 'cause they know he went back to Canada."

"Cathy, why did you tell them that? I don't know if Tom is coming over here at all."

"Oh well, how will they know? It's not going to hurt anyone."

She switched her plaid book bag from one hand to another.

"Hey, it's bread baking day. Wanna come in and have some?"

We were standing in front of my house. Renee was shaking a rug over the porch railing.

"No, thanks. I have to go in and figure out what kind of science project I'm gonna do. I'll see you tomorrow."

Renee followed me back into the house.

"Don't track snow in here, take your shoes off. You really shouldn't be using the front door anyway."

"Well, you already had it open, so I just came in."

"For once I'm glad you didn't make your bed. It gave me a chance to see your sheets. They were covered with scales and blood streaks. I can't believe you were sleeping on them!"

"Leave me alone, Renee. I have more to think about than your crazy cleaning obsession. Why don't you go write a play about zombie maids or something?"

I stormed up the stairs to my room and Renee stood at the bottom and yelled up to me.

"Well, your sheets are in the dryer. Don't you dare lie around on the bare mattress."

I threw my books down on the bed and looked at the wall calendar. In less than a week, Renee would be back at college. It would be such a relief to be alone with my mom again. I sat on my dressing table bench and pulled my knee socks down. The psoriasis patches were cracked and bleeding. I had scratched them a lot last night. In fact, the itching woke me up, so I guess my sheets probably were a mess. I put Vaseline and the heartbreak stuff on. It only helped a little.

I glanced up at the calendar again and for the first time realized that the psoriasis might not be gone by spring. I was as scared as I was mad.

Why me? Why not Renee? She had the same parents as me. Why didn't she get it? Why not Mary Lou? She had the picket fence, the perfect hair, a dad at home every night, and a scarf collection. Why did everything work out for other people just the way it was supposed to?

Renee opened the door and flung the warm sheets and mattress pad at me.

"Make your bed. If you hurry up, you can watch *Dark Shadows* with me."

"Get out of here, Renee. And don't just think you can bust in here any time you want. Knock the next time! And no, I do not want to watch anything with you. You can take your damn *Dark Shadows* back to Mt. Pleasant as soon as possible!"

"Ruth Ann Bloomfield, did you just say *damn*?"

"Yes I did, and you're not my mother, so damn, damn, damn!"

I slammed the door in her face, and turned around to see Cathy in the next door window. I looked away, and began pulling the sheets, blankets, and bedspread into place. She knocked on her window, but I pretended I didn't hear.

* * *

"How was your first day back at school?" my mom asked as she dished out left-over tuna casserole.

"It was okay. We have to come up with a project for the science fair by next Monday."

"Do you have any ideas?"

I thought of an idea right away, an idea that would keep me away from Renee after school.

"No, I better go to the Seymour Square Library after school tomorrow. Maybe I'll get an idea if I look through the encyclopedias there."

We owned one encyclopedia, "A." My mom got it free from the A&P Store when we lived in Saginaw. I had done every report imaginable that started with A. When I did one on Africa in fifth grade, I cut pictures of people out of it. They were from tribes that extended their lips by inserting plates. I glued them onto the cover and was worried I'd get in trouble for it. It turned out good, though. Mr. Lynch gave me an A-. I think the pictures helped.

"Well, you better go tomorrow, because I set up a guitar lesson on Wednesday night."

"A guitar lesson?"

I had almost forgotten about the guitar. It really bugged me how my mom and Renee had cooked that up without asking me, kind of like the time they redecorated my room while I was visiting my dad. I didn't get any say in the colors or patterns they chose. The room was a lot cuter than before, but it just wasn't what I would have picked.

"I told you that was part of the present, Ruth Ann."

"I don't think she's even picked that guitar up once, Mother," Renee said as she dabbed her mouth on her napkin.

"Well, I bet after she gets a lesson or two, she won't ever set it down. The lesson is at seven o'clock, so we'll need to eat and run."

"You don't have to worry about me on Wednesday. I'm going out for dinner with the Wurzburgers," Renee said as she slid her chair back.

Renee worked at Wurzburg's Department Store during the summer, so she and her two friends from work, called themselves the "Wurzburgers."

"Well then, we'll stop at Burger Chef. There's one right on the way."

* * *

Tom met me in the park the next day after I told him I was walking to the library. We kissed as we stood between two large trees that were close together, but stopped when a lady walking a poodle, came by and gave us a dirty look.

"Once you told me you were going to the library, all I thought about was meeting up and kissing you. I didn't even hear Fizzytits call on me in

English class. I think she said my name three times. You don't know how much I've missed you," Tom said before he kissed me again.

I glanced around nervously. As much as I was enjoying this, I couldn't stop thinking about Renee being a block and a half away and how I wouldn't put it past her to spy on me.

Tom walked with me to Maureen's house and then went home. Maureen and I spent over an hour at the library, looking in encyclopedias for ideas. I checked out a book called *Your Science Fair Project*, so I could think about it later.

My head, arms, and legs were itching like crazy and I was starting to feel worried about the guitar lesson. Maureen suggested we go over to Mitchell's Young at Heart, and look at the sale racks. I found a rust colored corduroy skirt and vest set for my mom's birthday. It would be a great way to mix and match with different tops and bottoms. I only had two dollars with me, but Mrs. Roshevsky said it was plenty to put it on lay-a-way. That gave me over two months to pay it off. If I got more babysitting jobs, I figured maybe I could buy a matching blouse for under the vest.

We went to Alger Variety after that, and Maureen bought some seafoam for us to share. Peg and Irene were there getting a birthday card for Irene's dad. We all walked back toward our homes together.

"Hey, I hate to say this, but it's kind of nice without Mary Lou," Peg said as she offered her Fruit Stripe Gum to us.

"You don't have to be sorry, it is nice without her. I like Angela, but Mary Lou has changed since the beginning of school," Maureen said as she handed the gum back to Irene.

"Maybe we should all talk to her," Peg said.

"I don't think she'd take that well," I said.

"How has she been since Maureen talked to her?" Irene asked me.

"Well, I've only seen her in science class, and she's been about the same. She doesn't say much to me, really."

"I wonder what *she'll* do for a science project," Maureen said. "Remember her igloo with the little Eskimos she put in the social studies fair? You could tell her dad built the igloo and her mom made those little costumes on the teeny Eskimos."

We all nodded, remembering the project. I added it to the other stuff about her that had made me so mad the day before. One more thing to add to the "Mary Lou List," I thought to myself.

Chapter Thirteen

"Are you sure you don't want fries with that?" my mom asked me.

I shook my head and looked up at the Burger Chef clock on the wall. In less than a half hour, I'd be at Farrell's Music Studio for a guitar lesson I didn't want. If Renee was with us, she'd probably say I was acting like a spoiled brat. I hated it when Renee was right about me, so I picked up my "Big Chef" burger, and tried to smile at my mom.

Farrell's Music Studio was brightly lit and the walls were lined with all kinds of instruments. A teenaged boy stood behind the counter, twirling drum sticks.

"My daughter has a guitar lesson set up for seven o'clock."

"Are you Ruth Ann?"

I nodded.

"Yup, you are scheduled with Pete. Follow me."

"I'll be back at eight. I'm going next door," my mom said.

I had noticed the used book store when we pulled up. It made me wonder if that's why she had bought me the guitar. My mom went through a couple of Harlequin romances or Mickey Spillane mysteries every week.

The boy led me through a back hallway and down a stairway, where we passed a few small rooms. In one of the rooms, a girl around my age had a violin on her shoulder.

"Pete will be here in a minute," the boy said as he gestured toward an empty chair.

Pete was about thirty years old, I guessed. He wore cowboy boots and a blue jean jacket. He tuned my guitar for a couple minutes, then handed it back to me and showed me his fingertips.

"You see these? They're calluses, and I'll be able to tell if you're practicing because you should have 'em too."

He asked me what kind of music I liked and then taught me a few chords and explained how to remember which letter went on which string. I tried to copy him, but it didn't sound at all the same when I did it. Then he set his guitar down and took off his jacket. I didn't blame him because the little room was too warm.

"Now don't you worry about this. It's not contagious or anything."

I couldn't believe my eyes when I looked at Pete's arms. They looked just like mine. It took me a few seconds before I could speak.

"Do you have psoriasis?" I asked.

"I sure do, Miss Ruth Ann. How the heck do *you* know about it?"

I hesitated and then pushed the sleeve of my sweater up.

"Well, wadda ya know about that? You & me got somethin' in common now, don't we?"

I nodded and smiled at him. It felt pretty strange having the same disease as this cowboy guy. Up to this point I was thinking I wouldn't come back for another lesson, but now I felt like we were practically related.

"It's no fun, is it? I imagine it's even worse for a young girl like yourself. I was nineteen when mine hit."

It felt like my head was underwater. This guy knew how I felt and for some reason that really got to me. Then my heart jumped because I understood psoriasis didn't always go away in a couple of months. I swallowed, blinked, then strummed down extra hard with the little red guitar pic.

"Hey, you got a good sound that time. Let's try it again."

My mom was standing by the counter, holding a couple of paperbacks when we came upstairs. We set up lessons for the next few weeks.

"Start workin' on those calluses, Miss Ruth Ann, and take care of yourself," Pete said, and he winked when I waved at him.

* * *

The phone was ringing when we came in the house. It was Maureen.

104

Gone Before Spring

She wanted to hear all about my guitar lesson. I told her about Pete having psoriasis and she could hardly believe it. My mom was upstairs and Renee was still out with the Wurzburgers. I was glad, because for some reason I didn't want them to know about Pete's psoriasis.

"Well, my dad has me talked into doing my science project on magnets. Have you decided on yours?" Maureen asked.

"No, not yet," I told her, and then we chatted about a few other things before hanging up.

Reddy was curled up next to me on the window seat.

"Damn, damn, damn the science fair," I said as I buried my face into his fur.

This was another one of those times when having a dad around would be really nice. I hadn't felt like this since the father-daughter breakfast last year when I had to go with Cathy and her dad.

I opened *Your Science Fair Project,* and flipped through the pages. For most of the projects, you needed things we didn't have, like big square batteries, electrical wiring, air hoses and stuff like that. No wonder all these dads loved helping.

* * *

On Thursday, most of the kids in my science class turned in their science fair ideas, even though we had until Monday. When Mary Lou brought her form up, Sister Barfalottoyou raised her eyebrows, smiled and nodded.

"Very interesting, Mary Lou. I'll be looking forward to this."

I had never been very sure what the word smug meant, until I saw the look on Mary Lou's face as she practically skipped back to her chair.

"Anyone else?"

Barfalottoyou was looking right at me when she asked that. I was glad my bangs had grown out enough to be pushed all the way over now. At least she couldn't pick on me for that.

* * *

After dinner that night, Tom and Marty stopped over. Renee was cutting a skirt pattern out on the dining room table and my mom was on the phone.

"Can Tom and Marty come in and look at the science fair book with me, in the basement?"

It was perfect timing. Renee's mouth was full of pins and since my mom was talking to Larry, I knew she'd be sweeter than usual.

"I guess it's all right if your homework's done."

I sent Tom and Marty down to the basement.

"Let me get the science fair book. I'll be right back."

When I came back down, the boys were flipping through a pile of National Geographic Magazines that my mom had brought home from work. Marty was sitting in a corner chair and Tom was at the table. He pulled me down on his lap and we began kissing. I was a little uncomfortable with Marty there, and Tom seemed to notice.

"Don't worry about him. He doesn't care."

Marty did seem distracted. I figured he had found one of the issues where the ladies were bare naked on top.

"I told my mom we were figuring out projects from this book," I whispered into his ear.

He smelled so good, I could barely stand it. We both heard the refrigerator door close in the kitchen, right at the top of the stairs.

Tom opened the book to the middle.

"I think this project on page thirty-nine is the one, Marty," Tom said, especially loud.

"Ruth Ann, what about this one for you? Or is that the one Danny Delaney is doing?"

He kissed the edges of my ear and then reached for the Yahtzee game that was on the shelf.

He opened it up and put the dice in the cup. We continued to make out and every few kisses, he shook the dice loudly, and spilled them on the table. I pulled his hand down every time he tried to reach under my sweater, even though Marty was in another world and probably wouldn't notice.

After a while, Marty yelled, "Yahtzee!" and we knew he'd found another "good page" in the magazine.

* * *

Cathy ran up to me when I was walking home the next day.

"Hi Ruth Ann. I saw Tom come over last night, huh?"

"Yeah, he and Marty came over. Why?"

"No reason. Did your mom let them come in?"

"She did. We were looking in a book for science fair projects."

"Oh. Did you find one?"

"Not yet. They all need tools and fancy stuff we don't have."

"You should just do the one my cousin Rose did last year."

"Which one did she do?"

"She grew mold on little pieces of food and just measured it and wrote it down. She didn't have to buy anything. She just took stuff from the kitchen."

Now that sounded like a good plan to me. Mold was disgusting, but I could handle it all by myself. You didn't need a dad to grow mold. When Renee was away at college, we had mold on stuff without even trying.

"Where does Rose go to school?"

"She goes to Our Lady of Sorrows. We always go to the spaghetti dinners there, remember, we took you before? Hey, I could call Rose and ask if she has any directions or anything. You want me to?"

"That would be great, Cath, thanks."

"Okay, I'll call her tonight.

Chapter Fourteen

I had just put David and Steven to bed when I heard a light tap on the front door of the Harrisons' house. Cathy was standing on the front porch. I was surprised because she had never come to my babysitting jobs before, even when they were on our street, like this one. The phone rang just as I opened the door.

"Hi, Cath. What are you doing out at night? Come on in, I gotta get the phone. It's probably Tom."

Cathy stepped in and stood on the mat looking around. She had a folded piece of paper in her hand. I told Tom to call back in twenty minutes.

"Shut the door and sit down, Cath. What's that?"

"I talked to my cousin, Rose, and wrote down some directions about the mold project."

We sat down on the couch and she handed me the paper with her handwritten notes.

"Hey, this doesn't look too hard. I'll only need to ask my mom for a couple of things from the grocery store, but we usually have most of this stuff. Thanks, Cath, you're a lifesaver."

"Well, I was thinking," Cathy said.

"Yeah?"

"I was thinking maybe we could say that I came over the other night when Tom was at your house."

"Who would we say that to?"

Cathy ran the zipper on her jacket up and down.

"You know, Teresa Sullivan and her friends."

"Geez, Cath, that's kind of strange. How 'bout you just *really* come over sometime when Tom is at my house?"

As soon as I said it, I thought of sitting on Tom's lap and the Yahtzee dice shaking.

"Well, I kind of wanted to tell her on Monday. I'm in her study group next week."

"Oh, okay. Go ahead. I guess it's not a big deal."

Cathy smiled and then pulled something out of her pocket.

"My mom and I went to Miracle Mart and I got this."

It was a light blue knitted head band like the black one I'd loaned her for skating.

"I know you hate my red hat," she said as she put it on.

"I don't hate it. You just look a little older in this, which is a good thing."

"Is the color okay?"

"It looks great. I wish Laurent could see you in it."

Cathy blushed right up to the headband and then she stood up.

"I better go. I promised Frankie I'd make popcorn and watch TV with him."

I walked with her to the door just as Steven came sleepwalking into the living room.

"Thanks again, for the project idea. Maybe we can go skating again soon."

I closed the door, turned Steven around, and led him to the stairs.

* * *

"Do a good job on that science project, Ruth Ann. Mom doesn't have time to help you and you're in the eighth grade. You shouldn't need any help. And listen, don't forget to change the kitty litter more often. And...you really need to let up on all that scratching. It seems like you're scratching every time I look at you lately. If you have to do it, vacuum afterwards, do you hear me? "

"Okay, okay," I said.

Renee was waiting for her ride to go back to college. I was watching

Top Cat and eating a bowl of Shredded Wheat. She'd been standing in front of the window with her coat on for over a half hour and I'd had all the extra mothering I could take. My mom was sitting on the couch filing her nails. When she got up and left the room, Renee turned to me again, and said, "You better practice that guitar. It wasn't cheap and Mom really can't afford to waste money on lessons if you aren't going to practice."

Thankfully, a horn honked outside, and my mom and I helped Renee carry her stuff to the car. She gave us each a peck on the cheek before she left.

"Why is Renee always in a bad mood?" I asked my mom as they drove away.

"She's not always in a bad mood. I hear the phone ringing, Ruth Ann. Run and get it."

I picked up the phone. It was my dad.

"Hey Sport, wadda ya up to? Did I miss your sister or is she still there drivin' ya nuts?"

"She just left. How'd you know she was drivin' me nuts?"

My mom gave me a big scowl.

"Hmmf, it's your father, no doubt."

"Well, Sport, our birthday's a week from Monday, so how bout I come there next Sunday and we go out for a real nice dinner, the two of us."

"Okay, that'd be great."

"What kinda present should I look for? Is there somethin' special you want? Are your sister's old skates holdin' up?"

"The skates are fine, I guess. I don't care about a present, Daddy. I just want you to come. That's all I care about."

"You're such a peach pie, ya know that? Well, we'll see what I can come up with. Expect me next Sunday around noon. You pick out a good place to eat and we'll have ourselves a real good time. Okay, honey, bye now."

110

"Dad's coming next Sunday for our birthdays," I hollered to my mom who was in the basement. I didn't wait for her reply. I went upstairs to get dressed.

The plan was for all the Tandem Riders to meet at Mister M's Sundae Shoppe in Alger Heights at noon.

* * *

I knocked on Maureen's door at eleven- thirty. When she answered the door, her face was all red and she was crying.

"Oh no, what's wrong?" I asked, as I stepped into her family room.

"Guess?"

"Johnny?"

She nodded and then burst into tears on my shoulder.

"He broke up with me! I can't meet those girls. You go ahead."

"Maureen, tell me what happened."

"Okay, but you have to promise you won't utter a single word to anyone."

"Of course not. Are your parents home?"

"She shook her head and reached for a Kleenex from the coffee table.

"Last night I went over to his house. His mom and dad were gone. Of course we were making out and everything, and well, he wanted to go farther than I did."

"Johnny? Wow, how far?"

Maureen looked out the window at a blue jay that had landed on the bird feeder.

"All the way."

"Holy cow! You're kidding. I can't believe it."

"He said I obviously didn't care about him as much as he thought I did and I couldn't convince him that I do." Maureen started crying again and said, "So he broke up with me!"

I put my arms around her. This felt like a story from one of the magazines I used to read when I went with my mom to the beauty shop. I didn't feel old enough to have a friend with this problem. Then I thought about that bulge in Tom's jeans when I was sitting on his lap and it made me nervous. Was he going to pressure *me* about this? Trying to hide my skin was enough to worry about.

I tucked Maureen's hair behind her ears. "You know what, he's gonna feel so sorry about this. I predict you'll be back together by tonight."

"I don't know if I want to get back together." Maureen began crying again. "I'm not sure I could ever feel the same toward him."

I pictured my Barbie doll slapping Ken and stomping out the door, which made me think of playing dolls on the grass in Cathy's back yard. Then Maureen lit a Winston. She offered me one, but I shook my head.

"You should get going if you're gonna meet the girls by noon."

"I think you should splash cold water on your face and come with me. Then you won't sit around here thinking about it."

The phone rang. We both stared at it for a few seconds before speaking.

"Should I get it?"

"I wouldn't. If it *is* Johnny, he shouldn't think you're waiting for him to call. Come on, hurry up and get ready. Let's go."

* * *

We all sat at a table by the window while we ate our lunch. Maureen told the girls she had a slight cold and that was why her nose was red.

"Guess who we saw going into the jewelry store?" Peg asked me as she squeezed a packet of mustard onto her hamburger.

I shrugged, "Who?"

"None other than your boyfriend. Marty told me on the phone last night they were going there to find you a birthday present."

I hadn't even talked about my birthday with Tom, so I was surprised he remembered when it was. Then I realized that his was only four days after mine. I would probably need to get him a gift too, and I had no ideas.

After lunch we all headed across the street to Mitchell's Young at

Heart, so I could put more money on my mom's gift. Tom and Marty walked by the store while I was giving Mrs. Roshevsky three more dollars for my lay-a-way. I noticed Mary Lou was buying a sweater we'd all admired in the window. At the last minute she handed a yellow scarf and a circle pin to the clerk.

"Just put it all on my mother's charge account," I heard her say. I tried to imagine what it would be like to buy something that I saw in a window without even planning it out.

"Let's get seafoam," Irene said as she headed to the door. I wanted to look for something for Tom, but I didn't want Maureen to feel bad. We entered Alger Variety through the back door, and as we made our way to the glass candy bins, I saw an olive green suede hat on a rack. It had a tiny feather in the ribbon.

"This would look great on my dad and he's coming for our birthday," I told Maureen. "I'm not really sure which size he'd wear, but this one looks close enough."

"That's right, your dad almost always wears a hat, doesn't he? I noticed that in all the pictures you've showed me."

"Yeah, except in the summer. I usually just send him a card, but since he's coming to take me out for dinner, I really should get him a gift, don't you think?" Maureen nodded. I was excited to have found the hat without even searching. It seemed like it jumped out at me. Tom was the one I wondered about. I felt a tap on my shoulder. It was Tom. He and Marty were standing behind me.

"Nice hat," Tom said.

"It's for my dad. He's coming for our birthday next Sunday. I told you we have the same birthday, didn't I?" Tom nodded and smiled at me like he had a big secret.

"Can you go skating tonight?" he asked.

"If I don't get another babysitting job, I probably can."

"Okay, we're going at six, so hopefully, I'll see you there."

I could tell he wanted to kiss me by the look on his face, but there I was, standing next to a lady wearing a plaid babushka, as Grandma Gertie called them, and I was holding a man's hat.

He gave me his most romantic look and then followed Marty out the door. I wanted to look around for a birthday gift for him, but then I saw Maureen was standing by the other girls in the nail polish aisle. She looked so sad that I decided it wasn't a good time to shop for *my* boyfriend. Angela came walking toward us, wearing a huge pair of lady's pink underpants on her head.

"Since my cousin can't decide on bridesmaid veils, I think I just solved the problem."

We all screamed with laughter, especially since Angela had such a straight face when she said it. All of us, except Maureen. She had a half-hearted smile, while the rest of us were holding our stomachs and practically crying.

"Oh no! Is there a bathroom here? I'm gonna pee my pants!" Peg said as she crossed her legs and hopped up and down."

"You girls should be ashamed of yourselves," the plaid babushka lady said to us.

I scurried to the cash register to pay for the hat. Maureen followed without saying a word.

* * *

"I'll see you in an hour," my mom said as she locked the car door and headed into the used bookstore. I stood in front of Farrell's with my guitar. This sure was different than last week. I shrugged and went in by myself. The drumstick kid was behind the counter, polishing a trombone.

"Hey there. You can go on down to the studio. I think Pete's waiting for you."

I noticed the same girl with the violin was in the room next to me. We smiled at each other when I passed. The hour went by pretty fast. Pete took hold of my right hand and looked at my fingertips.

Gone Before Spring

"I don't see one hint of a callus, Miss Ruth Ann. It shows you're not puttin' enough time in. Try a little harder this week. You been busy?"

"Well, I have this science project to work on and I've been babysitting a lot so I can buy birthday presents."

"Speakin' of birthdays, I happened to see here on your form, that you've got a birthday in a few days." I smiled and thought to myself what a nice guy Pete was to notice that.

"Yeah, it's the same day as my dad's and then my boyfriend's is four days after mine."

I was grateful that Pete didn't tease me or act all goofy about me saying that I had a boyfriend.

"Well, I guess you do have some important gifts to buy."

"I got my dad a hat that looks just like him. I have no idea what to get my boyfriend."

"He likes music, doesn't he?"

I nodded.

"I always say, you can't go wrong with the gift of music. By the way, is your skin lettin' up on ya, at all?" I shook my head.

"Well, neither is mine, Miss Ruth Ann. You and me are in the same boat." He stood up and stretched his arms behind his head. I could see the psoriasis on his neck and on his arms when the sleeves of his western-style shirt inched up.

"Now practice those new chords and think about singin' a little when you play that song. It helps some people learn guitar better when they sing. And don't you worry, we'll have ya' playin' cooler songs in no time at all."

That was a relief to hear because "There's a Hole in My Bucket," was not something I even felt like playing, much less singing.

* * *

I decided to take a bath when I got home. I brought my transistor radio into the bathroom and set it on the counter. I couldn't use my mom's bubble bath anymore because it made my psoriasis burn. It didn't bother me so much when I only had a few spots, but now that there were so many, I just couldn't stand it. The spots were very red and sore and it was getting closer and closer to spring.

I leaned back and thought of Pete's neck. So far, I didn't have it there, but I still felt scared and sad. A tear rolled down my cheek and I sniffed loudly to make myself stop. After all, I still had the cutest boyfriend at St. Boner's, didn't I? I looked down at my body and thought of that cute boy seeing this horrible skin and wondered if he'd look at me the same way if he knew. Then *Happy Together,* by the Turtles came on the radio and I started singing along. Even though the song made me feel sad, because of the mood I was in, I knew it was the perfect birthday present for Tom.

Chapter Fifteen

"Ruth Ann, that guy's outside, honking the horn," my mom hollered down to me.

I was in the laundry room sprinkling a few drops of water on my science project. It had been almost a week and there still wasn't any mold growing on my pieces of food. They just looked a little shriveled.

"Okay, I'll see ya later." I headed out the door. Ralph's dad had called me the night before to babysit. When I got into the car he looked at my school books and said, "Well, how do you like that? We finally got our TV fixed and it looks like you've got a pile of homework to do."

"I do have quite a bit, but I'm glad you got your TV fixed. I bet Ralph's *really* glad."

I hadn't babysat for Ralph since New Year's Eve and I did need the money. The Tandem Riders were going to see "Gone with the Wind" and I still needed to buy Tom's gift.

"Oh yeah, Ralph loves his Saturday morning cartoons."

Ralph's mom was in the kitchen wearing a black and turquoise maternity top with black stretch pants. I was surprised that I hadn't noticed she was pregnant the last time I'd seen her. She still had her usual cat's eye make-up on, and her beehive hairdo. She didn't look anything like the pregnant ladies in our new Spiegel catalogue.

Ralph and I played Tiddlywinks and Candyland and I made him some toast before I put him to bed. I was asleep on the couch when I heard his parents unlock the back door. I had finished my history paper, watched *Star Trek* and talked on the phone to both Tom and Maureen before falling asleep. When I glanced at the sunburst clock on their wall, I noticed it was ten after two in the morning. *No wonder I had fallen asleep*, I thought to myself.

I was barely awake when we pulled up in front of my house. Ralph's dad stretched his arm out so it was almost touching my shoulder. A big piece of his Elvis hairdo had fallen down on his forehead and he smelled like beer and cigarettes.

"I guess you noticed my wife is expecting."

I scooted closer to the door.

"I did notice and I think it's great. It'll be so nice for Ralph to have a baby brother or sister."

"It is nice, isn't it?" He leaned toward me. Thankfully his wife had paid me in the kitchen before we left. I opened the car door.

"Well, thanks a lot, Mr. Taylor. I'm sure we'll be talking soon."

* * *

My mom let me sleep in the next morning because I'd been out so late. I was in the kitchen making toast, when I heard her complaining about it to Mrs. Cicerelli on the phone. I was worried that she wouldn't let me babysit for Ralph anymore, and I needed to make several more payments on her birthday outfit. She mentioned going to Miracle Mart, so I decided to ask her if I could tag along. Even though she was going with Cathy's mom, it was probably my only chance to get Tom's gift. When I opened the car door of the Cicerellis' Ford, Cathy was in the back seat. She didn't look happy to see me at all.

"Hi Cath."

She let out a puff of air when she looked at me and turned toward her window. I wondered if she was mad that I hadn't asked her to go skating again.

"Ruth Ann, this a surprise to see you. Your mama didn't say you were coming with us," Mrs. Cicerelli said to me.

"I hope it's all right, Francesca," my mom said. "Ruth Ann asked me after we got off the phone. I suppose she needs a card for her dad. He's coming tomorrow for their birthdays."

"I bought him a hat at Alger Variety yesterday."

118

"You bought him a hat? What kind of hat?" my mom asked.

"That's right, you've got a birthday on Monday," Mrs. Cicerelli said. "Maybe I better make some cannoli for the occasion, or better yet, come over for dinner *and* cannoli,"

Even at the mention of my birthday, Cathy didn't turn to me.

"Well, *we* have a special reason for going to the Miracle Mart today," Mrs. Cicerelli announced to all of us.

"My Caterina is getting her first bra. She finally sprouted little *mammalines*."

Cathy put her hands over her face and shook her head. The last time I'd asked her if she had a bra yet, she hadn't answered me directly, but she'd made it sound like she did have one. That was almost a year ago. I couldn't believe she was in the middle of seventh grade and still didn't have a bra. I could tell she was mortified.

"Hey Cath, look what I found. I took my Choco-Mint Lifesavers out of my purse. They had been one of our favorites when we first met. She looked at them and shook her head.

"C'mon take one."

She took the Lifesavers from me and put one in her mouth. My mom started talking to Mrs. Cicerelli about how she needed to buy cat food and litter. I lowered my voice and leaned toward Cathy.

"Getting a bra isn't that big of a deal, Cath. At least *you* get to go and pick it out. Remember when Renee just brought one home for me from Wurzburg's when she worked there? And then I had to come downstairs and model it!"

Cathy nodded and looked a little relieved. She probably figured that I'd forgotten about the time we'd talked about *her* bra situation.

"I'm going for Tom's birthday present," I said to her even more quietly, although our moms were talking loud enough that they wouldn't hear anyway. I knew she'd enjoy being in on that information, and I was trying to lift her mood.

"You know, I'm four days older than him." Cathy gave me another nod.

When we got to Miracle Mart, I found the *Happy Together* record right away and picked out a funny card for my dad. I handed Cathy a new roll of Choco-Mint Lifesavers in the car.

"Here's a little gift for your Bra-Day."

She smiled at me and said, "I got two and one of them is pink."

* * *

We went to an earlier Mass than usual the next morning, since my dad was coming at noon. I found a box to fit his hat and wrapped it up with the comic pages from our Sunday paper. I decided to wear my corduroy suit with the green tights, because I didn't want my dad to see how bad my skin was. I knew he'd ask, and my plan was to just pull my sleeves up a little to show him. If he saw how bad it really was getting, he'd probably have Wally the pharmacist, call me or something weird like that.

We got home just before eleven. I was hungry, but decided I shouldn't eat anything so I could save my appetite. I hoped we could go to the Pantlind Hotel for lunch and then maybe to a movie. We'd gone to the public museum the last two visits, so I figured we should do something different. My mom and I were at the dining room table, reading the paper, when the phone rang. I was looking at the movie section. I wanted to see *The Graduate*, but I knew my dad would rather see a western.

'Hey, Sport, it's your ol' man. I don't know what kind of weather ya' got over on your side, but over here, it looks like the North Pole."

I looked out the dining room window to our back yard. There were a few clouds in the sky, but the sun was shining.

"It looks good here. Haven't you even left yet? Does this mean you're not coming?"

"Well, Sport, I planned to leave at nine thirty, but that's when this snow got started. I called a bunch of times, nobody answered."

I felt like I'd been punched in the stomach. My mom lit a Salem and walked into the kitchen.

"We went to church early 'cause we thought you were coming."

"Well, I was planning to come, Sport, but I wouldn't be able to see a foot in front of me with this snow comin' down. And that Highway 46 is bad enough in good weather. Don't worry, I'll get there in a couple of weeks. I shoulda known better than to think we could do this in January. As soon as this lets up a little, I'm gonna drop your card and some money in the mail. It won't get there for a couple days, but just think of this as our birthday *week*."

"I have a present for you," I said, as I swallowed hard.

"Well, isn't that nice? Just hang on to it, Sport. I'll get there soon. Now Happy Birthday to us, huh? And tell your mom how bad this snow is, hear?"

I hung up the phone and sat down on the window seat. I could hear the can opener in the kitchen. Ruff and Reddy galloped in at the sound of it and I thought of the day my dad brought them to me and my sister. We met him at a park and had a picnic that my grandma had packed. The tiny kittens with dark brown faces were in a box with a screen over the top. Renee had put my hair up in a bun that day and pinned daisies around it. Tiny red ants crawled out of the flowers and down my back while we were eating Grandma Gertie's fried chicken. We used to see my dad a lot back then. He didn't visit as often since we moved to Grand Rapids. Or, maybe he didn't love me as much as he used to, because I was a teenager. I wondered if it really was snowing in Saginaw.

My mom came into the dining room. I hadn't felt like crying until I saw the look on her face. For a second, I thought about hugging her, but other than good-night kisses on the cheek, my mom and I didn't show affection.

"What kind of soup do you want with your tuna sandwich?

"None," I said, and I picked up the wrapped hatbox and walked upstairs to my bedroom. It was almost worse that she hadn't made any mean comments about my dad like she usually did.

* * *

Tom whispered *Happy Birthday* to me as we circled our way to classes the next morning. Otherwise, it didn't feel much like my birthday. Maureen came home for lunch with me, even though my mom usually didn't like me to bring anyone to the house during lunch hour. I'd asked her while she was spraying Aquanet on her hair, and she'd said okay since it was my birthday. I knew she felt sorry for me because of my dad not showing up.

"I talked on the phone to Johnny for two hours last night," Maureen said as we walked toward my house. "I guess we're back together."

"I knew your break-up wouldn't last. Do you think he'll keep trying for, you know?"

"He better not. That's partly what we talked about for two hours."

"You're kidding? Were your parents home?"

"No, they were next door playing cards. I smoked a half of a pack of Winstons while we were on the phone. I think we're going to the movie on Saturday. You and Tom should come with us."

I brought our sandwiches to the dining room and saw a gift on the table.

"Open it," Maureen instructed. It was a box of Ambush scented stationary. "Hey, you haven't told me how your dad liked the hat."

"I can't tell you how he liked the hat, 'cause I didn't give it to him. He didn't end up coming."

Maureen came over to me without saying a word, and gave me a long hug. After we put the food away, we took a quick look at my science project which was finally growing mold. Then we got on the beep-line for about fifteen minutes before heading back to St. Boner's.

Tom caught up with me after school when I was standing on the corner with the Tandem Riders. "C'mon, I'll walk home your way," he said to me.

"Sorry, I didn't call last night, but I thought your dad might still be there, plus *my* old man was in a terrible mood and made us all work practically 'til we went to bed. Did you have a good time with your dad?"

"He didn't show up. He said there was a blizzard in Saginaw, so he didn't come."

"Dang, Ruth Ann, that's really too bad. You got him that hat and everything, right?"

I nodded and blinked a bunch of times, and I'm pretty sure Tom noticed. He shook his head and put his arm around my shoulder more like a friend than a boyfriend.

When we got to my house he asked if he could come in for a minute.

"I'm afraid if my mom finds out, she won't let you come in when she *is* here."

"How will she find out?"

"Believe me, the neighbors around here don't miss a thing. I really got in trouble when you came in on Christmas Eve day."

"Yeah, but wasn't that because of your sister? Okay, well, I just wanted to give you this."

He handed me a small box wrapped in twinkle tissue, and held my books while I unwrapped it. It was a pair of tiny gold earrings with garnets in the middle.

"My birthstone, how pretty." I smiled up at him. He gave me a quick peck on the lips.

"I know, I know, the neighbors are callin' your mom right now."

"Stop it," I said, as I pretended to kick his foot. "But, really, thank you. I love them."

"And I love *you*. Happy birthday."

He kissed my cheek and I went in the house.

There was a gift from Renee in the mail and a card from Larry with ten dollars. When my mom came home from work, she could hardly contain herself, she was so excited. She pushed the vacuum cleaner out of the way and pulled a box out of the coat closet.

"Open it now. We're having dinner at the Cicerelli's and it's too big to take over there."

It was a set of 1968 World Book Encyclopedias. My mom stood with her hands over her nose and mouth to keep from exploding.

"Just think, you can do your reports right at home from now on. Aren't they nice?"

"They're great, Mom, really great. Thanks so much, but where are M through Z?"

"I bought them from a door-to-door salesman on the two-year payment plan, so we'll get a couple more, every time I make a payment. You might as well open your gift from Renee now too. And before I forget, Larry's taking us to dinner when he gets back from Toledo."

Renee's package contained a box of Siamese cat bookends, and two booklets, *How to Be Popular* and *Necking and Petting, and How Far to Go*. I was really glad I hadn't opened those at the Cicerelli's.

Chapter Sixteen

"If you don't like coconut, I'll trade you," Maureen said as she bit into her third chocolate.

"I love coconut."

"You do, really? Hardly anyone likes coconut. I told you, we are *so* much alike, and that is why I love you." Maureen popped a caramel into my mouth and I popped a raspberry cream into hers. Two heart shaped candy boxes were in front of us on the table. Tom and Johnny had met us at the park and given them to us for Valentine's Day. We'd spent a half hour goofing around on the playground with them, but then came back to my house to make posters. The boys wanted us to stay longer, but the science fair was on Friday night and we needed to set our projects up tomorrow.

We opened the bottles of poster paint and began to carefully fill in the stenciled letters. After I finished painting the word "MOLD" in green, I turned the record over on the stereo.

"I can't wait for Amy Jo's party on Saturday night. What are you wearing?"

I hadn't thought about it, but without a doubt it would be long sleeved. My arms and legs had so many new spots I couldn't even keep track of them anymore.

* * *

I ended up with a B on my science project, and I felt good about that. It was obvious that most of the kids had lots of help. Mary Lou and her dad had made two models of heads and lungs out of paper mache. One of the heads was smoking and his lungs were dark and bumpy. They even had it rigged so smoke came out of the cigarette. Of course, she took first place.

When I looked around the auditorium for my mom, I figured she had gone outside to smoke a Salem, even after she'd seen those lungs.

"Hey, look at our moms," Maureen said.

"Oh yeah, what do you know?" The two of them were standing together in a corner, drinking punch and laughing. Maureen took my hand and squeezed it. We had talked about introducing our moms, but hadn't figured out a way to do it.

"We should plan a Mom Day, and all four of us do something, okay?"

"That's a great idea, let's do it."

I felt really lighthearted, and for once, it didn't bother me that my dad was on the other side of the state while everyone else's was right in the room.

* * *

Amy Jo had gone all out for her post-Valentine/birthday party. Her entire basement was decorated in pink and red and even the cake was heart shaped. I hadn't talked to her much since we'd made her pee at the slumber party. I kind of figured this party was her attempt to make us all forget about that. *It Hurts to be in Love* was playing when Teddy Zukowski sat in the middle of the floor with an empty O-So Grape bottle.

"Gather round, one and all, for spin-the-bottle," he announced. I could tell he and Gerard Waterman had cooked the whole thing up 'cause Gerard plopped down instantly. Then a bunch of other boys joined them.

"C'mon girls, wadda ya waitin' for?" Teddy waved his arm around.

Tom walked over and held his hand out to me. I got off the couch and he led me to another room and shut the door. I had seen Maureen and Johnny enter the room a few minutes before. Tom jumped backwards onto the dryer and sat on its edge. He helped me onto the washing machine. Maureen and Johnny were behind the furnace and I could hear them whispering. We kissed a few times with our legs dangling and then he leaned me backward so that I was lying across both appliances.

"What about the parents?" I asked him.

126

"Hey, if they come down, they're gonna blow up about spin-the-bottle. They won't even look in here."

Tom was breathing fast like he did after racing at the skating rink. His hand was on top of my bra and I could tell his "bulge" was back again. He was trying to reach under me to unhook my bra.

"Tom, don't. Okay? If the Burkes do come in here, I don't want to be all undone."

He tried to wedge his hand into my bra from the top. He was pretty determined.

"All right, kids, lights on!" It was Amy Jo's dad coming down the steps. My heart was beating like mad. Then he knocked loudly on the door to the room we were in.

"Anybody in there?" We held our breath.

" The pizzas are here." We waited for a few minutes until the door opened slightly.

"Hey, all, the coast is clear, better get out before he comes back," Marty said.

I was relieved that we didn't get caught and that somebody had put the brakes on Tom. I would have to talk to Maureen about this since Johnny had put even more pressure on her. I liked the feelings I had when we kissed, but they were getting even stronger than the Barbie negligee feeling. I was a little worried that if we were alone, only one thing would stop me. And with spring just a few weeks away, I was afraid that one thing was no longer going to be a secret.

* * *

"Well, Miss Ruth Ann, I do believe you've got yourself an honest to goodness callus here. Nice goin'. Now, let me hear your Irish tune."

It was the last guitar lesson before my mom's birthday. My mom was born on St. Patrick's Day and she's Irish, so when Pete asked me to pick out a song, I decided to try and learn an Irish one for her by March 17th. I had been practicing a very simple version of *When Irish Eyes Are Smiling*, but only when she wasn't home. I wasn't great at it, but in the past week, it was starting to sound better.

"Now, I told you last week, you gotta sing for me, like it or not. I gotta see that these chords and lyrics match up. And *you* gotta get used to singing with an audience."

So far, I'd only sung the song when I was alone. I felt shy about singing in front of Pete, but then he took off his jean jacket and I saw his arms that were even more covered with psoriasis than I remembered. For some reason, that made me feel like I could sing the song. I knew I didn't have a great voice, and I could only play it fairly well, but the words matched up okay.

"Hey there, Miss Ruth Ann, that sounded real pretty. You gotta keep at this. Your mama's gonna love it."

* * *

Maureen was rolling my hair up on her giant curlers when I heard a car pull up and the front door open.

"Oh no, my sister's home. You were right, we should have stayed at your house."

I'd no sooner said that, when my bedroom door opened. It was Renee.

"Ruth Ann, there are two inches of dust on every solid thing downstairs. Couldn't you even come through for Mom's birthday?"

"Nice to see you too, Renee. In case you didn't notice, I have company."

"I don't know how you can invite anyone over to this pigsty. Hi, Maureen. Glad to see somebody's trying to do something with that hair. And I hope you figured out a birthday cake like I told you to. I have a thousand lines to memorize."

Renee shut the door before Maureen could even say hi back to her. She looked at me in the mirror with wide eyes.

"Sorry, Maureen. She's so embarrassing. I'd give anything to have your sisters."

128

Gone Before Spring

Maureen closed her eyes and shook her head. "I can't even believe you two are related," she whispered.

Maureen's older sisters seemed like a dream come true. One of them was married, and the other had an apartment. They were funny, and kind to Maureen, and really seemed to like me, and our other friends. Sometimes it felt like Renee was another one of my "crosses to bear," as Sister Marie Frances had taught me in first grade.

"So you're responsible for your mom's cake? Do you have a plan?"

"Yeah, I mentioned it to Cathy on the way home from school. She said I can bake one over there tomorrow."

* * *

On Saturday night while Renee was out with the Wurzburgers and my mom was on a date with Larry, Cathy and I baked the birthday cake over at her house. Mrs. Cicerelli gave us her pistachio frosting recipe and she donated the pistachios so the cake would be green for St. Patrick's Day. I noticed that Cathy was quieter than usual while we were baking. I hadn't seen much of her the past few weeks, except for walking home from school. The ice rink had melted in late January, so we hadn't gone skating again.

"Gee, I think this is the first time we've hung out since your Bra-Day," I said to her after closing the oven. I regretted saying it right away, because she blushed.

"Well, you were here for your birthday, a couple of days after that."

I felt bad that I'd forgotten the birthday dinner that the Cicerellis had given me. Since it wasn't the greatest birthday, maybe I was even trying to forget the one or two good parts.

"Oh yeah, how could I forget? Your mom made all my favorites and you made the cherry chip cake. Hey, *Get Smart* will be on in a few minutes. Let's make popcorn."

* * *

Renee made beef stroganoff for my mom's birthday dinner. I helped with the salad and Larry brought pistachio ice cream. After my mom opened her gifts, including the outfit I'd had on lay-a-way for two months, I ran upstairs to get my guitar. I hadn't told anyone about my plan, just in case I chickened out. When I walked into the living room with my guitar, they all stopped talking.

"I have one more surprise for you, Mom. I hope it's not a disaster." I sat down and played and sang, *When Irish Eyes Are Smiling*. I goofed up once or twice, but kept going anyway. When I looked up, my mom was wiping the corners of her eyes with her sleeves. Larry stood up and clapped and Renee actually smiled at me.

* * *

I was digging through my drawer, trying to find clean knee socks when I realized my mom hadn't left for work yet. She was usually out the door, shortly after attacking her hair-do with clouds of hair spray, but I could still hear the television playing downstairs.

I found her sitting on the couch in front of the *Today Show* with an unlit Salem between her fingers.

"Martin Luther King Jr. was assassinated last night," she said without taking her eyes off the TV set.

I sat between her and Ruff and listened to the report of how he was shot on the balcony of a motel in Memphis. I didn't know a lot about Martin Luther King, but I'd seen him leading Civil Rights marches on the news many times. I also remembered my dad's friends at his old pawn shop talking about the important work he was doing and that they were afraid he'd be shot like Kennedy.

During school Mass that morning, the priest said a special prayer and we were all asked to bow our heads and be silent in remembrance of him. I felt quiet and sad for the rest of the day.

* * *

All of the Tandem Riders were invited to a sleepover in the room above Angela's garage, where her slumber party had been, last fall. The

130

week before, our class was told to come up with ideas for the eighth-grade talent show that would be in late May. Angela thought we could use the overnight to figure out an act that we could all do together. Mary Lou suggested a modern dance number to the theme song from *Peter Gunn*.

"No, we can't do that," Maureen said. *Peter Gunn* is the song the high school girls use every day for exercising in gym class. Plus, you're the only one who's taken modern dance lessons."

"Yeah, we need something that we can all do," Peg said.

"I wonder if we could do some kind of tribute to Martin Luther King," I said.

"No. We're *not* going to sing about someone who died," Mary Lou said. "That would be too depressing."

"I think we should sing a Beatles song," Angela said.

We tossed a few ideas back and forth about which song would be a good choice and I mentioned that we needed some action with the song. We decided that we'd sing, *When I'm Sixty-Four* and instead of acting sixty-four, we'd do little kid things while we sang, like playing ball, jacks, jumping rope, hula hoop and blowing bubbles.

"We should all wear spring dresses," Irene said.

Mary Lou added, "With matching bows in our hair, and nylons."

At the mention of nylons, I looked over at Maureen.

"Not nylons. Let's wear white tights, so we look more little girlish," Maureen said as she squirted cheese from a can onto her cracker.

Everyone but Mary Lou nodded in agreement. I wondered if she was pushing nylons on purpose, because of me. Earlier in the evening, I had ducked into the bathroom to put on my pajamas, hoping that nobody would notice. When I walked into the party room, Mary Lou made a point of looking at me and saying, "Ruth Ann, you're the most modest person I've ever met."

"But aren't those the cutest PJs you ever met?" good old Maureen asked. I was wearing the polka dot pajamas that Aunt Dorothy had sent for my birthday.

* * *

The next morning as we rolled up our sleeping bags, we all agreed to buy spring dresses for the talent show. I would need a few babysitting jobs, for sure, because we also needed a dress for the May procession, and one for eighth grade graduation.

I mentioned the dress problem later to my mom while we were making dinner.

"Get your dad to buy you a dress or two," she said as she sliced a cucumber into the salad.

Spring break was in a week, and I was going to Saginaw the day after Easter.

"It's about time he realized how many things you need. We're just lucky you have to wear a uniform. Tell him *that* when he complains about Catholic school," she said as she dished out the macaroni and cheese.

Chapter Seventeen

I was happy to have a window seat on the Greyhound Bus but was disappointed that both of my parents said no to Maureen coming with me to Saginaw. It was surprising they agreed on something, and they also agreed they would think about it for my summer visit.

We pulled into the Saginaw bus terminal where I saw my dad standing on the platform with a cigar in his mouth, his hands in his pockets. Of course, he was wearing a hat. Before standing up, I reached into my bag and put the hat on my head that I'd bought him for our birthday. As I came down the steps of the bus, he looked at me with a big grin.

"What's that on your head, Sport?" He gave me a bear hug and then removed the cigar to kiss me. I took his hat off and replaced it with the olive green one I was wearing.

"Happy late birthday. Hey, it looks good on you."

As soon as we got out of the car, I could smell Grandma Gertie's roast chicken. It made me feel cozy and little and I wondered if I was too big to slide down the bannister. Grandma came waddling toward me with her toothless grin.

"Oh my Got, you're all grown up," she said in her Yiddish accent. She kissed both my cheeks.

"Are you hungry? What do you want to drink? How about a Vernors? Would you rather have a root beer? Danny, you want a cup of coffee?"

"No, Ma. Just fix Ruth Ann up here."

That's how it would be for the next five days. My grandma couldn't stop offering food and drinks. On the table, there was a box of Manischewitz egg matzas. Passover had begun a couple of days before, so I wouldn't be eating bread, noodles, or anything like that while I was here.

"Grandma, can I have a matza with sweet butter?"

Grandma looked at my dad and put her hands up in the air. "Danny, did you hear that? She wants a matzah with sweet butter."

It didn't seem like my grandma could ever see me as anything but a Catholic girl. She always acted surprised whenever I acknowledged something Jewish. I sat at the kitchen table and helped myself to a matzah and two kosher for Passover macaroons.

My dad's wife, Wilma, didn't come over to Grandma's for dinner. I'd actually never seen her there. My dad told me that we'd have dinner with her at their apartment the next night. Aunt Dorothy and I cleaned up the kitchen and then went up to her room so she could show me her newest clothes. She never got married and had always lived with Grandma. Like my mom, she was a secretary. She loved dancing and chocolate, but mostly she loved shopping.

"Honey, when the *Carol Burnett Show* comes on, I want you to watch it with Grandma, and make sure she doesn't see me go upstairs. I bought a few things that I don't want her to know about. I left them in the car so I'll come in the side door after the show starts. There's something for you, too."

"Okay, sure." I tried not to laugh because Aunt Dorothy had trained me to do this when I was three years old, and she always acted like I never did it before.

After an hour or so, Aunt Dorothy called me upstairs. She was wearing a shiny, sleeveless dress in her favorite color, which she called "cerise".

"Oh, you look beautiful!" I told her as I sat on the large, wooden window seat next to the telephone. Their house was Victorian with lots of oak and leaded glass. They rented it from the Catholic church across the street, where I attended Mass when I visited. I was glad that I was going home on Saturday this time, so I wouldn't have to go.

Aunt Dorothy handed me a bag. Wrapped in tissue was a pink skirt and top that I would have loved in fourth grade, but we could tell instantly that it was too small when I held it up.

"Well, I'll have to take it back to Heavenrichs," she said.

* * *

My dad picked me up from Grandma's the next afternoon. I hung around the car lot with him and then we went to his apartment. The day had turned very warm for April, and I rolled up the sleeves to my blouse, without thinking.

"For cryin' out loud, Ruth Ann, you didn't tell me your arms had gotten *so* bad. Is it like that in other places?"

"It's a little worse, here and there. It's no big deal, Dad."

I rolled my sleeves back down.

"I better give Wally a call," he said, as he headed toward the phone.

I plopped down on the couch and opened up a copy of *True Romance*.

Wilma walked in just as my dad was removing homemade french fries from his deep fryer. She headed right to the bedroom, calling over her shoulder, "Hi Ruth Ann. Let me get out of these clothes. Danny, be a doll and make me a drink."

After dinner, when my dad and I were clearing the table, I leaned over Wilma to get the cap to the mustard.

"I took tomorrow afternoon off because I want to take you shopping," Wilma said as she set her empty martini glass on the table. She ate two french fries and then pushed her plate back, ignoring the hamburger and salad.

"I want to buy you a new dress. Would you like that?" she asked.

"Sure, that'd be great. Maybe I can return the outfit Aunt Dorothy bought me while we're at it. Will we be going to Heavenrich's?"

"Not so fast," my dad piped up. "We have a date with Wally."

* * *

My dad picked me up from Grandma's house at noon the next day and we drove to Wally's Drug Store. It was a small shop with a creaky

135

wooden floor. Wally was a slight man with thin, graying hair that was combed straight back. He took us behind the drug counter to a small room lined with shelves full of medicine.

"Well, Ruth Ann, you sure have grown up since the last time I saw you."

I recalled the summer before when I got my period and I made my dad go in for products without me. I hoped that wasn't the grown up part he was talking about.

"Let's have a look at this "heartbreak" crap you're dealing with," Wally said as he sat on a stool. I rolled my sleeve up and he held my wrist, then he turned my arm over to see the other side.

"Both arms?"

I nodded.

"Legs too?" I nodded again and scooted my pant leg up a few inches. He parted my hair and looked at my scalp.

"Do you have it on your back and trunk?"

If I hadn't been so mortified, I might have found "trunk" amusing. I wished my dad wasn't standing so close by.

"Some," I answered.

He picked up a tube of the "heartbreak" stuff and some shampoo with the same name.

"This is about the best stuff out there, but I'm not saying it works all that well. They really don't know what causes this. Most folks just have to ride it out and see. It's a damn shame it hit you at this age, sweetheart."

"How long does the riding it out take? I thought it would be gone by now."

I hadn't wanted to face the fact that spring was here and this was not going away. I could tell Wally thought so too, especially when he'd called me sweetheart.

"I wish I could tell you that, Ruth Ann, and I'm sure your doctor has said the same thing."

"Oh, he hasn't seen it. I haven't been sick or anything".

Wally looked over at my dad, "She hasn't been to the doctor? How long has it been like this?"

"This all started when I hurt my leg on a bleacher last fall."

"It's very common for an injury to kick this off, as well as strep throat."

"What about this?" my dad asked as he turned something over in his hand.

"It can't hurt, but I don't know how much good that'll do, either," Wally said.

It was a bar of pine tar soap. Oh great, more tar stuff, I thought to myself. I already smelled like a patched up pothole.

* * *

We met Wilma downtown at the Home Dairy for sandwiches and malts. Then my dad went back to the car lot. I had never been alone with Wilma and I wondered what my mom would say if she knew. I felt pretty uncomfortable, but I knew it was making my dad happy and I sure didn't mind if she wanted to buy me a dress.

"I think we should go to Jacobson's first," Wilma said as she crushed her cigarette into the ashtray that was attached to the wall of our booth.

We looked in the junior miss departments at three stores, before I found a dress that I liked. For one thing, it had to have long sleeves and that limited the choices. Wilma liked the one I chose too. It was empire style in yellow dotted swiss and she didn't even question me when I tried it on with white tights. I told her that we were all wearing tights for the talent show, and that I'd buy them, but she insisted. My dad had probably told Wilma about my psoriasis, but she never mentioned it. The white tights hid it for the most part, but not completely.

As we passed through the housewares department, I saw a blue teapot I thought my mom would like.

"I think I'll buy this for my mom," I told Wilma.

As weird as it felt being with Wilma instead of my mom, it also felt strange to buy a gift for my mom in front of Wilma. Everything inside my heart felt so mixed up.

* * *

I woke up the next morning and headed right to the telephone in Aunt Dorothy's room. This was the day Mimi and I had planned to get together. Mimi was the only friend I had in Saginaw. We'd known each other our whole lives because our parents had been friends before we were born. Her real name was Mary Jane, but I couldn't say that when I was little. Only Mimi came out. So, it stuck and everyone always called her that. It felt so good to hear her voice when she said hello. We sent letters to each other every month, but we never made long-distance calls.

My dad dropped me at her house before he went to the car lot. We listened to records and talked all morning and then her mom took us to lunch at their country club. After that, we rode bicycles around her neighborhood and looked at all the pretty houses. My dad called in the late afternoon.

"Hey, Sport, how'd you girls like to sleep on the houseboat tonight?"

Mimi and I had wanted to sleep on my dad's houseboat for as long as I could remember. He had built it himself by putting a travel trailer on a pontoon. He kept it parked on the Saginaw River and in the summer, he took us for rides on it.

"We'd love to, but I don't know if Mimi will be allowed."

"It's all set, Sport. I talked to June and Don already. Tell Mimi to pack a bag and I'll be there at five."

Mimi and I jumped up and down screaming, like we did when we were six-years-old.

We stopped at Grandma's so I could pick up my stuff and then we went straight to my dad's boat which was named, *The Whole Megillah*. It was especially warm for April, so my dad grilled hot dogs and we ate on the dock. Passing boats honked and we waved at the people going by.

"Hey Ruth Ann, remember when we used to play *West Side Story* and *Gypsy*?"

"Oh yeah, and we'd sing *Let Me Entertain You*, and dance around in those chiffon scarves for bras. We had so much fun playing in your basement."

"We had lots of fun at your house too. Remember when your mom took us to the drive-in movie and all we did was watch that couple make out in the car next to us?"

I nodded, thinking back to that time.

"Just think, we have been friends our whole lives," Mimi said.

"I know, my friends at home all think it's so cool, especially how we write letters all the time. Hey, how do you like my Ambush scented stationary?"

"I love it, didn't I tell you?"

"I got it for my birthday from Maureen, the new friend I've been writing about."

"Hey, do you think we'd be such close friends if you still lived in Saginaw?"

"I don't know, maybe. I do know we'll be friends even when we're old ladies."

"*And* don't forget, there are movies of us together in the *playpen*."

We slept in the double bed that was surrounded by knotty pine at the back of the boat. My dad rolled a mattress out on the floor in the front of the boat, where the tiny living room and kitchen were. I knew he couldn't have been very comfortable.

"I love your dad," Mimi whispered in the dark. "He's the funniest person I've ever known, and it's so nice of him to sleep on the floor out there, so we can spend the night."

My dad usually made our sides split with laughter, but he hadn't done that tonight. He seemed quieter than I ever remembered. On the way to the boat, he'd turned the radio up when *Ode to Billy Joe* came on. "Have you girls listened to the words to this song? It's a sad one, listen."

Mimi fell asleep before me, and I looked out the little window at the stars. The boat was rocking gently and I wondered if my dad was afraid my skin was never going to get better. Then I realized that was probably why he got the idea for us to sleep on the boat. If he was worried, I knew I better be worried too.

* * *

I spent the next day helping Grandma around the house. I followed her from room to room, watching her large bottom sway back and forth. Renee and I always said it was like a small table that you could set a tea service on and it probably wouldn't fall off. I helped her to make potato kugel and brisket for dinner.

"So, did you get any sleep on that boat last night? What did you eat? Did Danny feed you enough? What did you eat at the lawyer's house yesterday? Did her mother take you out to the fancy country club? You weren't dressed for that place."

I just nodded and let Grandma talk while I grated the potatoes and popped macaroons into my mouth. My dad came over shortly after Aunt Dorothy got home from work, and we had dinner in the dining room.

"Wilma's niece is going to a dance at the Y tomorrow night. She thought maybe you and Mimi would like to go," my dad said as he broke a matza in half.

I had never met Wilma's niece, but she'd mentioned her to me several times because we were the same age. I also had never been to a dance. St. Boner's didn't believe in them, it seemed, because other Catholic schools in town had dances all the time. I had hoped to see Mimi again before I left on Saturday, so I said I'd call her.

It ended up that my dad talked to her dad and they set it all up for us to go to the dance. We'd spend the night over at Grandma's after, because it was closer to the Y.

* * *

140

Gone Before Spring

Aunt Dorothy met me at Heavenrich's department store the next day on her lunch hour. Grandma's house was only a few blocks from downtown and I'd been allowed to walk there by myself since last year. I brought the pink outfit so we could exchange it for something else. It was different than shopping with Wilma, because Aunt Dorothy would sooner die than look at something that wasn't on sale.

The one lucky thing about the sale rack, was that most of the stuff had long sleeves because they were from last season.

"Look at this dress, Aunt Dorothy. It would be great for the talent show."

"Oh that's cute, and it's on fourth mark-down. Go try it on."

The dress had a dropped waist and pleated skirt. The material was a red and black pattern on white and it fit perfectly.

"I'm all set now," I said as I came out of the dressing room with the dress on over my jeans. "I'll wear this for the talent show and the yellow dress from Wilma for the May procession."

"What about shoes?" she asked me.

"Daddy gave me shoe money. I need to get white shoes so I can use them for graduation too. If you have to get back to work, I'll look for some myself."

Aunt Dorothy looked skeptical about me picking out shoes, but then she glanced at her watch.

"All right, I do need to go. Make sure they fit good, and don't pay full price."

It was a good thing she was in a hurry, I thought to myself. She didn't even ask why I left my jeans on.

I had never shopped for anything by myself, but it turned out to be fun and I found white shoes with squashed heels, on sale.

* * *

Aunt Dorothy told me not to worry about helping after dinner. She wanted me to go upstairs and get ready for the dance. I decided to wear the

141

new talent show dress with my garnet earrings from Tom. It felt strange to not talk to him for so many days. He had gone to Canada for spring break to visit Laurent. It seemed like he was a million miles away.

I applied a little extra blush and my whitish-pink lipstick and then Aunt Dorothy called upstairs, "Mimi's at the door."

Mimi was wearing a pale peach matching skirt and sweater that reminded me of the outfits I'd seen at her country club. I noticed she was wearing different glasses that matched her outfit.

"Who'd have ever thought we'd be going to our first dance together?" she asked me, as I took her overnight bag and set it by the stairs.

Mimi was right, I wouldn't have guessed we'd be doing this, either. I felt a little nervous in the car as her dad drove us to the Y. Wilma had phoned and told me that her niece, Paula, would wait for us in the front lobby with her friend. We spotted two girls on a bench with their heads together after we walked in the front door. They got up and walked toward us when we caught their eye.

"Hi. Are you Ruth Ann? I'm Paula, and this is my friend, Ellen. Aunt Wilma has wanted me to meet you forever."

"Hi. This is Mimi. She lives in Saginaw, too." I felt really dumb as soon as I said that.

I noticed that Paula and Ellen were both wearing very short skirts and squashed heels. Paula had chin length brown hair and Ellen had a scarf tied around her ponytail which made me think of Mary Lou.

"This is a good night for you to come because the best DJ is here. They hardly ever get him."

"Do you come to dances here a lot?"

"They have dances here once a month, but we also go to this place called Daniel's Den." She looked at Mimi. "Do you go to the Den?"

Mimi shook her head and looked kind of scared. I was starting to wonder if coming to this dance was such a good idea after all, and then we entered the auditorium. Groups of kids were clustered here and there, some standing, some sitting on benches. Mimi sat on the only empty bench that was left. I sat next to her and Paula stood by us. Ellen had stopped to talk to some other kids.

"Ellen's probably trying to find out if Brian's coming," Paula said.

"Is Brian her boyfriend?"

"She wishes. She's been in love with him for two years. But he's in love with Penny Donaldson and she breaks up with him all the time. It's like *Peyton Place* around here. Is it like that in Grand Rapids?"

I thought of Cathy's friends who were in love with Tom.

"Yeah, it is sometimes."

The first two songs the DJ played weren't ones I particularly liked, so I wondered why Paula thought he was so great. Then *A Girl Like You* by the Troggs came on.

"I love this song," I said to Paula and Mimi.

"Wanna dance?" Paula asked us.

I got up right away. Mimi shook her head and Ellen was off dancing with two other girls. So, Paula and I went out on the dance floor and began dancing. Colorful circles swirled on the wall behind the DJ and sometimes on the other walls and the floor. The next song was *96 Tears* by ? Mark and the Mysterians.

"Oh, they had to play this, didn't they?" I said to Paula. "I always tell my friends that they're from Saginaw since it's my home town."

I motioned for Mimi to come out and join us. She got up and walked over to us and then to my relief, started dancing. I knew she was proud that *96 Tears* was such a popular song everywhere. Two really cute boys had just entered the room and were standing together looking around. I saw Paula look over at Ellen. Mimi stayed up and we danced to the Doors, Cream, and Jefferson Airplane.

"Do you want to get something to drink?" Paula asked us.

We walked back out to the lobby and Ellen ran to catch up with us.

"You girls were right," I said. "This DJ does play great music."

"Guess what? Penny broke up with Brian again," Ellen said after she came up from the drinking fountain.

"So what else is new?" Paula said.

We bought candy bars at the vending machine and compared stories about our schools and friends.

As we headed back to the dance, *Get Off of My Cloud* came on. When we got on the dance floor, all four of us sang *hey! hey!* while we danced. Even Mimi was singing, and I knew she was not a Rolling Stones fan. After our intense Beatlemania phase, she'd veered down more of a Monkees path. We were all cracking up, and I could tell Mimi was having fun now. It crossed my mind that Wilma would probably get a charge out of us all getting along so well.

A slow song by the Temptations came on and we needed to catch our breath after all that laughing, dancing and singing, so the four of us plopped down on the bench. The next song was *Strangers in the Night* by Frank Sinatra. As hard as I fought it, I liked this song, which was weird since Frank was from my parents' era. The next thing I knew, one of the cute guys that I'd noticed earlier was standing in front of me with his hand slightly extended.

"Do you wanna dance?" he asked me.

I was surprised and confused. I'd never thought about slow dancing with somebody that wasn't my boyfriend, especially somebody I didn't know, and I wasn't sure how to handle it. I was sitting between Mimi and Paula and could feel them both looking at me. I glanced at Mimi and saw a look on her face that reminded me of Cathy. It's just a dance, I thought to myself. Besides, the boy looked like Johnny Crawford from *The Rifleman.*

"Okay," I said.

He led me to the middle of the floor and when he took me in his arms, I could tell he had danced with lots of girls. He held me very close and when the song ended, he smiled and just said, "Thanks."

When I looked at the bench where I'd left the girls, it was empty. I walked out to the lobby and Mimi was standing by the coat room.

"What's going on? Where are Paula and Ellen?" I asked her.

"Paula took Ellen into the bathroom 'cause she's crying."

"Why is she crying? What happened?"

"She's very upset because *somebody* was dancing with her heartthrob."

"Oh. Wait. What are you talking about?"

"That stranger you just danced with is *Brian!*"

"Well how should I know that? And besides, I thought he wasn't her boyfriend."

Mimi didn't even answer me, but she followed me into the girls bathroom. Ellen was blowing her nose on a wad of toilet paper. I decided to play dumb.

"I can't believe it's almost ten o'clock and my dad will be picking us up soon," I said.

Ellen gave me a dirty look and walked out of the bathroom.

"Is she okay?" I asked Paula.

"No, she's really mad because you just danced with Brian!"

"I did? How should I know that was Brian?"

"Well, why would you dance with our boys anyway? You're from another town and Mimi told us you *have* a boyfriend!"

I looked over at Mimi, who had her arms crossed, and gave her my best *thanks a lot* look.

"I didn't realize out of towners couldn't dance with the boys here and even if I have a boyfriend, I wasn't going to elope with somebody just 'cause I danced with him."

"We better go out and watch for your dad," Mimi said.

"*I* better go find Ellen," Paula said. She walked out ahead of us.

"It was nice meeting you, Paula," I called after her. "Please tell Ellen I didn't know that was Brian."

"Okay, bye. Nice meeting you too," she said without even turning around.

When we got in the car, my dad asked, "So, how did you Rockettes make out at the dance?"

"It was fun, wasn't it Mimi? Wilma's niece is really nice."

Mimi didn't say a word. I couldn't figure out why *she* was mad at me. When Aunt Dorothy and Grandma asked us about the dance, she barely answered them. They sent us to bed because they thought she was tired. She continued to give me the silent treatment while she was putting her pajamas on.

"Mimi, what's wrong?"

"Nothing."

"C'mon, I haven't seen you like this since I hid your Mickey Mouse ears in second grade."

I could tell she was fighting off a smile when I said that.

"I don't know, it was just weird when you danced with that boy you didn't even know. And then those girls got mad and I was alone with them and I didn't know what to say. And plus, you already *have* a boyfriend."

Mimi sat on the edge of the bed and looked down at the floor.

"I'll probably never, ever get asked to dance. You don't realize this, but girls with glasses are invisible."

Mimi's voice was a little shaky and I noticed her chin was trembling. My stomach felt all knotted up and my heart was beating faster than it did on the dance floor.

"Don't feel bad about glasses, Mimi. You could maybe get contacts someday. I might have a boyfriend *now*, but I probably won't when he sees this."

I reached back, unzipped my dress, and stepped out of it. I stood in front of her in my tights, half-slip and bra, then turned around so she could see my back. Mimi opened her mouth to say something, but then I pulled my slip and tights off so she could see my legs. She closed her mouth.

"See, glasses aren't so bad, are they?"

146

"Ruth Ann, what happened?"

"I have psoriasis. It started last fall and I thought it would be gone by spring, but today is April 19th and here I am. You don't have to worry. I promise it's not contagious."

She walked over and put her arms around me and we both started crying. I took a step back and looked at her. "I love you."

"Me too, I love you, too."

We started laughing and she pointed to the screen door. "I forgot how good you can see that sign from up here."

"I know, I love that sign," I said as I put on my polka dot pajamas. Then we stepped out on the little balcony and held hands as we looked up at the Rainbo Bread sign that flashed in the sky.

"Ruth Ann, I've never watched *Peyton Place*."

"Know what? Neither have I.

Chapter Eighteen

Mimi and I were waiting on Grandma's porch swing when my mom pulled our Oldsmobile into the driveway. When she got out of the car, she threw her Salem butt down and crushed it under her foot. My dad had warned me she was mad when he'd called that morning. He said she was upset that I'd gone to a dance without her permission. It seemed that my dad's permission didn't count in her eyes. His fatherly behavior was hard for her to get used to. I pretended that I didn't notice she was mad. It seemed like I was doing that a lot lately.

Aunt Dorothy and Grandma both had their hair in pin-curls with bobby pins when they stood on the porch waving good-bye. Even though Aunt Dorothy was smiling, her eyes were filled with tears.

We drove to Roy's Steak House to meet Mimi's mom for lunch. She asked us all about the dance. I tried to downplay that Wilma's niece had been with us and didn't mention the way the night ended and thankfully, neither did Mimi.

"Our girls sure have grown up, haven't they, Marla?" Mimi's mom said after she lit her cigarette with Roy's Steak House matches. My mom seemed to lighten up about the dance by the time lunch was over, mostly because Mimi's mom had such a different attitude.

Mimi and I had an extra long hug in the parking lot when we said goodbye.

"I'll see you this summer," I said to her. She just nodded because she was trying not to cry. That got to me and then I was fighting tears. And just like the night before, we both started laughing about crying.

"Well, we better hit the road, Ruth Ann. I told Renee we'd be there by four so we could see her before the show," my mom said before turning to Mimi's mom. "I'll be shocked if her father makes it at all."

Gone Before Spring

We all hugged again and then my mom and I got in the car and headed to Mt. Pleasant because we were going to see Renee star in the college play, *The Corn Is Green*. I felt grouchy because the last thing I wanted to do was hang out with Renee and my mom. I wished more than anything we were going right home. I was dying to talk to Maureen and find out what she'd been doing all week. I missed Tom, my cats, and even my radio station.

Renee was a nervous wreck when we got to her apartment. I tried to stay out of her way because I knew she'd find fault with whatever I said. I was glad her roommate, Karen, came home because Renee was a little nicer to me in front of her. My mom invited her to go out to eat with us, but she had a date. I was sorry to hear that.

Our food had just been placed in front of us when my mom told Renee about Mimi and me going to the dance.

"Ruth Ann, you were out with Wilma's niece? How could you do that to Mom?"

"Do what to Mom? I didn't adopt her or make her my best friend. What was I supposed to do? Daddy set it up!"

The man in the booth behind us turned his head around. I could tell my mom loved the way Renee was defending her because she was dipping her french fries in ketchup and not saying a word. At that moment I hated them both. I thought of Wilma and Aunt Dorothy taking me out to buy dresses and how my dad had let us sleep on the boat.

"Of course *Daddy* set it up," Renee said in her meanest voice.

"Well, guess what? For once, I didn't feel like I was in the way! It felt like people wanted me around. I never, *ever,* feel that way with you two!" I threw my napkin on the table and walked out of the restaurant. The car was locked so I just leaned against the trunk and cried. A father and mother with three little kids walked by and the school-aged boy was staring at me.

"It's okay, Bruce, you have days like that too," the mother said as she gave the kid a little shove so he'd stop looking.

"What is wrong with me?" I thought to myself. I knew I was behaving like an eight year old and wished I could just bury my face in Tom's sweet-smelling neck. For some reason, that made me think about showing my body to Mimi the night before and then I started sobbing.

"Ruth Ann, pull yourself together and come back inside," my mom said.

"Renee shouldn't have been so hard on you. She's just nervous about the show tonight. They've had problems with the costumes and a couple of the actors."

"*Costumes and Actors*? Oh my God, that's all made-up stuff. Who cares? I have real problems, Mom! My psoriasis is a lot worse and I can tell Dad's friend Wally doesn't think it's going away, like you do."

"Your dad took you to that quack pharmacist, Wally? What would he know? I *had it* Ruth Ann. It didn't last more than a year. I've told you over and over, it has a cycle. Now come back in and eat something."

"No, I want to wait here."

She unlocked the car and walked back into the restaurant without saying a word to me. After about twenty minutes, Renee opened the back door of the car and handed me a white sack with my turkey sandwich in it. She rolled her eyeballs at me and said, "I cannot believe how you behave. You're the one who should be on the stage, not me."

* * *

I knew my mom was really mad at my dad because he didn't sit with us at the play. He sat in the back row and met us backstage when it was over. He was wearing our birthday hat and he had a bouquet of yellow mums for Renee. My mom didn't even look at him while we were waiting for Renee to come out of the dressing room.

"Hey, Sport, how'd ya like this one?" My dad was snickering as he usually did after Renee's plays. It made her furious that he didn't take her acting seriously.

Gone Before Spring

After he kissed me goodbye in the lobby and was walking away, he turned around, reached into his pocket and handed me the pine tar soap. "Oh yeah, I almost forgot about this, Sport. Just try it anyway. Like Wally said, it can't hurt."

Renee was going to a cast party, so we left right from the theatre. When we were about halfway to Grand Rapids, my mom started humming with the radio, so I could tell she was in a better mood. I knew the car was a safer place to talk with her because that's where we were when she tried to tell me the facts of life back in sixth grade. We had just pulled into the garage and she asked me if I knew how girls got pregnant. She got pretty mad when I told her that I'd known for two years.

"Hey, Mom, remember you told me to get Daddy to buy a couple of dresses? Well, I'm all set now except for a graduation dress. Aunt Dorothy bought one for me that's great for the talent show and Wilma bought one I can wear for the May procession."

I looked sideways at my mom to see her reaction, especially about Wilma. I hadn't mentioned it earlier because Renee would have blown her stack if she knew I'd gone shopping with Wilma. Since she didn't say anything back, I thought I better keep talking.

"Maybe I'll get enough babysitting jobs to cover the graduation dress. Oh yeah, and Daddy gave me shoe money, so I got those already too."

"Well, for heaven's sake, I'll buy the graduation dress. I was always planning to do that. It was the other two that threw me for a loop, Ruth Ann. You know, the house needs a new roof, and I haven't gotten a raise in two years."

We unlocked the side door just before midnight. When my mom switched on the lights, Ruff and Ready stretched, blinked, and jumped off the couch to rub against my legs. It felt like I'd been gone for a month and it hadn't even been a week. I carried them both up to my bed and then dug Tom's school picture out of my pocket. I kissed it and placed it on my dressing table against my pierced earring tree.

151

* * *

It seemed so good to have toast the next morning because Passover at Grandma's had started to get on my nerves. While I was eating my third piece with butter and honey, Maureen called to tell me that the Tandem Riders were meeting after lunch at Angela's house so we could practice our song for the talent show.

I looked around for Tom when we got to Mass, but either he had come earlier or wasn't home from Canada yet. When I thought about him, I got the grabby feeling in my stomach that I had when we first met. This was the longest we'd gone without talking or seeing each other since September.

* * *

Everyone was sitting on the floor in a circle. We were in the slumber party room over Angela's garage and we were all wearing old hats that we'd plucked from an antique rack in the hall. Mary Lou stood up and put her hands on her hips.

"Okay, so you all got dresses and white tights, what about the bows? Don't forget we agreed to wear matching bows in our hair."

"Chill out, Mary Lou," Irene said. "We still have over three weeks."

"Yes, I know, but we do need a dress rehearsal at some point. What if somebody's dress doesn't look right? Ruth Ann, I hope yours has long sleeves. You did think of that, didn't you?"

Angela's dad walked in with a bowl of popcorn.

"What's all this chatter? I thought you Beatle-ettes were here to sing."

"Beatle-ettes?" Maureen said. "Oh my gosh, you guys. That's it. What a great name! Thanks Mr. Droski." Angela took the bowl from her dad and kissed his cheek. Then we heard him down the hall, singing, *Love Me Do* just like he had at our first slumber party last fall. Angela set the popcorn down in the middle of the circle and then Maureen said, "Now let's see, where were we? Oh yeah, now I remember." She walked over to Mary Lou and put *her* hands on her hips. "Mary Lou, I thought you got it

152

straight that night at ice skating."

Mary Lou wrinkled her forehead. "Got what straight?"

"That you were gonna stop being a bitch to Ruth Ann about her psoriasis."

Mary Lou opened her mouth and rolled her eyeballs.

"Oh my God, I didn't mean anything by it. I was just trying to make sure we had every problem figured out."

"Problem? Did you say problem? Since when is anything about Ruth Ann a problem? If there are any problems in this group, it's you!"

Mary Lou lifted the hat off her head and tossed it on the floor. She turned toward the door and walked toward it.

"Wait! You two need to call a truce right now. This is ridiculous," Angela said as she grabbed Mary Lou's arm.

"Yeah, C'mon. The show must go on," Peg said as she reached into the popcorn bowl.

I felt like climbing out the window. I couldn't believe this was happening again. They both held their hands up in defeat and sat back down. Maureen shot me a knowing glance which let me know we'd be talking later.

"Let's just sing already," Irene said as she threw her head back. The giant flowered hat she was wearing fell off and everyone but Mary Lou laughed.

"Well, I vote we call ourselves the Beatle-ettes," Maureen said.

"I second it," I added.

"I third it."

"I fourth it."

"I fifth it."

There was a pause and we all looked at Mary Lou.

"Fine! I sixth it. Can we sing the damn song now?"

Chapter Nineteen

Pete took hold of my fingertips and shook his head. "This callous is going soft, Miss Ruth Ann. You didn't take your guitar with you to visit your daddy, did you?"

"I couldn't, Pete. I had to take the bus there. And besides, I wouldn't have had time to practice anyway."

"You gotta get back in the saddle here, darlin'. This guitar's gonna get mighty lonely if you don't pick it up more often."

"I'm sorry, Pete. And in two weeks, I'll be gone again because our graduation talent show is that night."

"Talent show? You didn't say anything about a talent show. Are you playing your Irish song?"

"Oh, no. I'm singing a Beatles song with all my best friends. We're calling ourselves the Beatle-ettes."

"Is that right? What Beatles song?"

"We picked *When I'm Sixty Four* because it's the one Beatles song our parents like and the nuns approved."

When I'm Sixty Four? Well, you're gonna accompany them, right?"

"You mean on guitar? Not a chance. I could never play that, especially in front of my whole school and everybody."

"It's an easy song. I can grab the sheet music right now and if you practice enough, you could get it down."

I shook my head. "I can't, Pete. It's gonna be hard enough to sing and blend in up there. I have plenty to worry about just keeping my skin covered."

"It's not gettin' worse, is it?"

I nodded.

"Shoot! I am so sorry to hear that, Miss Ruth Ann. If it makes you feel any better, mine got lots worse before it improved any. Course it's gone up and down since then, but don't give up hope. I know there's a little light at the end of your tunnel."

As much as I wanted to believe Pete, I was pretty sure he was just trying to make me feel better. And there was something about Pete that always did make me feel better.

* * *

"I'm telling Mom, Cathy. You'll be sorry too!" Frankie bumped my arm with his lunch box when he ran past.

"Ouch! Watch where you're going, Frankie Cicerelli," I hollered to him as I rubbed my arm.

I turned around and saw Cathy with a scowl on her face.

"What's his problem?" I asked her.

"Nothing new. He's just being his usual bratty self."

"Hmm, what do I smell? Is it what I think it is?"

"Oh yeah, my mom is baking today for a baby shower. Wanna come in and have some?"

I couldn't remember the last time I'd been in Cathy's house, so I decided to go in for a little while.

"Well, well, look who's here," Mrs. Cicerelli said. It's the prodigal neighbor. How was your visit to Saginaw? How's your grandma doing?" She set a plate of anise cookies in front of us.

"Saginaw was fun and Grandma's fine.

"You are almost a St. Bonaventure graduate. Do you have your dress yet?"

"Not yet, but I got the two other dresses I need while I was in Saginaw."

"Well, good for you. That helps your mama out."

Mrs. Cicerelli left the room to answer the telephone. I could hear her talking in Italian as I bit into my third cookie. Cathy poured two glasses of milk and then slapped Frankie's hand as he grabbed a cookie from the plate.

"Go wash your grubby hands and get out of here. Can't you see, I have a friend over?"

Frankie looked as confused as I was. I'd always thought of myself as Cathy and Frankie's next-door neighbor, not Cathy's friend. It crossed my mind that I needed to ponder this later.

"Are you going shopping for your graduation dress this weekend?" Cathy asked."

"Yes, but it won't be Friday night."

"Why? What's on Friday night? Are you babysitting?"

"I *am* babysitting on Saturday night for Ralph and for his brand new baby sister, which kind of scares me, but Friday night, Tom's new band is rehearsing for the talent show. A bunch of us are going over to Marty's house to watch."

"Wow!" Cathy said. You didn't tell me that Tom's in a band."

"Yeah, they've only rehearsed a couple of times. Their name is Optical Illusion and the talent show will be their debut. But anyway, my mom and I might go shopping on Saturday for my dress. We're thinking about looking at the new mall."

I was feeling better about graduation because a note had gone home that no sleeveless dresses were allowed. I knew there would be some short sleeves, but I probably wouldn't be the only one in long sleeves.

"My cousin went to that new mall. She said it's huge."

I could tell that Cathy was hinting around to go with us. And I also knew she'd do anything in the world to go to the band practice. That would never fly with the Tandem Riders and she'd probably end up pretending she went anyway.

* * *

On Friday night, it was chilly enough to wear my mod print blouse again. I was getting sick of it, but it sure had helped me out on many occasions. I stopped at Angela's house so we could walk over to

Maureen's together. Mary Lou came out of the front door with her when I rang the bell. I hadn't expected her to be there. She was wearing a brand new spring jacket. I decided to be nice and compliment her on it.

"Thanks, I just got it. Are you warm enough in that?" She was looking at my blouse and I could tell she was thinking about how often I wore it.

"Oh, I'll be fine."

"Did you hear that Danny Delaney is having a graduation party at his cottage?" Angela asked. "And he's inviting the entire class. I guess it's a family tradition. All his older brothers had one there when they graduated too."

"I was the first person he told," Mary Lou said. It'll be *so* much fun. In fact I already got a new bathing suit. I got it at Beverly's at the new mall. Have you gone to the new mall yet, Ruth Ann? My mom and I went the first day it opened."

I didn't even answer because I spotted Maureen on her porch steps. She was blowing on her fingernails. Just seeing her there made me feel better.

"Hi guys," she said. "How's this for a summery look?" She held out her nails which she'd just painted with white nail polish.

"Cool," Mary Lou said. "Speaking of summer, did you hear Danny Delaney is having a party for the whole class at his cottage? That's seventy-two kids. Just think about it."

Maureen and I walked behind Mary Lou and Angela on the way to Marty's house.

"How can I go to a cottage party, Maureen? My skin is a lot worse. I'm pretty much covered now." Maureen squeezed my hand.

"Don't worry about it, sweetie. We'll figure something out."

When we got to the side door at Marty's house, we stopped and listened to the band for a minute. Peg and Irene walked up the drive and joined us.

"Should we knock?" Maureen said. "They won't hear us."

"Just go in, I guess," Peg said.

We all walked down the basement steps and then stood together in a group. They stopped playing.

"Come on in," Marty said.

Marty was playing guitar and so was Johnny. Gerard Waterman was on the drums and Tom was holding a tambourine. A boy named Rick, from Burton School, was their lead singer and he played harmonica. He lived across the street from Tom and Marty and Tom said that he'd been trying to form a band for quite a while.

"Okay, girls, you're our first audience, so we're kind of nervous," Gerard announced from behind his drums. "Take a seat if you want."

"Or, feel free to dance, if you're so inclined," Rick added.

We sat on the floor and they started playing *Gloria*, just as Teddy Zukowski and some other boys came down the steps.

"Those guys are from Burton," Maureen whispered. "I remember them from the park last summer." I wondered what my mom would say if she knew I was hanging around with Burton kids. Burton was the public school in our neighborhood that lots of St. Boner's parents thought was full of juvenile delinquents.

Angela turned around, "Yeah, they all live by Teddy."

The band started and stopped over and over and I wondered if they'd ever get through the whole song. Tom sang along with Rick while he played his tambourine. I couldn't help but notice that he was the cutest boy in the band.

"Let's take a break, you guys," Rick said as two girls came down the steps. "Hey, everybody, this is Cindy and Leta." He walked over to Leta and gave her a kiss. She had long dark hair with bangs and was very pretty. She smiled at us and then he took her by the hand and led her up the basement stairs. The other girl said hi to us and then walked over to the boys from Burton School. One of them put his arm around her.

Gone Before Spring

"I guess we don't sound too hot yet," Tom said as he laced his fingers through mine. "We thought an audience might help, but maybe we should have waited."

"You'll get there," I said.

It was the first time we'd been together since before spring break. I felt like diving into his midnight blue eyes.

"I see what you mean about Rick's girlfriend," Teddy Zukowski said into Tom's ear as he passed by. Tom wrinkled his forehead and shook his head.

"What about Rick's girlfriend?" I asked.

Tom opened a bottle of RC Cola on a bottle opener that was nailed to the wall and then took an extra long drink from the bottle. "Who ever knows what Zukowski's talking about?"

"Do you know all these Burton kids?" I asked him.

"I've met a couple of 'em. They're Rick's friends."

I was about to ask another question when Rick and his girlfriend came back down the steps. You could tell by the looks on their faces that wherever they'd been, they'd been making out. Rick walked over to Tom and they started to pretend fist fight. They were both laughing and seemed really friendly.

Then Rick said, "Hey, LaBelle, you've met my girlfriend. When are you gonna introduce me to yours?"

Tom introduced me and Rick bowed from his waist. Then they started shoving each other around and the two Burton girls shook their heads and rolled their eyes like they'd seen them do this before.

Gerard sat down at the drums and the other band members returned to their instruments. They finally managed to get through *Gloria*, and they played a couple of other songs with several starts and stops.

"My dad's picking us up at ten, so we better get back to Peg's," Maureen said.

We left while they were still playing, so Tom and I didn't get a

159

chance to be together again. I waved to him before I went up the basement steps. He lifted his tambourine to me.

* * *

My mom and Larry were playing cards at the dining room table with another couple when I got home.

"How was talent show practice?" my mom asked. I knew she wouldn't have let me go if she thought I was just going to watch some boys in a band. And since their first performance would be in the talent show, I figured it counted as talent show practice.

"Everybody needs more rehearsal, if you ask me. Well, good night."

I scooped Reddy up from the window seat and took him upstairs to my room. I laid in my bed, listening to the radio, looking at the moon, and scratching my legs until they bled.

* * *

"This really is quite a place, isn't it?" my mom said, looking up at the ceiling.

We were standing at the fountain in the middle of the new mall, watching kids throw pennies in.

"Yeah, it's a lot bigger than the other two malls, that's for sure."

"We didn't even make it to half the stores."

"Well, I'm just glad I found a dress."

I felt lucky to have found a long sleeved, white dress that I actually liked. We were required to wear white dresses for graduation at St. Boner's. My favorite part of the dress was the row of white daisies on the empire waist. The sleeves were sheer, but not so sheer that my psoriasis showed through. As we walked past the shops, I tried not to look at all the bathing suits in the windows. I had decided to be like Scarlett O'Hara about the cottage party. Every day I told myself that I'd think about it tomorrow.

* * *

I made sure to get my homework done because I figured there

wouldn't be time at my babysitting job. I had no idea what to expect with the new baby and I hoped that Tom would call since I'd told him I was babysitting there.

I walked to the babysitting job because it was staying light out now until much later. I could hear the baby crying even before I got to their house. Ralph was pushing the screen door open as far as he could.

"My baby sister is screaming. Can we still play Tiddlywinks?"

I ran my hand over his little brush cut as his mom came into the kitchen, jostling a mint green bundle.

"This is Orna Lee and she cries almost constantly," Ralph's mother said. "I hope you can handle her 'cause I need to get out of here. The bottles are in the fridge. Just heat 'em up in that pan of water. Her diaper stuff is over there and put her to sleep in that bassinet. *If* you can get her to sleep, that is."

She thrust the screaming bundle at me and walked out the back door. I looked inside the blanket at the tiny baby with a pointy face and black hair. I tried rocking her, feeding her, and changing her diaper, but nothing worked.

While I walked the floor, Ralph colored in his coloring book on the coffee table and I could tell he was getting frustrated because he was scribbling on every page. At nine o'clock I set Orna Lee down in her bassinet even though she was still crying and took Ralph upstairs to get ready for bed. I felt sorry for him, but I turned out the light without even reading him a story. Ralph's parents came home together at midnight. The baby hadn't stopped crying until eleven o'clock. I didn't know who I felt the most sorry for, the baby or me. And, I was disappointed that Tom hadn't called, but I really couldn't have talked to him anyway.

He finally called the next day. He told me he had been at band practice until eleven the night before and said they had improved on all their songs.

"I wish you could hear us now. We're a lot better."

I wondered how much better they could sound only one day later.

* * *

On Monday, we stayed after school to practice our song with the hula hoops, jump ropes and jacks. Peg and Irene's moms were in charge of the show. They told us we needed to add ten more girls to our group and sing an additional song. Mary Lou was furious.

"It's not fair. Just because they couldn't come up with their own ideas, they get dumped on us," she said.

"Girls, you need to be diplomatic about this. It will help out the whole show and make your class look that much better," Peg's mother said in her New York accent.

I didn't see why Mary Lou was making such a fuss. It seemed to me that we'd probably sound better with sixteen voices than six. We decided to add *Sgt. Pepper* and open the show with it. *When I'm Sixty Four*, would come later on in the program. We rehearsed with the new girls until after five o'clock and were told we'd be rehearsing on several more days.

* * *

Maureen and I took the bus downtown the next day and headed straight to the budget basement at Herpolsheimer's. I bought my mom a sleeveless, print dress for Mother's Day that came with a daisy brooch right on it, which made it feel like two gifts in one. I figured it would be great for her to wear to work in the summer.

"Good thing I babysat again last night," I told Maureen.

"Did that baby scream again the whole night?"

"Not the whole time, but probably for two hours."

Maureen shook her head, "I'd pull my hair out."

After I paid for the dress, we went to the snack bar to get soft serve ice cream. We looked up at the Santa train that was parked on the ceiling above our heads.

"Doesn't it seem like years ago that we rode that down here?" Maureen asked me as she licked her cone and looked up.

"Yeah, it does. Here we are practically in high school. Was that just in December?"

It did feel like time was either going really fast or really slow. So many feelings were crowded into my mind and heart. Lately it felt like I was in one of those dreams where I was chasing something that I couldn't catch up with.

Chapter Twenty

The summer dress I'd bought for my mom fit perfectly, and it was warm enough on Monday evening for her to wear it to the May procession. I felt so good in my yellow dotted swiss dress that I wished I could wear it for graduation too. I also wished I could send a picture of myself in the dress to Wilma, but I would never tell my mom that, especially since we'd had such a nice Mother's Day. I made her pancakes for breakfast and she opened the dress and her gift from Renee while Renee was on the phone. She didn't even care it was a long-distance call. I could tell by her smile that she especially liked the brooch on the front of the dress. Renee had made her a lime green skirt that wasn't even crooked and there was a matching striped Ship 'n Shore blouse.

The tradition at St. Boner's was to have the eighth-grade girls sit in the choir loft and wear blue lace mantillas on their heads for the May procession. They would follow the girl who crowned Mary and stand in a circle around her as she placed the crown on the statue's head.

When we got to the church, my mom gave me a kiss before I went up the steps to the choir loft.

"You look very nice," she said.

I could tell that seeing me in the mantilla had gotten to her and she was a little choked up.

The church began to fill quickly as I looked down. They had run out of seats and people were standing against the walls under the Stations of the Cross. I spotted Frankie and Mr. Cicerelli standing under the fifth station, the one where Simon is helping Jesus to carry the cross. Tom turned around and smiled up at me. I couldn't tell if he was glad to see me or if the mantilla looked as ridiculous as it felt. He looked very handsome in his white shirt and tie. We still talked on the phone almost every day, but he had been busy with band practice and I was babysitting a lot lately. We really hadn't spent much time together since before spring break.

Margaret Gallagher had been picked to crown the statue of Mary. Four girls were chosen by the nuns each year, and then the eighth-grade girls would vote from the four. I had voted for Marie Trojanowski because she'd always helped me with my math, but Margaret was tall and blonde and her family had more money than the Trojanowskis. At least that's what my mom had said to Mrs. Cicerelli when we were cleaning up the Mother's Day dishes.

Margaret wore a wedding gown and a ring of blue flowers in her hair. Four first-grade girls walked beside her, each holding a ribbon from a corner of the pillow that Margaret carried the crown on. We all stood on cue and descended the choir loft steps behind them as quietly as possible, as Barfalottoyou had instructed us at all four rehearsals the week before. Just as we rounded the last bend of the staircase, Amy Jo Burke slipped and rode down the last four steps on her butt, causing several other girls to topple backwards.

Margaret, the first-graders, and a few of the eighth-grade girls had already started down the aisle. The rest of us were in a heap on the stairway, laughing. As hard as we tried to stop, we couldn't. Amy Jo stood up, rubbing her backside. I knew somebody should ask her if she was okay, but nobody could get it out. When she turned around and glared at us, it made it even worse. I thought I was going to choke from laughing so hard.

I looked up to see people in the pews turning their heads to see where the rest of us were. They were singing, *Oh Mary, We Crown Thee with Blossoms Today*, but not as heartily as they had before the fall.

"Get *up*, you guys! Go!" Mary Lou whispered loudly.

Our principal, Sister Mary Edith suddenly appeared in the vestibule, and came flying toward us with a round red spot on each cheek. If I hadn't known better, I would have thought she was wearing rouge.

"Get moving, this instant!" she said as she pointed a stiff arm toward the sanctuary. I could hear the second line of the song, *Queen of the Angels, Queen of the May,* but now it sounded like less than half of the people were singing.

Stifling our laughter was almost impossible, but we brushed off our pastel dresses, pressed our lips together, and marched down the aisle as soberly as we could. I noticed that several of the mantillas were lopsided and crooked. They no longer looked like bridesmaid veils, but more like old party decorations that had fallen from the ceiling.

We all stood around Margaret and watched as she handed the pillow to Marie Trojanowski. The other two runners-up held her hands as she stepped onto the stool. I tried to get serious by thinking about sucking on a lemon as Renee had once advised me, but felt like I was going to burst from holding back the laughter. I could tell by the red faces around me that I wasn't the only one.

As Margaret Gallagher placed the crown on Mary's head, I realized that I would never forget this, even when I was as old as Sister Mary Edith.

* * *

On Saturday, the Tandem Riders rented tandem bikes. Maureen was my partner this time instead of Mary Lou. Each couple took turns taking the lead as we cycled down our favorite streets.

"Let's go down Jefferson Drive," Maureen said to me over her shoulder.

Jefferson Drive had large, older homes with very interesting architecture. A few families from St. Boner's lived on the street.

"Don't go down there," Mary Lou yelled from behind. "It's too close to Burton Woods!"

"What in the world do you think is gonna happen to six girls on bikes, Mary Lou?" Maureen called back to her.

Burton Woods had a bad reputation. There were lots of rumored stories about scary things happening there, especially to girls. Nobody ever dared to walk alone there. Maureen pedaled slower as we approached the opening path to the woods. The other girls were a block behind us.

"Hey, look," she said.

Cindy and Leta, who we'd met at band practice, were coming down the path with the boys who had also been there. I looked away quickly, not knowing if we should say hi. They didn't seem to recognize us as we pedaled down the street.

"Did you see who that was?" I asked.

"Yeah, I wonder what they were up to and I wonder where Rick is," Maureen said.

* * *

I told Tom about it on the phone that night. I was holding Orna Lee and giving her a bottle with the phone on my shoulder.

"Well, they live on the other side of the woods. They were probably just cutting through the park to Marty's house. They came to band practice."

"Oh, they did? Do they always come?"

"Not all the time."

I hadn't known that kids came to band practice other than the time I'd gone. I wondered why Tom hadn't mentioned it or why he hadn't asked me. I was pretty sure Maureen and Peg didn't know either, and their boyfriends were also in the band. I had a funny feeling in my stomach.

"I better hang up. The baby needs to go down and I promised Ralph I'd read to him."

"Okay, see you tomorrow," Tom said.

Maureen and I met Tom and Johnny in the park and the four of us walked to the Four Star to see *Bonnie and Clyde*. It was a really good movie and I was fascinated with Faye Dunaway, who was playing Bonnie. She'd been in lots of magazines lately and I loved her accent, but Tom didn't care about the movie at all. He only wanted to make out, and his hands were all over me. He reached his hand inside the back of my shirt and started to unhook my bra.

"Tom, please don't. This isn't a good place."

It felt weird to me that he didn't care we were in public, plus the psoriasis on my back had gotten worse. It felt itchy and irritated.

"C'mon, there's hardly anyone here. It's been so long since we were together like this."

"I want to watch this," I said and turned to face the screen. He pulled his arm from around me and leaned toward the other armrest. He looked over at Maureen and Johnny, who weren't watching the movie at all, and then let out a very loud sigh.

"I want you to know I cancelled band practice to come here."

I didn't even answer him and we watched the movie without exchanging another word.

We walked down Burton Street, and Tom and Johnny walked behind us.

"What's going on with you guys?" Maureen whispered.

"He was an octopus at the movie and I really wanted to watch it. Making out is one thing, but he seemed to forget where we were."

"Yeah, they get like that, that's for sure."

Maureen and I stopped walking when we reached the corner. I turned around and saw Tom and Johnny were almost a block behind us and they were talking loudly about music and not paying attention to us at all.

"I'll see ya tomorrow," I hollered to Tom.

"Okay, see ya," he answered.

I was hoping he'd say that he'd call me later, but he didn't. I heard him as he started up again about the keyboard player from The Doors.

* * *

In history class the next day, Marty handed me a note from Tom when Miss McHeartland was writing our homework assignment on the board. I didn't dare open it because I was afraid of getting the teacher's manual on my head, so I waited until I was in the bathroom after class. All it said was, *Sorry. I love you.* I took a deep breath and my stomach settled for the first time since our phone conversation at my babysitting job.

We had our final rehearsal for the talent show after school. I had a hard time concentrating because my skin itched so badly. My hands, feet, neck, and face were still okay, but the rest of my body was covered in psoriasis. I just wanted to go home, take off my uniform, lie on my bed and listen to the radio.

* * *

The talent show went off without too many problems. A string of beads broke in the Charleston number and two girls stopped dancing and ran all over the stage trying to pick them up. Tom's band played *Gloria* and *Open up Your Door* and only started over once. They all wore paisley shirts and jeans. I wished I could have watched them from the audience, but we were back stage.

The Beatle-ettes got loud applause after both songs and everyone laughed when Irene's hula-hoop rolled off the stage. Mr. Droski handed it back to her and winked at all of us. The "Casey at the Bat" skit seemed to be the favorite of the night, probably because everybody was so excited about the Detroit Tigers. After the show, the folding chairs were stacked so we could have a reception.

"You girls sounded really good," Tom said before he took a drink of punch. He offered me a Pecan Sandy from his handful.

"Thanks. And you were right, all your band practice did pay off. I thought *Open up Your Door* was especially good."

"Well, believe it or not, we have a gig on Friday night. Rick's aunt hired us to play at her daughter's birthday party over on the west side."

"Seriously? That's really cool," I said before I bit into my cookie.

"Yeah it'll be a bunch of little kids 'cause his cousin is only turning twelve, but a job's a job. By the way, I like your dress."

"Thanks, I got it in Saginaw. That's where I got my May Procession dress too."

"Wow, I still can't believe all you girls wiped out on the stairs. I thought Waterman was gonna roll in the aisle like he did when Fizzytits took her blouse off."

"Yeah, but you weren't even there when *that* happened," I said.

"I've heard the story enough times that I feel like I was," Tom laughed.

I thought back to the day that happened in homeroom. The very first day of eighth grade when my skin was clear and smooth and just like everybody else's.

Chapter Twenty One

By the time we got out of school on Friday night, it was eighty five degrees. As much as I'd dreaded this, I had to give in. I opened up my bottom drawer and took out a pair of last summer's shorts and paired them with my lightest, long sleeve blouse. Maureen was going to babysit with me for Ralph and Orna Lee. I decided it didn't matter how I looked for any of them.

Ralph's parents were going to a bowling tournament and would be gone for several hours. They said they didn't mind Maureen coming over at all. They had warned me on the phone there was a new batch of puppies in the basement.

"Just make Ralph this macaroni and cheese, and give Orna Lee a jar or two of baby food," Ralph's mother said with her hand on the open cupboard door.

"And remember, don't bother with the puppies," Ralph's dad said. "They're just fine on their own in the basement. We'll be back around midnight."

I had thought about mentioning my psoriasis to the Taylors, in case they thought it was contagious, but neither of them even looked at my legs. As usual, they were in a hurry to leave.

I watched them out the window. Ralph's dad pulled a comb out of his back pocket, combed his greasy hair back and then rubbed a spot off the toe of his boot with his thumb before getting in the car. His wife threw her cigarette butt in the driveway and stepped on it.

Maureen knocked on the door while I was putting the dishes in the sink.

"Hi, you're just in time to play Cootie with me and Ralph," I told her.

"That's cool. I used to love Cootie. Hey, how come that baby's not screaming?"

"She's much better than she was before, plus I think she really likes me."

Maureen followed me into the living room and the three of us played a couple of games with Orna Lee propped on my lap, drinking her bottle.

Ralph looked at my crossed legs, "How'd you get so many ouchies?"

"It's a rash, sweetie."

"Does it hurt?"

"Sometimes it does. But now I need to put your sister to bed. Then it's your turn."

"C'mon Ralph," Maureen said as she took him by the hand. "I want to see your room."

We closed Ralph's door and then heard a loud thump somewhere in the house.

"What the heck was that?" I said to Maureen as we headed down the stairs.

"Hey girls, how's it goin'?"

Teddy Zukowski, Gerard Waterman, and two of the boys from Burton School were in the kitchen.

"Zukowski, *what are you doing here*?" I asked.

"Just checkin' on you girls to make sure you're doin' a good job."

"How did you even know about this?"

"Oh, a little bird told me."

The other boys were in the living room and had turned on the TV. Gerard was turning the dial to change stations. Running back to the living room, I cursed myself for wearing shorts. I needed to get them all out before anyone noticed my skin.

"Where's the stash of *Playboys*?" Teddy asked from the other room. "There's no doubt this guy has 'em. Check out his record collection."

"Hey, look," Waterman said as he turned up the TV. "*Wild, Wild West* is on."

"Shh, turn that down. The kids are asleep."

I turned off the television. Teddy walked back into the kitchen.

"Hey, they got anything to eat here?" The other boys followed him and Gerard opened the top cupboard.

"Whoa-ho, exactly where my ol' man keeps his pal, Jim Beam!"

He brought the whiskey bottle down and held it up.

"Anyone care to join me?"

"Are you kidding me, Waterman?" Maureen reached for the bottle. "Put that back right now!"

My heart was racing and sweat was pouring down the backs of my legs. Then I noticed a cigarette tucked behind Zukowski's ear.

"Where did *that* come from?" I asked, remembering the cigarettes they usually kept in the desk drawer. I rushed into the dining room, opened the drawer, and saw with relief that the pack of L&Ms was still there.

"If I can't drink the hooch, can I have some Nestle Quick?" Waterman peered into the cupboard.

Both of the boys from Burton were shaking their heads and grinning. One of them picked up the sugar bowl and poured sugar into his mouth.

"You guys have to go," I said. "C'mon, this is my steady job."

"And anyway, Waterman, how come you're not playing drums at that gig?" Maureen asked him.

"Oh, I was only in the band for the talent show. Those weren't even my drums. Another guy is the regular drummer. I didn't want to be in Casey at the Bat."

He laughed and gave Teddy a sock on the shoulder since he *had* been in the skit.

"What the hell is on your legs?" Teddy asked me.

"It's a condition I have called psoriasis."

"Wow, if I had that crap on my legs, I'd cut 'em off," one of the Burton boys said.

173

I was mortified and hated his guts, but tried to act like it didn't bother me.

"You guys need to go. I'm *not* kidding."

They were all shoving each around and opening the cupboards and refrigerator when I heard Ralph calling me and Orna Lee crying.

"Get out now!" I pushed them toward the door. They left while laughing their way down the back steps.

"Those guys are total jerks. Let's check on the kids."

I locked the door, then Maureen and I went upstairs and got them both settled down.

We straightened the house and watched a movie on TV. Ralph's parents got back at eleven-thirty.

Maureen came home with me because she was spending the night. A few minutes after we got our pajamas on, the phone rang. When I picked it up, Ralph's dad started yelling at me.

"Look here, Ruth Ann, I know you had some kinda wild shindig over here, and I wanna know what the hell went on, and who it was. Somebody took the puppies out of the cages and two of my Elvis records are gone. And the room divider must have got knocked over 'cause now it's upside down *and* the time's wrong on the living room clock, so somebody messed with that. I'll tell you what! If those puppies die, you're the one responsible. I want names. NOW! Who'd you have in my house?"

My heart was pounding so hard, I wondered if I was having a heart attack.

"A couple of boys did come in, Mr. Taylor, but I kicked them out right away. They never went in the basement, so I don't know how the puppies got out of their cages. I didn't see the room divider fall. I'm not sure what you mean. They don't even like Elvis, so I *know* they didn't take your records."

He was so quiet when I said that, I could tell he was insulted.

"First of all, you will never set foot in my house again, and second of

174

all, I want names. You either give me names or I call the cops, you hear me? And you better get those records back to me or I *will* call the cops, names or no names!"

I spelled Zukowski and Waterman for him and then hung up the phone. I didn't know the boys from Burton and they weren't the instigators. Maureen and my mom were standing next to me and I could barely speak.

"Oh no! What about Ralph and Orna Lee?" I started crying. "I'll never see them again. That stupid greaser. Nobody took his dumb old Elvis records or let his puppies out. And that damn room divider would look the same right side up or upside down. It's the ugliest thing I've ever seen."

"Watch your language, Ruth Ann. Whatever possessed you to let those boys in?" my mom said.

"I didn't let them in. They just came in while we were putting the kids to bed. Didn't they, Maureen?"

Maureen nodded. I could tell by the look on her face she'd be lighting a Winston as soon as she had the chance.

"Well, why in the world didn't you lock the door? This was your best job, Ruth Ann. You've really gone and screwed things up. They'll never have you back, and he sounds like the kind of guy who won't drop this."

I had dreams all night about the sunburst clock on the Taylors' wall. The hands kept going around and around and wouldn't stop.

* * *

I called Zukowski and Waterman the next day and warned them. The guy had really blown the whole thing up, so I wasn't even that mad at them. I was worried about him calling the police, but I believed them when they said there was no way they'd stolen the records or even gone in the basement. I started to realize that Ralph's dad was "off his rocker" as my mom said. He called Sunday night and I told him what the boys had said. He barely responded.

175

Marty told me that Tom had yelled at the boys before school and told them they owed me an apology, which they both gave me later on.

"Well, since nothing's happened, let's hope he decided to forget the whole thing. Not that I'll ever get the job back though," I said to them.

Maureen called that night after dinner.

"Did you hear anything?" she asked.

"No, it's so strange. I'm hoping he decided to forget it. He probably remembered who he loaned his dumb records to and maybe his wife admitted she forgot to lock the puppy cages."

* * *

On Tuesday, I was just finishing a history quiz when Sister Mary Edith stepped into the classroom and looked directly at me. She had a scowl on her face and was curling her finger toward herself. Everyone turned to look at me and half of them had heard the babysitting story by now. I thought as hard as I could about what else she might want me for. Maybe my uniform was too short or maybe she'd heard I wear make up on weekends. When I got in the hall, Zukowski and Waterman were both standing there. They looked as terrified as I felt. I'd never seen Teddy without the grin and the crazy glint in his eye.

"You three will not graduate eighth grade!" she snarled.

Then she led us down the hall with her rosary swinging at us from her belt. She opened the door to a tiny room across from her office that I'd never seen opened. Behind a desk sat two Grand Rapids Police Officers. We were ordered to sit down and then were grilled with questions about the puppies, records, and supposed broken items. We answered truthfully and the boys admitted that I hadn't let them in and had begged them to leave. Even though I was scared, it was kind of exciting, like being on *Perry Mason* or *Peter Gunn*.

We were dismissed after about twenty minutes of questioning. When I returned to history class, the room fell into a hush, and after school, the three of us were surrounded by kids wanting to know every detail. Nobody called my mother that night and I didn't hear from Ralph's dad. I wasn't sure if I should be relieved or worried.

When I looked out at the moon from my bed, I took a deep breath and decided I'd put it behind me. I just wanted eighth grade to be over, even if I didn't graduate.

Chapter Twenty Two

"Well, yer Mr. Taylor sounds like quite a character," Pete chuckled after I told him the babysitting story. "And this guitar is so outa tune here, you can't possibly have been playin' it."

"We have all kinds of final tests coming up and papers to write, Pete. But I did practice once or twice, really."

Pete squinted at me like he didn't believe me. I'd missed last week's lesson for the talent show and hadn't thought much about the guitar lately.

"How's this hot weather on your skin? I see you're still wearin' jeans and long sleeves."

"I did wear shorts the first day it was hot, but this kid said something so mean, I'm not doing it again, and there's a cottage party for graduation in a couple of weeks. I hope we have a huge storm that day."

"Ya know, the sun works real good for some people with psoriasis."

"I've heard that before, but I don't have time to test it out before the party. It's only about two weeks from now."

"You're a right pretty girl, Miss Ruth Ann. Inside and out. And we both know inside is what really counts. Your friends, your real friends, already know that. You didn't ask for this and they better not judge, 'cause nobody ever knows what's comin' their way."

I pictured Mary Lou with boils all over her face and then felt really mean and guilty. But one thing I suspected was that she wasn't so pretty inside.

* * *

Tom and Marty rode their bikes over after dinner on Thursday night. Now that it was nice out, I had no excuse to have them in the basement. My Yahtzee making out days with Tom were on hold for now.

"You sure you can't go to the park?" Tom asked me while we

watched Marty pop three wheelies in a row.

"I can't. My mom's been making me hit the books all week. She's still pretty mad about the whole babysitting mess, so she's trying to be stricter, I guess. It's a good thing I'm babysitting for David and Steven this weekend." I glanced across the street at the two boys who were playing catch.

"Then I can prove to my mom I'm still a good babysitter. Plus, I need the money with all this stuff coming up."

"Yeah, I'll be so glad when school's finally done," Tom said. "I've had my fill of St. Boner's. At least you've only been there four years. I've been there since first grade."

"I bet you were so cute in first grade. Bring me a picture sometime."

Tom leaned over from his bike and gave me a one second kiss. Even after all these months of being his girlfriend, his midnight blue eyes still gave me the grabby feeling.

"You're asking for it," I said, looking around to be sure that David and Steven didn't see him.

"Hey, we're practically in high school. Your neighbors need to get over it."

"Yeah, but they all think we're the black sheep around here. You can't imagine how evil divorce seems to everybody. I feel sorry for my mom 'cause she always has to prove herself to people."

I had never even thought about my mom doing that, but as I said it, I realized it was true. I felt sort of wise and wondered if it had something to do with almost being in high school.

* * *

Renee came home on Friday night. She would be here all summer driving me crazy. Thankfully, her old job at Wurzburg's would be starting on Tuesday, after Memorial Day. She'd would be gone all day, at least. When I got up on Saturday morning, she was vacuuming the living room drapes. I couldn't even make toast because she'd taken the whole toaster apart to clean it.

We spent most of the weekend cleaning the garage, pulling weeds, and planting petunias.

"Some holiday," I said to Tom on the phone.

Maureen had gone to her cottage, and Tom's family had him working around the house, too. In fact, he had just mowed the lawn before he called me.

"Did I tell you the band has another gig tomorrow night?" he asked me. "We're playing at a Burton School graduation party."

"Oh, I suppose Rick got that job, huh?"

"Yeah, it's one of Cindy and Leta's friends."

I got a weird feeling when he said Cindy and Leta so easily, like he said it all the time.

"Ruth Ann, get off the phone. Larry's here," my mom called from the front porch.

"I gotta go. My mom's boyfriend has a new car and he's taking us for a ride and out for olive burgers at Mr. Fables. Have fun at your gig tomorrow."

* * *

When we got back to school, we were bombarded with reviews and graduation rehearsals. At lunch on Wednesday, the Tandem Riders made plans to meet and rent tandem bikes on Saturday.

"We need something to look forward to after this grueling week," Peg said.

"Just think," Irene said. "This is our last real weekend as eighth-graders."

"Hey, I was going to get my hair done for graduation," Mary Lou said. "But it'll get ruined if I swim the next day at Delaneys' party. What do you think?"

The girls all started talking at once about hairdos, bathing suits, and which parents were chaperoning at the cottage. Since the party was on a

Monday, my mom would have to work, and it was just as well. I was still trying to figure out a reason not to go.

I dug around in my bottom drawer when I got home and found the two-piece bathing suit I'd worn last summer. I remembered buying it with Cathy when our moms had taken us shopping downtown. I decided to try it on to see if it still fit.

When I looked at myself in the mirror, in the turquoise checkered suit, all I could see was a monster. There was very little skin left that wasn't covered in psoriasis. I remembered how excited I was when I got the suit and touched the tiny row of daisies that trimmed the top of it. Then I thought about how I never appreciated my clear skin when I had it. It was hard to even imagine how it looked then. If I ever got clear skin again, I swore I would clean the oven and defrost the refrigerator every week. Maybe I'd even tell Renee she was smart and kind and funny. Well, maybe not.

"Hey, Ruth Ann."

It was Cathy calling me from Frankie's window. I grabbed my robe and put it on over my bathing suit, then I parted the curtains, "Hey Cathy, what's going on?"

"I wondered if you wanted to come over. Since Monday was Memorial Day, my mom didn't bake bread 'til today. Are you sick? How come you're in your robe?"

"I'm not sick. I was trying something on. I can't come over 'cause I have to study for final tests and I have to start my book report 'cause I want to get it done before the weekend."

Cathy looked down and it looked like she was writing on the window sill.

"I'm sorry," I said. "I'll come over another time soon. Are you okay?"

"I just really wanted to tell you something," Cathy said.

"What is it? You can tell me now, can't you?"

"Well, I have a babysitting job on Friday. My Aunt Mary got it for me."

"Oh that's good, Cath. You'll be a great sitter."

Cathy glanced over her shoulder and then held her finger up. She turned around and closed the bedroom door quietly before coming back to the window.

"There's something else I wanted to tell you," she whispered loudly.

"What is it?"

She looked toward the street and the back yards before speaking. "I got my period."

"Cathy! You did?"

She nodded, blushing. "It was there when I woke up this morning."

"Congratulations. You're now a full-fledged woman."

We both laughed. "Hey, Cath, remember when our Barbies got their period?"

"Yours got it. Mine never did."

I used to embarrass Cathy by using Barbie's elbow-length glove for a Kotex. I would keep it in place with the belt that came in the accessory pack. I thought about moving here in fifth grade and how Cathy came over and introduced herself the first day. We were playing Barbies and eating Italian bread an hour later.

"You know, I guess I can come over for a little while. Give me five minutes."

* * *

When I got home from riding tandem bikes on Saturday, my mom was ironing in the living room while she watched an old movie.

"Maureen and all the girls are getting their hair done for graduation," I told her. "I think I want to get mine done, too, and I can pay for it."

"That's fine, Ruth Ann, and don't worry, I'll pay for it. I'll call Dodsons Beauty Shop and see if I can get you an appointment for next Saturday."

I had decided that I better look good at graduation, since I wasn't sure

182

if I was even going to the cottage party. I took my graduation dress out of the closet and held it up in front of the mirror. I hadn't worn a white dress since back in first grade when I made my First Communion. The row of white daisies on the graduation dress made me think of the ones on my bathing suit and then I felt like exploding. Why did those old Delaneys have to go and give a stupid cottage party?

"Damn, damn, damn," I said. "It's not fair! I hate my body!"

I threw the dress on my bed and sat down on the bench in front of my dressing table. Just when I started to cry, I looked down and saw a paw reaching under my door. It was Reddy. When I opened the door, he jumped on the dressing table and started purring. No matter how rotten I felt, he could always make me smile.

* * *

The next few days seemed to fly by as we finished all the tests and papers and handed things in. On Wednesday morning, before Mass, Peg turned around as I slipped into the pew.

"Did you hear what happened?" she asked. I shook my head.

"Bobby Kennedy was shot last night. He's probably going to die."

Father O'Hara asked everyone to pray for him before he started Mass. I couldn't believe it. Martin Luther King had been shot in April. Our president, John Kennedy, was shot when I was in the fourth grade. Now, his brother, who might have been our next president, had been shot. The world felt scary and confusing to me. I couldn't even stand to watch the news anymore with all the pictures from the war in Vietnam. I wished I could talk to my mom. I knew she wanted Bobby Kennedy to run for president and would be taking this hard. I even kind of wished I could talk to Renee.

Mrs. Fizzytits had a portable TV in her classroom. She kept us updated all day on Bobby Kennedy's condition. It didn't look good. My mom, Renee, and I watched the news after dinner, hoping we'd hear of his improvement.

In the morning, I found my mom and Renee crying in front of the TV. He had died during the night. I sat next to my mom and she put her arm around me.

"What's wrong with our world?" I asked her.

She just shook her head and squeezed my shoulder. That sure didn't make me feel any better.

Chapter Twenty Three

Maureen and I sat side by side at Dodson's with giant curlers on our heads. Her beautician was Polly, mine was Dolores. My last haircut was from Dolores and she was really nice about the psoriasis on my scalp.

"Tomorrow at this time, we will be fully graduated." Maureen sighed. "I'm excited, but a little sad too."

"It almost feels like a dream," I said. "We've been talking about it for so long, it's hard to believe it's finally going to happen."

The radio was playing and they were reporting about funeral arrangements for Bobby Kennedy. Dolores shook her head. "What a shame." Then she took a swig from her bottle of Coke. The whole incident was hard for me to understand and it felt like a shadow had been cast over our graduation. Even my psoriasis felt less important than before.

Polly began to unroll Maureen's hair. "So, what are all your graduation plans, girls? Is there a dance tonight?"

"Are you kidding? At St. Boner, I mean St. Bonaventure's?" Maureen said. "No, they would never allow such a thing. My parents are taking me to dinner at the Pantlind Hotel and there's a big party on Monday at somebody's cottage. That's about it."

Maureen turned to me while Polly was spraying her hair. "Have you decided to wear your bathing suit?"

"I guess so. I don't know what else to do." I got mad every time I thought about it. Maureen gave me a sympathetic look in the mirror as Dolores began coiling my hair into piles of loops on top of my head.

"Now, listen girls," Polly told us. "If you want these hairdos to last for tomorrow, wrap your heads in toilet paper before you go to bed, you hear?"

* * *

I carried the dishes carefully from the table, because I was afraid I'd ruin my hair if I moved my head too much. My dad called while I was scraping the plates.

"Well, good luck, Sport. Be sure your mother takes some pictures. Wilma would like to see you in the dress she bought."

"I already wore that dress, Dad. We have to wear white tomorrow. The yellow dress was for something else."

"Oh. Guess I got it mixed up. Sure wish I could be there, Sport, but I got all kinds of problems at the car lot. I'm gonna have to spend the whole day trying to figure it out."

"That's okay. I didn't plan on you coming anyway."

"Yeah, I guess you're used to my business shenanigans by now. That's what happens when you're the boss."

"Yeah, but you're only the boss of yourself, Dad. Nobody else works there."

"You know that's the *only way* my cookie crumbles, Sport. All right then, we'll talk soon. Now don't trip in your squashed-up heels when you get your diploma."

"Not squashed-*up* heels, Dad. Just squashed. But don't worry, I'll try not to trip. Say hi to Grandma and Aunt Dorothy for me."

* * *

The next morning, my hair had somewhat flattened, even though I'd used the toilet paper. I figured my hair was probably not the right type for an up-do. After breakfast, I got dressed and sat at my dressing table, trying to redo the loops the way Dolores had done them. Renee poked her head in when she heard me sighing.

"Here, let me fix it," she said. She sprayed Aqua-Net on my hair and inserted a few bobby pins to secure the hair-do, then she walked down the hall to her room. "Thanks," I called after her. She came right back with her hand extended.

"I'll let you wear these, if you're really careful, and you take them out

186

as soon as we get home."

I was shocked. Renee was offering to loan me her daisy earrings. I had coveted them for over two years.

"Wow, thanks, Renee. I'll be really careful, I promise."

The earrings polished off the whole outfit just right. If you looked hard, the red lesions on my arms showed through the sheer long sleeves. I figured that maybe Renee noticed that, and had loaned me her earrings because she felt sorry for me.

* * *

The graduation ceremony was right after eleven o'clock Mass. Maureen squeezed my hand before we marched down the aisle.

"This is it," she whispered. No more Fizzytits, no more St. Boner's."

"And most important, no more Barfalottoyou," I whispered back.

"I am going to fall right over if I look at Johnny one more time, Maureen said. "He knocks me out in that shirt and tie."

"Don't you dare fall down. This is *not* the May Procession. And in case you didn't notice, my boyfriend looks rather dreamy too."

Unlike the May Procession, graduation went smoothly. We'd been given lots of warnings about the behavior that was expected this time. There was a rumor going around that next year's May Procession would be completely different and that we were probably the last class to ever wear the blue lace mantillas.

After we got our diplomas, everybody gathered in the school auditorium for coffee, juice and donuts. They took pictures of the whole class on the stage and Peg's mom had all the Tandem Riders stand together for a group shot.

"Cute earrings, Ruth Ann," Mary Lou said. I started to tell her they belonged to my sister, but since it was the only compliment she'd ever given me, I changed my mind.

"I thought about wearing just one big hoop earring," Maureen said. "You know, like Lulu did in *To Sir, with Love*. You guys said I look like

187

her."

We all laughed and I felt a twinge in my heart and stomach when I thought of all the stuff we'd done together. What if the Tandem Riders were only friends in eighth grade? What if Maureen found a new best friend when we got to high school? Somebody with beautiful skin who had her own Winstons.

"Who's planning to water ski tomorrow?" Angela asked us. "I know I am."

"Hmm. I smell Ambush," Tom whispered over my shoulder. "You look really nice." And *I* can't wait 'til tomorrow. I'm hoping we can find a way to ditch the party and go off by ourselves."

I turned around and faced him. "Okay, sure. I guess we can try."

My mind began racing. If only I could come up with a reason not to go. I had to think of something. Maybe I could say that I got my period. On second thought, that would be almost as embarrassing as my monster body. All I could do was hope for a catastrophe of some sort. But that would mean something bad would have to happen.

"Is that okay with you, Ruth Ann?" Peg asked me.

"Is what okay?"

"If my mom picks you up at nine-thirty?"

"Oh sure, thanks. I'll be ready."

Tom was looking at me like he was confused. "Where were you just now? I don't think you heard a word of that conversation."

"I heard them. Peg's mom is driving us in their station wagon."

He was still giving me a funny look.

* * *

I changed into jeans as soon as I got home. Larry was going to barbecue hamburgers in our back yard. My mom had invited the Cicerellis over.

"Ruth Ann, get down here to help peel potatoes," Renee called up to me. "And be sure you put those earrings back in my jewelry box."

Gone Before Spring

I turned my left ear toward the mirror while I took the earrings out. The daisy earrings were so cute and Renee hardly ever wore them. I was hoping she'd let me wear them all day, but I should have known better.

* * *

I heard Larry dumping charcoal into our grill so I went downstairs to help.

"Wow, how does it feel to really be in high school?" Cathy asked me as she helped herself to another pickle. I was putting the hamburger buns into a basket.

"Not much different. At least not yet."

Cathy followed me out the back door. She carried a bowl of chips and I had the condiments.

"Aren't you excited about tomorrow's party? I can't believe your whole class got invited. Are they really all going?"

"I suppose *a few* people might not go. I don't know."

I didn't mean to sound irritable, but I could tell by the look on Cathy's face that I had hurt her feelings.

"I feel kind of funny about going because I've never water skied before," I said. "Maureen and Angela have cottages, so they do it all the time."

"Oh well, at least Tom's going, right?" Cathy asked. "That'll make it fun."

Mrs. Cicerelli set a plate of anise cookies in front of me and Cathy got up to get the Betty Crocker cherry chip cake that she'd made. She'd probably still be making those when she was an old lady.

After we finished dessert, Larry handed me a small gift box. Inside was a wristwatch.

"Now that your school is downtown," he said, "I want to be sure you get yourself there on time."

'Thanks, Larry. This will help." I kissed his cheek.

Renee gave me a beach bag and matching beach towel which she'd bought especially for the cottage party. I wished it was a beach tent that zipped up to my chin. My mom gave me a pearl ring she knew I'd been looking at in the jewelry store window. I was really surprised because I knew it was $29.95. The Cicerellis gave me a pair of summer pajamas with Siamese cats.

"I love these! Now I won't miss my flannel ones all summer," I told them.

"Yeah, our mom went crazy when she found them at Miracle Mart," Frankie said. "And Cathy got a bathing suit there with a bra built right into it."

Cathy's face turned bright red and Frankie laughed behind a slice of watermelon.

Everyone sat around on lawn chairs after we ate and some people played badminton in the Cicerelli's back yard. It felt like a real party. Even Renee's work friends, the "Wurzburgers," stopped by. The four of them had pitched in and bought me a gift of pearl earrings, since they'd heard from Renee about my pearl ring. Ruff and Reddy were napping under the spirea bush and Frankie was running around with Bugles on his fingers, poking me and Cathy with them.

"Mom, make him stop!" Cathy shouted. I knew she was still mad at him for the bra remark and would probably torture him later.

Even though I was having a good time, I couldn't stop worrying about the cottage party.

* * *

"Do you have all your stuff ready for tomorrow?" my mom asked me. We were putting food away from the cook-out after Larry went home and Renee left to go bowling with the Wurzburgers. I thought about telling my mom that my skin was worse and that I couldn't go, but just as I started, the phone rang and it was my Aunt Maxine. I knew they'd be on forever, so I finished in the kitchen and went up to my room. When I turned on my radio, *Light My Fire* was playing. I remembered how Tom said we should

Gone Before Spring

think of each other every time we heard the song until the end of time. Right now, the end of time sounded like the only way out.

Chapter Twenty Four

My heart was racing as soon as I opened my eyes the next morning. A muffled voice hummed through the wall from my mom's room. It sounded like a weather report, probably from her clock radio. I heard a light rap on my door.

"It's quarter to eight, Ruth Ann, and it sounds like the weather's going to be perfect."

I groaned and pulled the covers over my face. Ever since I'd heard about this party, I'd held out hope there would be an earthquake, a flood, or at least a tornado alert.

My mom opened the door. "I have to go, sweetie. Have a wonderful time and I'll see you tonight."

"Thanks," is all I managed to croak. Sweetie? I couldn't ever remember my mom calling me that. Did she suspect my situation or was she just glowing that I graduated? My mouth felt parched. The last time I remembered looking at my clock was at 1:30 a.m. When I finally got to sleep, my dreams were exhausting. The only part I remembered was running down a beach with a picnic basket that got heavier and heavier. The Wurzburgers were expecting me and I couldn't find them. The first time I looked in the basket there was a litter of puppies, and the second time there were two bowling balls. At some point, I realized Mr. Taylor was chasing me and asking me where I'd put Ralph and Orna Lee.

I set my feet on the floor and looked down at my legs. The miracle I'd prayed for hadn't happened. In fact, my skin felt like it was on fire when I put on my jeans and blouse. I knew I should apply lotion to get a little relief, but that would make it look even redder, and I sure didn't want that today.

Gone Before Spring

I made my way down the stairs, hoping we had lemonade left from yesterday. Renee was in the kitchen packing her lunch. I poured the rest of the lemonade into a glass and drank it all without stopping.

"That sure doesn't look like a beach outfit," she said as I put a slice of bread in the toaster.

"What do you expect, Renee? Have you seen my body lately? Oh, come to think of it, you've been too busy sterilizing the house to notice anything else."

I felt so bitchy the minute I finished saying that, I wanted to go upstairs and start all over. Renee had actually been nice the day before, loaning me something for the first time ever and fixing my hair. I was just about to apologize when she said, "Grow up, Ruth Ann, it's not a tragedy. You could be in an iron lung or something. Be grateful that you can even leave the house. Some people can't, you know."

It felt like she'd punched me in the stomach.

She left the kitchen for a few seconds, then returned with her purse and sweater.

"I have to catch my bus."

She picked up her lunch and went out the side door. "Have fun," she called over her shoulder.

I threw the toast in the trash and went back upstairs to pack my beach bag. Before rolling my checkered two-piece bathing suit in the beach towel, I decided it would be a better idea to wear it under my clothes. When I got it on, I looked at myself in the mirror and shuddered.

"Maybe I should run away to Hollywood. I'm sure somebody would cast me in a horror movie."

I looked at the row of daisies along the top of the suit and thought about Mary Lou actually complimenting me on Renee's daisy earrings. For some reason, they had given me confidence yesterday. I thought about them nestled in the blue velvet of Renee's jewelry box. She would never miss the earrings. I could sneak them back in as soon as I got home. Ruff followed me into Renee's room and watched me as I put them on.

"Shhh, don't you tell on me, Ruff."

The earrings made me feel slightly better. Maybe they would help me get through this day that I'd dreaded for weeks. A car horn honked in the driveway right after I'd stepped into my jeans and buttoned my blouse. I grabbed my flip-flops and beach bag and hurried down the stairs.

I was the last Tandem Rider to be picked up, since everyone else lived closer to Alger Heights. As usual, Peg's mother looked like Jackie Kennedy. She was wearing large sunglasses and a floppy orange hat.

"We saved you the seat with Maureen, in the way back," Peg said as she lifted up the back door of the station wagon.

I had never ridden in a seat that faced the back window, but I'd always wanted to. It probably would have been fun if I was going somewhere that didn't require a bathing suit.

"I can't believe Renee loaned you her earrings again," Maureen said.

"She didn't exactly loan them again."

Maureen's eyebrows shot up and I nodded. Angela started us up singing our Beatle-ette songs and then we branched out from there to every Beatles song we could think of. I usually enjoyed singing, but each song filled me with more and more dread as we got closer to the Delaneys' cottage on Big Whitefish Lake.

The car wound through the woods on the dirt road that led to the cottage. The girls were calling out names from signs that were nailed to trees and fence posts.

"McKinley, Howard, Robertson, Delaney! There it is!" Angela yelled.

The cottage was made from field stones and had dark green shutters. It looked like a picture in a storybook.

"Look how many cars are here already," Mary Lou said.

That made my heart race even faster. I wondered if there would be a way for me to sneak back to the car before everyone changed into their suits. I was sure Maureen would cover for me. The one problem would be when Tom asked for me.

Mary Lou was the first person to get out of the car. She was wearing a plaid scarf that matched the shift she had on. I figured her bathing suit underneath was the same material. She said it was the Ladybug brand when Irene gave her a compliment. It would take months of babysitting for me to even afford one Ladybug item, much less a whole outfit. As the other girls left the car, I noticed that, like Mary Lou, Angela and Irene were wearing beach shifts. Maureen and Peg had on shorts and t-shirts. I felt ridiculous in my jeans, and the denim was rubbing the sores on my legs.

The cottage was filled with kids from our class. Through the windows that faced the lake, I could see others playing volleyball and some wading into the water. A few moms and even a couple of fathers were sitting at a picnic table.

Crepe paper and balloons hung from the ceiling in our school colors, green and white. Mrs. Delaney greeted all of us and showed us which room the girls could use for changing.

"I already have my suit on," I told Maureen as she and the other girls headed into the room. She nodded and smiled to let me know that she understood.

"Can I help you with anything, Mrs. Delaney?" I asked her. She was squeezing a tube of frozen orange juice into a pitcher.

"Thanks, Ruth Ann. You can put this on the table over there next to those Dixie Cups. I thought I'd put some breakfast stuff out to hold everyone over until lunch, knowing how you teenagers blend one meal into another."

I placed the pitcher on the table next to packages of English Muffins and jars of apple butter and strawberry jam, while looking out the window to see if Tom was anywhere around. Peg's mom was standing next to me, blowing on a cup of coffee.

"Aren't you going to put your suit on?" she asked me.

"I already have it on under my clothes. I just thought I'd wait 'til it warmed up a little."

"It's supposed to be eighty-five by noon and keep climbing after that. Of course, here, we'll get a breeze from the lake."

She sipped her coffee and we both turned as the Tandem Riders exited the bedroom and Tom, Johnny, and Marty arrived. All three boys were holding rolled up towels. Tom walked right over to me. I twisted the left daisy earring around in circles and did my best to smile.

"Hi. How long have you been here? Want to go swimming?" he asked.

"We just got here a little while ago. I'll swim later. You go ahead."

Mary Lou and Angela stopped at the food table to get some juice. Tom glanced at them and said hi. As I suspected, Mary Lou's two-piece suit was the same plaid material as her shift.

"Where's *your* suit?" he asked me looking down at my jeans. Somebody turned the radio on outside and *How Can I Be Sure* was on. It was the song that was playing the first time that Tom and I danced. I wondered if he remembered that.

"Hey LaBelle, you're last on skis," Gerard Waterman ran by us and snapped Tom with his towel.

"Oh no I'm not!"

Tom and the other boys headed into the opposite bedroom to change, and Maureen walked over to me.

"Hey, are you gonna wear your jeans all day?" she whispered.

"I don't know what to do. I'm not going to stand around in my suit."

"Come with me." Maureen tugged on my blouse.

I followed her into the bedroom and she closed the door. I looked over my shoulder to make sure no one was watching us. Most of the kids were going outside to join the others. A few quieter kids that I wouldn't have expected to come were selecting board games from a shelf next to the fireplace.

"I brought this for you," Maureen said.

She held up a striped, cotton beach blanket.

"I figure you can wrap up in this, and say you're chilly or that you're allergic to the sun or something. Why not?"

"Okay. I guess it's worth a try. I don't know what else to do."

"Cute suit," Maureen said after I removed my clothes.

"It's from last year. When I didn't look like this." I held my arms out and looked down at my stomach and legs. Maureen gave me such a sympathetic look, that I felt like crying.

"Well, look how good this'll work." She wrapped the blanket around me, and I held it together in the front. It covered so well, I felt silly for not thinking of it myself.

"You're a lifesaver. I can't believe I have such a good friend."

My bottom lip trembled and I felt like a little kid.

"Don't you dare cry. You hear me? You're my best friend ever, and that's all there is to it. Now, let's get outside before anyone wonders where we are."

I followed her through the cottage and out the door. The other Tandem Riders were sitting on the dock with their feet dangling off the edge. Angela was applying suntan lotion to Mary Lou's back.

"What took you guys so long?" Mary Lou asked.

"Ruth Ann was helping Mrs. Delaney with some breakfast stuff, so I had a bite to eat," Maureen answered.

Mary Lou looked at me and held her hand over her eyes to shield them from the sun. "Are you cold?"

The other girls looked away, so I knew they had figured out why I was wearing the blanket and I had a pretty good idea Mary Lou also knew the reason.

"I'm always cold. Have you guys tested the water?"

"I don't even care," Angela said. "I'm gonna water ski, no matter what."

"Well, you better get in line with the boys," Irene said.

I looked at the group of boys standing in the water. They were waiting for Mr. Delaney to circle the boat back to them. Tom turned around when he heard screaming. Teddy Zukowski was trying to pull Margaret Gallagher into the lake and she looked furious. She had a blue bathing cap covering part of her hair, but it was crooked and most of her golden locks were trailing down her back.

"Looks like our May procession queen doesn't want to get her hair wet," Peg said.

Tom trudged through the water when he saw me on the dock. He leaned in and gave me a quick kiss with his cold, wet lips. I looked over at the parents who were still sitting at the picnic table to make sure they weren't watching.

"What's up with the blanket? Are you cold?"

"A little. I also have to be careful of the sun. You know, with my skin condition." I hadn't planned on mentioning my skin, but once I'd said it, I decided he might as well be warned.

"Oh. Well, I'm gonna ski for a while, but I'm hoping we can sneak away later. Nobody will miss us, 'cause there's so many people here. Okay?"

"All right. That's a good idea," I lied.

The boat pulled up and Johnny got on the skis.

"I'm gonna ride with these guys. See ya soon."

Tom climbed into the boat and they took off with a loud roar. As soon as the noise was gone, we could hear the radio playing *Will You Still Love Me Tomorrow* by the Shirelles. Angela started singing and the other girls joined in. I'd always loved the song and had never really thought about the words before. I tried to sing along because I knew it would be more noticeable if I didn't, but it felt like the song was about me and Tom. How *would* he feel about me after today? A lump formed in my throat and made it hard to sing. Maureen must have noticed because I could tell she had turned her head in my direction.

The sun was almost directly overhead. Dozens of kids were in the water, playing catch and dunking each other. The boat came back over and over, to pick up new water skiers. Mary Lou had found a raft. She was floating on it and paddling the water with her hands. One by one, Angela, Peg and Irene went in and they took turns pulling Mary Lou around. I was glad that Peg eventually dumped her off. When they were a safe distance away, Maureen asked, "Are you going in at all? It's up to our necks here. You could just jump in. Seriously, nobody's looking."

I looked around and saw that nobody was paying any attention to us.

"Okay, I guess this is as good a time as any," I said. I let the blanket fall from my shoulders and I dropped from the dock into the water. Maureen joined me and we floated around. The cool water felt heavenly on my parched, burning skin.

"If only I could stay like this all day and it was just you and me here," I said as I leaned my head back and looked up at the cloudless sky.

"Well, you are definitely going to my cottage as soon as I get home from our vacation to the Black Hills."

"I forgot about you going. When are you leaving?"

"Day after tomorrow. If it wasn't for this party, we would have left already. I'll be back the week after next. Maybe we can figure out a way to get Tom and Johnny to my cottage. Wouldn't that be cool?"

"We'll see if Tom and I are still together."

"Are you kidding? He loves you so much. Johnny tells me all the time."

Maureen ran up to the beach and grabbed two inner tubes for us. We leaned on them and floated for nearly an hour. Peg and Irene swam near us for part of the time and a few other kids were nearby, but it was deep enough that only my arms were showing. I was pretty sure that the psoriasis on my arms wasn't a secret anyway. The boat was back at the dock and Tom was getting on the skis. He waved at me in the water before they took off.

"I'm getting hungry," Maureen said. "Want to go up there and eat now?"

I looked at the kids carrying paper plates back to their beach blankets. I wanted to just stay in the water, but knew I couldn't do that.

"You go sit on a chair and save one for me. I'll bring food over so you can keep your blanket on," Maureen said.

I got back on the dock and covered up as quickly as possible. When I looked up I saw Peg's mom walking toward the water. I couldn't tell if she was looking at me because of her hat and sunglasses, but I had a pretty good idea that she was.

"Better get up there girls. The lines are getting long," she said.

"Here, take my towel and save me one of those green chairs," Maureen said.

I held the blanket together and watched my classmates. Some of them were still playing volleyball, others were eating, and several were still in the water when the boat returned. Maureen handed me a plate with food and sat down. "Mrs. Delaney said there are over fifty kids here. That's pretty good out of seventy-two, don't you think?"

"I guess so," I said. "I'm completely wrecking this party for you, aren't I?"

"Will you stop? You are *not* wrecking anything. I'll go back and get drinks. What do you want?"

"It doesn't matter. Whatever you're having."

While I tried to take a couple of bites from a cheese sandwich and still keep my blanket together, I saw Tom coming toward me. He squatted down next to my chair and I noticed there were beads of water on his eyelashes.

"Listen," he said. "There's a little row boat behind those bushes down there. When the time's right, we'll grab it and get away, okay?"

"Okay," I agreed reluctantly. I couldn't think of any way out. I wished with all my heart that I'd stayed home. I could have said somebody died or something. This felt like probably one of my biggest mistakes ever.

Ode to Billy Joe came on the radio and I remembered my dad telling me and Mimi how sad it made him feel. I would have given anything to be with my dad right now. Even if it meant going to Wally the pharmacist and making martinis for Wilma.

"Well, I'm starved, so I'll look for you in a while."

I was glad Tom left. The song was really getting to me and I was having a hard time keeping tears back. Maureen was talking to the Tandem Riders and some other girls. Mary Lou turned around and looked over at me and then said something to Maureen. I saw her shrug and then she came back with two bottles of root beer and sat down.

"The girls are going water skiing. Do you want to just ride along in the boat?"

"No, that's okay. Tom's got a plan for us to be alone. Don't ask me how I'm supposed to handle that."

"Well, consider yourself lucky. Johnny has barely said hi to me all day. I guess I'll go ahead and ski, since *you've* got plans," Maureen said as she shifted her eyebrows up and down. On a different day, it would have made me laugh.

"Anyway, when you come to *my* cottage, we're gonna go on the water toboggan and maybe I'll even get you to ski."

We sat on the sand and watched Tom and Johnny play volleyball.

"Johnny looks so good without a shirt. I can't take my eyes off him," Maureen said. "I'll tell you what, if he doesn't ask me to take a walk in the woods, I might ask *him*. Is that what you guys are doing?"

"No, I guess we're...."

"We're taking off, Maureen. Come on!" Mary Lou hollered.

"Her highness is calling, I better go," Maureen said as she stood up and brushed the sand off her legs. "See you in a while, and try to have fun, hear me?" I nodded and tried to smile.

201

Maureen turned around and looked at me as she got into the boat. Mary Lou was the first girl to water ski. I watched as the boat pulled away and she and her plaid two-piece suit got smaller and smaller. Tom was standing next to the trash can, finishing a piece of watermelon. I watched him throw it in, wipe his hands on his bathing trunks, and walk toward me.

"Hey, come on. Let's get going before anybody notices."

I looked over at the crowd on the grass, sand, and in the water, half hoping that someone would notice us. I held my blanket together and tried to keep up with Tom. He darted behind the cottage next door and then down the road a bit. My heart was racing even faster than it had when I first woke up. I took a couple of deep breaths, trying to make it slow down. Tom led me down a path toward the bushes he had pointed out earlier.

"The boat's right over here," he said.

"Whose boat is it? This isn't the Delaneys'."

"It's okay. We're just borrowing it. We skied by this cottage a bunch of times, so I'm sure nobody's here. We'll bring it back."

"Won't everybody see us when they come by skiing?"

"No, I timed it right. We'll get to the secret spot before they come this far. It's a huge lake and anyway, I'm not sure he'll take the girls as far as he took us."

In the distance, we could hear the kids at the party laughing and shouting. I had a sick feeling right in the pit of my stomach and I longed to be back there with them. A little voice in my head was telling me to say I'd changed my mind, but then I looked at Tom's long, muscular arms, as he pulled the row boat toward us. With his hair falling over one eye, he looked so handsome that I still couldn't believe he was my boyfriend. I thought of how Cathy and her friends had envied me all through eighth grade. How just a year ago, I had practically no social life. And here I was, thinking of walking away.

"I'll get in first to steady it," Tom said. He sat on the little bench and I did my best to hold the blanket together with my left hand, using my right arm for balance. He took my hand and I sat on the other little bench facing him. He picked up the oars and turned the boat around.

"We'll go down to this lagoon place I saw earlier," he said as he rowed away from the tall bushes. The party voices grew fainter and fainter, until we couldn't hear them anymore. The sun was hot and the water so still that it barely lapped the sides of the boat. I stared into the water and thought about diving in and staying under. Maybe forever. We had gone by several cottages, and in and out of very tall weeds. He kept rowing until we were beyond all of the cottages and there was just woods on the shore.

"This is the place," he said. "Good thing it's so sunny. There shouldn't be any mosquitos."

He turned the boat into a circle of tall grasses and stopped rowing.

"Nice, huh? As soon as I saw this spot, I couldn't wait to get you here."

My whole life, I had always loved cozy places. When I was little, I made secret hideouts behind furniture, played in closets, created tiny rooms in basements and attics and made snow or branch forts outside. Part of me had to admit, this was a lovely, secret lake room and the boat was the furniture. I trailed my hand in the water, trying to grab a lily pad that was just beyond my reach.

"Wow, thats so pretty. I don't think I've ever seen one in real life."

Tom was sitting on the bottom of the boat. I glanced at the dark hair on his legs. I'd never even seen his feet bare before this. My own toes were painted pale pink, and thankfully, my feet were clear of psoriasis. I wiggled them as if to distract Tom, who had stretched out on the floor of the boat.

"Come down here."

I scooched off the bench and sat facing him. He kissed my lips, ears and neck. Breathing fast, he leaned over me, almost pushing me, so that I was lying down on the bottom of the boat. He began to peel my fingers back so I'd let go of the blanket.

"You have to take this off," he said.

"I can't. Please just leave it." The sun was beating down on us and my skin felt like it was cracking under the blanket. A needle-like insect hovered over us. It darted away and another followed it. I sat up on my elbows and looked into his midnight blue eyes. I thought about the first time I realized they were that color. We were by the swings in the park. He hadn't even kissed me yet. Right now I wished I'd never gone to the park that day. I wish he'd never handed me that cup of ice at the football game where this all started.

"What do you mean, you can't? Are you kidding me? This is all I've thought about for weeks. Ever since we got invited here. Come on. I haven't even seen your bathing suit."

I had no idea what to say to him so I just held the blanket even tighter.

"Ruth Ann, this isn't fair. You can't do this to a guy. I'm not kidding. What can be so bad?"

A tear rolled down my cheek and into my ear. He sat up.

"Oh my God, you're crying? Why the hell are you crying?"

I turned my face sideways to dry the tear. I was embarrassed to be crying and worried that Tom was mad at me.

"Look, if this is about your skin, I don't care. If you loved me enough, it shouldn't matter. Now come on. When will we have a chance like this?"

He opened the blanket and looked at my whole body, from top to bottom. I could tell he was trying not to act shocked. He unhooked my bathing suit top and then he pretty much put his hands wherever he wanted. He didn't say anything and kept his eyes closed. Part of me felt horrified. A smaller part wondered if maybe I didn't look as bad as I thought. Or maybe Tom loved me so much that he really didn't care about my psoriasis.

My skin felt so raw and burned, I could hardly stand it. The weight of his body made my skin feel like it was on fire. I stopped thinking about Tom and what we were doing because the pain was so bad. I came back to reality and jumped when his hand touched the inside of my thighs.

"Are you shivering?" he asked.

All I could do was shake my head. It was taking all of my strength not to cry. I felt like swinging my legs over the side of the boat and dipping into the cool water. I concentrated hard on that idea and whether it was the smarter thing to do. When I looked up at the first cloud I'd seen all day, I noticed the sun had moved very far from where it had been when Maureen and I had been floating on the inner tubes.

"I think we should get back. It must be getting late," I said.

"Yeah, we better." I hooked my bathing suit top and gathered the blanket around me. Tom got up on the bench and started rowing. We put the boat back where we'd found it and ran up the path to the road.

"I wonder what time it is? How long were we gone?" I asked.

"It can't be that late. This party goes 'til seven, right?" We started running when we got to the road. When we came around the side of the Delaneys' cottage, there weren't nearly as many people as when we'd left.

"There they are," someone shouted. A group of parents were standing by the picnic table and I saw the Tandem Riders on the dock with Peg's mom.

"I'll tell the Delaneys," one of the fathers hollered out as he opened the cottage door and went inside.

"Uh-oh," Tom said softly. "I think it's later than we thought."

Peg's mom came toward us. I could see Mary Lou gloating behind her.

"Where have you two been? The Delaneys were about to call your parents."

"We found a little row boat and took it for a ride. I guess we took it further than I thought," Tom said.

"You had us all worried to death."

"I'm really sorry. I didn't know we were gone so long," I said. I could tell by the way she was looking at me that she had a pretty good idea of what we'd been up to.

"Well, go up to the barbecue and get something to eat."

Tom headed right over there and I saw Gerard Waterman and Teddy Zukowski poking him with their elbows. Mr. Delaney was standing by them with a spatula and he looked over at me. I wanted to die on the spot. Food was the last thing I wanted.

Maureen came over to me. "Oh boy, you guys caused quite a commotion." I wanted to ask her more, but the other Tandem Riders came up behind her.

"Where *were* you guys?" Mary Lou asked. "Another five minutes and the Delaneys were gonna call the police."

"They were not," Maureen said to her.

"Yes they were. I went inside for more plastic forks and I heard them."

"Well, I'm going inside to change," I said.

As I walked away, I heard Mary Lou say,"Out of her blanket?"

When I got inside, Mrs. Delaney reprimanded me for giving her a scare and I apologized. All of the other parents and the kids were staring at me. I felt like Hester Prynne from *The Scarlet Letter*. As soon as I opened the bedroom door, Maureen followed me in.

"You have to tell me everything," she whispered.

"It was awful. Tom found this boat and took us way out in some weeds. I tried to keep my blanket on, but he wouldn't let me, 'cause he had big ideas. Next thing I know he's all over me. I didn't know what to do."

"You guys didn't...?" I shook my head. "But not 'cause he didn't want to." I pulled my jeans on over my scorched skin. "I seriously wanted to drown. I'm not kidding."

Maureen hugged me and then stepped back with her hands on my shoulders.

"You are going to be fine. I mean it. You're a lot stronger than most people 'cause you've had to be."

The door opened and Peg stuck her head in. "If you guys are ready, my mom wants to get going."

Mary Lou and Angela had already claimed the seat facing backwards in the back of the station wagon. Maureen sat between me and Irene. I was glad to have a window because I didn't feel like chatting.

The news on the radio was still about Bobby Kennedy's assassination. We listened in silence until a song came on.

"I see you took Renee's earrings out. I hope you put them in a safe place," Maureen said.

"What?" I felt my earlobes. The right earring was gone. "Oh no. Please tell me I didn't lose it."

"Lose what?" Peg said from the front seat.

"One of my sister's earrings." I felt like swearing, crying and throwing up all at the same time. This day had turned out even worse than I'd imagined.

Chapter Twenty Five

When I got home, Renee was watching *I Dream of Jeannie*, and filing her fingernails. She barely looked at me when I came in the door.

"Where's Mom?" I asked.

"At the store."

She shook a bottle of clear nail polish and stared at the TV. I figured there was no way she'd be ignoring me if she missed her earrings. I went to my room and hid the one earring in my old Barbie case in the back of my closet. After buckling it shut, I sat down on the floor and cried into a cardigan sweater that had fallen off the hanger. I felt like staying in the closet forever. When I heard the phone ring, I held my breath and stopped crying. After it rang three times, I crawled out and tried to listen. Nobody called my name, so I knew it wasn't for me.

I went into the bathroom to blow my nose and looked in the mirror. My face was bright pink from the sun. I locked the bathroom door and peeled off my clothes and bathing suit. I rolled the bathing suit up, buried it under all the stuff in the waste basket, then turned on the cold water in the bathtub. I sank down slowly into the freezing water. It only gave me a little relief because my skin looked and felt even worse than it had in the morning.

"Ruth Ann? Hi. How was the party?" My mom was on the other side of the door.

"It was fine. I'm a little sunburned, so I'm taking a cold bath."

"Well, it was a hot one, that's for sure. The radio said it was ninety three earlier. Do you have any idea why Peg's mom wants me to call her back?"

My heart started to thump in my chest. I could hear it beating in my ears. Should I give her a heads up or pretend I had no idea? I'd wasted too much time worrying about the damn lost earring when I should have been concentrating on what to say if somebody called my mom.

"Ruth Ann, Cathy's here," Renee called up the stairs.

"She's in the bathtub, Renee. I'll go see what she wants," my mom said.

I leaned my head back, closed my eyes and let out a long breath. Boy, did I owe Cathy a big favor. She'd saved me, at least temporarily. Toweling off was too painful, so I just patted my skin as gently as possible. I applied lotion, but even my softest pajamas felt rough. I looked at the cats who were washing themselves on my bed, and envied their simple, uncomplicated lives. Renee stopped at my bedroom door. "Cathy brought some bread over."

It was Monday. Mrs. Cicerelli's bread-making day. Something about that didn't feel real or it felt too real. Maybe that's what they meant by surreal. I turned on my radio and *Do You Believe in Magic*, was playing. I needed some magic right now. It was the only way to get out of all this. I wondered if my mom was downstairs talking to Peg's mom.

"Hey Ruth Ann." I heard Cathy at Frankie's window. I parted the curtains and knelt down.

"Was the party fun? Did they try to make you waterski?" she asked.

I had to take a deep breath so I wouldn't sound irritated or upset. Then I remembered that I'd told Cathy skiing was the reason I wasn't excited about the party. Was that only yesterday? The barbecue and graduation felt like weeks ago.

"The party was all right, I guess. Skiing wasn't an issue. I just swam with Maureen and stuff like that."

"What about Tom? Didn't you swim with him?"

My mom opened the bedroom door. "Ruth Ann, I want you to come in my room."

"My mom needs me, Cathy. I'll talk to you later." I stood up and followed my mom into her room. She pointed to the bed and told me to sit down.

"I want you to tell me everything that happened in that boat, and I mean everything. Right now!"

"Boat? What do you mean?"

"You know exactly what I mean, Ruth Ann. What happened with that boy when you disappeared for the *entire* afternoon!"

There it was. Peg's mom had snitched, after all. For some reason I had been hoping, she might not, but I should have known better. After all, even if she was from New York, she was a parent.

"We just took this little row boat for a ride. It was no big deal. Tom loves fishing and he knows a lot about plants on the lake and stuff."

"Ruth Ann, do you think I was born yesterday? Come on. Give me a little credit. This is a very embarrassing situation. It's bad enough trying to raise you without a father and now you go and do something like this. I want to know exactly what happened. You can't tell me you looked at plants for four hours!"

"Mom, listen. Tom felt bad for me 'cause all the other girls knew how to waterski and they took off in the speed boat. What was I supposed to do, twiddle my thumbs?"

"I don't believe for one minute there wasn't hanky-panky going on. I'm not that stupid, dearie!"

Renee stopped in the doorway, "I think you should send dearie to Villa Maria. *If* they'd even take her!"

"Shut up Renee! This is none of your business!" I was screaming. Villa Maria was a place they sent "bad girls." The Tandem Riders always made jokes about it, especially Mary Lou. We never knew of anyone who went there, but it was way over on the west side and we'd heard there was a large brick wall around it.

"Well, you better think long and hard about this, young lady. And you are grounded until further notice. Do you hear me?"

I nodded and strained my ears to try and hear if Renee was opening her jewelry box across the hall. The only thing I heard were hangers rattling in the closet.

"Get in your room and stay there. Right now. Hear me?"

I got up and walked back to my room. My feet felt like cement as I made my way down the hall. My mom started to go down the stairs.

"Wait a minute," she said and walked into my room. "Mrs. Langedon told me you stayed wrapped up in a blanket all day. And she said when you got out of the water, you were covered with sores. Has the psoriasis gotten worse?"

I sat on the edge of the bed and closed my eyes. Everything bad that I'd worried about for all of eighth grade was dumping on me right now. All at the same time. For some reason, I could hear Barfalottoyou screaming at me, "Just look at yourself!" Then I saw myself sitting in that little room with the police officers and Sister Mary Edith. I stuck a finger in each ear. I couldn't listen to anything else. I shook my head back and forth and started crying. Really hard. It was like a dam burst. Even with my ears plugged, I could hear myself. It was probably true, I thought. Maybe I should be sent to the Villa Maria.

"Ruth Ann, let me see your skin. All over. Right now!"

I put my hands over my face and shook my head.

"Here, blow your nose." My mom handed me a bunch of toilet paper. She only bought Kleenex in August, when I had hay fever.

"Come on. I need to see these sores she told me about."

Still crying, I rolled up my pajama bottoms to show her my legs.

"That is a lot worse. How far up does it go? Is it on your thighs?"

I nodded and tried to find a dry spot on the toilet paper, so I could blow my nose again. By this time, Renee was in the doorway. She brought me some new toilet paper. Probably not to be nice. She just wanted to see my skin.

"Where else do you have it? Lift up your pajama top."

I only lifted it high enough to show my stomach. There was no way I

211

would let them see my boobs.

"Ruth Ann, why didn't you tell me how bad this has gotten? Is it on your back?"

I stood up and turned around so they could see my back. I hated having Renee there, but I felt too beat up to protest.

"I think we should call a dermatologist," Renee said.

"Is it on your breasts? What about your bottom?" my mom asked.

"It's *everywhere* except for my face, hands, and feet."

"Why didn't you tell me, Ruth Ann?"

"You kept telling me it would go away like yours did! And anyway, it wasn't all over until a few weeks ago. It was just on my arms and legs for a long time. I thought it would be gone by spring like you said."

"Well, I'll call Dr. Carter tomorrow and see who he recommends. We better get you in somewhere. I still don't know what they can do. But we'll see anyway."

They both went downstairs and my mom came back with a sandwich, a glass of milk, and two aspirin. "Mrs. Langedon said you didn't eat any dinner."

She set the dishes on my dressing table. I took two bites of the sandwich and Reddy lapped up milk from the top of the glass. I wondered if I was still grounded and if I'd be allowed to talk on the phone in case Tom called. I fell asleep at ten o'clock and the phone never rang.

* * *

The next morning, I waited until my mom and Renee had left for work before getting out of bed. My skin felt like it was cracking with every step I took. I was watching Captain Kangaroo and eating Wheat Thins when the phone rang. Part of me wanted it to be Tom, but part of me didn't. My stomach felt kind of sick when I thought about him. It was Maureen.

"Oh my God, I couldn't wait to call you. What happened? Did anybody call your mom?"

212

"Oh yeah. Mrs. Langedon did her parental duty. My mom pumped me for details which I had to lie about, and I think I'm grounded for life."

"Oh no, don't tell me that. She'll let you go to my cottage, won't she?"

"Maureen, I'm in so much trouble. She might even send me to Villa Maria!"

"Oh, Fiddle-de-de. They all say that. You have to be some sort of criminal before they send you there. Don't worry."

"Well, Mrs. Langedon also told her about my skin and the blanket, so now she's gonna send me to a special skin doctor and everything."

"Well, good. I think you should have gone to the doctor a long time ago. Guess what? My parents got everything packed and ready yesterday, so we're leaving for vacation right after lunch."

I sat down on the window seat.

"I thought you were leaving tomorrow."

"We were going to, and then they just changed it on me. So I guess we won't be talking 'til I get back in a couple of weeks. Hey, I almost forgot. What about Renee's earrings?"

"So far, she hasn't missed them. That's the only good thing that's happened. Knowing Renee, though, it's just a matter of time. When they find that out, they probably *will* send me to Villa Maria. Renee would never think of it as borrowing. To her it would be stealing. Even though I *am* her sister."

"Yeah, I think you're right. Well, if you have to be grounded, I'm glad it's while I'm gone. I'm sure Tom's not happy about it, though."

"He doesn't know yet. I haven't heard from him."

"You haven't? Hmm...I wonder if they called his parents. Maybe he's grounded too."

"I wondered about that. Maybe he'll call me if his parents both leave or something. Well, have a good time in the Black Hills. Say hi to the presidents for me."

213

I spent the morning cleaning out my closet and drawers. When I saw the Barbie case, I decided to put the one daisy earring back in the jewelry box. I thought it was a better idea to let Renee think she'd lost one. Cathy came to the side door when I was in the kitchen feeding the cats. She picked up Ruff and asked me if I wanted to go to Miracle Mart with her and her mom, so I had to tell her about being grounded.

"Wow, did Tom get in trouble too?" she asked while setting Ruff down by his dish.

"Of course," I fibbed. "We have no idea when we'll get to see each other."

All of a sudden I pictured the daisy earring nestled by itself in the blue velvet. I could see Renee lifting the top of the jewelry box and exploding.

"Hang on, Cathy. I'll be right back."

I headed straight for Renee's room, snatched the earring back out, and practically dove into my closet to put it back into the Barbie case. Sweat was rolling down my arms and legs, so I decided to change from my jeans and blouse into something cooler. Cathy hollered up the stairs.

"Well, I guess you're busy and we're going to Miracle Mart pretty soon, anyhow. So I'll see you later."

I had almost forgotten Cathy was downstairs, but I was glad she was leaving because my skin looked horrific. I was so hot that I had to put on shorts and a sleeveless top, and I just hoped nobody else stopped by. While I was folding my tops and laying them in the drawer, I heard boys on bicycles coming down the street. My heart skipped a beat and I ran to the window in the bathroom that overlooked the driveway. I could hear them laughing. It had to be Tom and Marty. I looked out and saw the boys riding no-handed. They went right by the house and I didn't recognize them.

My heart sank and I kicked the waste basket, which made me remember my bathing suit was in there. What was I thinking? My mom or

Renee would find it and ask all kinds of questions. I fished it out from the bottom and crammed it into the Barbie case with the earring. The phone rang and I answered it in the hall.

"Ruth Ann, I was able to get an appointment with a dermatologist at two o'clock. I'll be home in half an hour to pick you up."

"But what about work? How can you leave?"

"The doctor had a cancellation. If we don't take this appointment, we'll have to wait a whole month. Mr. Horton told me I could take the rest of the day off and come in Saturday morning. So get ready and I'll see you soon. And mix me up a glass of that instant iced tea, would you?"

I felt bad because on Saturdays, my mom and Mrs. Cicerelli usually drank coffee together in their robes. In the afternoon, she washed her nylons in the sink and ran errands. Now, because of me, she'd have to go into work. I changed back into my jeans and blouse. The last thing I wanted to do was sit around in a doctor's waiting room and look like I came from the side-show at a carnival.

My mom smoked two Salems in the car and didn't say much. I thought about Maureen on her way to South Dakota, and wished I could go to her house after this and smoke a Winston. It felt lonely with her so far away, especially since Tom felt far away too.

The doctor's office was in a modern looking building by Reed's Lake behind the new Jacobson's Department Store. I had gone to the store once with Aunt Dorothy when she'd come to town with my dad. As we walked toward the medical building, I glanced longingly at some girls my age who were headed into Jacobson's. They all had smooth, tanned legs, and I figured their biggest problem was what they were going to buy, mini skirts or culottes.

The dermatology office was in the basement of the building. As we went down the stairs, my heart quickened, especially when we passed a teenage boy with really bad acne. After we registered, we sat down and I watched feet walking by the windows. People were casually flipping through magazines while they waited. I couldn't tell what was wrong with any of them, so I was glad I wore my jeans and blouse.

The nurse called us back and we followed her to the end of a long hallway. She took my temperature and blood pressure and told us the doctor would be in shortly. I wondered if the doctor would say the same things that Wally the pharmacist had told me. I thought about the tar soap my dad had given me at Renee's play. Maybe Wally had been wrong and the soap would have helped. The last place I remembered seeing it was in my suitcase.

Dr. Sheffield came into the room and shook both of our hands. He was around my mom's age and had wavy black hair. He opened a folder and looked at the only piece of paper that appeared to be in it.

"It says here that you have psoriasis. When did you get this diagnosis?" He glanced at me and then my mother.

"Well, she didn't really get a diagnosis. I've had it myself, so I knew what it was."

"When did you first notice it?"

"It started at the beginning of school when I banged my leg really hard on a bleacher," I answered.

He rolled my left sleeve back and looked at my arm. "That's a common way for psoriasis to start. It's called the Koebner Response. Why don't you slip your blouse off, Ruth Ann, and I'll take a look at your front and back."

He looked closely at my stomach and chest, and I was relieved that he didn't ask me to take off my bra. After that, he turned me around so he could see my back. Now it did feel like I was in a side show at the carnival. Standing in my bra, in front of my mom and the doctor, felt as bad as hiding in the blanket at the cottage.

"Old Dr. Koebner figured out psoriasis formed on injuries, after his patient kept getting it when his horse bit him. You can go ahead and put your blouse back on. Can you roll up those pant legs for me?"

Gone Before Spring

I sat back down and rolled my jeans up as far as I could. Dr. Sheffield crouched down and examined my legs closely. I looked over at my mom who had a funny look on her face. It reminded me of the look she had when I was in fifth grade and caught her and Larry kissing.

"I see Dr. Carter gave you the referral here, but he never saw you for this?"

"Mine went away on its own and I really thought hers would," my mom said. "I used that tar stuff in the tube and she's been using it for months. I figured there wasn't much else we could do."

"My dad had it when he was in the army," I said. "And his just went away too."

"Well, you didn't stand a chance having two parents with this. It runs in families, but we don't know the cause. Do you have siblings?"

"Just one sister, but she doesn't have it. At least not yet."

Doctor Sheffield stood up and put his hand on my shoulder.

"I bet the pain and itching are driving you crazy."

I nodded and swallowed hard.

"You know, the word psoriasis comes from the Greek word, psoro, which actually means itch." He turned toward my mom. "Mrs. Bloomfield, I'm not even going to let you take Ruth Ann home. This is a very serious case and she needs hospitalization."

My mom stood up. "Hospital? What can they do? Doctor, it just got this bad. She had some patches on her legs and arms all winter, but nothing like this."

"A severe outbreak like this can come on suddenly, which I imagine is what happened here. But, we need to stop it as soon as possible before it spreads to her face, hands, and feet."

"Those are the only places I don't have it," I mumbled, almost to myself.

"The other risk we need to think about is infection," he said. "Some of these patches are already split open."

Dr. Sheffield picked up a phone from the wall. "Nancy, call over to St. Anthony's and see if they have a bed in pediatrics. Tell them I need to admit a young girl for Goeckerman." He hung the phone back on the wall and turned to us. "What they'll be doing is the Goekerman regimen. They'll be applying coal tar and using ultra-violet light."

He examined my scalp. "We'll need to apply the coal tar here as well."

"How long will she be in the hospital?" my mom asked.

"It usually takes about three weeks to be successful."

"Three weeks?"

"Ruth Ann is suffering with this. She has close to 90 percent coverage. With this treatment, she stands a good chance of clearing."

A chance, I thought. This was supposed to be gone by spring, and now there's a *chance* it won't ever go away. I leaned back in the chair and looked up at the ceiling. Ever since I got into the car for that damn party, my life had been out of control.

The doctor put his hand back on my shoulder. "Since it's summer, you won't have to miss school."

The phone rang and the doctor picked it up. "All right, Nancy. Thanks."

"Your bed is waiting just down the street."

"Can't we go home first and pack a bag?" my mom asked.

"We need to get her settled right away. They only have two empty beds on the whole ward. I don't want to take a chance on losing hers. You can bring her you what she needs, which won't be much. Maybe some reading material."

Chapter Twenty Six

"Well, I never expected that," my mom said as we walked to the car. "I sure hope my hospitalization policy covers this."

That figures. I'm going in the hospital, and all she's worried about is how to pay for it.

"Of course, your father doesn't have any insurance, so he better be prepared to pick up this tab if we need it."

I felt like I was sinking in quicksand. There was no way out of this. We drove by Reeds Lake and I imagined diving off the dock and swimming away. The thought of the cool water made me think of floating on the inner tube with Maureen. That was the calmest my heart had been in a long time.

The first thing we had to do at the hospital was stop in the admitting office and fill out lots of forms. It felt so weird sitting in the office when I knew summer was just outside the door. This had to be a dream. I wasn't really going into the hospital. I'd be waking up anytime now. I dug my fingernails into my palms as hard as I could, while we walked to the elevator. We got off on the fourth floor and followed a nurse with a large pointy cap down the hall that said Pediatric Ward. I looked into rooms, and all I could see were little kids. I panicked. This couldn't be right. How could they put me on this floor? I hadn't felt like a little kid since the fourth grade.

"Since this room is empty, you can have the bed by the window," the nurse said as she took a hospital gown from the nightstand.

I could barely get the words out. "I think this is the wrong floor. I'm going on fifteen."

"No, you're in the right place." She handed me a hospital gown. "This floor goes up to seventeen. Put this on with the ties in the back, and I'll come back to take your vitals. You can hang your clothes in that closet."

She pushed her glasses against her nose, pulled the curtain around the bed, and practically ran out of the room.

My mom waved her hand toward the door. "Well, isn't she delightful?"

I could tell she felt sorry for me because she was trying to be funny. It was the type of thing she'd say to Renee, and I would feel left out. Kind of how I always felt when I had to ride in the backseat of the car.

I took my jeans and blouse off in front of my mom. I didn't even care, since she'd already seen most of my body at the doctor. I left my bra and underpants on because there was no way I'd be going without them under the huge gown with ties in the back. The nurse hurried back in and stuck a thermometer under my tongue.

"Do you have a smaller gown, by any chance?" my mom asked. "She's drowning in that one."

The nurse was pressing my wrist and looking at her watch. She shook her head. When she was done, she looked up and said, "Sorry. She's too big for the kids' gowns, but she's a very small adult. You'll find a toothbrush, toothpaste and comb in the emesis basin in the top drawer. I'll bring you some ice water."

I opened the top drawer after the nurse left and asked, "What kind of basin?"

"It's for vomit. In case you have to throw up."

"Oh, that's nice. I probably will need it when I'm covered with tar."

My mom sat in the corner chair with her purse on her lap for a while. Then she started pacing from the window to the doorway.

"Well, at least there's a television. I wonder how you're supposed to turn it on," she said as she looked up at the set mounted high up on the wall.

I lifted the remote control that was on the nightstand. "With this."

"That's pretty modern. When I had my gall bladder out, the only TV they had was in the lobby. Of course that was 1956. Did you eat lunch?"

"Yeah, I guess so."

Lunch. I couldn't believe she'd asked me that. I'd never really cared that my mom wasn't the hugging type. Until now. I knew I needed a hug, and it felt weird. I couldn't remember feeling like this since I was eight years old and my cat had been hit by a car. Thankfully, the neighbor had hugged me.

"Can you bring my transistor radio when you come back tonight?"

"Sure. Can you think of anything else?"

"Not right now."

"I better get going, honey. Renee probably wonders where we are. I'll come back with your things in a couple of hours." She kissed my cheek. "Maybe Renee will come with me."

Oh, boy. Just what I wanted. A visit from Renee. After she left, I walked over to the window and looked out at the parking lot. I watched her get into the Oldsmobile and drive away. I'd been lonely for a lot of my life, but never this bad. The lump in my throat was so big, I could barely hold back the tears. But I was determined not to cry on this damn *pediatric ward*. I got into the bed and used the remote control to turn on the TV. *Leave it to Beaver* was on. It was the episode when Beaver gets his head stuck in a fence at the park. I completely sympathized with him, since I also felt trapped, scared and on display. The grouchy nurse finally came back with a plastic glass, a straw, and a pitcher of ice water. She looked up at the show.

"Oh, I remember this one. The fire department has to come and rescue him. Your dinner tray will be here in an hour."

At least he didn't have to wait three weeks.

"When are they putting the tar stuff on me?" I asked her before she left the room.

"We'll find out when the doctor comes. Maybe tomorrow."

I looked at the telephone next to my bed and wondered if I could make calls, even though I wasn't sure I wanted anyone to know I was in the hospital. I wondered what my mom would tell my friends. She'd probably hang up on Tom. If he ever called again. More than anybody, I wanted to talk to Maureen. It was just my luck that she left for vacation a day early. There was a hard knot in my stomach that I'd only had one time before. The time my mother's co-worker decided I should be friends with her granddaughter. I had never even been to her house and they had me sleep over. I was scared of her neighborhood because the houses were all new and there weren't any trees. When we got into her bed, they didn't have pillows. The friend fell asleep and I started crying. My mom had to pick me up at midnight and I never saw the friend again.

I fell asleep before Beaver got rescued by the fire department. The sound of the dinner tray woke me up. The food looked like a TV dinner, but it was on a plate instead of a foil package. A slice of turkey, peas, mashed potatoes and canned peaches. I poked at the food with my fork, taking two bites of each thing. The one good thing was the carton of chocolate milk. A small child screamed down the hall during dinner. The phone rang at seven o'clock. It was my mom.

"Ruth Ann, I can't make it up there tonight. The car won't start. Larry told me last week my starter was going. So, I guess now it's gone. It'll have to be towed in the morning and I'll need to find a ride to work. If it's not fixed by tomorrow night, I'll get up there somehow, don't worry. Did they start the tar treatment?"

"No. They have to wait for a doctor to come in. Probably tomorrow."

"Well, in the meantime, just do what they say. Don't act like you're down in the dumps."

"Okay, Mom. I'll keep that in mind."

Back to her old self. So much for the sympathy act. She and Renee probably loved having me out of their hair. I hung up the phone and changed the three TV stations back and forth. A woman's voice on the loudspeaker constantly paged the doctors. I wondered if that would go on all night. How could anyone sleep through that?

"Hi, are you new?" A pale, thin boy with an IV pole stood in my doorway.

"I just got here a couple of hours ago."

"Well, I've been here a month and the food's terrible. Especially breakfast. Just wait and see." He rolled the pole back down the hall.

Breakfast was worse? Great. And were kids gonna stop and gawk at me whenever they felt like it?

At eleven o'clock, I was still watching TV when a new nurse came in. She sat on the edge of my bed and told me her name was Carolyn.

"It looks like your leg is bleeding. Can I take a look?"

She rolled the sheet back. A couple of the worst patches were bleeding.

"Are you in pain?" she asked me.

"I'm pretty used to it."

"Well, you don't have to be brave around here. I'll be right back."

She came back with aspirins and a jar of thick, white cream. She applied gobs of it to my legs, arms, chest and back. Some of the skin came off the psoriasis patches. She left the jar by the bed and said I could put it on other places if I needed to. Then she brought me some ginger ale and graham crackers. After that, I fell asleep to the sound of *Doctor Jones and ten-million other doctors, please call number number number*, over and over and over.

I was dreaming that Orna Lee was crying and I couldn't find her.

"I'm sorry to wake you, but I need to take some blood."

I opened my eyes and a young woman was standing at my bedside with a metal box full of tubes. I didn't know where I was at first, and then I remembered I was in the hospital. I heard a baby crying down the hall. That's why I was dreaming about Orna Lee. The lady looked at the psoriasis on my arm before turning it over for a vein.

"It's not contagious," I told her.

223

"I know. Looks like it hurts really bad."

She tied a strip of rubber around my upper arm.

"What time is it?" I asked her.

"It's three o'clock. The order came in late. Sorry, here's a poke."

Doctor So and So was still going on the intercom system, even at three in the morning. In addition to the baby crying, another small child began whimpering. I thought about my quiet room at home, where I would only hear crickets. Ruff and Reddy were probably sleeping on my bed right now. Without me.

Chapter Twenty Seven

"Trays," I heard someone say. When I opened my eyes a black girl in a blue uniform set a tray on my overbed table. She smiled and said, "Good morning, here's your breakfast."

"Thank you." I tried to sound friendly, but I felt groggy and confused. Under the metal cover on the tray was a plate of unappetizing scrambled eggs, soggy white toast and shriveled bacon. Thankfully, there was a small box of Raisin Bran and a carton of milk. I drank the grapefruit juice and ate the cereal. The grouchy nurse came in when I finished eating and took my blood pressure. As she removed the stethoscope from her ears, a man with a white coat came in. He had a grey mustache that turned up at the corners, and he introduced himself as Dr. Ording.

"Are you ready to get tarred but not feathered, Ruth Ann?"

"I guess." I shrugged.

"Somebody will be in shortly to start the process. We'll do our best to have it over with for three o'clock visiting hours. Okay?"

"Okay."

As soon as he left, the boy with the IV pole rolled into my doorway.

"How'd you like breakfast? I should've told you to get your emesis basin out first." He laughed at his own joke and then went right back to his glum face. "What are you in here for, anyway?"

"I'm getting a coal tar treatment in a few minutes. I have really bad psoriasis."

"You mean like the heartbreak? Wow. I've got leukemia. So does Sam and so does Charlie."

He rolled away without telling me his name or asking mine. Of course somebody had to say heartbreak. I'm surprised it hadn't happened sooner. But I did feel bad that the kid had leukemia. I flicked on the TV. Barbara

Walters was demonstrating the latest electric can-opener on the *Today Show*, but then I changed it to *Captain Kangaroo* which always made me feel cozy. Ping Pong balls were falling on Bunny Rabbit's head when a nurse came in pushing a cart with several items.

"Ruth Ann? Hi, I'm Nurse Penny and I'm going to be applying your tar today."

"Oh boy, aren't you lucky?"

"It's not so bad, once you get used to the smell."

She opened a large, plastic tub that said Crude Coal Tar on the label.

"First we have to test you to make sure you're not allergic to the tar. So, I'm going to apply a small amount to the back of your neck and then we'll check it in a couple of hours to make sure there's not a rash or any other reaction. If everything is fine, we'll give you a full treatment."

She applied a small amount of tar.

"How can anyone stand this all over?" I asked her. "This little bit smells bad enough."

"It's really strong, you're right. Is there something good on TV? Do you have a book to read?"

"I had to come here right from the doctor's office. I don't have a book or my radio or anything."

"Let me see if I can hunt something down."

She came back with four magazines. "This is the best I could do. They're from the visitor's lounge. All the books we have are for little kids. I'll be back to check on you soon."

All the magazines were at least a year old. I read about no-fuss hairdos, make-ahead meat loaves, and what to do when your kids complain of "Nothing to do!" I felt like throwing the magazines out the window, but the window didn't even open. My mom called and said the car wouldn't be ready until tomorrow, but she'd be coming to see me tonight one way or another.

"Please don't forget my radio. I'm going crazy with *nothing to do!*

226

Gone Before Spring

A mother walked by my room pulling a child in a wagon. The toddler was wearing a helmet and the mother looked like she needed a nap. Doctors and nurses scurried up and down the hallways. The loudspeaker continued to constantly page doctors. It was weird to feel lonely when I was surrounded by so many people.

"You are in the clear," Penny said as she checked the dab of tar on my neck. "No sign of an allergy."

She put on a paper gown and some rubber gloves and pulled the curtain around my bed. She applied the tar all over my top half, front and back. She acted like it was no big deal when she was putting it on my boobs, so I started talking about Ruff and Reddy, so she'd think I was okay with it too. But I wasn't okay. I was so embarrassed, I wanted to die. Then I had to put on a paper shirt with three sets of ties. The tar felt thick and gooey and smelled terrible. I could just hear my mom saying, "It stinks to high heaven."

Next, I had to stand up, so she could apply it to my entire bottom half, front and back, and I put on paper pants. I don't know which was worse, having her put it on my boobs or my butt.

"You're lucky not to have it on your face, hands and feet. Those are terrible places to get it," Penny said. "But I guess you don't feel so lucky about anything right now, do you?"

"Well I feel lucky that you were the one to do the tar and not that grouchy nurse."

Penny laughed, "Oh, you mean, Nurse Blackburn? She's an R.N., you know, registered nurse? They make us LPNs do the stuff like this. Or the nurse's aides. Well, how do you feel?"

"Like my street when it got tarred last summer."

"You're right. It smells exactly like the tar they use on roads. You'll get used to it, I promise. Put your light on if you need anything."

It was hard to be so close to a phone and not call anyone. I wondered what Tom was doing and if anyone had called his parents. For some reason, being in this hospital bed covered in this terrible stuff, was making me remember how awful I felt in the boat. I swallowed hard to keep from crying.

I watched *Love of Life* while I nibbled on a cold grilled cheese sandwich and fruit cocktail. It was pretty disgusting to eat while I reeked of tar. The same girl who had brought my breakfast picked up my lunch tray. She stopped in her tracks when she caught wind of me.

"*What is that smell?*" She looked around the room, like she expected a backhoe or a bag of fertilizer.

"It's me."

"I'm sorry, but you didn't smell like that this morning. I thought it was the electricity or plumbing or something."

I explained about the tar and what it was for. She shook her head.

"That's too bad. I hope it works. I watch that story too," she said, looking up at the TV. As she carried the tray out to the hallway, Penny came in.

"I hate to make this worse, but we have to apply the tar to your scalp now. I decided to wait until after lunch. After today, we'll put it all on in the morning."

She applied a different kind of tar, thinner, like brown shampoo, to my scalp. Then she covered my head with a plastic shower cap. The stuff on my head smelled even worse than the other tar. Maybe because it was closer to my nose. At two thirty, I was taken down the hall to a room where there was a tub and shower. Penny gave me a bottle of oil to remove the tar from my hair and body. It was hard to get the tar off and it made my hair feel stiff, even after the shampoo. I put on a cloth hospital gown and pants and followed Penny to a room where I had to lay on a table with my clothes off. The only thing I could wear was goggles over my eyes and a strip of cloth over my nipples because they said the skin there was more sensitive. I couldn't even wear underpants because the psoriasis was on my upper thighs, private parts and bottom.

Gone Before Spring

"The ultra-violet rays will help your skin to heal," the light operator said. "But it's very strong, so we start out with one minute on each side. We'll increase it a little bit each day."

I was mortified a man was operating the light treatment, even though I knew it was his job. I looked at the door and pictured myself running down the hall screaming, *Nooooo*. Then I looked at the window, and thought jumping out might be a better idea.

Instead, I put the goggles on and tried to close my whole mind and pretend to dissolve. I imagined a black cloth covering my brain. Even though my eyes were closed, the light beating down reminded me of the sun when Tom and I were in the boat. I wanted to wrap myself in Maureen's beach blanket and never show my body to another human being again. It was overwhelming when I thought about doing this every day, for longer and longer times, for three weeks. One tear squeezed out of the goggles and rolled into my ear.

* * *

When I got back to the pediatric ward, visitors were getting off the elevator and going into rooms. The toddler with the helmet was being pulled down the hall by an older couple, probably his grandparents. Just as I got into bed and reached over for the remote control, I heard a familiar voice.

"Well, well, well, I don't see a guitar anywhere around here. What's your excuse, Miss Ruth Ann? Didn't it fit in your suitcase?"

"Pete! What are you doing here?"

"Hey, when your mom called to cancel the lesson, she told me you were in here, and I said if that don't beat all. I gotta get up there for a visit. So I skipped the lunch hour at my day job and got off early. How ya feelin' anyway?"

He pulled a chair up to my bed and sat down.

"I just had a whole body coal tar treatment and a light treatment. It was pretty awful, but they say I'll get used to it. Did you ever have to go

229

in the hospital for tar treatments, Pete?"

"Never did. You have to be more than fifty percent covered, I think. Mine's always been bad, but stayed below that. You're lucky, Miss Ruth Ann. This will give you a head start."

"You're the second person to tell me I'm lucky today. I guess I need to get a different outlook. I keep thinking about my friends on vacation and the ones hanging out at the park. I'm so bored I could die, and they said I might be in here for three weeks!"

"You'll be gettin' all kinds of company. Don't you worry none. Time will go by quicker than you think."

"I don't know, Pete. My best friend is in the Black Hills, so she doesn't even know I'm in here, and this hospital is pretty far from where I live. I don't know if any of my friends will be able to get up here."

"I know it's not the same as friends, but your family will be comin' too, don't forget."

"Yeah, if my sister finds out what I did, she'll come up. That's for sure. She'll come up to murder me."

"Now, come on. What could you have done that was so bad?"

"Well, first of all, I got in a bunch of trouble for taking off in a row boat with my boyfriend at a party, and being gone a long time. I never should have done it, Pete, 'cause now he knows how bad my skin is and how I look like a monster, and I got grounded and he hasn't called, and he doesn't know I'm in the hospital and I don't know if he's grounded."

"Whoa there! Hold on for just a second. That all sounds like a pack of trouble, but what about your sister? Where does she fit in?"

"My sister already hates me. To her, I'm the biggest mistake ever born. And I did the stupidest thing. I borrowed her daisy earrings without asking, and lost one that day of the party. Probably in the row boat. I didn't tell her 'cause I was way too scared. I can't believe she hasn't noticed, but when she does, I don't want to think about what she'll do. She already thinks I belong in the Villa Maria." Pete leaned toward me with his elbows on his knees.

"Miss Ruth Ann. I know this feels like the end of the world. I used to get myself in all kinds of scrapes at your age too. But you shouldn't worry so much. It's not good for you right now. You need to concentrate on getting well. I just know it'll all work out. And as far as that boyfriend is concerned, he was just lucky he *ever* had you for his girl. If he quit callin' on account of your skin, you're a lot better off without him. There's my two cents on that. Oh, yeah, I picked this up for ya', 'cause it's got stories about the Beatles *and* the Rolling Stones."

He handed me a rolled up magazine that he'd been holding on to. I'd have to straighten it out after he left.

"Thanks, Pete. I needed something to read. This is great." He stood up and stretched.

"Well, take her easy now, and stop worryin' about everything. I'll catch ya later."

I spent the next hour reading every word of the magazine, even the ads.

Chapter Twenty Eight

I heard familiar voices in the hall when the elevator opened at seven o'clock. Cathy, Mrs. Cicerelli, and my mom walked in with big smiles like it was my birthday or something. Cathy was holding a paper plate covered in Saran Wrap.

"Hi, Ruth Ann. I made this for you."

I could tell through the plastic that it was her cherry chip cake.

"That's really nice, Cathy. Thanks."

Mrs. Cicerelli kissed my cheek and lifted a lunch bag up in the air.

"Here's some anise cookies. I know how you love them. How are you feeling?"

"Fine," I lied. "Thanks for bringing my mom up."

My mom kissed my cheek too and handed me my radio, which *I* kissed when she handed it to me. I turned on WLAV and *Let's Spend the Night Together* was on. I remembered my slumber party when all the girls were singing it and Cathy walked in. I looked over at her, but she didn't seem to make a connection. I turned the radio off because my mom gave me "the look."

"Here's a few of your things," my mom said, and she set my paisley suitcase on the window ledge. "Renee picked up a book for you at Wurzburg's and that's in there too. She had her bowling team tonight, but she'll come up tomorrow."

I doubted that Renee would have picked up anything for me if she knew I'd lost her earring. She must not have missed it yet, which meant I had more time.

"Let's see if there's any coffee in the visitors' lounge, Francesca," my mom said. I figured she was also due for a smoke. As soon as they left, Cathy sat in the chair that Pete had sat in.

"Why didn't you tell anybody your skin was so bad?" she asked. "Were you afraid to go to the doctor?"

"I don't know, Cathy. It's hard to explain. I really thought it would be gone by now but then it got a whole lot worse. The doctor said that can happen practically overnight."

"What did Tom say?"

"Tom doesn't know I'm here yet. Maureen doesn't even know 'cause she's on vacation."

I still wanted Cathy to think this was no big deal and that nothing had changed between me and Tom.

Our mothers came back with their coffee and my mom looked a little more relaxed. I heard her talking about the car repair and what it might cost. They asked about the treatment, but I decided not to mention the part about being naked under the lights. Cathy got her old saucer eyes, anyway, even though I had only talked about the tar. Then they switched the topic to some new neighbors who had moved in on the corner.

"Oh, I almost forgot," my mom said. "Peg called and she's going to try and come up for a visit."

"Mom! I'm not sure I want the whole world to know I'm in here."

As soon as I said that, I regretted it, because Cathy's mouth was open a good five inches.

"Oh for heaven's sake, Ruth Ann," my mom said. "Three weeks is a long time. You're going to need all the company you can get. Especially since you don't have a roommate yet. That reminds me. I better call your dad when I get home." She turned toward Mrs. Cicerelli. "Not that he'll make any effort to visit or anything."

I felt a little stab in my heart when my mom said that. Why did she always act like I couldn't hear those kinds of comments?

A voice on the intercom announced that visiting hours were over. It was a relief to have them say goodbye and walk out the door. I wasn't comfortable with Cathy and her mom knowing how bad my psoriasis had

233

gotten. Plus I wondered if my mom had told Mrs. Cicerelli about Tom and me and the boat. I figured that Cathy probably would have mentioned it if she knew. Just as I realized this, Cathy ran back into the room, "Look, I almost forgot these were in my pocket."

She handed me a roll of Choco-Mint Life Savers.

"Thanks, Cath. And thanks for coming up."

"It's okay. And I hope your skin clears up really fast."

It was getting harder and harder to stay irritated with Cathy. Maybe she really was growing up.

I switched on the TV and *Peyton Place* was beginning. It made me think of Mimi and the night in Saginaw when I showed her my skin and we both admitted we'd never watched the show. The girls at the dance had talked about it like everybody watched it all the time. I got bored and switched off the show, and turned my radio back on.

My skin had gotten so much worse since the trip to Saginaw. I kind of wanted Mimi to know, but I didn't dare make a long distance call. I never even did that at home. I reached over and picked up the receiver. I dialed 0, but the voice that answered said, "Main Switchboard. Can I help you?"

"Oh sorry, wrong number," I said, quickly hanging up. It wasn't a regular operator. It was the hospital operator. *What was I thinking? I needed to stay out of trouble.* Nurse Blackburn came in to take my "vitals" just as I placed the receiver on the phone. She glanced at my radio.

"You better turn that down a notch or two." Then she shook the thermometer and aimed it at my mouth.

"Would you like a cookie? My neighbor from Italy baked them," I asked her just before she jammed it in.

"No thank you. Looks like you need more water."

She grabbed the pitcher from my table, and flew from the room. If I didn't know better, I would have thought psoriasis *was* contagious, the way she acted. Or maybe it was teenagers that she didn't like and I seemed to be the only one on the floor. After she took the thermometer out and brought my water, I decided to see what my mom had brought in my suitcase. It felt weird to open it on a hospital bed, when it had been taken to so many overnights with friends.

The Siamese cat pajamas that the Cicerellis had given me for graduation were in the suitcase, several pairs of underpants, my other bra, and a small Wurzburg's bag, which contained a paperback copy of *Rosemary's Baby*. "Holy cow," I said out loud. This was the most grown-up gift Renee had ever given me. I climbed into bed and started reading the book. It was so good, I barely looked up when Nurse Blackburn took my blood pressure.

Nurse Caroline came in right after eleven o'clock. "Ooo, *Rosemary's Baby*. I read that. Be careful, it's pretty scary."

I smiled at her. What a relief to have her back. I fell asleep reading and dreamed that Mr. Cicerelli was grilling steak in his back yard. There was a tub of tar on the picnic table and he was spreading it on the steaks. Dark clouds of smoke were hanging in the air and all the neighbors were holding their noses. I turned around and Tom was standing there, holding a Doors album.

"Here, take this. It's not mine," he was saying. When I reached for it, he dropped the daisy earring in my hand.

* * *

"Do you have your period, dear?"

"Yes."

"We'll get that pad changed for you, right now."

Wait a minute. Those are real people talking. It's not part of the dream.

When I turned my head, I could see a curtain drawn around the bed next to me. A soft light was shining behind it and I could hear Nurse Caroline and a few others. Then I heard someone crying.

"We'll get you something for the pain right now."

I was very curious about who was in the bed, but they kept the curtain

235

drawn and I fell back asleep.

I woke up much earlier than the day before, and could see the girl sleeping in the bed next to me. Her leg was in a cast, hanging above the bed from chains. She had a large bandage around her head and a black eye. I got up to use the bathroom as quietly as possible, so I wouldn't wake her.

"Hi," the girl said when I opened the bathroom door to come out.

"Hi. I was trying not to wake you."

"That's okay. I'm Susie."

"I'm Ruth Ann. Were you in an accident?"

"That's what they told me. I can't remember anything."

Just then, two nurses came in and drew the curtain around Susie. I climbed into bed and went back to reading *Rosemary's Baby.* I was just beginning chapter four when my breakfast tray arrived. I was glad it was the same girl who had brought it the day before.

"Look at you," she said. "You got yourself a roommate and a scary book. Things should be gettin' interesting around here now."

"Yeah, we've barely been able to talk yet." I pointed at the drawn curtain. "But the book's great so far."

Doctor Ording came around the curtain, twisting his mustache. "Well, it sounds like you tolerated your treatment very well. Ready to do it again?"

"Okay." I said. But I felt like saying, *It would have been nice if you'd warned me, Dr. Mustache, that I'd be completely naked in front of a strange MAN!*

Chapter Twenty Nine

Susie could only have apple juice and a few sips of tea for breakfast. She was trying to be brave, but I could tell her leg was hurting a lot. After she got a shot for pain, I put my book down.

"I think I should warn you that pretty soon, it's going to smell really bad in here. I have a skin disease called psoriasis, and they cover me in tar every day for hours."

"I live on a farm. I'm used to all kinds of smells."

"You do? Wow, I've never known anyone from a farm. Do you have animals?"

"We have cows and chickens and a goat. And we grow corn and other stuff too. But mostly corn. How long have you been in here?"

"I just got here the day before yesterday. How old are you?"

She told me she was fifteen and we chatted for a few minutes about school. She fell asleep while I was in the middle of a sentence. That was okay with me because I wanted to get back to my book. It felt really good to not be the only teenager in the pediatric unit. I also didn't feel so bad about the tar and lights. At least I didn't have to use a bedpan, especially with my period.

Nurse Penny came in and applied the tar, first to my scalp, and then my whole body. It felt even more irritating than it had the day before.

"Can I use that white cream before bed tonight? I used it the first night and it helped the pain and itching."

"I'll have to check with the doctor," she said. "Let me know if you need anything else."

"Look. I can't believe the smell didn't even wake Susie up," I said.

The itching seemed worse than yesterday. I told Nurse Penny when she checked on Susie, and she brought me a pill that she said would help. I didn't know there were pills for that. It was a good thing that *Rosemary's Baby* was so interesting, because it helped to distract me. An hour later, Susie was moaning in her sleep and then she let out a shriek. It nearly scared me to death, especially since my book was getting creepy.

"Susie, are you okay?" I put the call light on and two nurses came in. Susie woke up and was trembling all over. I could tell she was remembering the accident. The IV pole boy was standing in the doorway. He shook his head and lifted a hand to wave at me. The tired mom pulled the wagon by with the toddler in the helmet. Penny and another nurse put washcloths on Susie's face and got her some ginger ale. I dove back into my book to find out why Rosemary was having the horrible pain in her abdomen.

"I hope I didn't scare you," Susie said when we were alone again. "I think the shot gave me a weird dream."

"I had a weird dream last night," I said. "And I wasn't even in an accident."

"I just wish I could see my brother. He's upstairs on the adult floor."

"Oh, was he driving? Is he hurt bad?"

"Yeah, he was driving, but I guess I'm in worse shape. A pick-up truck ran a stop sign and hit my side. I don't even know if anybody told my boyfriend yet. Do you have a boyfriend, Ruth Ann?"

"Well, I did. Right now, I'm not so sure."

Our lunch trays were delivered by the usual girl. I introduced her to Susie and she told us her name was Vivian.

"I hoped you'd be watching my story," she said, glancing up at the television.

"I'll turn it on and tell you what happens," I said.

Susie was trying to eat Jell-O, but she was having a hard time, so Nurse Penny came in to help her.

"I should probably eat somewhere else, so Susie doesn't have to eat with this terrible smell," I said.

Gone Before Spring

"You don't need to leave, Ruth Ann," Susie said. "I got used to it right away and it doesn't bother me."

Vivian came back for my tray and I filled her in on what was happening on *Love of Life*.

"Okay then. You get back to your scary book and I'll see you tomorrow," she said.

My mom called and I asked her to bring my two triangle scarves, Dippity-do, pink hair tape, and my bottle of Ambush. My hair was a mess yesterday after the tar treatment and I thought maybe the Ambush would make me feel better.

It seemed like I had to scrub even harder to get the tar off this time, and after the shower I soaked in an oatmeal bath to help the itching. When I was on the table, getting the light treatment, I tried again to imagine the black cloth around my brain, to help me forget about being naked in front of the guy running the light.

Susie's parents and sister were visiting when I got back to the room. After she introduced me to them, I got back into bed so I could find out what was happening with Rosemary.

"Hi, Ruth Ann. We hope you're in the mood for company."

Peg, Irene and a girl that looked slightly familiar were standing at the foot of my bed.

"How are you?" Irene asked. "Do you remember my cousin, Denise?"

I remembered that I'd met Denise at a couple of basketball games in seventh grade when St. Boner's played her school.

"Hi, Ruth Ann, "she said. "I just live around the corner from here, so when Irene said she was coming up with Peg, they said I should come. Hope you don't mind."

Denise was a really chubby girl. She was so cheerful and funny that you barely noticed. In fact, it didn't even seem to bother her. She had freckles on her nose and her brown hair was in a ponytail. She was wearing the Ladybug earrings we'd seen at Wurzburg's.

"No, it's great," I said. Thanks for coming up and I love your earrings."

"Denise will be in our class, you know," Peg said. "And she and her buddies hang out in the cafeteria here all the time."

"Here?" I asked "At the hospital?"

"Yeah, the food's cheap and those boys eat constantly," Denise said. "Plus we all live around here. You probably met them at the games."

"Hey, Ruth Ann, Did you hear about Mary Lou's brother?" Irene asked. I shook my head.

"I haven't talked to anybody since I got in here."

"He got killed in Vietnam," Peg said softly.

I was shocked to hear those words. Mary Lou talked about her brother Kevin all the time.

"That's awful," I said. "When did they find out?"

"When she got home from the party on Monday night," Irene said.

Monday night. Just hours after she was mean to me, she found out her brother was dead. While Renee was saying that I should be in the Villa Maria, Mary Lou got the worst news ever. Even her perfect hair and picket fence didn't stop this from happening.

"We went to her house to talk to her," Peg said. "She wouldn't even come to the door."

I felt sad and scared. We heard about boys dying in Vietnam every time we watched the news, but we never knew them. Until now.

"They'll probably have the funeral next week, "Peg said. "Will you be home by then?"

"I doubt it. They've been saying I'll be here for three weeks."

"Wow. That's a long time," Denise said. "I will definitely be up to visit more. If that's okay, I mean."

"Sure, if you want. It's pretty boring up here, though."

"Looks like your roommate was in an accident," Irene whispered. "Is she nice?"

Gone Before Spring

I looked over to be sure Susie and her family didn't hear us. They were all laughing about the new kittens in their barn.

"She just came in the middle of the night, but yeah, she's nice," I said. "Her brother was driving and he's upstairs on the adult floor."

The girls stayed until afternoon visiting hours were over. We talked a lot about high school starting in the fall and how different kids would come there from so many grade schools. Denise had a really contagious laugh and I liked her a lot.

* * *

My mom and Renee came up for the evening visiting hours. I was reading when they walked in.

"You're reading that book awfully fast," Renee said after kissing my cheek. "Are you sure you're absorbing it?"

"First of all, I'm a fast reader, Renee. And second of all, what else do I have to do? But, it is really good. Thanks for buying it for me."

"It looks like you'll be needing another one," my mom said. "Here's your hair stuff."

"Good thing you brought it," Renee said, looking at my hair.

"By the way, I called your father last night and told him you're in here, "my mom said.

Renee was running her finger along the window sill to check for dust. "Why did you even bother?" she asked.

I looked in the bag of stuff my mom brought, and when I saw the bottle of Ambush, an instant lump formed in my throat. I thought about Tom's sister wrapping it, and Ruff and Reddy playing with the ribbon while we made out on the couch. Right now Christmas Eve seemed like a million years ago.

I put on my paisley triangle scarf to cover my hair. I was tired of Renee looking at it, and I didn't want to bother with the Dippity-do and hair tape until tomorrow.

"That's better," Renee said after I tied the scarf. I felt like sticking my

241

tongue out at her, but then I remembered that I'd lost her earring. She was sitting on the edge of the chair filing her fingernails, only because she couldn't find anything to clean. My mom looked really tired.

"You guys don't have to stay until eight-thirty," I said. "You're both probably tired from working all day."

They left shortly after I said that. Susie's family was still visiting, so I got back to *Rosemary's Baby.* Since I had less than a hundred pages left, I tried to read slowly to make it last through tomorrow's tar treatment.

I found myself sneaking peeks at Susie's parents. Her dad straightened her covers, got her fresh ice water, and when he talked to her he leaned over the bed rails and looked right into her eyes. Her mom decorated her bulletin board with get-well cards and photos, and since Susie could eat regular food now, she'd baked peanut butter cookies. I wondered what it felt like to be in a family like that. They never even raised their voices to one another.

* * *

The next day, they wheeled Susie's brother down to visit her. His arm was in a sling and he had a cast on his foot, but he was going home in a day or two. Just after Susie introduced him to me, Denise came in.

"Hi. I thought I'd stop by to see how you're doing," she said. "Oh yeah, and these are for you."

Denise handed me a small box. Inside were a pair of tiny seashell earrings.

"Denise, these are so cute. You shouldn't have gotten me anything."

"I'm kind of an earring fanatic. I have way too many. You looked sort of sad yesterday when Peg and Irene talked about going to the beach in Grand Haven. So, I thought I'd bring a little beach to you."

"Thanks so much. You're way too nice," I said.

Denise stayed for the whole afternoon visiting hours. She made me laugh over and over, which felt really good because I hadn't laughed in a long time. She said she would come tomorrow and maybe bring the guys she hung out with, because they wanted to meet me. Even though I wanted to meet them, I hoped she would wait a day or two. I wanted her to come alone because I had decided by the end of our visit that she would be a good person to talk to about Tom. Neither Peg nor Irene had mentioned him the day before, and I was relieved, since I was embarrassed about the boat incident and I didn't want to tell them that he hadn't called.

I finished *Rosemary's Baby* right after dinner.

"The first thing I'm going to do when I get out of here, is see this movie," I told Susie as I held up the book. "Do you want to read it?"

"I don't feel good enough to read yet," she said. "Thanks anyway, though. Mind if I turn on the TV?"

My mom came by herself for visiting hours. She brought me an Almond Joy and a book called *Junkie Priest.*

"I just finished this book," she said. "And I think you're going to really like it."

I had my doubts, but I could easily see through my mom's plan. She probably hoped that a priest who worked with drug addicts would seem so cool to me that I'd lose interest in boys and music and any other possible temptations. Maybe she really did think I was headed to Villa Maria.

"This came today," she said as she handed me a big envelope. It was an extra large greeting card that said "Get Well" on the front and when you opened it, a goofy guy popped up at the top holding a sign that said "Soon." It was from my dad. At the bottom he had written:

Sorry to hear the news about you being in the hospital, Sport. Keep your chin up and do what they tell you. Maybe you can finally get rid of this nasty stuff. Love, Dad XOXO

"Did he mention anything about you going to Saginaw this summer?" my mom asked after I set the card on my nightstand.

"No, but I'll probably go in August like I always do. And I hope you both remember that Maureen gets to come with me this time."

"I knew I was forgetting something!" my mom said. "A package

243

came from Maureen and I left it on the dining room table."

"A package?" I asked. "From the Black Hills?"

"Yes, darn it, from South Dakota. I'll bring it tomorrow."

I was surprised to hear Maureen had sent a package, since I'd only expected a postcard.

My mom kissed me good-bye after the end of the TV show we were watching.

Susie's boyfriend was visiting her for the first time. His name was Gary and he was very tall and thin. He brought her a bouquet of daisies which made me feel sad. Where was Tom *right now*, I wondered. It was hard to believe how close we had been just a few weeks ago. I envied Susie. Her leg would heal, her black eye and cut were already getting better. Maybe if she had psoriasis, Gary wouldn't be holding her hand right now. Maybe there wouldn't be a vase of daisies. All I had was a daisy earring at home in my Barbie case.

Chapter Thirty

Saturday morning was no different than the other days. I still got slathered with tar, had to wear the shower cap and goop on my head, and lie naked under the lights. Susie and I watched *American Bandstand* and picked out the cutest boys and our favorite outfits. After the show, I started reading *Junkie Priest* and once I got past the introduction, it was actually pretty good. Anything that was set in New York City interested me. I wanted to go there more than anywhere else.

My mom called and asked if I would mind if she skipped the afternoon visit. She had to mow the lawn and go grocery shopping. I was kind of glad, because I was hoping to talk to Denise. But, right at three o'clock, Denise walked in with three boys, Michael Fitzpatrick, Charlie Callahan, and Eddie Steffens.

"Okay, now I remember who you are," Eddie said as he plopped down on the foot of my bed.

"I think I met all of you back in seventh grade," I said. "Thanks for coming up."

"Are you kidding?" Michael asked. "This hospital is our second home. We finally have an excuse to really be here."

"Yeah, Fitzpatrick is addicted to the french fries in the cafeteria. He can't go forty-eight hours without 'em or he'll go through withdrawal," Charlie said.

"Speaking of withdrawal," Michael said. "What are you reading here?"

He turned over my copy of *Junkie Priest,* and read the back cover. He wore black glasses and his hair fell over to one side. He was the first boy in glasses I'd ever thought was cute. Susie didn't have company and was looking over at us, so I introduced her to everyone. Denise sat in a chair by Susie's bed, and the boys moved back and forth from my window sill to the foot of my bed, and to my chair. We played the radio and talked about music, books, and people we knew in common. I told them about the police coming to school because of my babysitting job and I felt sort of cool when I saw how fascinated they were with the story.

These boys seemed much smarter and funnier than the boys from St. Boner's. I wondered if there was a chance I'd be hanging out with them when we all got to high school in the fall. Eddie put on my triangle scarf and we all burst out laughing for the third time in five minutes.

"Ruth Ann, if you and your visitors don't quiet down, they'll have to leave," Nurse Blackburn said from the doorway.

"We're also *Susie's visitors*," Eddie said, still wearing the scarf. Susie grinned from ear to ear. Nurse Blackburn let out a huffy sound and said, "I mean it, Ruth Ann!"

After Denise and the boys left, Susie looked over at me and said, "Those boys are really fun and I like your friend Denise a lot."

"The funny thing is that I didn't even know any of them a week ago. There's six of us in the Tandem Riders and I've only seen two of them since I got here."

Susie knew all about the Tandem Riders and she had told me about her close friends from 4H club. There was a girl named Darla in her group that sounded a lot like Mary Lou. It was still so hard for me to believe that Mary Lou's brother had been killed. Whenever I thought about it, I wasn't sure where to put it in my mind. It seemed like life was more confusing every day. Is that what growing up meant? Would more confusing stuff just keep piling up every time I turned around?

* * *

Susie and I both took a nap after dinner. I had a feeling that the pills for itching were making me a little sleepy. I woke up when I heard Renee's voice in the hall. She walked in with my mom. Susie's boyfriend and her parents were right behind them.

"Your hair looks a little better," Renee said as she gave me her obligatory kiss on the cheek.

"Gee, thanks. I think."

"Did you have company this afternoon?" my mom asked after *her* obligatory kiss.

I told her all about Denise and the boys coming up, and I noticed her expression was less than pleased.

"What's the matter? Aren't you glad I'm making friends with kids I'll be going to school with?"

"Well, I've just never heard of a girl who travels around with a group of boys all the time."

I leaned back on the pillow and closed my eyes. There was no use trying to explain this to my mom or Renee. They were going to twist around anything I said, anyway. I hadn't told them that Denise was very overweight or that she was the funniest person I'd ever met.

"Did you bring the package from Maureen?" I asked.

"Oh, shoot. I didn't see it, so I forgot," my mom said. "If it had still been on the table, I would have remembered. Did you see it, Renee?"

Renee was chewing gum really fast and flipping through a *Woman's Day* magazine she had brought with her.

"Yes, I put it on her dressing table," she said without looking up.

"*Thanks a lot,*" I said to her. "Has anyone called me at home since I've been up here?"

"Just Peg and Irene," my mom answered. "Before they came up to see you."

"Are you sure nobody else called?" I asked.

"She must be talking about that boyfriend," Renee said, as she tore a page from the magazine. "What I want to know, is your skin getting any better? It would be so nice if we didn't have to follow behind you all the time, cleaning up piles of your flaky skin."

"Oh my God! Why did you even come up here, Renee? To make me

247

feel worse?"

"Stop it, you two," My mom said, as she jerked her head toward Susie and her family.

"I'm going to look for the drinking fountain," Renee said and left the room.

"Why is she always like that?" I asked my mom. "I swear she hates my guts."

"Ruth Ann, that's not true. Renee loves you very much. She just gets nervous, that's all."

My mom sighed and looked up at the TV. I decided to stay quiet because she looked so worried and tired. Susie's family were all talking about the kittens again and their Collie, Jake.

Renee came back in with more magazines from the lounge.

"These are really old. You'd think with the prices that hospitals charge, they could order some new ones. Mother, didn't you have something from Larry?"

"That's right, I do," she said while reaching into her purse. "Larry sent this book for you. He also says hi, but he can't stand hospitals. Now, promise you won't start this until you finish *Junkie Priest*."

"I read a few chapters this morning. It's not bad," I said.

The book from Larry was a thin paperback called *The Creeping Siamese* by Dashiell Hammett. On the cover was a horrified looking lady with a plunging neckline and a bloody knife. A note was sticking out of the top.

Ruth Ann, I hope you're doing okay. Please forgive me for not visiting, but I'm not very good company at hospitals. I saw this book at the drug store and thought of you. I don't know if there are any Siamese cats in it, but I know you like mysteries, and I figure you've outgrown Nancy Drew. I hope the treatments work for you and maybe you can even do a little writing while you're in there. I've always thought of you as a future writer. All my best, Larry

"That was so nice. Tell him thanks for me, okay, Mom?"

"Sure, I'll tell him. He's taking us to the Fiesta Cafe Monday night. Do you want me to bring you some tacos?"

"Yes. That would be great. I'm really sick of the food here. Hey, Renee, can I have a stick of gum?"

Renee opened her purse for the gum. "Oh my gosh. I guess I did bring your little package from your friend. I forgot it was in here."

Somehow I didn't believe Renee had forgotten. Knowing her, she enjoyed holding out on me. My mom passed me the paper covered box, which I tore into. Inside was a silver keychain with the Mt. Rushmore president faces. Underneath the keychain was a tiny folded piece of paper, and under that was cotton batting. I held up the keychain.

"I told Maureen to say hi to the presidents for me. I guess that's why she sent this."

"That was thoughtful of her," my mom said.

"I wonder why she mailed it," Renee said. That's a lot of trouble on her vacation. She could have just given it to you when she got home. Does she even know you're in the hospital?"

I unfolded the tiny piece of paper and it said: *Hi Ruth Ann, here's the presidents to say hi 'til I get back. There's also something under the cotton, but don't lift it up 'til you're all alone. I'll explain when I get home. See you soon, Maureen*

I was dying to lift up the cotton, but since Renee and my mom were both staring at me, I just set the keychain back in with the note and closed the box. I couldn't imagine what it was. The box was too small for even one Winston.

"Did she say she's having a good time?" my mom asked.

"Yes. She is," I hoped my face wasn't giving anything away.

"We should go, Mother," Renee said. "We both have to figure out what we're wearing to work all next week."

"Not just yet, Renee. Visiting hours aren't over for forty minutes and

I couldn't make it up here this afternoon."

I thought I'd go crazy waiting for them to leave. They both leafed through magazines and talked about their bosses. I even thought about sneaking the box into the bathroom.

I finally got my obligatory kisses and they left. I waited until I heard the elevator doors close and then I opened the box, tossed the keychain onto my bed, and lifted up the cotton. At first it looked like there was nothing there, and then I saw something stuck to the underside of the cotton. When I pried it loose, it felt like my stomach jumped into my throat. *It was the lost daisy earring!* I couldn't imagine how or where Maureen had found it. I was dying to ask her, but there was no way. She probably imagined that I'd run right into Renee's room and put it back in her jewelry box. But I wasn't going home for more than two weeks. I had never felt so relieved and frustrated at the same time.

* * *

I read *Junkie Priest* the next day while my tar was on. It was so depressing to read about the horrible lives of the women in the book. I put it down and looked over at the phone. Denise had left her number, and I was dying to tell someone about the daisy earring. I decided not to bother her on a Sunday, in case she was busy with her family. I thought about calling Peg, but I was still pretty embarrassed about her mom being at the cottage party when everything happened. I even thought about calling Cathy, but then I remembered my mom telling me the Cicerellis had rented a cottage on Diamond Lake for the week.

Now that I had the earring, I kept thinking about Tom, and getting the weird feeling in my stomach. I wondered if he was thinking about me at all. Maybe he had completely forgotten how he used to feel about me. Before he saw me in the boat. Before he saw what I really looked like.

* * *

On Monday, I started reading *The Creeping Siamese*. Larry had probably guessed right about there being no cats in it. It was about

Siamese men. It was pretty entertaining, anyway. I felt antsy and longed to go outside, even though the guy on WLAV was talking about it being really hot. I felt impatient with the radio. It seemed like they were playing all of my least favorite songs. Susie had been gone for tests all morning.

"You don't look too happy today," Vivian said as she set my tray down.

"I feel like I'm going crazy in here. I can't believe I've only been here since last Tuesday. It feels like forever."

"That plastic cap looks mighty uncomfortable, and all that stuff on your skin. You deserve to feel crazy if you ask me."

"Thanks, Vivian. I'll tell you what happens on *Love of Life*. Or maybe you can come back and watch a little."

"Oh no. If old Mrs. Maguire found that out, I'd be history. She'd just as soon get rid of all the black tray girls." She looked over her shoulder. "In fact, she'd probably fire me for just chattin' with you. I better go."

I felt sorry for Vivian. She worked all day and then babysat for her little brothers and sisters when she got home, so her mom could work. Here I was feeling sorry for myself because Tom hadn't called and because I had to be cooped up.

The shower felt especially good when I was done with my tar treatment. While the water was splashing over my shoulders, I thought about being in the inner tube at the party and how good it felt. It was so hard for me to believe that was only last Monday. Exactly a week ago from today.

I climbed on the table in the light room, took off the hospital pajamas, and put on my goggles.

"The doctor's coming in today to observe," the light guy said as soon as I was lying down.

"The doctor? What doctor?"

"Good afternoon, young lady," a deep voice said that I wasn't sure I recognized. "I've brought some students in to observe your case. This is

Ruth Ann Bloomfield, fourteen years old, admitted last Tuesday with severe, acute plaque psoriasis with possible erythroderma."

I opened my eyes behind my goggles and saw "Dr. Mustache" with eight or ten people in white coats. They were all looking at my body. My naked body. I closed my eyes and thought about the inner tube again. But this time I pictured myself letting go and drowning. And right now, I wished I had.

Chapter Thirty One

I was relieved that I didn't have any afternoon visitors. I needed time to think and to decide if I should tell anybody about the students "observing me," or if I should just keep it to myself. Usually, if something really bothers me, I can only hold it in for so long before I felt like exploding. I still hadn't told anyone about the damn daisy earring, and that was bad enough. How much more could I hold in?

My hair was frizzier than usual, so I just put a triangle scarf over it. And then I started crying really hard. At first I thought it was my hair that was making me cry. But I hadn't cried about my hair for at least a year. I knew it was about those people all looking at me naked. It was even worse than Renee and my mom teasing me about pubic hair. Way worse.

I splashed cold water on my face and took a bunch of really deep breaths. When I came out of the bathroom, Susie was talking on the phone, and I heard her say she was being transferred to a rehabilitation hospital in a day or two. I was looking out the window at the parking lot when I heard Vivian walk in.

"Hey there, just thought I'd say a quick hi since I'm up here."

"Hey, Vivian," I said. "What are you doing up here when it's not lunch or breakfast?"

"They sent me up with a special tray for some new kid that just got here. These scarf things you wear are so cute," she said pointing to my head. "Where do you get those from?"

"Oh lots of places, I guess. Even Woolworth's has them. And they really come in handy with my problem hair."

"*Your* problem hair? Don't talk to *me* about problem hair. Well, I better get back down there. See you in the morning."

I felt a little better after Vivian left. I wished she didn't always have to run off so fast. When Susie hung up the phone, we talked about her being transferred, and I thought of telling her about the observing students and maybe even the whole daisy earring thing. Just when I opened my mouth, Dr. Sheffield walked in.

"Hi there, Ruth Ann," he said. "Now that you've been here for almost a week, I thought I should stop in and see how your treatment is going."

He pulled the curtain around.

"I really don't see any difference yet," I told him as I swung my legs up on the bed.

"That's typical," he said. "You don't usually see results for a couple of weeks. Your body is used to reproducing cells very fast and those cells build up and cause the plaques. For some reason, the tar and lights slow down that whole process. But it's not an overnight deal."

He examined my arms, stomach and back, but thankfully, none of my private parts.

"It looks like you're tolerating the tar and the lights just fine. I don't see any allergic reactions, so that's good."

"Well, today when I had my light treatment, a bunch of students came in to watch, when I didn't have any clothes on. It was really embarrassing."

"This is a teaching hospital, Ruth Ann. You're contributing to science and possibly helping another psoriasis patient down the line."

"Oh," was all I could say. Then I felt embarrassed for complaining.

"Keep up the good work, young lady, and I'll stop in next week. Glad you got a roommate that's close to your age."

He smiled at Susie as he pulled the curtain back, and then walked out the door. I looked over at Susie and suddenly realized that if she left, I might get a little kid for a roommate.

"I didn't mean to eavesdrop, Ruth Ann," Susie said. "But I heard you say that students came in during your light treatment. That's awful. Did they even warn you?"

"No. They didn't warn me. I guess I was contributing to science." Tears welled up in my eyes and I turned toward the window.

"Hey you two," the IV pole kid said from the doorway. "I heard we're getting caramel pudding tonight. It's the best thing they make in this dump. Way better than tapioca." He wheeled away and I heard him tell the same thing to the kids in the room next door.

A nurse came in to adjust the weights that were hanging on Susie's traction. My phone rang and it was my mom.

"Hi, honey. Remember, Larry's taking us to Fiesta Cafe. How many tacos do you want?"

"Two is fine, thanks."

"Do you want Spanish rice with that?"

"Sure. Hey, Mom, could you get five dollars from my purse and bring it up?"

"I guess so, but do you think that's a good idea? What do you need?"

"It's fine, okay, Mom?"

The dinner tray looked less appetizing than usual, so I was glad they were bringing me tacos. I saved the caramel pudding and set it aside.

Nurse Caroline came in and saw my untouched dinner. I explained about the tacos.

"Okay, Ruth Ann, but are you sure you're all right? Does your skin hurt or something?"

"There were some students who came in during my light treatment," I said. "And there I was with nothing on. Nobody even warned or asked me."

"Gee, they should have. Was there a doctor with them?"

"Yeah, that one with the giant mustache."

"Dr. Ording?"

"I guess that's his name."

"I'll look into it, sweetie. And I'll see that it doesn't happen again."

"Thank you."

* * *

"Well, I tried to get Larry to come with us," my mom said as she and Renee walked in. "But he said he had to trim the hedges at his mother's house."

"That's okay," I said as I opened the bag with my tacos and rice in it. "This looks so good. Thank you."

"He sent this up for you," my mom said. "Don't open it 'til you're done eating." She set a package on the nightstand that was wrapped in newspaper.

Renee was pushing her cuticles down with the little wooden stick she always carried in her purse. I told them about Dr. Sheffield's visit while I ate. I decided not to mention the observation thing. The tacos were delicious and I thoroughly enjoyed them. I opened the package from Larry when I was done. It was a charcoal sketch of Ruff and Reddy curled up together sleeping.

"He did that the other day when he was over. He said he never expected them to stay in the position long enough, but they did."

"It's really good. Wow. Please tell him thank you very much, okay?"

I thought of the time Larry sketched my loafers, back when we lived in the apartment. It was right around the time he'd taken me to see *A Hard Day's Night*. That seemed like a lifetime ago or maybe like it happened to somebody else.

"Did you finish *Junkie Priest*?" my mom asked.

"Not yet. I started the book from Larry."

"I told you she'd never read that," Renee said as she fished a nail file from her purse.

"I will too, Renee. MYOB, would you? Hey, Mom, did you bring my wallet, or at least my money?"

"Here it is," she said, "But I don't think it's such a good idea. What do you need it for, anyway?"

"I don't know. I just want it. It's my babysitting money."

"She'll probably give it to those boys who come up with that girl," Renee said. "What's her name again, Diane?

"Oh my God. Mom, make her stop. Why would I give my money away? And besides, none of them even need my money."

I propped the picture of the cats on my lap and stared at it so I wouldn't make a bigger scene. I felt like choking Renee with my bare hands. Maybe I wouldn't put those earrings back. Maybe I'd keep them forever and wear them to her funeral.

"Let's go, Mother," Renee said. "I need to iron your blouse, remember? See you later, Ruth Ann. I hope you're in a better mood the next time I come."

* * *

They came to get Susie the next afternoon while we were watching *Let's Make A Deal.*

"Good luck, Ruth Ann. I hope everything works out," she said after they transferred her to a stretcher. I knew she was talking about Tom and the earring because we'd talked in the dark until after one in the morning.

"Same to you, Susie. I hope your leg heals fast and you make it home for part of the summer."

"Remember to call me."

"Okay, I will. Bye."

After she was gone, they stripped her bed and put all new linens on it. The room felt still and lonely. I tried to read one book, and then the other. The smell of the tar seemed worse today. I felt like jumping out of my skin. Grandma Gertie called it "feeling utsy." It was one of her Yiddish words. I never left the room with the tar on, but I stood in the doorway, looking down the hall. Nurse Penny came by with a clipboard.

"Is everything okay, Ruth Ann?"

"Do you think I could take the tar off a little earlier today? It's really bothering me."

"Doctor's orders are 'til two-thirty. You know that."

257

"Just this once?" I asked. "I feel gross. I think I need to soak in an oatmeal bath."

"Well, it's almost two. I guess it's okay if you're not feeling well."

As I gathered my bath things together, Nurse Penny came in and said, "There's a note here that says you'll be going in the light booth today instead of your usual light treatment. I'll come down in half an hour to take you there, okay?"

The light booth was totally private. Nobody could see me when the door was closed. It was like standing in a little closet with light bulbs all around. I still wore the goggles to protect my eyes. I wondered why they switched me to the booth. Was it because I had said something about the observing students? I had a pretty good idea that it wasn't Dr. Sheffield, but that Nurse Caroline had suggested it. I was glad that I had said something to her. I decided right there in the booth, that keeping things inside was not a good idea. Renee was always telling me that I had a big mouth. Maybe she was right. But if you ask me, this time, my big mouth was a good thing.

* * *

The room felt lonely with Susie gone. There was an envelope on my nightstand from Grandma and Aunt Dorothy. It was a card with a teen-age girl on the front. She was in bed with a thermometer in her mouth and a bag of ice on her head, and inside it had the usual get-well-soon message. There was a note written in Aunt Dorothy's fancy penmanship:

We're so sorry to hear you're in the hospital, honey. Get well soon and when you come in August, I'll take you out to lunch at the Amberwood. All our love, Aunt Dorothy & Grandma Gertie XOXO.

I wouldn't be holding my breath about the lunch at the Amberwood. Aunt Dorothy had taken Renee there dozens of times. I'd only been there once, on my seventh birthday. It was a fancy place with little lamps on the tables and the waitresses wore black and white uniforms with ruffly aprons. It seemed like Renee had worn out the fun side of Aunt Dorothy.

By the time I came along, nobody was interested in entertaining another little girl.

* * *

I fixed my hair just in time before Denise walked in with Eddie and Charlie. I was disappointed that Michael wasn't with them which sort of surprised me.

"My sister was done with these, so they're all yours," Denise said as she handed me a couple of *Teen* magazines.

"Thanks, Denise," I said. "I need more distractions, especially since I lost my roommate."

"Yeah, I noticed that," Eddie said. "Good thing we're here to keep you company."

He picked up one of the magazines and plopped down on Susie's former bed.

"Wow, I need to read this article," he said. *Vacation Love: How to Play All the Angles*. I need angles since I plan on getting some vacation love."

While Eddie read, Charlie flipped the stations on the TV. Denise had me laughing in no time about her weekend babysitting jobs.

"I bet kids love you, I said. "No wonder you get so many jobs."

Denise shrugged as she pulled on the bottom of her T-shirt. I was still amazed at her confidence, even though she was overweight. The only chubby girls I'd ever known were shy and seemed embarrassed all the time

Every now and then Eddie began reading out loud from the magazines.

"Hey, there's an article in here called, *Are You Headed for a Broken Heart*? Does anyone need me to read that one aloud?"

I almost said yes, but changed my mind. I made a mental note to read it as soon as they all left.

Nurse Caroline opened the door and walked in. "Ruth Ann, you need to keep this door open."

Then she looked at Eddie on the bed. "Young man, I'm sorry, but you'll have to get off that bed. We've made that up for the next patient."

"Oh, sorry," He said. "I never undid the covers and my feet have been hanging off this edge the whole time, so you can still use it."

Nurse Caroline smiled and shook her head.

"Go ahead and use this chair," she said as she slid the chair over from Susie's side of the room.

"We need to go anyway, you guys," Denise said. "I'm cooking dinner tonight for my mom, and I should get started. I'll try and come up tomorrow, Ruth Ann. Let me know if you need anything."

"Can I think about it and call you later?" I asked her.

"Sure. I'll be around tonight."

My phone rang as they were leaving. It was Peg calling to apologize for not coming up to see me again and also to tell me about the funeral for Mary Lou's brother.

"It was the saddest thing I've ever gone to," she said. "Mary Lou was a mess. I don't think she'll ever be the same."

"Poor Mary Lou," I said, and actually meant it.

"Do you know when you're getting out?"

"It'll be at least a week," I told her. "Have you seen Tom around?"

"I saw him yesterday going into Marty's with the other guys from the band. I've hardly seen any of them since Marty and I broke up. He's been up to see you though, right?"

"Actually, no," I said. "I haven't heard from him at all. In fact, I don't even think he knows about me being in here."

"Wow, I can't believe it," Peg said. "You guys were *the* class sweethearts."

When she said that, I felt my chest tighten up. How could everything have changed so fast?

"Yeah, well, I think that might be over," I said, wishing I hadn't even brought Tom up. "What have Irene and Angela been up to? As soon as I get out and Maureen's back from vacation, we need to have a Tandem Riders day."

"Okay," Peg said. "Maybe we should rent tandems. For old time's sake, right?"

"That sounds really fun. I'll call you as soon as I get home, and Maureen will definitely be back by then."

"Yes, please do, and hey, Ruth Ann, I wish I could visit you again. I just haven't had a ride and it takes two busses to get there. I looked on the bus schedule."

"Oh, that's okay. Irene's cousin, Denise has been up a bunch of times. Sometimes she brings her guy friends and they're pretty cool."

"Oh good. I really like her, don't you? Listen, I'll keep an ear out about Tom, and if I hear anything, I'll call you, okay?"

"Okay, and thanks for calling. Even if you can't get up here, phone calls are the next best thing. Say hi to Irene."

After I hung up the phone, I closed my eyes and tried to imagine Tom going into Marty's house. For some reason, I couldn't picture his face. I could remember his smell clearly. A mixture of Brut and his own sweet scent. I took my bottle of Ambush out of the nightstand drawer and opened it. All I could think of when I sniffed it, was making out with Tom. I thought about our first kiss at the Four Star Theatre, and then sneaking into the laundry room at the party in Maureen's basement.

At the thought of that, I started crying really hard. That party was the first time I'd ever tried to hide my psoriasis and it made me feel scared to think of it. How could I go to high school like this? I had this terrible disease and it would be a whole different school with tons of new kids.

"Are you crying because your skin hurts? Or are you sad that your roomie left?"

It was the IV pole kid in my doorway again. "I've had twelve different roomies while I've been here. It gets easier, don't worry. I heard

261

we're having Swiss steak tonight. Yuck!"

He wheeled away and I blew my nose. It took several Kleenexes before I was done.

After I picked at my dinner, I called my mom and told her I had a headache, and she didn't need to come up. I did sort of have one from crying and I knew my mom was getting tired of coming up all the time, especially after work. I read *Are You Headed for a Broken Heart?* and a few chapters of *The Creeping Siamese*. I gathered from the article that I was more than *headed* for a broken heart, and just as Larry had said, there still weren't any Siamese cats in the book.

I called Denise just after eight o'clock to ask her if there was any chance she'd be shopping somewhere the next few days.

"Could you pick up a couple of those triangle scarves for me?" I asked her. "It doesn't matter what color."

"Sure, I could do that before I come up tomorrow. I'll ride my bike over to the D&C Store. I've seen them there."

"Thanks, Denise. I'll pay you back when you get here."

* * *

"You know what?" Nurse Penny said the next morning as she applied tar to my back. "I think your back is starting to look better."

"That's good, but I wish my arms and legs looked better."

"I know, but you have to be patient."

I felt anything but patient. I watched TV while my tar was on and I read an article in one of the teen magazines called, *The Family Fight: How to Win*. Nothing in it applied to my crazy family. I was a born loser, no matter how you looked at it.

"You feelin' okay? "Vivian asked as she cranked the handle on my overbed table.

"Not really. I can't stand the smell of this tar anymore. My skin looks exactly like it did when I got here. And it seems like my so-called boyfriend forgot I'm alive."

"Well, you are right about that tar stuff not smellin' so good. I can't see your skin, so I don't know if it's better or not and I didn't know about the so-called boyfriend, but I guess if you're saying he's so-called, he's up to somethin' that's not good."

"You're right about that. Do you have a boyfriend, Vivian?"

"Me? I don't have time for boyfriends. Between this job and all I got to do at home."

Somebody called Vivian's name from the hall, so she left quickly. I felt sick to my stomach from the tar smell. I ate a few bites of fruit cocktail, and then pushed the tray and table away. By one o'clock, I was begging to take the tar off.

"Ruth Ann, you can't do this every day," Nurse Penny said. "The tar needs a certain amount of time or it won't work."

"But it's giving me a headache and I can't eat with it on."

"Let me get Nurse Blackburn," she said.

"Oh, never mind." The last thing I needed was Nurse Blackburn yelling at me."

Chapter Thirty Two

As soon as I turned on the faucet in the shower, I started to cry. Really hard. The scales on my skin were pretty much gone, but the large red patches were the same size they were when I came into this place. I started to wonder again about the tar soap from my dad. Maybe if I had used it, like he said, I wouldn't be standing there with gobs of tar running down my legs. Thinking about my dad made me cry harder. I didn't know until then that I missed him so much. He hadn't even called me. I thought about the silly card he'd sent and decided I'd throw it away when I got back to the room.

I took longer in the shower than I realized, because Denise was waiting for me after my light booth treatment. I walked in with the towel wrapped around my head and saw her reading one of the *Teen* Magazines by the window.

"Look at you, all sparkly clean," she said.

I looked at myself in the mirror and grinned. "Yeah, I look like my sister when she does her talent show act."

"No kidding? What's her talent show act?"

"She sings, *I'm Gonna Wash That Man Right Outa My Hair*. She comes out on stage in this fluffy, pink robe with a towel on her head and really washes her hair while she's singing. She's taken first place two times, in high school and college."

"I know that song. It's from the musical *South Pacific,* right?"

"That's the one," I said as I took the towel off my head and combed my fingers through my hair.

"I gotta meet this sister of yours. She really sounds like a character from what you've told me."

"She's a character, all right, and character is spelled B-I-T-C-H."

Denise laughed, "Here's your scarves. I hope you like the ones I picked."

I opened the brown sack that said D&C Stores on the front. One scarf was orange with white daisies and the other was baby blue eyelet.

"These are great, Denise. Thanks for picking them up," I said as I opened my wallet to pay her.

"It was hard to choose, but I thought you'd look good in both of those."

"Oh, they're not for me. They're for Vivian, the girl who brings my breakfast and lunch. She's really nice. She's black and she says her hair is a big pain in the neck, too. Even worse than mine." I reached for my Dippity-do.

"I'm so glad I met you, Ruth Ann. We're even more alike than I thought. And it's so damn cool that we'll be in the same class this fall."

"Well, you remind me of my friend, Maureen. I can't wait for the two of you to meet. Boy, speaking of Maureen, I could really go for one of her Winstons right now. I can't wait to get out of here and get back to my life. Even though I have some big problems to deal with."

"What kind of problems? Anything I can help with?"

I opened up to Denise and told her the whole story about the party at the cottage, including the earring situation.

"Holy cow, Ruth Ann. From what you've told me about your sister, I can't believe she hasn't missed her earrings. Yikes, you've gotta put them back as soon as possible. And as far as Tom goes...." Just then Michael and Eddie walked in. I was glad to see them, but sorry Denise didn't finish her comment about Tom.

"Today's french fries were not up to snuff," Michael said. "Apparently, the usual cook is on vacation."

"Well, hello to you, too," Denise said to the boys.

"Oh, sorry. Hello, hello," Michael bowed to each of us and then picked up *The Creeping Siamese*. "Well, now you're reading Dashiell

Hammett. You certainly have eclectic taste in reading material. By the way, have either of you read *Catcher in the Rye*? I stayed up until three o'clock this morning finishing it. You *have* to read it!"

Michael sat on the edge of Susie's bed flipping through my book, and not a minute later, Nurse Caroline walked by my door. Before I could say a word, she turned around and came back.

"Ruth Ann, we've already talked about your visitors staying off this bed. Please don't make me say it again."

"Michael wasn't here yesterday," I said.

"Yes, but you were here."

Michael stood up and walked over to the chair. Nurse Caroline left the room.

"Sorry," he said. "I didn't mean to get you in trouble."

"Didn't you say she was the nicest one?" Denise asked.

"She is," I said. "Nurse Penny's pretty nice too. But she's always gone by the time you guys come."

Eddie turned on my radio and *Ode to Billy Joe* was playing.

"My dad loves this song," I said.

"Really?" Michael asked. "Your dad likes moody, broody stuff, huh?"

"Well, not usually. He's the funniest person I've ever met, but he likes this for some reason, so it makes me think of him."

"That's right," Michael said. "Didn't you tell me your dad lives in another city? Hey, talk about good moody songs. Remember that song they took off the radio last year, *Society's Child?* My sister has that record. I've been playing it a lot lately."

"That's right, it was banned," Eddie said. "Even in Chicago."

"Why?" Denise asked.

"Because it was about a white girl and a black boy going steady," Michael said. "Can you believe it's illegal for people to get married if they're not from the same race?"

I was impressed that Michael seemed angry about that. I'd never met

266

boys who cared about important stuff. I told them all about Mary Lou's brother, partly because I wondered what Michael thought about the war in Vietnam. Just as I figured, he was angry about that too. Nurse Blackburn poked her head in and told us we were making too much noise and that she was going to limit my visitors if she had to tell me again.

"Well, she'd be happy to know I won't be back up for a couple days," Denise said. "I'm going to be helping my grandma clean her house."

* * *

I felt much better after they all left. It was so different to know boys who talked about books and things that mattered in the world. I wondered what Michael really thought of me and if I'd actually be hanging out with these kids in the fall. Our high school class was going to have over four hundred kids, which was a huge difference from the seventy-two at St. Boner's.

Pete stopped by on Thursday afternoon. He brought me a pack of gum and some Sweet Tarts. He didn't stay long, but he told me the sun was helping his psoriasis and that I should try it when I got home. He also told me that I should have my guitar at the hospital, so I could practice.

I tried calling Maureen's house, in case they'd come home early, but there was no answer. I asked Nurse Caroline for some paper and started to write a letter to Mary Lou. It didn't seem right that her brother had died and I hadn't even seen her or talked to her. It was hard to find the right words. After three tries, I gave up and decided that it would be better to call her when I got home.

Friday was the first day I'd seen Vivian since Denise brought the scarves. After she set down my breakfast tray, I handed her the paper sack and she peeked inside.

"These are for you."

"What'd you go and do that for?" she asked.

"Well, it's been so good to see someone else around here that's my age. Especially someone who knows about bad hair days. But, also you

267

said you liked mine, so I wanted to get you some."

"Thank you *so* much," Vivian said. "And you are right about me havin' bad hair days. I'm putting one of these on right now."

She tied the blue eyelet scarf over her hair.

"That's a really good color on you," I said.

She looked in the mirror and turned her head from side to side. "It is, isn't it? I've seen these on other people, but I never thought to try 'em myself. Well, old Mrs. Maguire will probably make me take it off, but I'm leavin' it on for now, anyway."

At one o'clock, I began to pace around the room. Ninety more minutes with the tar sounded like eternity. There was nothing good on TV. I'd finished all my reading material and nobody answered at Maureen's house or Peg's. I decided to try Irene, but her mom told me that Peg's mom had taken all the girls to the beach at Grand Haven. That sounded so fun, I could hardly stand it. But then I realized that even if I wasn't in the hospital, I wouldn't go to the beach the way I looked.

On Saturday, I groaned when Nurse Penny came in with the tar.

"Is there any way, I could have a day off?" I asked her. "Could I just do the light treatment today?"

She shook her head. "Ruth Ann, you're not helping us or yourself with all this complaining. It's our job to follow the doctor's orders."

"I'm sorry. It smells *so* bad and it feels awful on my skin. Can I at least not put it on my head today? My hair feels like straw from all of this."

"Please, don't make this any harder," Nurse Penny said.

I gave in and stopped asking. At least I had a fairly good distraction today. I'd found a Nancy Drew in the playroom the night before when I'd wandered in with my mom during visiting hours. It was on a top shelf under a pile of old *Highlights* magazines. It felt like I'd found an old friend when I spotted it.

So, after the plastic shower cap was in place over my tarry hair, and my entire body was coated in the stuff, I settled down to read *The Haunted Bridge*, which happened to be one Nancy Drew book I hadn't read. Just as I got to the part I always looked forward to where they recalled her previous mysteries, Dr. Mustache walked in with four other people in white coats. I had a feeling they were students and had probably all seen me naked the week before.

"Well, young lady," he said, "I'm getting reports that you haven't been very cooperative these past few days."

It felt really unfair that he said I was uncooperative. I wanted to yank on his ugly mustache or at least smear tar on it, but instead, I just said, "The tar makes me feel nauseous after a few hours and it gives me a headache."

"If you want the tar to do its job, it has to stay on a certain amount of time. There's no reason for you to be here otherwise."

He examined my arms, legs, and back while the others in white coats wrote on their clipboards. I doubted he could even see anything through the tar, but I figured he had to show off his doctor gimmicks.

"I'll have the nurse bring you some aspirin and ginger ale with ice. Sip on it slowly and it should help."

It was a relief to get back to the *Haunted Bridge*. This time, Nancy was a champion golfer who, as usual, amazed her "chums," Bess and George. The book kept me distracted until it was time for my shower and light treatment.

I had just changed out of my hospital "uniform" and into my Siamese cat pajamas when Eddie, Michael and Charlie walked into my room.

"Ruth Ann, the french fries are at their peak perfection today," Michael said. "I almost brought you some, but Charlie said I should ask you first."

"Thanks anyway, but I'll pass this time."

"Not feeling so good?" Eddie said. "Well, never fear because we are here to cheer you up *and* to compliment you on your snazzy PJs."

Before long we were all holding our sides from laughing. Eddie was telling us how he and another altar boy would insert swear words into the Latin prayers and the priest wouldn't even notice. Nurse Caroline came through the doorway at the loudest outburst.

"Ruth Ann, you and your guests need to go to the visitor's lounge. There are too many of you in here."

"Okay," I said. "We can do that."

I thought it was odd that she thought there were too many of us, since I often had that many visitors. I wondered if it was because they were all boys. A large group of people were leaving the lounge as we came in, so we had the room to ourselves. We sat on chairs at a round table. There was an ashtray on the table with a pipe resting in it.

"Wow, this is a fantastic pipe," Michael said as he picked it up. He put it between his teeth and grinned. "I bet I look pretty debonair, huh?"

"Yeah, you're about as debonair as Donald Duck," Eddie said as he shuffled a deck of cards. "Anybody wanna play Setback?"

"I can't stay long," Charlie said. "I gotta mow the lawn."

An elderly man entered the room and walked over to the table. "Pardon me, I left my pipe in here. In the ashtray, I believe."

"There's no pipe in this ashtray," Michael said quickly. "Is there an ashtray over there?" He pointed to a small table in the corner.

"No, I left it in this ashtray," the man said. "Now if you boys know where it is, I'd like it back."

Eddie spoke up, "We're sorry sir, there was no pipe in here."

My heart started pounding really hard. I couldn't believe the boys were doing this. I kept thinking they were joking and would pull the pipe out. I felt sorry for the man because he knew one of them had it. He looked over at me with a pleading sort of look. I didn't know what to do.

The man turned around and walked out.

"Hey, Michael," I said, "Maybe you better give it back, okay?" He grinned and shook his head.

"That old man probably has ten more at home."

Nurse Caroline walked into the lounge. "All right, you guys, which one of you has the pipe? Hand it over."

"Just like we told the man, there wasn't a pipe in here," Eddie said.

"Ruth Ann, who has it? Which one of them?"

I didn't want to tell on Michael because I was afraid he'd hate me for it. I felt angry at him, but I had four years of high school ahead of me. If I told on him, it could ruin me for life.

"I didn't see a pipe," I said. I hated lying and felt like a terrible person, but didn't feel like I had a choice.

Nurse Caroline closed her eyes and shook her head.

"Your friends need to leave right now, Ruth Ann. I know one of you has the pipe and I hope you'll hand it to that man when you pass him in the hall."

The boys said good-bye and left. I went back to my room and my stomach felt even worse than it did from the tar. I wished Denise had come with them. I wondered if she would have told on them.

* * *

My mom came up for the evening visiting hours. She looked tired and started talking about the roof as soon as she sat down.

"I couldn't make it up here this afternoon," she said. " I had to get a couple of estimates. Don't ask me how I'm supposed to pay for it."

I didn't have it in me to cheer her up because I was feeling so crummy myself. We watched *The Dating Game* and *The Newlywed Game* and then they announced that visiting hours were over. We had barely talked, even during the commercials. She bent over and kissed my cheek.

"Okay, honey," she said. "I'll see you tomorrow."

"It sounds like you have too much to do, Mom. I'll be getting some company. Don't worry about coming up."

"We'll see," she said, which was her answer to most things in life.

After she left, I tried to get back into the Nancy Drew book, but found

271

it impossible to concentrate. I kept thinking about Michael keeping the man's pipe and the other boys going along with it. But I had gone along with too. And there was no way around the fact that it was stealing. I felt terrible. I had chosen to let myself down instead of letting Michael and the boys down.

I had a sudden wish to be in Cathy's bedroom cutting out her ballerina paper dolls. So what if she'd stolen my Barbie's blue birdcage hat back in fifth grade? So what if she looked goofy half the time and hid under the bed for tornado alerts? I closed my eyes and thought of the aroma of bread baking in their oven. I thought of Mr. and Mrs. Cicerelli arguing out in the kitchen in Italian while we watched *Walt Disney's Wonderful World of Color* in the living room. Why had I always longed to be a teenager? All those fantasies I had about wearing make-up, going to dances and making out were so overrated. This was too hard. I fell asleep wishing with all my heart to be back in fifth grade, or maybe even fourth.

* * *

"We've brought you communion, dear," said Mrs. Fizzytits who was standing at my bedside with my Flintstones lunch box from second grade. Someone else came running into the room.

"She can't have communion. She's a thief! Here's what she deserves."

Sister Barfalottoyou was standing over me with the giant clip from her clipboard. "She's not only a thief, her hair is in her eyes again."

"No it's not," I said. "I don't have bangs anymore. Please don't make me wear the clip!"

When I turned away from them, Wilma was standing on the other side of the bed and she was wearing the yellow May procession dress she had bought for me. "These are from Grandma Gertie," she said. "But don't tell her I'm the one who brought them." She set a box of matzahs on my table and walked away.

"But wait," I yelled after her. "It's not even Passover and how come you're wearing my dress?"

I heard the blind going up on the window and I opened my eyes.

"Your breakfast is here. Were you having a bad dream?"

Nurse Penny touched my forehead with the back of her hand and left. Vivian was standing at the foot of my bed with my breakfast tray.

"I was having a really strange dream," I said. "Was I talking or something?"

"You were kind of moaning and it scared me, so I got the nurse," Vivian said. "Here, drink some juice."

She handed me a small glass of orange juice which tasted better than anything else I'd had in the hospital. I drank the whole thing without stopping.

"Better?" Vivian asked me.

I nodded. "Thanks, Vivian. You really make it bearable around here."

"Well, I don't know about that, but I'll see you at lunch."

Nurse Penny came back and took my temperature and blood pressure and listened to my heart and lungs through her stethoscope.

"You seem fine. I guess it was just a bad dream, after all."

I only had a couple of chapters left in the *Haunted Bridge,* so even though I was still feeling bad about Michael and the pipe, I decided to find out if Nancy won the golf tournament and if Mortimore Bartescue was going to succeed in swindling old Joe Haley. Less than an hour later, I closed the book with everything resolved and looked up to see it was after ten o'clock. I usually had my tar on way before this. I wondered if there was an emergency on the floor.

I turned on my radio and the disc jockey was talking about the hot weather and how everyone should head to the beach. I hadn't even been outside in twelve days. I decided to walk down to the playroom to return the Nancy Drew book. Maybe I'd find another one, or at least maybe I could find out where everybody was. The hall was eerily quiet and there was nobody behind the counter at the nurse's station. I walked into the playroom and placed the *Haunted Bridge* facing out on the shelf, so somebody else would spot it easily. As I was scanning the shelves for something else to read, I heard someone enter the room behind me.

"Here you are," Nurse Penny said. "I wondered where you'd wandered off to."

"Well, I was wondering where *everyone* had wandered off to. I was looking for another Nancy Drew. Where is everybody, anyway?"

"Have a seat," she said as she pulled out a chair for me. "Jimmy passed away a little while ago."

"Jimmy?"

"The eleven year old with leukemia."

She was talking about the IV pole kid. I felt woozy, like I had when I woke up from the crazy dream. How could he just up and die like that? He'd talked to me almost every day. How could he just go and die? And I didn't even know his name was Jimmy.

"That's awful. I thought he was getting better."

"We were hoping that he was going to turn a corner, but it just didn't happen and then he took a turn for the worse."

I picked up a puzzle piece from the floor and placed it on the wooden puzzle that was in the middle of the table. My eyes were swimming with tears.

"What about my tar? Are we going to skip it today?"

"That's the other thing I came to talk to you about."

"What do you mean?"

"As soon as we can get in touch with your mother, we're going to have her pick you up."

"Pick me up for what?"

"To go home, Ruth Ann. Nurse Blackburn called Dr. Ording and they decided that you aren't benefitting from the treatments."

"But I haven't been here for three weeks," I said. "It's less than two."

"That's right," Nurse Blackburn said as she entered the room. "We're not seeing enough improvement *and* you have been very difficult these past few days. Complaining about the tar and the lights and you appear to be more interested in entertaining boys than getting well. You're wasting everyone's time around here when we could give the bed to someone else. I'm going now to call your mother, so I suggest you go back to your room and pack."

After Nurse Blackburn walked out I said, "This is all about that missing pipe, isn't it?"

"It's a lot of things, Ruth Ann, "Nurse Penny said.

Part of me wanted to open up and tell her the truth about the pipe. But I decided there was no point. It wouldn't bring the pipe back and I'd never see any of these people again. My thoughts and feelings were swirling so fast, I couldn't decide anything or even talk. Nurse Penny leaned over from her chair and gave me a hug. I got up, and in a fog, walked down the hall.

When I got back to my room, a song came on the radio I'd never heard before. It sounded a little like The Supremes, but I knew it wasn't. The words stopped me in my tracks, *nothing but a heartache...* The singing and the words meshed perfectly with all of the crammed-up emotions that made my own heart feel like lead. I threw my suitcase onto the bed, cranked the radio and tossed in my books, pajamas, triangle scarves, Dippity-do, Ambush, and the box that contained the president's keychain and the daisy earring.

Chapter Thirty Three

My mom barely talked on the way home. I could tell she was mad at me. After speaking to Nurse Blackburn, she'd marched into my room and said, "Let's go!"

By the time we reached the parking lot, my fear of her anger was overshadowed with the feeling of freedom. I felt bad that I didn't get to say good-by to Vivian and I was worried about what to do with the daisy earring, but the thought of no more stinky tar was worth it. The cicadas were singing and the air smelled like summer. I had never been Tom's girlfriend in the summer and I got a fluttery feeling when I thought about it. The boat incident didn't seem so bad right then, and the thought of making out with him under the trees in the park sounded like heaven.

"I don't know what kind of new friends you think you made," my mom said when we were a couple of blocks from our house. "But they better not come near me *or* you. Imagine. Stealing an old man's pipe. And since when do you know more than the doctors, Missy?"

"I don't think I should be judged by anybody who hasn't had a tar treatment," I said. "Or twelve tar treatments, for that matter."

"You better watch your lip. In case you've forgotten, you were grounded before you ever went in the hospital."

When we walked into the kitchen, Ruff and Reddy brushed against my legs and purred. I squatted on the floor and encircled them in my arms.

"Hi, you guys. I missed you."

"By the way," my mom called up the basement steps. "I'm throwing a load in the washer and the dryer is shot, so you can hang the laundry out when it's done."

It was beginning to feel like I'd never been gone.

"Okay, I will. Where's Renee?" I hollered back down to her. Reddy lifted his chin to be scratched.

"She's at Bonnie's cottage with the other Wurzburgers."

Before I even opened my suitcase, I crawled into the back of my closet and opened the Barbie case. Sure enough, the earring was still there in the little accessory drawer. I was half surprised that Renee hadn't scoured every inch of my stuff. I took the other earring out of the little box in my suitcase and tip-toed down the hall to Renee's room. I opened the top of her jewelry case as quietly as possible so I could place the little daisies in the corner she always kept them in. I had a very funny feeling right before I set them down. It was hard for me to believe that she hadn't noticed that the earrings were gone, because the empty space looked like a smile with a missing tooth. But, knowing Renee, she would never have kept her mouth shut this long if she knew. I felt so relieved that I barely noticed that my legs, scalp and butt itched like mad.

I skipped to the upstairs phone and dialed Maureen's number. It rang eleven times before I hung up. I had hoped there was a chance they'd be back from vacation. I thought for a second about calling Tom, but decided against it. It seemed like his parents were strict about the phone, and a lot of people at St. Boner's thought only girls with bad reputations called boys. I was sure that my reputation was as bad as it could get after the boat incident. I didn't need to make it any worse. I turned on my radio and started unpacking my suitcase.

"Hey, Ruth Ann!"

It was Cathy calling me from Frankie's bedroom window. I opened the curtains and knelt down to talk to her.

"I heard your radio. How come you're out of the hospital already?" I turned the radio down even though they were playing *You've Got to Hide Your love Away* by the Beatles.

"It's a long story. It doesn't really matter. I thought you were all at a cottage."

"We got home yesterday, and my mom's leaving tomorrow. She and my Aunt Mary are going to Detroit until Friday to help with my grandpa. I guess he lost his memory or something."

"Oh," I answered. "Who's gonna stay with you and Frankie?"

"Nobody. At least not during the day. My dad's home by six and I can take care of Frankie. I do it a lot."

I knew for a fact that she didn't watch Frankie a lot, but I had more important things to think about, so I told Cathy I'd see her later.

It felt good to hang the sheets and towels out on the line. It was a perfect temperature, sunny with a breeze. The white flowers on the Spirea bushes were already turning brown, and I felt sad that I didn't get to see them when they were snowy white. They were my favorite because they looked like candy nonpareils.

I decided since it was so sunny that I should try Pete's suggestion and lie in the sun to see if it would help my skin. I went into the house and crawled back into the closet to get my bathing suit out of the Barbie case. As soon as I got it out, all of the humiliation of the cottage party flooded over me. I just couldn't put it back on. I settled for shorts and a sleeveless top, took my radio outside and fell asleep in the sun.

"Here's another load for you to hang up," my mom said. I looked up and she was standing over me, lighting a Salem.

"You know, Francesca's going to Detroit to take care of her father, so now that you're home, it'd be nice if you kept an ear out for Cathy and Frankie when I'm at work this week."

I hung the clothes on the line, taking note that none of them were mine, since I hadn't been here. I wondered if she and Renee liked it better with me gone. My mom probably made caramel corn at night like it was a slumber party. I went into the living room and glanced at the book shelf for something to read. I spotted *Marjorie Morningstar,* which I had started the summer before. It opened right up to the page where I'd smashed an Oreo in it and part of it was still there. I scraped it off, made a peanut butter sandwich, and took the book back out to the yard. I didn't really

278

expect the sun to help my psoriasis much, but it felt lovely to be outside after being inside a building for almost two weeks.

The sheets on the line offered some privacy from the Cicerelli's yard, which was good because I didn't feel like having anyone gawk at my skin. I read twenty five pages and then dozed off again. I woke up when I heard Mr. Cicerelli dumping charcoal into his grill, so I went back to the book. Just when I was reading about Marjorie smoking a Turkish cigarette on page 53, I heard someone walk up behind me.

"How many of those treatments did you skip? Your skin doesn't look much better than when you went in."

I turned around, sat up and faced Renee. "I didn't skip any treatments! Did that old biddy Blackburn say that? All I did was ask to take the tar off a little early once or twice. You would too, Renee, if you ever smelled it! You never even saw the stuff. It was awful!"

"You keep your voice down, young lady," my mom said from the upstairs window, as she glanced over to the Cicerelli's. "I'm warming up last night's goulash. Would one of you please make a salad?"

"I need to rinse off the sand," Renee said. "You make it."

I put a dandelion in my book this time instead of an Oreo, and went into the kitchen to make a salad. I was setting the table after chopping lettuce, cucumber and a tomato. Renee came downstairs in white shorts and a yellow blouse. She walked over to the stereo and put on a Kingston Trio record. I knew she did it to annoy me. I could even stand Barbra Streisand over the Kingston Trio. When I went back into the kitchen for napkins, Renee was squeezing a tube of frozen lemonade into a pitcher.

"Well," she said, "I heard those boys you thought were so wonderful didn't turn out that way after all."

My mom carried the goulash to the dining room table and I stuck my tongue out at Renee's back as she walked out with the lemonade. I put the salad down and pulled out my chair.

"But I guess you have a lot in common with one of them, huh?"

I looked across the table at Renee. There she sat with a huge smirk on her face. She was wearing the daisy earrings. I was speechless.

"Did you really think I didn't miss them?" she asked. My mom stopped chewing and looked at Renee and then at me.

"No," I said. "But why didn't you say anything?"

"And let you off the hook that easy? You're a little thief, Ruth Ann. Just like your new boyfriend that stole the man's pipe. No wonder you like him so much."

"I *borrowed* your earrings, Renee. I didn't steal them. And for your information, Michael is not my boyfriend."

"Would you mind telling me what's going on?" my mom asked.

"Your darling daughter stole these earrings," Renee said. "And I was beginning to think she'd never give them back."

"I borrowed them for the cottage party. I meant to give them back. In case you've forgotten, Renee, I spent the last two weeks in the hospital."

I decided to skip the part about losing one of them. What was the point?

"Ruth Ann, you've never borrowed your sister's things without asking," my mom said. "What got into you?"

"She loaned them to me for graduation the day before," I said. "I didn't think she'd mind if I borrowed them again. But I didn't think of it until after she left for work."

"My mistake," Renee said. "I will never offer anything of mine to you again. I guess I thought you were more mature than this. I hope you extend her punishment, Mother. If you were planning to un-ground her, you better think twice now. I'm surprised she bothered to give them back at all." She turned to me. "I'm actually shocked you didn't lose them."

I carried my dishes into the kitchen. I felt like smashing them on the floor. I *had* lost one of the damn earrings. Maybe I really was immature and a big loser. I tried to think of one good thing about myself and started crying. How could I face the whole summer with Renee around?

Gone Before Spring

"Ruth Ann, pull yourself together," my mom said. I could hear Renee putting her record back into the cabinet in the other room. "I want you to promise me you'll straighten up and behave yourself. You hear me? Now, go blow your nose and take the clothes off the line." I walked out the back door.

"And stay out of your sister's stuff!" she called after me.

I was trying to figure out if I was grounded or not. She hadn't said one way or another, and I decided it was better not to ask. Just as I took Renee's petti pants off the line, my mom called me in. "Your dad's on the phone."

I started toward the house, but I went back and got the laundry basket. It would be just my luck that dogs would run off with it.

"Hey there, Sport," my dad said. "How the hell are ya? They fix you up in there?"

"Well, not really," I answered.

"C'mon now, it's gotta be a little better."

"Well, my skin isn't as scaly as it was. And I was all red and puffy when I first went in. I guess that part's better. But my patches are all still there. All over. Way worse than when I was in Saginaw."

"Speaking of Saginaw, we need to get you here in August. Maybe they'll have another dance and you and Mimi can play like Rockettes again."

I didn't bother to mention that Maureen was supposed to go with me to Saginaw in August. I decided that I needed to mind my Ps and Qs with everyone. And August was a long way off.

"That would be great, Dad. How's the car lot? Have you taken the boat out yet?"

"Not much new at the car lot. Business is kind of slow. I took Grandma and Dorothy out for a boat ride last Sunday. We pulled over at Ojibway Island and had a little picnic."

"And Grandma brought her fried chicken, potato salad, and dill

281

pickles, right?"

"Yes she did. And her pineapple upside down cake."

I could hear Wilma in the background.

"I better hang up, Sport. Her highness wants me to make her a martini. Be a good girl and follow the doctor's orders, hear me? I'll call you soon."

After we hung up, I tried calling Maureen, but there was still no answer. I dialed Denise's number, but hung up before it began ringing. I wasn't sure what to say about Michael and the pipe, so I thought it would be better to wait. I also considered calling Mary Lou to tell her I was sorry about her brother, but decided that could wait too. Especially since the last thing I needed right now was Renee listening in on my conversations.

I turned on the radio and the song, *Nothing but a Heartache*, was playing again. Was that only this morning that I'd first heard it, while I was throwing everything into my suitcase at the hospital? That meant that the IV pole kid was still alive at this time last night. I tried to picture his family around his bed saying good-bye. I could have been a lot friendlier to him. But he always seemed to show up at my door at a bad time. I wondered how Susie was doing at the other hospital. We talked about calling each other, but we probably never would. Vivian would be surprised when she brought the breakfast tray and my bed was empty. Maybe it wasn't empty anymore. They would give my bed to someone first, since it was by the window. I had a funny feeling in my stomach. I was a loser patient too. Renee was right. I messed up everything.

I hadn't even finished that thought when I heard someone scream. I ran down the stairs and into the kitchen to see my mom holding a bloody napkin around her hand. A pointed shard of glass was on the counter.

"Good move, Ruth Ann," Renee said. You didn't rinse your lemonade glass and Mother cut her hand trying to get the pulp out. I think she needs stitches!"

"How do you know it was my glass?" I asked.

282

"Who else would leave a glass by the telephone? You're the only one who would do that."

She was right. I had left my glass on the window seat. More confirmation that I was a loser.

"I'm so sorry, Mom. Should we go to the hospital?"

"Just get me a bandage. I don't need stitches."

"Where are bandages?" I asked.

"Go ask Francesca for one."

Of course, we didn't have any. Just like all the other household necessities we never had. What did we do before we lived next door to the Cicerellis?

* * *

Even though I was awake, I didn't get out of bed until I was sure that my mom and Renee had left for work. I didn't feel like seeing either one of them. I found an envelope of Carnation Instant Breakfast in the cupboard. While I was stirring it into the milk, the phone rang. It was Maureen.

"I don't even care if I woke you up," she said. "I couldn't wait to talk to you. In fact, I wanted to call you when we got home last night, but it was almost twelve o'clock."

"Well, you won't believe it, but I just got out of the hospital yesterday."

"What? The hospital? You're kidding me, right? What happened?"

"What do you think? My skin. But, before I tell you all that, how the hell did you get my earring *and* how can I ever thank you for sending it to me? You saved my life!"

"Ruth Ann, it was the weirdest thing ever. We pulled off at this little roadside park to have lunch and my mom told me to spread out that beach blanket for Teeny to lie on. You know, the blanket you wore at the cottage party. Well, I decided to sit by Teeny while I ate, and as soon as I sat down, I felt something sharp, and there was your earring."

"Oh my God, I can't believe it," I said.

"So, I thought about what to do all the way to Mt. Rushmore. The only thing I could figure out was to mail it as soon as possible. My parents thought I was nuts because I was so desperate to buy you a gift and find a post office."

I went on to explain the dilemma I had when I received it in the hospital and I filled her in on my entire ordeal of the last two weeks. Maureen couldn't believe all that had happened and especially that I hadn't heard from Tom. She said she was going to call Johnny and try to get the scoop.

"Can you come over later?" Maureen asked.

"I think so. My mom never brought up whether or not I'm still grounded, even after Renee flapped her big mouth. You know what, though? I'd like to go somewhere and buy a record. Have you heard *Nothing but a Heartache*, by the Flirtations? It's my new song, Maureen. I need to own it."

We made plans to talk again in the afternoon. My mom had left me a note to mow the lawn and change the kitty litter, so I went upstairs to get dressed and make my bed. As soon as I turned on my radio, Cathy called me from Frankie's window.

"Hi," she said. "Want to come over for lunch? My mom is gone to Detroit and she left a bunch of good food. Frankie got asked over to his friend's house, and I have a cherry chip cake in the oven."

"I'm going over to Maureen's later," I said.

The last thing I felt like doing on my first real free day, was hang around Cathy. Then I remembered my mom asking me to watch out for her and Frankie while their mom was gone. I needed all the Brownie points I could gather right now. If I got back in good standing, my whole summer could be better. And after all, I needed to eat lunch.

"Well, okay. Sure, I'll come over. What time?"

"Twelve o'clock sharp," Cathy said.

Twelve o'clock sharp. Cathy would be a dork forever, no matter what.

While I mowed the lawn in my jeans, it got pretty hot, so I tried to figure out what I would change into before I went to Maureen's later. I needed to get creative. I felt proud of myself as I wheeled the push-mower into the garage. It was the first time I'd done both the front and back yards.

I got out my old summer clothes and decided to try brown tights on with a pair of burnt orange shorts. I found an old blouse with elbow-length sleeves that had a little brown and orange in the print. It covered my arms pretty well, and the cloth was light enough so that I wouldn't die from the heat. The tights and shorts kind of looked like fall, but I decided that it was a better idea than jeans. To give the outfit a summer touch, I added the sea-shell earrings that Denise had given me in the hospital. I also decided that I would call her later and thank her again for visiting me so often. Even though Michael had let me down, it wasn't Denise's fault. Without a doubt, those kids had made my time in the hospital way more bearable.

When I got to Cathy's, I couldn't believe she was wearing her mother's apron. She was spreading pink frosting on the cake and humming when I walked in.

"Well, look at you, playing house," I said. "Do you really have the whole place to yourself?"

"I sure do. My brother is staying at his friend's house 'til after dinner, so my dad's taking me to Uncle Alfredo's pizzeria tonight. Just the two of us."

"That's nice. You know what? I could *drink* your mom's salad dressing," I said as I poured it all over my salad.

"She'll give you the recipe when you get married," Cathy said.

"Well, then I'm outta luck, 'cause I'm never getting married."

"Not even to Tom? You wouldn't even marry Tom?"

"Don't be ridiculous, Cathy."

I reached for the green Pyrex bowl that was filled with pasta, and helped myself. After my first bite, I said, "This rigatoni is delicious. Your mom is the best cook in the world."

Cathy wiped her hands on her mom's apron like she was thirty-five years old.

"What are you going to do at Maureen's house?"

I felt like saying smoke marijuana or practice our strip tease act, but I just shrugged.

"I don't know. Nothin' special. She's been on vacation the whole time I was in the hospital. She didn't even know I was in there. Can you turn on the radio or something? It's too quiet in here."

I went back home after the cherry chip cake. I'd stayed longer than I meant to, because I could tell Cathy was nervous about being alone. She said she was going to cut out a pattern for a skirt, so I figured that would keep her busy. After I fed the cats, I called Maureen and she told me to head over. I called my mom at work and told her about eating with Cathy, so when I said I was going to Maureen's, she'd be more okay with it. She probably thought I should still be grounded, because Renee had pressured her.

I cut through the park on my way to Maureen's. Kids were lined up for the pool, running around with nose plugs and flip-flops, snapping their towels at each other. A group of older kids from Burton School were sitting on the steps of the community building. A couple of them looked familiar. One of them got up and walked over to me. She had a piece of leather tied around her forehead, and was stepping on her bellbottom pants.

"Hi. I'm taking a survey. Who do you like better, Bob Dylan or Donavon?"

"They're so different, I like them both."

"Okay. Cool," she said.

I could tell this was going to be an interesting summer.

Gone Before Spring

Maureen was lying out in the backyard on a chaise lounge. *Light My Fire* was playing on her radio, and it made me wince to hear it. All I could think of was Tom saying that we should think of each other every time we heard it 'til the end of time. Maureen took one look at me, switched the radio off, got up, and hugged me.

"Want some Bugles? A Coke?"

"No thanks. I just had a huge lunch at Cathy's. How about going to Alger Variety? I want to see if they have that record."

"Okay, I need some blush, anyway. C'mon in while I change. You haven't mentioned Cathy in ages. How's she doing? Are you still trying to give her a makeover?"

"No, I kind of gave up on that idea. She'll be a Mademoiselle Don't all her life. She's okay, I guess. Still afraid of everything."

"Did you get hold of Johnny to ask about Tom?"

"Oh yeah, I tried to call Johnny, but his mom said he went camping with his dad and won't be back until Thursday."

"That's okay," I said. "I guess I wouldn't want it to get back to Tom that I was spying or anything, anyway."

"Hey, I almost forgot," Maureen said. "Angela called and said all the other Tandem Riders are going to the park around three. I told them we'd try to come."

"So they all know I'm out of the hospital?"

"Yeah. It's no big deal, though, is it?"

"I guess not. I just feel like such a freak. Seriously, look at my outfit."

Maureen pulled an aqua Poor Boy over her head.

"I think it's cool. You put stuff together I would never think of. You know me, everything always has to match. Oh yeah, another thing that Angela mentioned was that Tom's band has been practicing a lot because they've had a couple more jobs."

"Oh. Probably with the Burton kids again," I said.

Maureen didn't say anything. She turned around quickly to the mirror and applied lip gloss, before dropping it into her purse. I was about to ask her what else she'd been hearing when Mrs. Abraham hollered up to us that she was leaving for a hair appointment.

"Oh good. I'm dying for a Winston," Maureen said.

"You're not the only one," I said back to her.

* * *

It felt good to walk to Alger Heights, but it also felt weird.

"If I was still in the hospital, it would almost be time to take my tar off and get a light treatment."

"I can't believe that all happened to you while I was gone. It sounds unreal, like a bad dream or something."

"It feels unreal to me too. But so does being out of there."

It turned out the record wasn't available in the United States because the Flirtations were from England. The guy at Alger Variety said he didn't even think radio stations were playing it yet.

"Wow," I said. "Everything is turning out to be unreal. Maybe I imagined the song. The tar probably affected my brain."

Maureen gave me a funny look, and offered me a stick of gum.

"You've been through a rough time. But everything's gonna be better now. You'll see. How soon can you go to my cottage? How about this weekend? I can't wait for you to try water tobogganing."

I didn't want to say no to Maureen, but the last thing I wanted to do was wear a bathing suit again. My skin felt so sore that I wished I had put the gunky hospital cream on before I left the house. I had brought it home, figuring I paid for it, and they'd just throw it away when I left. The tights were beginning to feel hot and uncomfortable.

* * *

"Hey, let's drop this stuff off at my house and head over to the park," Maureen said. "It feels like ages since The Tandem Riders were together. I'll just take a minute and put on some of my new blush before we go. You want to try it?"

"Sure, why not? Maybe if I put on some make-up, this crazy outfit will look better."

"Will you stop that? You look cute."

Before we climbed the stairs to Maureen's room, I glanced into the living room at the couch where Tom and I had our big make-out session last fall. We were in the dark that night, but it didn't really matter because my psoriasis wasn't that bad yet. My skin had looked so horrible in the boat that *I* couldn't stand to look at it. No wonder he hadn't called me since then. I never should have gone to that party.

"Nice color, don't you think?" Maureen asked. She handed me the blush.

"On second thought," I said, "I think I'll just skip the park and go home. I'm not feeling so great."

Maureen put her hands on my shoulders and looked right into my eyes. "C'mon, Ruth Ann. You know what they say. When you fall off a horse, you should get right back on and ride. It'll do you good to see the girls. Now tell me the truth. Is this blush too bright?"

* * *

We spotted Peg, Irene, Angela, and Mary Lou as soon as we got to the park. They were sitting on a large cement block by the fence around the pool. Angela waved us over.

"Hail, hail, the gang's all here," Peg hollered to us.

We jumped up on the cement block and all started talking at once like it had been years since we'd seen one another. I had purposely climbed up on Mary Lou's side.

"I'm really sorry about your brother, Mary Lou," I said to her. "It's so terrible that I don't know what else to say."

"Thanks," she said. Her eyes filled with tears, and I put my arms around her. She hugged me back and sniffled on my shoulder.

"I'm sorry I didn't come to see you in the hospital. Is your skin better?"

"Not really." I sniffled too. Then we both chuckled, which didn't really make sense, but I had a feeling we were going to get along better after this. We were the only ones in the group who had been through a rough time, like Maureen said.

I thought of last summer, before there was a group. Before the Tandem Riders. I would come to the park to swim, sometimes with Cathy, occasionally with Peg and Irene. So much had changed in my life since that time. I really was still a little kid back then. I wasn't sure if I liked this age better or not. It almost felt like I knew too much now. And that probably meant there was a whole lot more to still find out.

"Check out the life guard, you guys," Peg said. "It's Amy Jo Burke's brother, Steve."

"He is *really* cute." Maureen sat up straighter and looked toward the lifeguard chair. "I wish I had my binoculars."

"There's a bunch of Burton kids on the other side of the building," Angela said.

"Yeah, I saw them on my way to Maureen's house," I said. "In fact, one of them asked me who I liked better, Donavan or Bob Dylan."

"That's strange." Peg turned toward the direction of the building. "Do you know who she was?"

"I think I've seen her around. She's trying to look like a hippie, but not pulling it off very well."

"I bet she was high," Angela said.

I hadn't thought about anyone our age being high. I was about to ask her why she thought that, when Irene pointed toward the sky.

"Look, you guys. The sky's getting kind of strange over there."

Dark clouds were swirling and the trees were swaying.

"I'm glad I laid out in the sun earlier," Maureen said. "My parents never gave me a chance to work on my tan the whole time we were on vacation."

"Well, at least you have a cottage," Peg said.

"That's true. And hopefully, Ruth Ann will be going there with me this weekend." She gave me such a sweet smile, I knew I had to go.

"Oh look, that kid Zeke is over there." Mary Lou pointed toward Madison Street. "Call him over, so Ruth Ann and Maureen can hear him sing."

"Hey Zeke," Angela hollered. "Come here a minute."

A black boy who looked to be around ten or eleven walked over to our cement block with his hands in his pockets, trying very hard not to smile.

"Hello, ladies," he said. "How are all of you on this possibly stormy day?"

"We were just noticing that the sky looks funny." Peg looked up. "How 'bout a song, Zeke? These two girls have never heard you."

"Well, ladies, I do have a song that would fit the day, and I'd be happy to sing it for you."

Then Zeke just broke right into song. He sang *I Wish It Would Rain*, in a beautiful soprano voice, clear and full of emotion. He hit every note perfectly and lifted his face to the sky while pouring out his heart with his voice. His song made me feel like I wasn't alone. Lots of people had stuff that made them cry. Probably everybody, not just me and Mary Lou. We all burst into applause when he finished, and he took a dramatic bow from his waist. "Better head for home, ladies. Looks like my song worked some magic."

The trees were really blowing now, and the sky was getting yellowish.

"Wow," I said. "You guys were right. That kid can really sing. I wish Pete could hear him. You know, my guitar teacher."

"The funny thing is that he sings that song on sunny days too," Irene said.

Maureen tugged on my sleeve. "Hey, I wanna see who that hippie girl is you were talking about. Come with me to the drinking fountain and point her out."

"I know exactly who she's talking about," Angela said. The other girls all agreed with her.

"Well, I want to see," Maureen said.

"Okay. I'll go with you." We jumped down from the cement block and walked around the side of the building.

"Wait by these bushes, Ruth Ann. I just want a few puffs." Maureen lit a cigarette. We peeked around the building at the large group of Burton kids who had filled the steps and the sidewalk in front of the center.

"Oh, is that her?" Maureen asked. She pointed to the girl with the bellbottoms.

"Yup, that's her."

"Okay, I have seen her around before," Maureen said. "Probably not since last summer, though."

Candy wrappers and pods from the trees scuttled down the sidewalk. A paper sack blew right onto Maureen's cigarette and knocked the ash off.

"It does feel like a bad storm is coming," I said.

"Wouldn't you know it? I was hoping we could all hang out for a couple more hours. This is the best we've gotten along since last fall. Hey, look, there's Cindy and Leta. I think I heard that Leta and Rick broke up."

I looked toward the two girls who had been at band practice in the spring. Leta was even prettier than I remembered. The wind lifted her long, dark hair and brushed it across her face. They stood talking to the kids near the steps and we watched them while Maureen kept trying to re-light her cigarette. After her third try, the air grew very still. The voices of the kids sounded much louder.

"That's strange," I said. "The wind stopped. Maybe it's gonna blow over."

"Sometimes that's a bad sign," Maureen said. "My dad says it can mean a tornado is close by. But I doubt we'd get another one around here. Has it even been a year since the terrible one?"

"Over a year," I said. "It was April of seventh grade. I remember because we were out of town at Renee's."

"Same here. We were at our cottage. Now listen, Ruth Ann. Don't forget to ask your mom tonight about coming to my cottage this weekend."

"Only if she's in a good mood. I probably should wait for at least another day or two."

A huge gust of wind blew from the direction of Alger Street. A branch fell from a nearby tree and rolled past us toward the group of kids, just as two boys rounded the other side of the building and headed toward the group. Before Maureen even said anything, I saw it was Marty and Tom.

"Look, it's Tom," Maureen said. "Ohhh shit, Ruth Ann."

Tom had walked up behind Leta and encircled her shoulders with his arms. She turned her head slightly and smiled. Then she turned around to face him and they kissed. I felt like I'd been kicked in the stomach. The rigatoni and cherry chip cake started churning in my gut. Just when I thought it was all going to come up, Maureen threw her cigarette down and grabbed my arm.

"We need to get outta here. C'mon, let's go to my house."

As soon as she said that, a voice came on the pool loudspeaker.

"Please evacuate the pool at once. This is a tornado alert." A loud siren began ringing.

"C'mon, Ruth Ann. See, it really is time to go."

"Oh my God. I can't go to your house."

"Why not? It's closer than yours."

"Cathy! She's by herself," I said. "She's terrified of tornadoes. I gotta go!"

"Do you want me to go with you? You'll have to go by Tom to get there."

"Too bad. I'll call you later."

I broke away from Maureen and ran right by Tom and Leta. There wasn't time to take a different route. I saw him turn toward me with a shocked look on his face.

"Go to hell," I said breathlessly as I ran past him. I had no idea if he heard me with the siren going, but I didn't care.

I ran past the tennis courts, through the grass that was the ice rink in the winter, and headed toward Burton Street. My eyes and throat were burning hot. I thought of skating with Tom last winter, and Cathy skating with Laurent. She had looked so cute in my black headband, and I knew it was the best time she'd ever had. Why hadn't I tried to be nicer since then? Well, I would now, damn it!

I heard a crack and looked to my right as an entire tree fell over by the path I always took to Maureen's house. I could see all the tree roots in a huge chunk of ground that had lifted right up. I couldn't believe my eyes, and somewhere in my head, I thought of how badly I wanted to tell my dad about it. And then I thought of my dad kissing Wilma and how that was like Tom kissing Leta and was that just what boys and men always did?

The doors to the warm-up house blew open, and I looked at the gaping hole, wondering if I should go in. But I decided to keep running. It was more important that I get to Cathy, and it was only eight houses from the corner. The wind was pushing so hard against me, it felt like my feet weren't running anymore. A park bench bounced in front of me on its side and disappeared. Maybe this *was* going to be like last year's tornado. I wondered if I'd still have all my arms and legs by the time I got to Cathy's house.

I ran across Burton Street, down Prospect, and grabbed the handle on Cathy's door. Thankfully, she hadn't locked it. When I opened the door, it slammed against the house. I didn't even try to close it. A section of the skirt pattern was on the kitchen table and somehow, I noticed that it was pinned to some fairly cute material. Maybe there was hope for her yet. I ran up the stairs to her room, and sure enough, her feet were sticking out from under the bed. I got down and slid under, right next to her, barely able to catch my breath.

"Hey, Caterina Cicerelli. I guess you know there's a tornado alert. And I think you know the basement is a better place than under your bed."

I wanted to tell her about the tree falling, but caught myself. I had to remain calm and not let on to her how bad it was outside. Yet somehow, still get her down to the basement.

"What are you doing here? I thought you were at Maureen's house."

A door slammed across the hall, and I realized Cathy hadn't shut the windows. She gasped and buried her face in her folded arms.

"Well, I wanted to give you these." I reached into my pocket and pulled out the roll of Choco-Mint Lifesavers I'd bought at Alger Variety.

She lifted her head. "Thanks, but you could've given them to me later."

"I know, but I also know tornados are your least favorite thing, and you might need some company."

"Did you get to see Tom?"

"Yeah, I saw him."

Cathy let out a gushy sigh and got a dreamy look on her face, which made me think she was forgetting how scared she was. But then a loud crash came from downstairs and she hid her face again. I was afraid we weren't even going to make it to the basement.

"It's not like that anymore, Cathy."

"What do you mean?"

"I'll tell you all about it, but not under your bed." Beads of sweat were rolling down my face, under my tights, and dripping from my palms, but I was trembling. I bit my lower lip to keep my teeth from chattering.

"It's really nice of you to be under here with me," Cathy said into her arm. "Know what? I'm gonna give you the rest of the cherry chip cake. Know what else?"

I tried to keep my voice steady, even though I felt like pulling her out

295

by her feet. "No, what?"

"I'm the one who took your Barbie's birdcage hat right after you moved in. The one from your Aunt Maxine."

"You think I didn't know that?"

She looked up. "You knew all along?"

I nodded. "Why are telling me now?"

She started crying. "In case we're gonna die."

"We are not gonna die, silly."

"I'm really scared."

I reached over and rubbed her back with my sweaty palm. "I know. But I promise we'll be okay. *If* we go to the basement."

Cathy buried her face again. "If you really knew about the Barbie hat, how come you never said anything?"

"Because I knew you'd tell me when you were old enough. And when you really stopped playing with Barbies. But if you still have it, I want it back, damn it! Now can we go down to the basement? I'm getting claustrophobia under here."

Cathy lifted her face and turned toward me. "Well, okay. But let's grab the cake on the way down."

Acknowledgements

My daughter, Camille was involved in every single aspect of this book from beginning to end, and rightly so, as we often say to one another, "Stop having my thoughts! I owe a huge debt of gratitude to the West Michigan Writers Workshop. Without their eyes, ears, support, and needling, I would never have written this book or it's sequel. Thanks also to my husband, Gregg for listening to me read the book on road trips and helping me in every way possible, whether it was time, printing pages for writers group, or taking the dog out. Thanks to my daughter, Sonia for reading the whole book in one sitting and compiling and purchasing all of the songs in the book. To my readers, Jane Griffoen, Sheryl Cunningham, Teresa Thome, and the real Maureen, Maureen Barringer, for reading the book and giving me support, feedback, and enthusiasm. Thanks to my former bookstore boss and dear friend, Chris Byron, for nudging me to write this story and for practically pulling me by the ear to join my writers group. Thanks to my sister and the real Mimi for being good sports about their fictionalized depictions in the book. Thanks to the National Psoriasis Foundation for allowing me to teach improv at the 2013 conference and to read excerpts from the book. And a special thanks to Fred Finkelstein, for his films about real people with psoriasis who were the real inspiration for writing this book.

Authors Note

This is a work of fiction. Any names or characters, businesses or places, events, or incidents are fictitious. Any resemblance to actual persons, living or dead, or actual events is purely coincidental.

www.ingramcontent.com/pod-product-compliance
Lightning Source LLC
Chambersburg PA
CBHW020947120726
47905CB00008B/2708